科技英語論文寫作

◆ 作者｜俞炳丰 ◆ 校訂者｜陸瑞強

Practical Guide to Scientific English Writing

校訂序

科技英文論文寫作實用指南
Practical Guide to Scientific English Writing

　　近年來，隨著大專院校研究所廣泛的設立，將會有更多的研究生投入學術或應用研究，並期望能在國際學術期刊或在國際學術會議上發表論文，借此展現研究成果。然而，儘管許多學生研究成果相當出色，仍視撰寫科技英語論文甚或一篇中文的科技論文為畏途。究其原因，除因本身英文程度有待加強提升之外，實因在僅重視考試的升學制度之下，未曾受過相關訓練，以致不瞭解一般科技論文的基本架構及寫作要點。即使英文及寫作程度達一定程度者，仍會因文化差異而難以準確地表達出作者的原意，不但影響文章的可讀性，又易使讀者產生誤解或不知所云。

　　校者於上海參與國際學術研討會之際，有幸拜讀俞炳豐教授大作「科技英語論文實用寫作指南」。本書不但以論述與實例相結合的方式介紹科技英語論文各章節的寫作要點與基本結構，詳述論文中常用句型、時態及語態的用法以及標點符號的使用規則，並指出學生在撰寫論文時常易犯下的錯誤，在在皆值得需要撰寫科技論文之我輩參考。附錄中更列有在論文投稿時的投稿及致謝信函範本，以及在研討會中進行學術演講和圖表設計的注意事項等，亦頗值得研究。校者於就讀研究所時受教於前台大電機系主任王維新教授，王教授於批改論文時一向字字斟酌，常為尋求能精確達意之用字反覆再三推敲，其嚴謹治學之身影深深令人感動，在此向王教授致上崇高的敬意。

陸瑞強

2007年

科技英文論文寫作實用指南 **Practical Guide to Scientific English Writing**

科技英文論文寫作實用指南
Practical Guide to Scientific English Writing

　　隨著當今國際交流日趨增多，作為一種國際通用語言的英語越來越顯出其重要性。對於科研工作者和高素質人才來說，為了將他們的成果與經驗在國際上進行交流，必須掌握英語，學會用書面形式表述自己的研究成果和學術觀點。但是，由於文化差異和英語書面表達能力較差，國內不少科研人員、碩士生和博士生在撰寫英語論文和其他文體的文章時，往往難以準確地表達出自己的意思。文章中或存在「中文式」英語，或用詞不當，或出現嚴重的語法錯誤，這既影響文章的可讀性，又容易使讀者產生誤解或不知所云，從而降低文章的學術價值。針對這種普遍的現象，為了幫助科研人員、碩士生和博士生提高英語寫作水準，迫切需要為廣大讀者提供寫作，特別是論文寫作方面的指導，本書便是在此背景下應運而生。

　　通覽全書，沒有空洞的言詞，也沒有主觀的臆斷。每個觀點的提出，每個問題的分析，都基於豐富詳實的資料和廣泛的調查研究。本書參考了大量的相關文獻，典型的實例大多來自不同專業和領域國際學術刊物刊載的研究論文，具有很強的參考價值。要搜集整理這些珍貴的資料並非一日之功，本書凝結著作者多年的心血，確實令人敬佩。作者強烈的社會責任感和科學意識、敏銳的學術眼光、系統的研究方法以及紮實的語言功力使本書成為一部成功之作。

　　本書文字論述簡潔流暢，寫作風格樸實無華，編寫內容具有很強的針對性和實用性。它反映了作者長期指導研究生進行科技英語論文寫作的豐富經驗，但又並非只是經驗之作。作者採用論述與實例結合的方式，理論聯繫實際，使讀者能深入領會和掌握寫作方法並能舉一反三，觸類旁通。因此，針對性、指導性和實用性是本書的特色。

本書對提高讀者的英語寫作水準大有裨益，是現在和將來從事科研工作的人員的良師益友。讀者在寫作論文時，可以參考本書介紹的科技英語的文體特點、科技應用文寫作方法及常用表達方式、慣用表達方式、語法結構以及常用詞的用法，使論文的內容清晰準確，從而提高論文的嚴謹性和科學性。

著名哲學家培根說過：有些書要淺嘗輒止，有些書可以囫圇吞棗，少數好書則須深入鑽研，仔細揣摩。無疑，本書是值得「深入鑽研，仔細揣摩」的佳作。

王監龍

前言
科技英文論文寫作實用指南
Practical Guide to Scientific English Writing

　　隨著研究生培養水準的提高和科研工作的蓬勃發展，將會有更多的博士生和青年學者撰寫科技英語論文，並期望能在國際學術期刊上發表，或在國際學術會議上宣讀，借此展示自己的研究成果，並與國際同領域的專家、學者進行交流和切磋，同時達到提高自己研究水準的作用。撰寫的科技論文是否能被國際學術期刊或學術會議接受，基本上取決於論文作者研究工作的水準，但是，科技論文的英語寫作水準也是一個十分重要的因素。從目前的情況來看，大專院校內開設相應的課程以提高研究生的科技論文的英語寫作能力是一個迫在眉睫的任務。本書即是為因應這一要求而編寫的。

　　本書從實用性的角度出發，以論述與實例結合的方式介紹科技英語論文各章節的寫作要點、基本結構、常用句型、時態及語態的用法，以及標點符號的使用規則；並針對學生的特點，指出撰寫科技英語論文時常出現的錯誤與一些常用詞及片語的正確用法。在附錄中列出投稿信函、致謝、學術演講和圖表設計及應用的注意事項。

　　需說明的是：本書主要是以理工學科作為背景來進行論述和舉例的，但是本書介紹的科技英語論文的寫作原則、基本句型與語態及時態的應用規則同樣適用於其他領域論文的寫作，而且，在本書有些地方也有其他學科論文寫作特點的說明。此外，本書闡述的科技英語論文的寫作通則雖然對所有的論文寫作都基本適用，然而，由於各專業學術期刊都有體現其風格的體例規定，所以建議撰寫科技英語論文的作者務必參閱擬投學術刊物上已發表的若干篇論文，以使自己的論文寫作符合該刊物的具體要求。還有，儘管本書論述的是科技英語論文的寫作方法，但是閱讀本書的讀者會發現書中的內容對寫好中文科技論文也是有指導意義的，比如本書緒論中關於優秀論文的標準、關於論文各部分的寫作要點，以及附錄中的演講要求、圖表的設計與製作等對博士生、碩士生撰寫學位論文和準備學位論文的答辯都有幫助。

在撰寫本書時，作者曾經參閱了一些學者關於科技寫作的著作。這些著作在確定本書的寫作風格和內容安排上使作者受到啟迪，獲益良多。這裡要特別提到C. J. Fraser，他的著作寫作風格樸實無華、清楚簡潔，內容組織具有很強的實用性，而且反映了他長期指導研究生進行科技論文寫作的經驗和體會。他的著作為本書所介紹的不少內容提供了基礎。本書中的英文例句和段落摘自於許多學者的專著和五十餘種不同專業和領域國際學術刊物上登載的研究論文，其中極少數的例句和段落沒有直接引述原作者的寫法，而是經過作者的修改，以便使其簡單以適應本書的用途。這些專著與大部分的論文都在本書的參考文獻目錄中列出。

本書可作為大專院校博士生、碩士生的科技英語論文寫作方法課程的教材。大專院校的青年教師和研究院所的科研人員也可以通過閱讀本書，儘快掌握撰寫科技英語論文或研究報告的基本技能。本書還可以用於對國際學術會議與會人員的培訓。

編寫本書的整個過程實際上是一個不斷學習、不斷提高的過程。對此，作者深有體會。儘管如此，作為一個工程學科的教師來編寫本書，確實是一個不小的挑戰。由於作者程度有限，不當與錯誤之處在所難免，敬請廣大讀者及相關專家批評指正。

俞炳豐

科技英文論文寫作實用指南
Practical Guide to Scientific English Writing

科技英文論文寫作實用指南 **Practical Guide to Scientific English Writing**

1 緒論

　　科技論文是科學研究資訊的載體，主要是由文字和圖表組成的，在學術刊物上發表科技論文或在學術會議上作學術演講則是科研資訊傳播的主要途徑。

　　隨著科研工作的蓬勃發展，越來越多的大專院校教師、研究生和研究院所的專業人員必須使用英語撰寫科技論文或報告，並在國際學術界發表自己的重要研究成果，以促進國際學術交流，並藉此提升我國的研究水準。撰寫科技英語論文的目的，可能是研究人員期望和其他學者分享自己的研究結果，或者是描述自己業已發現的新的研究問題，企圖引起同行的注意與討論；也可能是論文作者為了提升職稱而積累自己的學術業績；對於博士生而言，可能是為了獲得國際學術界對自己研究結果的認可，以便達到規定的授予學位的基本條件。不管動機如何，撰寫科技英語論文的最根本的目的還是「交流」或「溝通」，即把自己研究工作的資訊傳達給全世界同領域及相關領域內的讀者。

　　每個科技論文的作者都希望自己撰寫的論文是一篇優秀的論文。那麼，什麼樣的論文才是優秀的論文呢？對於這個問題，不同的專家、學者可能會有不同的答案。但是絕大部分的專家、學者都認為一篇優秀論文必須具備以下四個基本因素，即具有創新性、資訊量豐富、可讀性強及優良的文字表達能力。具有創新性和豐富的資訊量是代表研究水準的標誌，而可讀性強及優良的文字表達能力則是代表論文寫作水準的基本要素。

　　所謂創新性，如果用最高標準來衡量的話，則是指：在已沈寂的研究領域提出新的思想，在十分活躍的研究領域取得重大的進展，或者將原來彼此無相關的研究領域融合在一起。當然，這個要求是辦刊人員的奮鬥目標和期刊的最高標準，要達到這些最高標準自然是很不容易的。大多數的科研人員或專業人員通常從事的是一項規模並不是很大的基礎研究或應用研究方面的工作。但是，只要研究工作比較深入，有實質性的進展，得到的最新研究結果可靠、深刻並能引起同領域或相關領域學者的關注，論文能反映研究者獨到的見解，那麼這樣的論文應該是高水準的、具有創新性的論文。

　　在篇幅有限的前提下，論文本身要能向讀者提供豐富的資訊量。論文的資訊量越大，讀者能獲得的新知識就越多。論文的資訊量是否豐富，一方面取決於論文所反映的研究水準，另一方面也依賴於論文的寫作方法。顯然，決定論文資訊量的關鍵是論文作者研究工作中是否有新的學術思想、新的實驗方法或者新的發現。當然，認真構思論文的框架、選擇最重要的素材、採用最恰當的表述方式，也能使論文的主題新穎、內容充實。

　　論文的可讀性十分重要，應當引起論文作者的高度重視。為充分體現研究工作的意義並使讀者對論文產生濃厚的興趣，作者要反復推敲研究背景的介紹、學術思想的解釋等論述方式，使論文結構嚴謹、內容充實、論述完整、邏輯性強。在論述方式上，要儘量做到深入淺出，表達清楚、簡潔，專業術語準確且前後一致。為了避免過多的文字說明和取得較好的效果，要注意圖表與文字的恰當配合。要嚴格按照學術期刊制訂可反映他們風格與特點的體例要求，特別要仔細斟酌論文的題目、摘要和關鍵字，切忌包羅萬象、大而空的題目和言過其實、空洞無物的摘要。如果一篇論文的可讀性差，那麼不僅會使論文失去許多讀者，而且會間接地給專業期刊的聲譽帶來一定的負面影響。

　　優良的文字表達能力對於撰寫科技英語論文的國內學者與學生而言尤為重要。首先，要有紮實的英語功底，學會「用英語思考」，避免不同程度的「中文式英語」問題，遣詞造句應當恰當、正確，不能出現語法錯誤；其次，應該採用清楚、簡潔、自然的方式表達自己的論點；還需要掌握科技英語論文的標準句型和論證模式。如果能透過學習達到上述要求，那麼就能很快地提高自己的英語文字表達能力，儘管我們之中大部分的人達不到以英語為母語的學者的英語寫作水準，但是也能寫出符合基本標準的科技英語論文。

有許多研究生的研究工作很有意義，且獲得了頗有價值的結果，論文投稿後，期刊的編輯會回信告訴作者論文很有新意，但是英文寫得太差，建議修改或請有經驗的專家指導重寫。出現這種情況的原因主要有以下三個方面：一是論文作者不瞭解科技英語論文的寫作本身是一門學問，不重視學習，僅僅靠參考所投期刊上已發表的論文「依樣畫葫蘆」的方式來撰寫科技英語論文；二是大學裡未開設科技英語論文寫作方法方面的課程，也未出版這方面的教材，因而，研究生沒有機會接受較有系統的撰寫科技英語論文的培訓；三是少數作者寫作不夠認真，缺少嚴謹的態度。實際上，如果我們不知道如何用英語正確表達自己的論點或研究結果，常常是因為我們的思維比較粗糙、比較模糊。由於思維與語言的使用之間存在密切的關係，所以訓練自己用英語寫出內容清楚簡潔、結構嚴謹的論文，也就是同時訓練了自己嚴謹的思維方式。值得注意的是，一個研究人員能使用清楚、簡潔、正確的英語來表達自己的想法，表明他具有某種專業能力，也能獲得其他專業研究人員的尊敬；相反，如果論文形式不夠合於規範，或內容籠統又模糊，則審稿人及讀者可能會懷疑作者的研究水準和專業能力。

提高研究生（特別是博士生）的科技英語論文寫作的能力是極待解決的一個問題，本書是為了因應這一要求而編寫的。

考慮到本書的實用性和本書的讀者群主要是我國青年學者及研究生的具體情況，本書的內容是這樣安排的：第二章至第八章分別闡述科技論文的導論（背景資料與文獻回顧，介紹研究主題）、理論分析、實驗與方法、結果、討論、結論等各部分的寫作方法，包括寫作原則、基本結構、常用句型、時態及語態的正確使用、注意事項和建議；第九章討論了如何撰寫一篇好的摘要；第十章敘述了參考文獻目錄的標準格式及相關事項；第十一章指出了科技論文寫作中常犯的錯誤；標點符號及一些常用詞或片語的正確用法則分別在第十二章、第十三章中列出。在本書的附錄1至附錄4中，依序介紹了投稿信函、致謝、學術演講和圖表的設計及應用。本書除了論述以外，還提供了大量的實例，供讀者參考。

最後，請讀者牢牢記住撰寫科技英語論文的三個重要原則（The Three C's）。"The Three C's"是英語修辭學最基本的原則，即正確（Correct）：每個句子的英語語法和論文的內容都必須正確；清楚（Clear）：作者的論點表達得既清楚又精確，以便讀者能容易並迅速瞭解；簡潔（Concise）：論文應該寫得簡潔、直接，避免重複和多餘的詞，每個句子中的每個詞都應該是句子中必不可少的。

2

導論部分之一
背景材料與文獻回顧

　　本章及下一章將討論如何撰寫科技研究論文的導論。導論有兩個主要的功能，即闡述研究的動機和說明研究的目的。在撰寫研究論文時，應確保論文的導論能精確而清楚地表達這兩個重點。通過閱讀導論，讀者可以瞭解論文的主題，以便對論文後面各章節的內容有個心理準備。導論往往被認為是論文最難寫的部分之一，因為作者必須採用適當的撰寫方法和組織形式來敘述論文的主題，同時必須在較少的篇幅內提及很多研究資訊。而且，導論的內容通常能反映作者對本研究領域的瞭解程度及其研究水準，因此，建議作者在撰寫研究論文時，要十分重視導論的寫作，應仔細擬定導論的草稿並不厭其煩地進行反覆修改。

　　在導論中，千萬不要直接重複摘要中的內容，更不要直接抄錄摘要中的句子。導論和摘要各自的功能與長度不同，因此這兩部分的內容與表達形式應有差別。況且，讀者通常不喜歡閱讀一模一樣的句子或段落。此外，在絕大多數期刊發表的論文中，導論的結尾處不簡述研究工作的主要結論。作者自己已經寫出清楚、適當的摘要，則摘要中已經以簡潔的方式敘述主要的結論。如果有些讀者需先深入瞭解這些結論的話，那麼他們可以先直接翻閱結論部分，然後再閱讀方法或結果等其他部分。

2.1 基本內容及組織形式

　　一般而言，一個好的導論應該清楚地說明以下四個項目：主要的研究工作，研究工作的目的，進行研究的動機或背景，以及本研究工作在相關領域中的地位。在撰寫導論時，通常先描述某個領域的近況，並指出進一步研究的理由，然後再敘述作者自己的研究工作的目的與內容。為了清楚地表達這些資訊，研究論文的導論常常至少包含下列的四個基本步驟：

步驟一｜背景資料。導論一開始，先介紹作者的研究領域，敘述有關該研究領域的一般資訊，並針對研究論文將要探討的問題或現象提供背景知識。

步驟二｜文獻回顧。介紹並評論其他學者對該問題或現象曾經發表的相關研究。

步驟三｜指出問題。作者指出仍然有某個問題或現象值得進一步研究。

步驟四｜介紹作者的研究目的或研究活動。最後，作者說明自己研究工作的具體目的，敘述自己的研究活動。

幾乎每一篇科技研究論文的導論中都會包含上述四個步驟。此外，導論有時還會包括一兩個其他的步驟，即下述的步驟五及步驟六。這兩個步驟的作用在於說明本研究工作可能的價值以及研究論文的組織結構。某些研究領域的論文導論中常出現這兩個步驟，但是在一些其他領域的論文導論中很少見到，因此，步驟五與步驟六是可有可無的。

步驟五｜指出本研究工作的理論價值或應用價值。作者解釋自己的研究對於相關領域的貢獻，例如指出可能具有的理論價值或實際應用意義。

步驟六｜說明本研究論文的組織結構。作者簡明地說明論文的組織結構，以便使讀者對作者介紹研究結果的方式有大致的瞭解。

請注意，步驟五往往會在一般的碩士學位論文或博士學位論文的導論中出現。但是，很多發表在專業學術期刊上的論文會省略該步驟。如論文篇幅很長（如8頁以上）時應該在導論中包含步驟六，以便使讀者獲知整個論文的組織結構。在某些專業領域，由於不同的研究論文有各自的組織結構，所以作者在撰寫導論時也常常採用步驟六。

下面的例2-1摘自一篇科技研究論文（發表在*Experimental Thermal and Fluid Science* 26(2002)）的導論，該導論包括上述的步驟一至四。

例2-1

Study of free convection frost formation on a vertical plate

→ 背景資料

Frost formation processes are of great importance in numerous industrial applications including refrigeration, cryogenics, and process industries. In most cases, frost formation is undesirable because it contributes to the increase in heat transfer resistance and pressure drop. Frost formation is a complicated transient phenomenon process in which a variety of heat and mass transfer mechanisms are simultaneous.

→ 文獻回顧

Typical frost formation periods have been described by Hayashi et al. [1]: an initial one-dimensional (1-D) crystal growth is followed by a frost layer growth peri-ods characterizes long time processes, in which the frost surface can reach the melting temperature. Each growth mode is characterized by peculiar values of frost density which in turn affects the other frost parameters (thickness, apparent thermal conductivity). Furthermore, as observed in several studies [2-5], the features of the heat transfer rate (through the wall-to-air temperature difference) and of the mass transfer rate (which depends on air moisture content too) affect the frost structure and control the length of the growth periods. Owing to the complexity of the phenomenon, the development of reliable frost formation models as well as of correlations to evaluate frost properties is a demanding task; experimental data are required to check both the assumptions made in the theoretical analyses and the predicted results.

As clearly reported in some review papers [6-8] frost formation during the forced convection of humid air has been extensively studied, while, on the other hand, only a limited number of investigations deal with mass-heat transfer during natural convection on a surface at subfreezing temperature. This problem was tackled by Kennedy and Goodman ([9], study of frost formation on a vertical surface), Tajima et al. ([10], flat surface with different orientations), Cremers and Mehra ([3], outer side of vertical cylinders), Tokura et al. ([4]. vertical surface). To the author's knowledge, no data are available for the natural convection in channels, despite the practical significance of this phenomenon in such devices as evaporative heat exchangers for cryogenic liquid gasification.

→ 研究目的與活動

The present paper reports the results of an experimental investigation of frost formation on a vertical plate inside a rectangular channel where ambient air is flowing due to natural convection. The experiments have been conducted in the range of low-intermediate values of the relative humidity (31-58%) for which frost temperature, during frost growth, is always below the triple-point temperature, thus acting as a further parameter of the study. The measured data have been compared with the results of a mathematical model developed for predicting frost growth and heat flux at the cold plate.

在本章的其餘部分，將討論研究論文導論的前半部分，即步驟一、步驟二的內容及常用句型。步驟三到六則在下一章再作討論。

2.2 背景資料（步驟一）

◆ 2.2.1 背景資料的介紹

在研究論文的背景資料介紹中，為了使讀者認識論文內容的重要性，作者必須說明研究論文的特定主題與較為廣泛的研究領域之間的關係，同時必須提供足夠的背景資料。論文作者可以採用一種約定俗成的方法，即先指出和論文內容所屬研究領域有關的一般事實；接著轉到此大研究領域中的其中一個次研究領域，並指出該次領域中某些特定的事實；最後應該把焦點轉到該次領域中的論文所探討的問題有密切關係的更狹窄的主題，並針對此主題再指出某些事實。所以，從介紹背景資料句子的內容來看，通常先有一兩個範圍比較廣的句子，然後句子內容的範圍逐漸縮小，最後一兩句的範圍應該相當狹窄。

例2-2

The separation of mixtures of alkanes is an important activity in the petroleum and petrochemical industries. For example, the products from a catalytic isomerization reactor consist of a mixture of lin-ear, mono-methyl and di-methyl alkanes. Of these, the di-branched molecules are the most desired ingredients in petrol because they have the highest octane number. It is therefore required to separate the di-methyl alkanes and recycle the linear and mono-methyl alka-nes back to the isomerizatio reactor. In the detergent industry, the linear alkanes are the desired components and need to be separated from the alkanes mixture.

Selective sorption on zeolites is often used for separation of alkanes mixtures [1-7]. The choice of the zeolite depends on the specific separation task in hand. For example, small-pore Zeolite A are used for separation of linear alkanes using the molecular sieving principle; the branched molecules cannot enter the zeolite structure. Both linear and branched molecules are allowed inside the medium-pore MFI matrix and the sorption hierarchy in MFI will be dictated both by the alkanes chain length and degree of branching.

在例2-2所示的背景資料中，作者所介紹的較為廣泛的題目是"separation of mixture of alkanes"，然後介紹較狹窄的題目是"linear alkanes separated from the alkane mixture"，最後，作者把焦點集中到一個更狹窄的小題目，即"selective sorption on zeolites used for separation of alkane mixture"。該小題目與研究論文具體的研究問題（entropy effects during sorption of mixtures of alkanes in MFI zeolite）具有非常密切的關係。

背景資料的內容通常都是該研究領域內一般學者都會承認或熟知的一

些普遍事實，因此往往不需引述參考文獻來說明這些內容。但是，有些作者也會引述一些參考資料，以表示這些內容的來源，如：

Flat plate heat pipes have attracted substantial attention lately due to their advantages over conventional cylindrical heat pipes, such as geometry adoption, ability for very localized heat dissipation, and the production of an entirely flat isothermal surface. Due to these advantages, flat heat pipes have become increasingly attractive for various applications such as the cooling of electronic devices［1］and space vehicles［2］.

撰寫導論的背景資料時，作者必須考慮研究論文的讀者對象，以確定背景資料的範圍。若大部分讀者可能是某個專業領域裡的專家，則背景資料可能會相當簡短（也許只有2至3個句子），而且往往省略較為廣泛的題目，在一開始就介紹較狹窄的題目。相反地，若某個學術期刊的讀者群包括來自幾個不同領域的學者，則此期刊所刊登的研究論文都會有較長篇幅的背景資料內容（也許有兩個段落以上），而且背景資料一開始介紹的是較為廣泛的題目。

◆ 2.2.2 時態與「先舊後新」原則

背景資料中的句子通常敘述有關某些現象或某個研究領域的普遍事實，這些普遍事實不受時間的影響，所以句子中的主要動詞應該使用現在簡單式，請參見下面的例句：

→ A few analytical models and simulations for conventional cylindrical heat pipe mainly concentrate on the startup operation involving liquid metal working liquids.

→ Heterogeneous distillation is involved in several industrial processes.

→ Delaminations in composite material result typically from impact damage or manufacturing imperfections.

→ Muscle pain in the shoulder/neck area and the upper extremities is common among computer workers, especially women.

然而，若在背景資料中指出作者專業領域裡最近發生的某種趨勢，或最近發生的某個事件，則使用現在完成式，如：

→ The study of scattering of elastic waves by subsurface defects has been the focus of interest of many recent studies due to its relevance to problems in nondestructive evaluation and material characterization.

→ Various approaches such as modular technique ［10］ and object oriented programming (OOP) ［11-13］ have been employed as programming tools.

「先舊後新」是一種可讀性原則。對撰寫背景資料而言，「先舊後新」原則是指在解釋較廣泛的研究領域與作者自己具體的研究題目之間的關係時，作者應該在每一個句子中先重複一項「舊」的資訊，即前面已述及的名詞或名詞片語，然後才提到「新」的資訊，即前面尚未提及的名詞或名詞片語。採用「先舊後新」原則的目的在於使讀者清楚地瞭解每項新的資訊與整個研究背景之間的關係。作者在提到「舊」的資訊時，可以直接重複前面曾經提及的名詞或名詞片語，也可採用代名詞或具有相同意義的其他名詞或名詞片語。例2-3表示出「先舊後新」原則的應用。請注意例中斜體字表示的名詞、代名詞或名詞片語。

例2-3

Delaminations in composite materials result typically from impact damage or manufacturing imperfections. In general, *they* cause a considerable *reduction* in compressive strength and therefore *reduce* the performance advantage of composite materials ［1］. One mechanism of compressive strength *reduction* in delaminated composites is *buckling out* of plane of the groups of plies above and below the delamination. This *buckling subjects* the remaining unbuckled plies to asymmetric loading, resulting in a reduced failure load for the laminate.

2.3 文獻回顧（步驟二）

文獻回顧是研究論文導論部分的第二個步驟。在文獻回顧中，論文作者會進一步說明自己研究工作的背景及動機。作者既要表示自己對同一研究領域裡其他學者曾發表的相關研究十分熟悉，也要反映自己的研究工作和這些其他學者過去的研究工作之間的關係。

有關專業期刊編輯問卷調查的結果顯示，科技研究論文投稿人最常犯的錯誤之一是論文中缺少對相關研究的引述，因而無法清楚地表示作者研究的動機及重要性。一篇研究論文的內容必須有創新並能增進相關研究領域的知識，才能為學術期刊所接受。若作者不能在導論中先清楚地解釋自己研究領域的近況，則審稿人和讀者無法看出作者的研究結果對所涉研究領域所作的貢獻。另一方面，作者在撰寫文獻回顧時，不應該引述一大堆不相關的參考文獻，只需引述適當的參考文獻以便指出作者自己研究工作的意義、動機及目的，並說明該研究能提供一些新的資料或解決某個需要解決的問題，而不是證明作者見聞廣博。

文獻回顧的長度視論文的類別與研究領域而定。在專業期刊上發表的論文中，文獻回顧有時只包含幾個句子，但是通常有一兩個段落。相較之下，博士學位論文中的文獻回顧則常常是一個完整的獨立章節。如果作者打算研討另一學者最近才提出的非常專業的實驗手段或數學問題，那麼只需引述一兩篇參考文獻即可。然而，假如作者自己研究的主題是許多其他學者曾經致力研究的問題，則可能要引述許多參考資料並進行評論。

文獻回顧的組織形式大致有三種類型：依照參考文獻的主題與作者研究論文關係的密切程度排列資料；依照時間順序排列參考文獻；依照所要討論的參考資料的不同類別排列參考文獻。

①依照參考文獻的主題與作者研究論文關係的密切程度排列資料。作者先提到和自己研究關係比較不密切的參考資料，然後再引述最密切的參考資料。在例2-4中，作者研究論文的主題是"Analyzing cloning evolution in the Linux kernel"。作者先描述"methods for identifying similar code fragments and/or components in a software system"，然後討論 "the evaluation of similar code fragments among several versions of the same software system"。

例2-4

In the literature there are many papers proposing various methods for identifying similar code fragments and/or components in a software system (〔2, 5, 11〕 and 〔17, 18, 21, 22〕). However, the information gathered accounts for local similarities and changes. As a result, the overall picture describing the macro system changes is difficult to obtain. Moreover, if chunks of code migrate via copy/remove or cut-and-paste among modules or subsystems, the duplicated code may not be easily distinguished from freshly developed one.

Indeed, only few papers have studied the evolution of similar code fragments among several versions of the same software system 〔1, 19〕. As a software system evolves, new code fragments are added, certain parts deleted, modified or remain unchanged, thus giving raise to an overall evolution difficult to represent by fine-grained similarity measures.

②依照時間順序排列參考文獻。在這種引述形式中，先討論比較早期的文獻，然後再敘述比較晚期的資料。下面的例2-5的作者採用的就是這種形式。

例2-5

Scattering of elastic waves by defects in anisotropic media has recently attracted attention due to the increasing use of composite materials in engineering design and its relevance to anisotropy of the medium on the response is useful in both qualitative and quantitative nondestructive evaluation of materials. Furthermore, the solution for surface displacements of a composite medium with defects (e.g. voids, cracks, etc.) due to a surface pulse can be used to compute the acoustic material signature of medium. Karim and Kundu (1991) considered the surface response of an orthotropic half plane with a horizontal subsurface crack due to a surface pulse. Datta et al. (1992) investigated the scattering of impact waves by a crack in a composite plate. Recently, Rajapakse and Gross (1995) examined the response of an orthotropic elastic medium with a circular cavity due to transient pressurization,

③依照所要討論的參考資料的不同類別排列參考文獻。把所要討論的參考資料分為幾個不同類別，例如根據不同的研究路線進行分類。當作者有很多參考資料需要討論時，常採用此種形式。在分類之後，又可以採用上述的形式①或形式②來引述各類中的文獻。在下面的例2-6中，作者把所要引述的參考資料分為兩類——"Free generalized thermoelastic waves" 和 "Guided waves"，然後針對這兩類的資料各採用依照時間順序的組織形式加以引述。

例2-6

Free generalized thermoelastic waves have been considered in isotropic media by Puri (1973; 1975), Agarwal (1979), and Tao and Prevost (1984). The interaction of generalized thermoelastic waves with anisotropic media was studied by Banerjee and Pao (1974), Dhaliwal and Sherief (1980), Singh and Sharma (1985), and Sharma et al. (1986; 1989).

Guided waves were considered by several researchers. Nayfeh and Nemat-Nasser (1971), Sinha and Sinha (1975), and Agarwal (1978) studied thermoelastic Rayleigh waves. Harinath et al.(1976;1978) studied Stonely-type waves. Mondal et al.(1973;1983), Massalas (1986), Massalas and Kaloakidis (1987a) ,and Massalas and Tsolakidis (1987) considered the propagation of generalized thermo elastic waves in thin plates. Erby and Sunhubi (1986) studied the problem of longitudinal waves in a circular rod. Massalas and Kalpakidis (1987b) considered a waveguide with a rectangular cross section.

In contrast, little work has been conducted on thermoelastic waves in layered and/or composite media. Sve (1971) used the classical theory of thermoelasticity to treat obliquely travelling waves in a bilaminated isotropic medium. His analysis was conducted by using potential functions. The results were given in the form of an exact dispersion relation resulting potential functions. The results were given in the form of an exact dispersion relation resulting from the vanishing of a twelfth-order determinant. Numerical results were given for the quasi-elastic modes in the form of dispersion and attenuation curves.

2.4 文獻回顧的常用句型

文獻回顧中的句子通常可分成下列四種類型：資料導向引述；研究領域的一般描述；多作者導向引述；論文作者導向引述。每一類型都有特定的句型，而且其動詞使用特定的時態。

文獻回顧通常以前三種句子之一開頭。在一兩個這種引述之後，作者往往會用第四種句子引述。若文獻回顧包含兩個或兩個以上段落，則作者會使用前三種引述句子作為每個段落的開頭。下面介紹這四種引述句子的句型。

(1)資料導向引述

文獻回顧中的第一個句子常常敘述與研究論文內容關聯的一般事實，這種句子稱為「資料導向引述」。在這種引述中，句子的焦點是某些資料，而被引述文獻的作者姓氏及出版年代則置於句末的括弧中。在資料導向引述中，作者需把自己正在討論的主題作為句子的主詞，見下例所示：

→ In some climates, control of house dust mite allergen loads has been found to be possible by seasonal regulation of indoor relative humidity [2].

→ This hypothesis is supported by cell morphology results in studies of myalgic trapezius muscle (Larsson et al., 1988; Kadi et al., 1998).

　　如上例所示，資料導向引述有兩種標準格式，其中一種格式是將參考文獻的序號放在括弧內，該序號是指參考文獻在論文末尾參考文獻目錄中的序號；另一種格式是把參考文獻作者的姓氏及出版年代置於句末的括弧裡。建議作者應先查閱擬投學術期刊的相關格式說明，再決定應使用的標準格式。

　　注意，文獻回顧的首句有時在形式上與資料導向引述完全一樣，但是省略了參考引述，只是陳述一些事實。這種寫法表示作者認為句子所陳述的資料是大家公認的事實，沒有必要引述參考文獻以支援自己的陳述。

　　在資料導向引述的句子中，最常用的時態是現在簡單式和現在完成式。現在簡單式表示所引述的資料是不受時間影響的普遍事實；而現在完成式則用於描述某種趨勢或變動的事實。此外，有時作者會用過去簡單式來陳述過去的事件或事實。使用的三種時態的句型見下例：

→ The supercritical CO_2 extraction of herbaceous materials generally results in a lower oil yield and a more complex final product profile (16-19).

→ Previous research has employed the MC methods to investigate uncertainty in air modeling estimates (Hanna et al., 1998; Jaarsveld et al., 1997; Smith et al., 1999).

→ Low-threshold MUs were found to show periods of inactivity in combination with direct recruitment of MUs of higher thresholds (Westgaard and De Luca, 1999).

(2)研究領域的一般描述

　　另一種常在文獻回顧中的前幾句或在文獻回顧中新的段落前面出現的類型，是對於某個研究領域的一般描述。該種句子的重點往往是在於表示該領域中對於某個問題的研究程度，即相關研究的多少。因為此種句子的內容通常是大家公認的事實，所以一般而言不需要引述任何參考文獻。由於所描述的內容是從過去到現在的一種研究趨勢，因此這種對研究程度的描述通常得使用現在完成式。此外，這種一般描述中討論的焦點是研究主題，而不是從事研究工作的學者。所以此種句子常常採用被動語態。標準的句型如表2-1所示。

表2-1　研究程度描述的標準句型之一

研究程度		動詞（現在完成式，被動語態）	主題
Much Little No A volume of	work research 不可數.	has been carried out on has been done on has been performed on has been published regarding has been conducted on has been devoted to	fuzzy voltage stability analysis
Much Little	attention 不可數.	has been devoted to has been directed toward has been focused on	the heterogeneous distillation.
Many A number of Several Quite few	studies experiments	have been conducted on have been done regarding have been performed on have been published on	the effect of delamination in flat laminates.

請注意：表2-1中第一、二行的主詞是不可數名詞，因而句子的動詞必須使用單數形式。第三行的主詞是複數名詞，因此句中的動詞為複數形式。還有，如果需指出確實有些學者曾研究過某個問題，則應該採用"several"或"a number of"等修飾主詞；相反，如果想要強調研究此問題的人極少，則應該使用"few"或"little"等詞作為主詞的形容詞。

在表2-1的例句中，研究主題都出現在動詞之後。然而，這種描述也可將研究主題當作主詞。此外，這種句子常常會提到特定的一段時間。研究主題作為句子的主詞時，應該採用被動語態還是主動語態，則要取決於特定動詞的含義。請參考下面表2-2、表2-3中的例子，參考時請注意句子的主動語態或被動語態的使用，還要注意句中主詞的單、複數用法。

表2-2　研究程度描述的標準句型之二

主題	動詞（現在完成式、主動語態）	研究程度	時間（可有可無）
The documentary structure of source code	has been	the subject of much research	in recent years. in the last decade. since 1995.
The effect of density fluctuations on the changes of azimuth	have been	the subject of few studies the focus of a great deal of research	
The documentary syructure of source code	have drawn have attracted	much attention much interest little attention	in recent years. in the last decade. since 1995.
The effects of density fluctuations on the changes of azimuth	has drawn has attracted		

表2-3　研究程度描述的標準句型之三

主題	動詞（現在完成式，被動語態）及研究程度	時間（可有可無）
The documentary structure of source code	has been widely discussed has been extensively examined has been thoroughly investigated has seldom been discussed	since 1992. in the last decade. in recent years.
The effects of density fluctuations on the changes of azimuth	have been widely discussed have been extensively examined have been thoroughly investigated have seldom been discussed	since 1992. in the last decade. in recent years.

還有一種常見的句型是使用 "There has been…" 和 "There have been …" 結構來指出對某個問題的研究程度。請注意下面例句中動詞單複數形式的用法。

→ There has been much research on the documentary structure of source code.

→ There has been little research on load margin and critical bus determination.

→ There have been many studies on the documentary structure of source code.

→ There have been few reports on load margin and critical bus determination.

在描述了相關領域中對於某個問題的研究程度後，作者通常會開始詳細介紹並評論個別學者曾經進行的研究工作。

(3)多作者導向引述

在文獻回顧開始時或在文獻回顧中新段落開始時，作者可以使用一個句子來討論兩個或兩個以上學者曾經做過的研究工作。此種句子稱為「多作者導向引述」。與研究程度的描述相同，多作者導向引述介紹一些學者從過去到現今的研究趨勢，因此句子中應該採用現在完成式。在這種引述中，可以把 "many investigators" 之類的名詞的片語作為主詞而採用主動語態（如表2-4所示），或者可以把研究主題當作主詞而採用被動語態（參見表2-5）。至於被引述文獻的資料則放在句末的括弧中。

表2-4　多作者導向引述常用句型之一

多作者	動詞（現在完成式，主動語態）	主　題	參考引述
Many investigators Several researchers A number of authors Few writers	have studied have investigated have examined have explored have reported on have discussed have considered	the fast decoupled continuation power flows	(3, 4, 5, 7).

注意，如果作者表達的意思是「有些學者研究過該問題」，則應該用 "several writers" 或 "a number of researchers" 作為主詞。只有當作者強調曾經研究此問題的學者極少時，才可以使用 "few writers" 或 "few researchers"。

表2-5　多學者導向引述常用句型之二

主題	動詞（現在完成式，被動語態）	多作者	參考引述
The effects of devices such as VDTs	have been studied have been investigated have been examined have been explored have been reported on have been discussed have been considered	by several authors by a number of authors by many investigators by few writers	(Brown,1982; Forman, 1986; McGee, 1988).

此外，有的作者採用多學者導向引述時，句子中還包含有以that開頭的名詞性子句。這種名詞性子句絕大部分是受詞子句，用於描述某些學者的研究結果（參見表2-6）。名詞子句中動詞時態的應用，在本章後面的內容中將加以討論。

表2-6　多作者導向引述常用句型之三

多作者	動詞（現在完成式，主動語態）	That	研究結果	參考引述
Several researchers	have found have shown have reported have suggested	that	muscle aches and joint pain can be reduced by the use of adjustable workstation furniture	(Kleeman, 1988; Roberts, 1990; Paul, 1993).

(4)主要作者導向引述

論文作者在資料導向引述、對研究程度的一般描述或多作者導向引述之後，通常需要用2～3個句子把焦點轉到與自己研究有關的一些參考資料,以介紹並評論這些參考文獻提出的研究結果。引述這些參考文獻的句子稱為「作者導向引述」。在這種引述中,往往把某個學者的姓作為句子的主詞。由於句中的內容是指文獻作者過去的行為,所以句子的主要動詞通常使用過去簡單式。被引述學者的研究結果,則在動詞後面的名詞子句中加以敘述。請參閱表2-7。

作者導向引述句子中,主句與名詞子句各有一個動詞。主句的動詞通常使用過去時態,而名詞子句動詞的時態取決於所表達內容的性質。本章2.5節中對此進行了討論。

表2-7　作者導向引述常用句型之一

作者姓及文獻年代	動詞（過去簡單式,主動語態）	That	研究結果
Hedge(1982)	showed found reported noted suggested observed pointed out	that	the open office caused too many disturbances and distractions.

作者導向引述還有另外一種表達方法,即第一句只描述某個學者的研究活動,第二句才敘述研究結果。這兩個句子的主要動詞都應使用過去簡單式。第二句的結構與表2-7中的例句一樣,必須包含以that開頭的名詞子句,但省略文獻年代。如表2-8所示。

表2-8　作者導向引述常用句型之二

作者及文獻年代	動詞（過去簡單式,主動語態）	主題	第二句為作者導向引述
Lee (1999)	studied examined investigated explored considered	the effect of environmental conditions on frost formation.	He found that....

值得注意的是,在人文學科的研究論文中,具有與作者導向引述相同

結構的句子卻常常使用現在時態。這是一種約定俗成的做法，其原因是句子用來概述某個文獻所表達的觀念，而不是描述某學者本人過去的行為。因此，即使被引述的人是很久以前的人物，仍然可以使用現在簡單式來表達其著作的觀點，例如：

人文學科‧用 作者導向句子時‧使用現在簡單式

Aristotle uses the term akrasia to refer to a person's failure to act according to his or her best judgment.

在管理學、經濟學、心理學、社會學以及其他社會學科的研究論文中，作者通常會遵循科技研究論文約定俗成的寫法，即在作者導向引述中使用過去簡單式。然而，有的作者也會如人文學科的做法一樣使用現在簡單式。因此，建議論文作者在撰寫研究論文之前，應該查詢自己專業領域普遍採用的標準，並參考擬投期刊上已發表的若干篇文章，以便在作者導向引述中使用正確的時態。

2.5 子句中的動詞時態

在作者導向引述和有些多作者導向引述的複合句子中，主句描述被引述學者的研究活動，子句敘述學者提出的資料或研究結果。主句中的動詞通常使用過去簡單式，而子句（主要是受詞子句）的時態應視句子表達的內容而定。下面將討論子句中時態的選擇。

(1) 子句中的資料為普遍有效事實

若作者認為以that開頭的受詞子句中所提出的資料是不受時間限制的普遍有效的事實，而不是只在所引述的研究情況下才有效，那麼子句中應該採用現在簡單式，如表2-9所示。

表2-9　受詞子句使用現在過去簡單式

作者及文獻年代	動詞（過去簡單式）	That	研究結果（現在簡單式）
Marks (1932)	showed found reported noted observed suggested pointed out	that	water boils at 100°C.
Gorden(2)			the gravity of the largest moon affects the orbits of the other moons.

　　當子句的內容是描述其他學者曾經提出的方法或技術時，若該方法或技術已成為一種標準的方法或技術，或者現在仍有人使用它，則此子句中可用現在簡單式。而主句中用過去簡單式，說明提出方法或技術是該學者過去的行為，參見表2-10。

表2-10　形容詞子句使用現在簡單式

作者及文獻年代	動詞（過去簡單式）	賓　語	形容詞子句（現在簡單式）
Davis (1991)	developed described	an algorithm a technique	that solves the problems quickly.
Rubinstein〔4〕	introduced designed presented proposed	a method	that produces more effect-ive results.

(2)子句中的資料僅在特定情況下才有效

　　假如論文作者認為所引述的某學者的研究結果只在某特定的研究條件下有效，並不是不受時間影響的普遍事實，那麼在子句中應使用過去簡單式。請參見表2-11。

表2-11　受詞子句中使用過去簡單式

作者及文獻年代	動詞（過去簡單式）	That	研究結果（過去簡單式）
Smith〔1999〕 Ludwig(2)	found suggested observed reported indicated	that	the predicted concentrations were in reasonable agreement with the experimental data.
			all the osmotic water fluxes measured were still far too small for practical application in the production of energy.

(3)子句中的資料只表示一種建議或假設

　　有時，論文作者所引述的資料在原來的參考文獻中就只用探討的語氣來敘述，或者這些資料僅僅是一些建議或假設，而不是十分確定的研究結果。此時，主句中的動詞需採用如suggested 或proposed 之類的推測動詞，而子句中的動詞通常使用**may**加原形動詞，如表2-12所示。

表2-12　表示建議或假設的受詞子句的時態

作者及文獻年代	推測動詞（過去簡單式）	That	資料（may + 動詞原形）
Merten (2000)	suggested hypothesized proposed argued	that	these contradictory examinations may result from differences in the column design, sparger configurations or measuring techniques.

(4)對引述資料的評語

　　有的作者在回顧文獻時，在描述某個學者的研究工作之後，還對研究做出評論。此時，在描述研究工作的句子中應使用過去簡單式。對於做出評論的句子，若評語是針對過去的行為或事件，則句子的動詞應使用過去簡單式，見下面的前兩個例句。相反地，若評語的內容，是指不受時間影響或目前仍然有效的事實，則應該使用現在簡單式，下面的第三個例句即是這種情況。

→ Rahil [5] proposed a model based on the Excluded Volume determined by Onsager [6]. With this model, the variations of porosity could be described according to the aspect ratio.

→ Aziz (1985) took into account the effect of these thermal resistances. However, his analysis was restricted to the longitudinal fin of two specific profiles.

→ John (1978) presented a method for solving problems of this form when x≤1.5. However, his method is not applicable to the general case.

3

導論部分之二
介紹研究主題

前面第二章我們討論了如何撰寫導論部分的步驟一及步驟二，即背景資料與文獻回顧。本章將介紹導論部分的步驟三至六的寫作方法。

當論文作者描述了論文的背景資料並評述了其他學者的相關研究之後，在導論部分的後半部分會集中到論述自己的研究問題上。介紹作者本人的研究主題通常至少包含兩個主要的步驟，即指出問題（步驟三）與闡明研究目的（步驟四）。在步驟三中，為了說明自己的研究動機，作者需指出過去相關研究中尚未處理或解決的問題，或所衍生的新問題，使讀者對作者的研究目的有一個認識基礎。在步驟四中，作者緊接著就可以闡述自己的研究目的或研究活動。此外，有的導論還會包含步驟五與步驟六。在步驟五中，作者指出自己研究的結果有何理論價值或應用價值；而在步驟六中，則說明本研究論文的組織結構。步驟五及步驟六不是導論的必要內容，不少研究論文的導論中不出現這兩個步驟。

下面將詳細地介紹並討論步驟三至六的基本內容及常用句型。

3.1 指出問題（步驟三）

導論的步驟三通常只需一兩個句子表達，用於指出下列四個項目的其中一項：

①以前的學者處理得不夠完善或尚未研究的重要題目。

②過去的研究所衍生並值得探討的新問題。

③以前的學者曾經提出兩個或兩個以上互不相容的觀點或理論，為了

解決這些互有差異的觀點或理論之間的衝突，必須展開進一步的研究。

④過去的研究自然可以擴展到的新領域或新題目，或者以前曾提出的方法或技術可得到改善或延伸到新的應用範圍。

請仔細閱讀下面摘錄自一篇研究論文的導論。請注意，在導論中，作者是如何結束文獻回顧和開始介紹自己的研究主題的。

Effect of soil compaction on sunflower growth

Generally, a good soil for crop production contains about 25% water and 25% air by volume. This 50% is referred to as pore space. The remaining 50% consists of soil particles. Anything, for example, tillage and wheel traffic, that reduces pore space results in a dense soil with poor internal drainage and reduced aeration. Intensive uses of machinery in recent years are increases in farm tractor power have resulted in heavy implements in the fields. Many problems arose as a result of heavy implements use one of them being soil compaction.

Compaction may significantly impair the production capacity of a soil. Many researchers have investigated the effects of wheel traffic on soil compaction and subsequent crop growth. Honsson and Reeder (1994) report a crop yield loss of 14% the first year after repeated wheel traffic on agricultural soils in seven different countries in Europe and North America. This may not immediately become evident. According to Moullart (1998), soil compaction particularly impedes root growth. The aboveground parts of the plants only rarely show a reduced dry matter production. Compaction, as evidenced by increased penetrometer resistance, reduces the penetrability of the soil for roots (Unger and Kaspar, 1994). Khalilian et al. (1991) reported that values of penetration resistance over 1000kPa caused reduction in yield. Ngunjiri and Siemens (1995) studied corn growth affected by soil compaction due to wheel traffic before secondary tillage. They found that corn yield from the treatment with wheel traffic on entire plot area was significantly lower than the yield from the other treatments.

In most studies the traffic has been applied across the entire experimental area. In some of the studies, on the other hand, traffic was applied especially after secondary soil tillage and pre-planting inter-row, intra-row and in entire plot area, and the effects compaction was observed. However, during especially pre-planting herbicide application tractor wheel creates additional compaction by pressing on intra-row or inter-row areas. Effects of this extra compaction happened after tillage but before planting operation have not been studied yet.

In this study, it was aimed to determine the effect of soil compaction due to wheel traffic on the vegetative and generative growth of sunflower, which is widely grown in Turkey. Pre-and post-planting compaction treatments were applied inter-rows; intra-rows and in the entire plot area. A control plot was used for comparison.

在該例中，第一段介紹背景資料，第二段則進行文獻回顧。第三段的後半部分以 "however" 開始的句子用於指出問題。這裡，"however" 這個詞的出現說明文獻回顧已結束，接下來作者將指出前面參考文獻中尚未研究的問題或缺少的資料，使讀者的注意力從其他學者過去的研究轉移到論文作者自己的研究上。例中的最後一段文字則說明論文作者的研究目的與研究活動。

絕大部分作者撰寫導論時，在文獻回顧結束，步驟三開始處使用however這個轉折副詞，以清楚地表示作者將要指出過去研究的缺點或不足之處。在however後面的句子則描述過去研究的缺點或不足之處，而且句子往往以具有few、little或no等修飾詞的主詞片語開始，而表示研究主題的名詞片語則放在句末。指出問題的常用句型列於表3-1中。

表3-1 指出問題的基本句型之一

轉折副詞	指出過去研究的不足	研究主題
However,	few studies have been done on few studies have reported on few studies have been published on few researchers have studied no studies have investigated little research has been devoted to little attention has been paid to little information has been published 　concerning no work has been done on little literature is available on there is little literature available on little is known about insufficient data are available on	the supercritical fluid extraction of oil from herbaceous substrates.

although.
while.

　　在步驟三中常用的另外一種句型是一個複合句，其中子句敘述研究領域中對某個問題的研究程度，主句則指出對於另一個相關課題的研究不足。這類句子通常以連接詞although或while開始。由於子句與主句的內容為一強烈的對比，所以子句中常出現如some、many或much等形容詞。請參閱表3-2所示的句型。

表3-2 指出問題的基本句型之二

連接詞	主題一的研究程度	主題二的研究程度
Although 　While	much research has been devoted to A, much work has been done on A, many studies have been published 　concerning A, many researchers have investigated 　A, much literature is available on A,	little research has been done on B. little attention has been paid to B. little information is available on B. little work has been published on B. few researchers have studied B. few studies have investigated B.

例如：

Although many researchers have investigated neural network and fuzzy logic based techniques, little work has been published on the RL based techniques.

這類句型也採用含有but或yet的並列複合句，如：

→ Many researchers have investigated neural network and fuzzy logic based techniques, but little work has been published on the RL based techniques.

→ Much research has been done on the effect of vortices on the frost growth rate, yet few experimental studies have been conducted in the range of low humidity conditions.

此外，有的作者在指出問題的複合句之後插進參考引述，例如：

Although significant advances have been made in the development of suitably robust ATPS process〔2, 3〕, their adoption in integrated processes is not widely reported.

除了表3-1、表3-2所示的兩種基本句型外，還可以採用其他的句型。不管採用哪種句型，一定要指出某個問題，使讀者能瞭解作者研究工作的動機。

在進行步驟三的寫作時，請注意下列三點：

①正確使用時態。步驟三的句子中，動詞時態通常採用現在簡單式或現在完成式。若敘述在過去已開始並持續到現在的事件或趨勢，則需使用現在完成式。請注意參考表3-1、表3-2中的例句。

②正確使用單複數形式。名詞study、paper、researcher及investigator等是可數名詞，它們具有複數形式，因此可用many、few或no來修飾這些複數名詞，如few researchers，many investigators，no papers等。這些複

數名詞之後的動詞也應採用複數形式。名詞work、literature、research及attention等都是不可數名詞，因此只能寫成單數形式並緊跟單數形式的動詞，修飾詞應使用much、little或no，而不能用many或few。但是可以用many literature works，因為這裡的work是著作之意，具有複數形式。也有的著作認為可以使用researches 這種複數形式表示學術研究。

③步驟二、三有時穿插進行。當文獻回顧很長時，常常可採用穿插進行的寫法，即先討論某研究主題一個方面的參考文獻，接著指出過去的研究存在的不足之處，然後討論研究主題另一個方面的參考資料，接著再指出另外一個尚未處理的問題或缺少資料的地方。

3.2 研究目的（步驟四）

在導論的步驟四中，作者常常使用一兩個句子來敘述自己研究的性質與目的，以說明自己要怎樣解決步驟三中指出的問題。

下例中，作者在步驟三指出問題之後，就立即敘述自己的問題。

→ 指出問題

In spite of several decades of intensive research, many important characteristics of frost growth cannot yet be accurately predicted. Moreover, few experimental studies have been conducted in the range of low humidity conditions, which indicate that the dew point of the incoming air is near or below the freezing point of water, these being typical air conditions in winter⋯

→ 研究活動及目的

In this study, an experimental investigation was undertaken to characterize the effects of environmental parameters on the frost formation occurring on a vertical plate in the entrance region. This study aims to present the effects of various environmental parameters on the frost formation, typical experimental data, and empirical correlations.

　　實際上，作者可以採用幾種不同的方式來介紹自己的研究活動和研究目的。大多數作者採用如purpose、aim或objective等名詞來直接敘述具體的研究目的，例如：

→ The purpose of the present paper is to obtain the explicit results for the phase change of the forward-scattered light in an isotropic chiral fluid.

→ The intent of the paper is to solve multiobjective thermal power dispatch problem having four objectives.

→ Another major goal of the study was to obtain quantitative data about the particle size distribution.

　　此外，作者也可只簡略地描述自己的主要研究活動，讀者自己可根據所描述的主要研究活動及上下文內容推斷出作者的研究目的。請參考下面的例句。

→ In the present paper, we consider the propagation of harmonic thermoplastic waves in laminated composites. The study is carried out in the context of the generalized theory of thermoelasticity.

→ In this paper, both water and solute flux through the membranes were measured using different Nacl solutions (<6 wt.%) and applying different hydrostatic pressure difference (<5.2 bar) between the high and low concentration sides.

→ This paper investigates alternative refrigerant mixtures to replace R22.

→ This paper describes a preparatory investigation into the effect of curvature on the compressive failure load of glass fiber reinforced plastic laminates containing embedded delaminations.

　　還有一種介紹研究主題的方法是通過主詞及動詞述語來描述主要的研究活動，同時利用不定詞片語來敘述研究目的，如：

→ A theoretical study was carried out to develop a fast-decoupled continuation method.

→ To obtain a proper evaluation on the interaction between porous pavement and the atmosphere, field experiments were conducted with various types of alternate pavement materials.

→ In order to verify that micron-size particles can be generated through direct injection of a cryogenic liquid into He II, and further investigate if the resulting particles stick to each other in the presence of motion, the present study was initiated.

　　上述第一種和第三種句子能直接表達作者的研究目的，不需要讀者自己推斷，所以使用得比較普遍。但有些作者習慣採用第二種句子。不管採用何種句型，作者應該要清楚地說明自己研究的目的與活動。

　　作者在介紹自己的研究目的與研究活動時，可以採用兩種導向方式，即論文導向和研究導向。

　　①論文導向。當研究論文的主要目的是分析某個問題，提出某種論證或介紹新的方法或技術時，通常採用論文導向方式。論文導向方式中，作者把論文本身當作強調的內容。此時，步驟四中的句子是要使用paper、report、thesis或dissertation這樣的特徵名詞直接提及研究論文本身，而且此類句子通常採用現在簡單式。請參見表3-3。注意：句子中用到purpose、aim或objective等名詞時，只能用現在簡單式。

表3-3　論文導向基本句型之一

論文導向（現在簡單式）	研究目的或主題
The purpose of this paper is The aim of this report is The objective of the present 　　paper is	to obtain quantitative data about the particles size 　　distribution. to model the dynamic behavior in the super-or 　　near-critical CO_2 extraction.
The present paper reports This report presents This thesis describes This paper discusses	heat transfer enhancement of the herringbone-type 　　micro-fin tube. the complexity of some decision and function 　　computation problems involving counterfactual 　　formulas.
This paper proposes This thesis describes This letter presents	a fossil-fuelled power plant simulator with an ITS. an intelligent tutoring systems (ITS) to enhance the 　　capabilities of a power plant simulator.

　　也可以使用we為步驟四中的主詞，如：

→ In this paper, we explore the possibility of putting vents in the ceiling of the third floor to allow hot air to rise into and circulate through the attic.

→ In this report, we discuss the effect of density fluctuations on the phase change in the critical region.

→ In this paper, we provide an extension of the boolean INN approach to more general constraint satisfaction by utilizing an encoding in terms of Potts spins, and present an annealing algorithm based on this approach.

　　上面所有的例句都採用主動語態，但是作者可以選用被動語態，例如：

→ In this report, an accurate model for coupled heat and moisture transfer in building envelopes and indoor air is developed.

→ In this thesis, the results of theoretical and experimental analysis of inclined wettable filtration systems are presented and further steps towards industrial design are discussed.

→ In this paper, two different ARCP-MC topologies previously proposed ［3］, ［6］ are briefly reviewed. A third alternative that overcomes some of the operational limitations of these topologies is introduced.

　　未來式也可用於論文導向的步驟四中，此時作者想說明句子所敘述的內容將在論文中被提出來，見表3-4。

　　②研究導向。若研究論文主要提出某些實驗或調查結果，則作者通常可以把研究活動作為步驟四的重點，即採用所謂的研究導向方式。在採用研究導向方式時，study、research、investigation或experiment等特徵名詞被用來強調研究活動本身。這類句子是表達已經過去的事情，所以使用過去簡單式。研究導向的兩種常用句型分別示於表3-5中。

表3-4　論文導向基本句型之二

論文導向（過去簡單式）	研究主題
This paper will propose	a new method for analyzing A.
This thesis will present	several approaches to improving A.
This paper will evaluate	a theory that attempts to explain A.
This paper will discuss	new equations for expressing A.
This paper will argue	that Chen's assumption is false.
This report will present evidence to show	that the conventional method causes errors in special cases.
This letter will present a proof	
In this paper, we will argue	how these material variables affect paste formation during mixing.
In this report, we will attempt to show	

表3-5　研究導向的常用句型之一、二

研究導向（過去簡單式）	研究主題
The purpose of the experiment reported here was	to determine the preferred viewing distance for work at a visual display unit
The aim of this study was	to examine the apparent osmotic behavior of some contemporary commercial reverse osmosis membranes.
The objective of this research was	

In the research described here,	we determined a new method for reducing variance in common case.
In this study,	
In the present investigation,	vertical nutrient mixing in late summer in a test area 20 kilometers off the coast was examined.
In this research,	
In the experiments reported here,	

　　需要指出的是，無論採用論文導向還是研究導向的方式，指出研究目的或敘述研究活動的句子中，一定要有this paper、the experiment reported here之類的名詞片語來明確作者本身的研究，而不是指其他學者過去的研究。也就是說，步驟四中的句子一定要明白無誤地使讀者清楚瞭解作者已經不再討論文獻回顧中的參考文獻，而是在說明自己的研究目的或研究內容。

　　另外，作者在步驟四中指出自己研究的目的時，如果表示研究目的內容的動詞不定詞中有受詞子句，或主句動詞後直接用受詞子句來介紹自己研究目的，那麼常利用助動詞could或would：

→ The aim of this research was to investigate whether the complex matrix structure of the herbaceous spearmint leaf would hinder the mass transfer inside leaf particles during the extraction process.

→ The purpose of this study is to determine how the baffles could affect the optimal number of tubes.

→ The experiment examined whether the friction loss at the vane speed of the tip contact could be increased with an increase in the rotational shaft.

3.3 研究價值（步驟五）

　　在導論步驟五中，作者指出自己的研究結果會有什麼樣的貢獻或應用前景，以說明自己研究的價值。理科方面的研究往往產生有價值的理論貢獻，而工科方面的研究通常會有某些具體工程實用的前景，因此理、工科領域中的論文導論常常包含步驟五。一般而言，碩士、博士學位論文也需在導論中指出自己論文的創新之處或研究價值，這樣才能符合學位論文的要求。

　　步驟五中，作者指出自己研究的理論貢獻或實際應用價值，或者兩者兼有。若指出理論上的貢獻，則作者要寫出自己的研究結果能協助某些領域中的研究者說明某種現象、解決某個理論問題或提供未來的研究方向。若指出實際應用價值，則作者需說明作者的研究結果能協助某個領域的專業人員解決某些應用上的問題或達到某些目標。請參閱下面的典型例句。

　　理論價值例句：

Our results may help to clarify whether the design of decentralized PI control system based on Nyquist stability analysis is effective.

The results of this study may help to explain how helpful the technique strategy can be in promoting the innovation culture in an organization.

The results of this survey may add to the literature on the factors that motivate engineers to prefer to remain in the traditional career paths (managerial and technical paths).

Further data of this kind are of importance for understanding how the behavior of individual team members can enhance or impede team performance.

Experiment similar to those reported here should be conducted using a wider variety of working conditions.

　　應用價值例句：

The methods reported here could be beneficial to research attempting to increase the performance of wettable filters.

The results of this study may be of interest to managers and educators attempting to develop programming standards and may help to increase programmer productivity.

The results obtained from this novel approach would provide better insight to planners and operators in the field of power engineering to handle the uncertainties affectively.

The results reported here could be used for qualitative and quantitative nondestructive evaluations and also for computing the acoustic material signature of a composite medium with defects.

也可利用介係詞片語、動詞不定詞片語或形容詞子句把導論中的步驟四與步驟五合併成一個句子，例如：

The objective of this study is to investigate the evaporative cooling effect of a roof lawn garden in order to understand and predict the transport of heat and moisture in the lawn.

The objective of this study is to empirically analyze the energy balance of a natural urban vegetated area to understand the resulting thermal and moisture regime and contribute to the knowledge of the physical urban environment in a tropical city.

The paper presents a diffuser modeling technique that may significantly increase the accuracy of the predicted results.

This report describes a new electro-hydraulic controlled high-pressure gas injection system that may be of importance in designing the internal engines with alternative fuels.

一般而言，科技論文的作者極少直接宣稱自己的研究結果能完全解決某個問題，而習慣用謙虛的口吻或試探性的態度來指出自己研究的價值，即使作者對自己研究結果的價值很肯定的時候，通常也只會表示這些結果能幫助大家解決某個問題或能提出一種可能的答案。細心的讀者可能在參考本節的例句時，已發現可以用助動詞may、could等來表述論文作者的這種謙虛態度。

下面介紹導論步驟四及步驟五中常出現的語氣助詞並指出這些助動詞所表示的確定程度。

①will表示論文作者絲毫不懷疑句子的內容，確定程度最高。如：

The results of this experiment will provide further data conserving the performance of the novel heat pipe/ejectors cooler.

②would在某些條件下很確定，即只要條件被滿足，確定性很高。如：

If a mathematical model for a flat plate heat pipe for a startup operation was developed, the transient heat transfer across the heat pipe walls and wicks and the temperature distributions in the heat pipe would be predicted.

③should確定性較高，但是不能完全確定。如：

The modification should improve the performance of the product, but it has not yet been tested in practice.

④may句子所表達的事情有可能發生，但作者不確定是否發生。如：

The results of this study may be useful to researchers attempting to gain more understanding of the behavior of the osmotic flow.

⑤might句子所表達的事情有可能發生，但比較不確定。如：

These data might help to clarify whether the steady state assumption is valid.

⑥could作者更不確定句子所表達的事情是否會發生。如：

Our findings could be beneficial to researchers in better understanding the adverse health effects of long-term exposure to whole body vibration.

3.4 組織結構（步驟六）

　　導論的步驟六為說明整個研究論文的組織結構，它位於導論部分的結尾處。通常只有在論文及讀者有可能不知道研究論文的結構時，才有必要在導論中包含步驟六。另外，工科領域中的研究論文有各種形式的組織結構，所以有些論文作者和有些期刊的編輯覺得這類研究論文的導論需要加一個段落以描述論文的結構。建議論文作者參閱自己擬投專業期刊上發表的一些論文，以確定自己論文的導論中是否應包含步驟六。

　　下面介紹三個典型的步驟六段落。請注意，這三個段落的作者都不採用同樣的句子結構，而且這些段落都提供了一些具體的資訊。

→ The organization of the paper is as follows. Section 2 highlights the basic facts about FST. Section 3 deals with the fuzzy modeling of input parameters considering trapezoidal and triangular MFs. In Section 4, the general procedure is outlined to obtain base case solutions by FPF. The necessary modifications for the development of the proposed FCPF algorithm are highlighted in Section 5. In Section 6, the procedure to obtain the proposed FVSI is presented. Section 7 outlines the simulation results obtained from the case studies conducted on standard IEEE 14-bus, 30-bus, and 57-bus test systems with proper justification.

→ The organization of the rest of the paper is as follows. In Section 2, we discuss how the AGC problem can be viewed as a stochastic multistage decision-making problem, and give a brief introduction to RL based control using the AGC problem as an example. In Section 3, we explain how an AGC controller can be learnt within this formulation. In Section 4, we present the two new RL algorithms for the AGC. Simulation results are provided in Section 5 and the paper is concluded following a discussion in Section 6.

→ Section 2 begins with background on documentary structure and on how simplistic tools attempt to deal with it. The expedients adopted by such tools, which never seem to work quite right, fail for reasons described in more detail in Section 3: the orthogonality of documentary and linguistic structure. Section 4 describes relevant characteristics of documentary structure and discusses its relationship to frameworks for program understanding, in which it has largely been ignored. Section 5 discusses architectural strategies for preserving documentary structure; and describes why it is so difficult to apply compiler-oriented approaches effectively. Section 6 reviews other approaches that have been taken in dealing with the 'comment problem' and argues that they are not likely to eliminate current mechanisms any time soon. Section 7 concludes with observations, implementation status, and open questions.

如上面的前兩個段落所示，若步驟六是一個獨立的段落，則該段落的第一個句子通常寫為：

→ The organization of the paper is as follows.

→ This paper is organized as follows.

→ The structure of the paper is as follows.

→ The paper is organized into the following sections.

→ The organization of the rest of the paper is as follows.

→ The reminder of this paper is organized as follows.

步驟六中的句子通常使用現在簡單式，主動語態或被動語態。請看下述例句：

In Section 2, we present a general derivation of the method for a generic CSP, based on information analysis.

Section 4 contains a description of the numerical explorations and the test beds, as well as a presentation and a discussion of the results.

The relevant procedure and theoretical analysis are presented in detail in

Section 2.

Finally, related work is summarized in Section 5, while conclusions and work-in-progress are reported in Section 6.

請注意，有些作者習慣在步驟六的句子中採用未來式，如"Section 3 will describe the test box and real test house for investigating the model performances." 還有，如果作者決定採用被動語態，那麼應該避免出現不平衡的句子。在這種不平衡的句子中，位於句首的主詞特別長，而句末的動詞述語很短，如：

In Section 2, a nonlinear theoretical approach that can provide a clear dynamical insight of how nonlinearity plays a role in such a flow system is presented.

這種不自然的句子應該改寫為：

In Section 2, a nonlinear theoretical approach is presented that can provide a clear dynamical insight of how nonlinearity plays a role in such a flow system.

或

Section 2 presents a nonlinear theoretical approach that can provide a clear dynamical insight of how nonlinearity plays a role in such a flow system.

科技英文論文寫作實用指南 **Practical Guide to Scientific English Writing**

理論分析部分

在數學、其他理學以及工學的研究論文中,在導論之後通常緊跟一個篇幅較長的理論分析部分。理論分析部分主要用於介紹論文作者所採用的或開發的理論模型,也有用來說明作者對某個問題的分析或作者所發明的技術的理論基礎。在本章中,我們將討論撰寫理論分析部分的基本原則,包括其基本結構、時態,以及寫作風格與常用句型。

4.1 理論分析的基本結構

對於不同領域或不同性質的論文,理論分析部分的內容有可能會有很大的差異,所以該部分的結構不像研究論文的其他部分(如導論、結果等)的結構那樣有一定的規則可遵循。但是,不管是對於數學分析類型還是對於模型介紹類型,它們各自所包含的資料項目還是有共同性的。

◆ 4.1.1 數學分析

在數學分析類型的理論分析部分中,通常會包含下列項目的資料:

①介紹題目及目的。

②敘述相關的假設、條件或定義。

③說明主要問題或基本方程式。

④進行分析並得出結果(該項目可能會多次重複)。

⑤說明或討論上述結果，或根據結果作出某種推論（該項目可能會多次重複或可能與前項穿插進行）。

下面的例4-1中，該段落的作者先介紹一個題目及目的（"Supposed that…"），然後再敘述主要的問題（"is it possible to…"）。接著，作者說明一些假設及定義（"Let…"及"we define…"），作者還列出一些方程式並進行一些分析及演算。最後，作者根據整個段落的內容得出一個結論（"and that this is…"）。

例4-1

Suppose that we want to estimate the expectation

$$\mathrm{E}X \tag{4}$$

of a real valued random variable X by Monte Carlo simulation. If X_1, X_2, $\cdots$ is an independent sequence of realizations of X, then we can use the unbiased estimator

$$\hat{s}_N = \frac{1}{N} \sum_{i=1}^{N} X_i \tag{5}$$

for Eq.(4). However, in many practical situations, especially in environmental modeling, we do not know the distribution of X exactly and we cannot sample directly from a distribution equal to that of X and must somehow obtain approximate realizations. Therefore we assume that for each $\triangle > 0$ independent realizations of a random variable $X_\triangle$ can be generated where $X_\triangle$ approximates X in distribution to order, $O(\triangle^p)$, $p > 0$ as $\triangle \downarrow 0$. Next we consider the estimator

$$\hat{s}_N^\triangle = \frac{1}{N} \sum_{i=1}^{N} X_i^\triangle \tag{6}$$

which is generally biased, and observe that

$$\mathrm{E}X - \hat{s}_N^\triangle = (EX - EX_\triangle) + (EX_\triangle - \hat{s}_N^\triangle) =: \epsilon_{\mathrm{syst}} + \epsilon_{\mathrm{stat}}, \tag{7}$$

so we have a deterministic systematic error $\epsilon_{syst} = 0$ (Δ^p)which is independent of N and a statistical error ϵ_{stst} for which $E_{\epsilon_{stst}} = 0$ and Var $\epsilon_{stat} = (1/N)$ Var X_Δ. To guarantee a certain accuracy in the evaluation of Eq. (4) by Monte Carlo simulation, we thus have to keep both the systematic error and the statistical error small. Obviously, we can make the systematic error smaller by taking Δ smaller, but the computational effort needed to generate an individual realization of X_Δ generally increases as Δ tends to zero. Once a small $\Delta > 0$ has been chosen, we then need to choose a number N, which is typically large, for the sample size in order to obtain a small statistical error. Consequently, we have an optimization problem: *Is it possible to choose Δ and N in such a way that the computational effort needed to ensure the desired accuracy is minimal?*

We will solve this optimization problem in the context of the following statistical model. Let $\sigma := \sqrt{VarX}$, $\sigma_\Delta := \sqrt{VarX_\Delta}$, and denoted by $C(\Delta)$ the computational time needed for one sample of X_Δ and by $C_{MM}(\Delta, N) := NC(\Delta)$ the total computational time need for the Monte Carlo method. Next, we define the total error of the Monte Carlo method by

$$\epsilon_{MM} := \epsilon_{syst} + \text{deviation of } \epsilon_{stat}, \tag{8}$$

and specify the model further by the following assumption.

There are $\alpha, \beta > 0$, and $q > 0$ such that for $\Delta \downarrow 0$

$$C(\Delta) = \frac{\beta}{\Delta^q}(1 + o(1)) \quad, \sigma_\Delta = \sigma(1 + o(1)) \quad,$$

$$\epsilon_{syst} = \alpha\Delta^p(1 + o(1)) \quad. \tag{9}$$

Within this model we thus derive

$$C_{MM}(\Delta, N) = \frac{\beta N}{\Delta^q}(1 + o(1)) \quad, \tag{10}$$

and

$$\varepsilon_{MM}(\Delta, N) = \left(\alpha\Delta^P + \frac{\sigma}{\sqrt{N}}\right)(1 + o(1)) \tag{11}$$

for $\Delta \downarrow 0$, and we have the complementary optimization problems:

$$C^*(\epsilon) := \min_{|(\Delta, N) : \varepsilon_{MM}(\Delta, N) \le \epsilon|} C_{MM}(\Delta, N), \tag{12}$$

and

$$\varepsilon^*(c) := \min_{|(\Delta, N) : C_{MM}(\Delta, N) \le \epsilon|} \varepsilon_{MM}(\Delta, N). \tag{13}$$

It can be verified by elementary asymptotic analysis〔7〕that the computation time will be asymptotically of order

$$C(\epsilon) = \left(\frac{1}{\epsilon^2 + \frac{q}{p}}\right) as \downarrow 0, \tag{14}$$

and that this is the most efficient order which can be achieved.

◆ 4.1.2 模型介紹

在介紹理論或數學模型類型的理論分析部分時，常出現的資料包括下列項目：

①模型的背景或理論基礎。該項目中，有時需要引述其他學者的著作。

②作者所用方法或所述類型的基本假設或根據。若此方法或模型有很多部分，則在介紹每個部分時都可能會提供這些資料。

③基本方程式與分析。

④模型的詳細描述。若模型有很多部分，則可能需分部討論，然後再作總結。

⑤說明或討論模型的重要特點。

⑥說明在特定情況下如何應用此模型，或討論一實際例子。

⑦對例子中的解答進行評論。

此外，為了確定模型的有效性，在介紹模型部分之後，常緊接著依據模型的計算結果與試驗資料進行比較的內容。

下面給出的例4-2與例4-3說明兩種不同的撰寫方法。例4-2在介紹模型時以文字敘述為主進行分析，而例4-3則是以列出方程式來詳細描述數學模型。

例4-2

We now modify the model to allow air to flow into and out of the system through the vertical and horizontal boundaries. This models air of a given temperature being pumped into and circulated through the attic.

We must ensure that mass is conserved in the system, so the amount of air we pump into the system must be the same as that which exits. We also attempt to account for the walls around the enclosure, since the thermal conductivity of the boundaries will affect the temperature distribution of the attic for given external (outside) temperature and given temperature of the rooms below. We therefore define further boundary conditions and modify the energy Eq. (15), since thermal conductivity is no longer constant over all space:

$$\rho c_p \frac{DT}{Dt^*} = \lambda \nabla^2 T \tag{15}$$

Our aim is to observe the effects of an inflow/outflow system on the temperature distribution of the attic. Such results could be of benefit for a variety of temperature related problems in buildings. Further, we may suspect that for sufficiently high inflow velocity, the instabilities observed previously should be reduced, so there is a chance that we may obtain results which are applicable to a real attic of appropriate Grashof number.

For fluids in which thermal conductivity is not constant, the energy Eq. (15) should read

$$\rho c_p \frac{DT}{Dt^*} = \vec{\nabla} \cdot (\lambda \vec{\nabla} T) \tag{16}$$

It may be noted that this is normally the case for compressible fluids since thermal conductivity varies with density.

After non-dimensionalisation, Eq. (16) may be rewritten to give a new energy transport equation:

$$\frac{\partial \theta}{\partial t} + \vec{q} \cdot \vec{\nabla}\theta = \frac{1}{\mu cp} \vec{\nabla} \cdot (\lambda \vec{\nabla}\theta) \tag{17}$$

We allow air to flow in and out at specific points on the boundaries. Consequently, the stream function must take a constant value on each section of boundary which does not have an inflow or outflow.

Consider a system with an inflow on the horizontal base and an outflow on the vertical wall. We suppose that the streamline passing from the centre of the inflow to the centre of the outflow corresponds to $\Psi=0$. We therefore expect that the stream function at the node to one side of the inflow will be the negative of that to the other side. Using the velocity equation (4), we may define values for stream function on either side of the inflow as follows:

$$\Psi_{i+1,0} = -v_{in}\Delta X \tag{18}$$

$$\Psi_{i-1,0} = -v_{in}\Delta X \tag{19}$$

For a system with an inflow on the horizontal boundary and an outflow on the vertical surface, we should therefore have the boundary stream function distribution shown in Fig. 6. The stream function may be derived in a similar manner for other inflow and outflow locations and for multiple inflow/outflow systems.

Since the boundary nodes in this model represent the solid walls surrounding the fluid rather than the fluid itself, we are now able to define vorticity as zero on all boundaries without loss of generality.

We require velocities on the boundaries to be zero except at the inflow and outflow points. We have already defined temperature on boundaries 1 and 2, and we solve for temperature on boundary 3 as before. The temperature of air entering the attic through the inflow is defined to be θ_{in}.

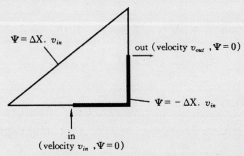

Fig.6   Stream function for an inflow on the horizontal boundary and outflow on the vertical boundary

We solve for temperature using the Peaceman-Rachford technique combined with an upwind scheme as before. However, we now need to incorporate variable thermal conductivity. The ADI technique now separates Eq. (17) into Eqs. (20) and (21):

$$\left[\frac{\partial\theta}{\partial t}\right]^{(t+\frac{1}{2},t)} + \left[U\frac{\partial\theta}{\partial X}\right]^{t+\frac{1}{2}} + \left[V\frac{\partial\theta}{\partial Y}\right]^{t}$$

$$= \frac{1}{\mu c_p}\left(\frac{\partial}{\partial X}\left[\lambda\frac{\partial\theta}{\partial X}\right]^{t+\frac{1}{2}} + \frac{\partial}{\partial Y}\left[\lambda\frac{\partial\theta}{\partial Y}\right]^{t}\right) \tag{20}$$

$$\left[\frac{\partial\theta}{\partial t}\right]^{(t+1,t+\frac{1}{2})} + \left[U\frac{\partial\theta}{\partial X}\right]^{t+\frac{1}{2}} + \left[V\frac{\partial\theta}{\partial Y}\right]^{t+1}$$

$$= \frac{1}{\mu c_p}\left(\frac{\partial}{\partial X}\left[\lambda\frac{\partial\theta}{\partial X}\right]^{t+\frac{1}{2}} + \frac{\partial}{\partial Y}\left[\lambda\frac{\partial\theta}{\partial Y}\right]^{t+1}\right) \tag{21}$$

例4-3

Consider a semi-infinite vertical plate with a leading edge at x=0 as shown in Fig.1. The plate is heated to uniform temperature T_0 above the saturation temperature T_s of the adjacent liquid which at large distances from the plate is cooled to temperature T_∞, $T_\infty<T_s$. As a result of heating, and for T_0 large enough, a vapor film is formed, separating the plate from the remaining liquid as shown.

The fluids are governed by the Boussinesq equations in each phase

$$\rho_0\left(\frac{\partial v}{\partial t} + v \cdot \nabla v\right) = \nabla p^* + \rho\nabla^2 v + \rho_0 \alpha g(T - T_L)Ee_x \tag{1}$$

$$\nabla \cdot v = 0 \tag{2}$$

$$\frac{\partial T}{\partial t} + v \cdot \nabla T = k\nabla^2 T \tag{3}$$

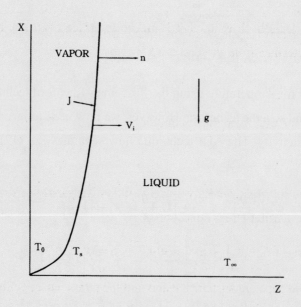

Fig.1　Sketch of the model system.

where the radiation heating is ignored. Subscripts v and l will label variables in the two phases. Here v={μ, ω} is the velocity, p* is the reduced pressure, T is the temperature, ρ_0, μ, k and α are the density, viscosity, thermal diffusivity, and thermal expansion coefficient of the fluid, respectively, $e_x = \{1,0\}$ and g is the magnitude of the acceleration of gravity. On the solid plate at $z=0$, $x \geq 0$

$$T_v = T_0 \tag{4}$$

and

$$v_v = 0 \tag{5}$$

Far from the plate at $z=l_*$

$$T_1 = T_L \tag{6}$$

and a non-zero velocity is allowed in order to mimic the infinite domain case.

$$v_1 = v_L = \text{ const.} \tag{7}$$

According to Burelbach et al. [9] on the interface $z=h(x, t)$, the mass flux J through the interface from the liquid is given by

$$J = \rho_{01}(v_1 - v_i) \cdot n \tag{8}$$

which equals the flux from the vapor side

$$J = \rho_{0v}(v_1 - v_i) \cdot n \tag{9}$$

where v_i is the interface velocity and n is the unit normal vector pointing out of the vapor. The normal-stress condition is

$$J(v_v - v_1) \cdot n - (T_v - T_1) \cdot n \cdot n + \sigma \nabla \cdot n = 0 \tag{10}$$

where σ is the constant surface tension and the stress tensor is given by

$$T = pI + 2\mu D \;,\; D = \frac{1}{2}[\nabla_v + (\nabla v)^T] \tag{11}$$

where p is the pressure, I is unit tensor. The shear-stress condition reads

$$J(v_v - v_1) \cdot t - (T_v - T_1) \cdot n \cdot t = 0 \tag{12}$$

There is the no-slip condition

$$v_v \cdot t = v_1 \cdot t \tag{13}$$

where t is the unit tangential vector,

$$t = \{1, h_x\} / \sqrt{1 + h_x^2} \qquad , t = \{1, h_x\} / \sqrt{1 + h_x^2} \tag{14}$$

The energy balance at interface takes the form:

$$J\{L + 1/2[(v_v - v_i) \cdot n]^2 - 1/2[(v_1 - v_i) \cdot n)]^2\}$$
$$+ k_1 \nabla T_1 \cdot n - k_v \nabla T_v \cdot n + 2\mu(D_1 \cdot n) \cdot (v_1 - v_i) \tag{15}$$
$$- 2\mu_v(D_v \cdot n) \cdot (v_v - v_i) = 0$$

where L is the latent heat of vaporization, and k denotes the thermal conductivity. Finally, one needs a relation that defines the interface temperature T_i; here, we shall assume local thermodynamic equilibrium, which gives that

$$T_i = T_s \tag{16}$$

◆ 4.1.3 方程式的位置及標點符號

(1)方程式的位置

　　當數學方程式與正文的其他部分區隔開來時，方程式上下應該至少空一行，而且方程式應縮進排印。縮排的距離應至少和該段落首行縮進的距離相同，最好比新段落首行縮進的距離還多一點（如0.5或1.0英吋），見上面例4-1中的方程縮進排印。若一個方程式較長，一行內排不下，則將方程式在運算符號處斷開，且使方程式的其餘部分縮進排印在接下來的一行上，如上面例4-2中的式(20)、式(21)及例43中的式(15)所示的那樣。此外，有些專業期刊規定把區隔開來的方程式排在頁面正中間（置中），而有些期刊則習慣把區隔開來的方程式靠左頂格排印（分別參見上面的例4-2和例4-3）。論文作者在投稿以前務必要查閱所投期刊的格式指導說明。

(2)方程式的標點符號

　　對於和句子其他部分區隔開來的方程式而言，是否採用標點符號沒有一個統一的規定。有些專業期刊在方程式後面一律不使用標點符號，原因可能是期刊的編輯認為明確含有方程式的句子意義並不需要標點符號，或是因為他們覺得在含有大量數學公式的正文中，標點符號的使用會使頁面顯得太擁擠，下面的一段例句中，方程式後面未有標點符號。

The first-order approximation for mean and variance are shown in Eqs. (3) and (4), respectively (Harr, 1987),

$$E[f(x)] = f(\overline{x}) \qquad (3)$$

$$V[f(x)] = [f'(\overline{x})]^2 V[x] \qquad (4)$$

where $f(x)$ is the model function, $\overline{x}$ is the best estimate of the input data, $f(\overline{x})$ is the sensitivity of the output to the input parameter, E [$f(x)$] is the expected value of the model result, and V [$f(x)$] is the variance in the modeled result.

　　但是，也有很多期刊在方程式後面加上標點符號，這些期刊的編輯認為標點符號的應用有助於明確句子的結構，以防誤讀，同時也可以增進論文的可讀性。例如：

In addition, we introduced the scalar SDE

$$d\Theta_t = \Theta_t \sum_{r=1}^{m} v_r(t, \tilde{X}_t) dW_t^r \ . \qquad (21)$$

Then, by Ito formula, it follows that

$$d[\mu(t, \tilde{X}_t)\Theta_t = \Theta_t \sum_{r=1}^{m} \left[\mu(t, \tilde{X}_t) v_r(t, \tilde{X}_t) + \sum_{i=1}^{m} \mu_{xi}(t, \overline{X}_t) \sigma_{ir}(t, \overline{X}_t) \right] dW_t^r \ , \qquad (22)$$

where μ is the solution of the corresponding backward Kolmogorov problem (18).

在這個例子中，"where μ is...."是修飾方程式(22)的非限定性形容詞子句，所以根據英文文法要求，方程式(22)的末尾應加上逗號。仔細的讀者會發現本章的例4-1、例4-2、例4-3中大部分方程式後面均使用標點符號，只有例4-1中的式(4)、式(5)、式(6)、式(11)例外。為什麼這些方程式後面不加標點符號？請讀者自己從英文文法的角度來回答這個問題。

對於未和句子其餘部分區隔開來的數學公式或方程式，若所在句子的結構有所要求，則也應該使用標點符號。

請作者先查閱擬投期刊所排印的格式指導說明，再決定是否在論文中的方程式之後使用標點符號。

4.2 時態

科技論文理論分析部分中的大部分資料都屬於有關數學或邏輯關係、不受時間影響的普遍事實。在英文中，此種事實以現在簡單式描述，所以理論分析部分中大多數的句子都使用現在簡單式，請參考下面的例句：

→ We consider now the case in which the dynamic link parameters and the environment stiffness are unknown.

→ Here we assume that beyond some critical rate of investment (per period), the marginal cost of backstop capacity increases.

→ Define the superheat ΔT across the layer:

→ Suppose that X_t is a solution of the SDE(1).

→ We have the complementary optimization problems:

→ Our aim is to observe the effects of an inflow/outflow system on the temperature distribution of the attic.

→ The solution can be obtained by solving Eq. (2).

也有的論文作者採用未來式以介紹新的題目或轉接到新的段落。未來式也常在條件副詞子句中使用，以說明可能的結果。例如：

→ We will solve this optimization problem in the context of the following statistical model.

→ Simplification of the system (1)-(16) will be sought appropriate for the situation where all the heat arriving at the interface is available for phase change.

→ Here we shall assume local thermodynamic equilibrium.

→ A pure controller will be proposed here to solve the resulting adaptive tracking control problem.

→ If X_t is a solution of the SDE (1), then the stochastic process will satisfy the stochastic equation.

在介紹理論模型或進行數學分析時，有的作者需要述及自己已完成的試驗結果。若實驗研究是作者過去的工作，則作者必須用過去簡單式來描述。下例中的最後一句指的是作者過去的實驗研究的行為，因此採用了過去簡單式。

It is assumed that the evaporation rate at the porous surface is proportional to the available moisture content. Then the right hand side of Eq. (9) is multiplied by a factor (θ / θ_s), where θ_s is the saturated water content at the ground surface. The lower boundary conditions are constant soil temperature and matric potential at 2m depth. Initial values for temperature and matric potential were specified from the observational data.

此外，有的作者在引用前人的數學模型時，也用過去式來提及原作者所作的假設，但假設的內容仍用現在式。例如：

For application of the first-order approximation applied herein the following assumptions were made:

1. Normal probability distribution describes the input and output data.

2. Linear relationship exists between the input and output data.

4.3 寫作要點與常用句型

◆ 4.3.1 寫作要點

(1)在撰寫理論分析部分時,作者應注意下述基本要素

　　應先清楚地敘述所用的假設及概念的定義,然後才可以應用這些假設或概念。而且在介紹基本方程式之前,應先把要解決的問題陳述清楚。若理論分析部分中需要討論多個小題目,則應該逐個地、有條理地介紹並討論。在介紹並討論某個小題目之後,應該清楚地敘述主要論點或作總結。而且在有必要時需清楚地表達不同小題目之間的邏輯關係。不要任意假定讀者一定瞭解理論分析中的所有細節,應該一步一步地清楚說明理論分析部分中的所有內容。

　　應盡量避免生硬、拙劣的寫作風格,而應採用自然、通順、易讀的寫作風格,如同經驗豐富的教授在教室裡解釋他的理論模型或數學分析一樣。同時,作者應注意不要使用任何俚語或不正式的言詞。

　　在介紹理論分析中,作者應盡可能地避免用it is、there is或there are這樣的句子。在許多實驗方法部分中,通常採用被動語態而不使用主動語態。然而,在理論分析部分往往採用第一人稱複數代名詞we為開頭的句子,如本章的例4-1、例4-2所示。

生硬:It is supposed that the streamline passing from the center of the inflow to the center of the outflow corresponds to $\Psi=0$.

自然:We supposed that the streamline passing from the center of the inflow to the center of the outflow corresponds to Ψ=0.

自然：Let us suppose that the streamline passing from the center of the inflow to the center of the outflow corresponds to Ψ=0.

自然：Suppose that the streamline passing from the center of the inflow to the center of the outflow corresponds to Ψ=0.

　　此外，在撰寫理論分析部分時，應防止出現垂懸的或誤置的修飾片語。若需表達作者自己的目的、動機或興趣等，則應使讀者容易看出作者本身是句子中行為的產生者。

差：After substituting this term for y in Equation (4), the equation can be rewritten as follows.

佳：After substituting this term for y in Equation (4), we can rewrite the equations as follows.

佳：If this term is substituted for y in Equation (4), the equation can be written as follows.

佳：Substituting this term for y in Equation (4) yields the following equation.

差：The relationship between ξ and q_{max} is now considered.

佳：Now let us consider the relationship between ξ and q_{max}.

佳：Consider the relationship between ξ and q_{max}.

佳：ξ and q_{max} are related in the following way.

(2)常用句型

　　論文作者應該多參閱自己研究領域中不同專家在相關期刊上發表的論文，以便獲得理論分析部分的撰寫方法和常用句型。下面列出一些理論分析部分常用句型的例子，供讀者參考。

→ Consider the case in which the dynamic link parameters are unknown.

→ Let us now consider the case the dynamic link parameters are unknown.

→ Suppose that X_t is a solution of the SDE (1).

→ Let d and V be scalings for the length and the velocity.

→ We assume that R_1/R_2=0.1724 under consideration here.

→ If m=1.2, then we have the following equations:（列出方程式）

→ Given that m=1.2, we obtain…（列出方程式）

→ The equation for A_t/A'_t becomes…（列出方程式）

→ The equation for A_t/A'_t can be written as…（列出方程式）

→ The equation for A_t/A'_t can be expressed as…（列出方程式）

→ The equation for A_t/A'_t can be written as follows:（列出方程式）

→ Substituting m into Equation 3, we obtain…（列出方程式）

→ The relationship between m and n is as follows:（列出方程式）

→ A is inversely proportional to B, as shown below.

→ Eq. (5) takes the form…（列出方程式）

→ From this equation, the relation between ξ and q_{max} can be expressed as…
（列出方程式）

→ If the same material is used, the above equation reduce to…（列出方程式）

→ We will now reduce Eq. (3) to a simpler form.

→ On substituting this equation into Eq.(16) and solving for x_2, （列出方程式）

→ The mass velocity G is defined as…（列出方程式）

→ The heat transfer area A on the airside is given by…（列出方程式）

→ Upon performing the integration using Eq. (19), substituting $r_v + l$ for r_w,
letting $z = l/r_w$, and simplifying, （列出方程式）

→ We will now integrate Equation(2)in order to derive the solution.

→ We can now derive the solution to Equation (2).

→ If Eq. (16) is solved for E_h, （列出方程式）

5

實驗與方法部分

實驗與方法部分在一些外國科技寫作專著中統稱為材料與方法部分（Materials and Method Section）。這部分要作者回答的問題是：自己做了些什麼？自己又是如何做的？它的作用，一是讓那些同領域的研究者在必要時也能重複和驗證作者的研究方法，二是證明作者所採用的方法是經過認真仔細的考慮的，能被認可的正確方法。對於其他領域的學者而言，他們會在研究論文的摘要中瞭解作者所採用的研究方法與研究結果，並只會略讀實驗和方法部分。然而，本領域的研究者會非常仔細地審讀實驗與方法部分，以對作者的研究工作質量做出判斷。因此，在展現研究結果的可信度和有效性方面，研究論文的實驗與方法部分是一個非常關鍵的部分。

在理、工、醫學學科領域中，研究工作通常包括必要的實驗，以證實自己提出的理論、模型或技術的可行性。本章將以實驗報告為主介紹論文中實驗與方法部分的寫作原則。這些原則對其他學科論文中方法部分的寫作基本上也是適用的。

5.1 基本內容及結構

研究論文的實驗及方法部分中，作者必須清楚、詳細地描述實驗方法及程序，其基本內容應該包含下列項目：

①對於所採用的材料、儀器儀錶、設備及測試系統所作的詳細介紹。

②對於實驗程序所作的清楚說明。

若有必要，基本內容還可以包含以下資料：

③對整個實驗的概述。

④選用特定材料、設備或方法的理由。特定材料包括工質、試劑、酶、催化劑、生物體等。

⑤實驗的特殊條件或工況，如特殊的溫度、速度或壓力範圍，特殊的高電壓或大電流，紫外線輻射等。

⑥特殊實驗設備或方法的詳細介紹。若採用的是標準的實驗設備或方法，則作簡略介紹。

⑦應用的統計、分析方法的描述。

對於人文及社會科學而言，基本內容可能還包含問卷或測試的內容，對於調查的樣本或總體的描述（樣本所屬總體的一般資料，抽樣的方法或準則，樣本的限制或特殊條件）。

在撰寫實驗及方法部分時，作者通常需按照實驗進行的先後順序來排列所介紹的內容。具體來說，在開始時對整個實驗作一、二句話的概述（包括實驗目的），並敘述該實驗的研究對象、樣本或材料；然後介紹測試儀器儀錶及測試系統（可用附圖）；接著描述實驗步驟；最後指出實驗結果的收集方式和分析結果的方法。但是，對於上述內容的排列順序，不同的研究領域、不同的學術期刊以及不同的作者都各有不同的習慣。

在某些研究領域中，作者會把實驗及方法部分的內容分成幾個小節，每個小節專門介紹基本內容中的一個項目。

下面是實驗及方法部分的一個典型實例。受篇幅所限，這個實例已經經過刪減，原文要詳細得多。

例5-1

Experimental Apparatus and Procedure

The objective of the present experiment was to investigate the heat transfer characteristics of flowing ice water slurry in a straight pipe, and thus to provide fundamental information for the new ice thermal energy storage system.

The schematic diagram of experimental apparatus is shown in Fig.1. The apparatus fundamentally consisted of a test section, an ice water slurry tank, a hot water circulating loop, and associated measuring instruments. The test section was a horizontal double tube heat exchanger of 2,000mm in length with an entrance section of 800mm in length. Ice water slurry flows in···

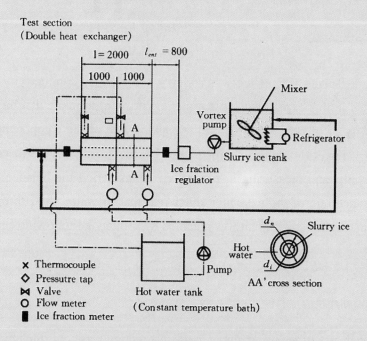

Fig.1　Schematic diagram of experimental setup

In this study, ice packing factor (IPF=volume of ice/volume of ice water slurry) of ice water slurry is a very important factor, so an IPF controller and an IPF measuring device were used. IPF controller, which was a double tube, is shown in Fig.2···

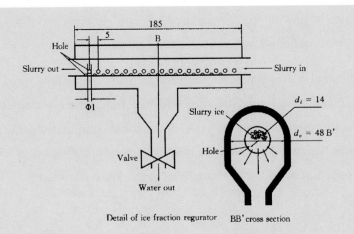

Fig.2 Detail of IPF controller

For measuring IPF of ice water slurry, the electric conductivity method was chosen in this experiment. It is a method using a principle that the electric conductivity of mixture depends on the packing rate of the components of the mixture····. Fig.3 shows the detail of the IPF measuring device. It consisted power supply, and measuring instruments··· Considering the balance between the resistance rate of the ice water slurry and that of water, the IPF of the ice water slurry in this experiment was obtained by solving the following equation:

$$IPF = \{A + B \times [(\Upsilon_{mix}/\Upsilon_{\omega}) - 1]/[(\Upsilon_{mix}/\Upsilon_{\omega}) + 0.5]\} \times 100$$

$$A = -0.001\ 6, B = 1.1$$

The velocity of ice water slurry in the test section was controlled by a vortex pump with an inverter. Thermocouples (C.A.: 0.1mm O.D.) were set in the test section to measure both the inlet and outlet temperature of the ice water slurry and the hot water····.

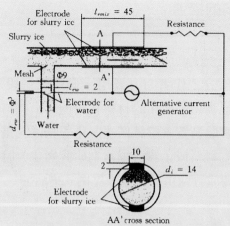

Fig.3　Detail of IPF measuring device

The experiments were performed using the following procedure. Ice particles were mixed with water in the ice water slurry tank. After controlled IPF and velocity of ice water slurry, it was passed through the test section and heated by hot water. The amount of melting heat transferred from hot water to ice water slurry was calculated with the difference between the inlet and outlet temperature of hot water. In addition, the behavior of the ice particles passed through the test section was recorded by a video camera for flow visualization.

For the present experiment, the ice water slurry velocity, u_i, ranged from 0.15 to 0.6 m/s, the IPF of ice water slurry at the test section inlet, IPF_{in}, between 0 and 15%, the hot water temperature, T_{hin}, between 20 and 30℃, and the hot water velocity, u_h=0.35m/s.

上面例子中的第一段為概述，說明實驗的目的；第二段介紹實驗系統；第三、四、五段敘述測試手段與資料處理方法；第六段敘述實驗程序；最後一段描述實驗的特定工況。

5.2 對設備或材料的描述

◆ 5.2.1 描述方法

在實驗與方法部分，作者有必要用一個或數個段落（包括文字和圖表）來專門描述自己實驗中所用的材料和設備。這些材料或設備包括被實驗的材料或工質、實驗裝置、儀錶儀器、化學物品、電腦軟體或數學公式等。在描述被實驗的材料或工質（通常為研究對象）時，先作概述，然後詳細介紹材料的主要成分或重要特性，見例5-2所示。

例5-2

Experimental Fuels

Two kinds of fuels (Zhejiang late rice straw and rice husk) were used in the experiment because of their abundance in fuel feeding and easy pretreatment. The data are shown in Table 1. Compared to coal, their volatile content is very high, but ash content is moderate. Table 2 shows physical parameters of biomass fuels. Thermal conductivity is very small with value only about 0.04W/m℃, apparent density is only 1/6-1/8 of coal, and energy density is also small. All these indicate that biomass should be used locally in medium/small scale plant and pyrolysis is sure to be good route.

Table 1　The analytical data of biomass fuels

biomass fuels	Ultimate analysis					Approximate analysis				Heat value (kJ/kg)
	C_{ad}	H_{ad}	N_{ad}	S_{ad}	O_{ad}	M_{ad}	A_{ad}	V_{ad}	FC_{ad}	
rice straw	33.96	5.01	1.07	0.10	34.67	9.96	15.23	69.11	5.70	15,175.2
rice husk	39.69	4.92	0.42	0.14	31.29	10.3	13.24	60.38	15.99	14,784.7

Table 2　Physical parameter of biomass fuels

Items	Diameter (mm)	Germetry (mm)	Pack density (kg/m³)	Thermal conductivity (W/m.℃)	Energy density (kJ/m³)
rice straw	0-4	2.5×10	59.3	0.035	900

Items	Diameter (mm)	Germetry (mm)	Pack density (kg/m³)	Thermal conductivity (W/m.℃)	Energy density (kJ/m³)
rice husk	0-3	9×3×0.2	122.9	0.036	1,870

當描述儀器、裝置、設備時，通常需要解釋它們的結構資料、功能與運行方式。請結合本章例5-1的圖1參考下例：

例5-3

The test section was a horizontal double tube heat exchanger of 2,000 mm in length with an entrance section of 800 mm in length. Ice water slurry flowed in an inside tube of the heat exchanger and hot water circulated in an annular gap between the inside and outside tubes. In this study, two kinds of heat exchanger were used. One was made of acrylic resin tube (inner diameter of inside tube: d_i=14 mm, inside tube thickness: t_i=2.0 mm；inner diameter of outside tube: d_0=37 mm, outside tube thickness: t_0=3.0 mm) for flow visualization and the other was made of stainless steel tube (d_i=14 mm, t_i=1.65 mm, d_0=37.1 mm, t_0=2.8 mm) for melting heat transfer measurement. The ice water slurry tank, which was covered with insulation material, was 500 mm in height and 500 ×500 mm in cross section with stainless steel plate of 2mm in thickness. An agitator was set in the ice water slurry tank to mix water and ice particles for getting prescribed ice water slurry which had uniform ice packing factor in the test section inlet.

注意，大部分情況下，對於材料或設備的描述是和實驗步驟的描述分開的。但是也有的作者將兩者合併在一起。在描述自己的實驗材料和設備時，作者應參考擬投學術刊物上的幾篇文章，以確保最合適的組織形式。

◆ 5.2.2 語態的應用

當作者不是描述自己的行為，而是描述實驗設備或材料的運行或反應時，通常應使用主動語態。注意，此時描述的是設備或材料自己的運行方式或反應，而不是描述作者操作的行為。

→ Two digital strain gauge pressure transducers measured the vapor pressure upstream and downstream of the test tube.

→ The lasers transmitted upstream signals on preassigned optical wavelengths.

→ A high-speed motion analyzer (Kodark Ekapro-1000) visualizes the bubble behaviors in the test sections.

　　作者也可以使用被動語態來描述實驗設備的運作，注意此時必須插入以by開頭的片語以表示哪些設備造成了句子中的動作。記住句子中的動詞是及物動詞時才可用被動語態。

→ The tube was uniformly heated by a 54kW DC power supply.

→ The flow rate was controlled by the volumetric pump.

→ The behavior of the particles was recorded by a video camera.

◆ 5.2.3 時態的應用

　　在描述實驗的研究對象或材料的句子中，若句子的內容是普遍的、不受時間影響的事實，則應使用現在簡單式；若句子的內容是特定的、過去的行為或事件，則應使用過去簡單式。例如，在描述自己領域中研究者通常採用的標準設備時，句子可採用現在簡單式，因為句子的內容和任何研究者都可使用的標準設備的普遍事實有關。

　　在研究工作中，有時候作者需要自行設計、製造或改造一些特殊的設備，以滿足實驗工作的要求。在描述這些特殊設備的句子中，通常應使用過去簡單式。因為這些設備是在過去為特定的用途而設計、製造或改造的，而不是一般研究者可以通用的設備。上面例5-3中對測試段的描述即是一個這樣的例子。再例如：

→ This refractory-lined research combustor was designed to simulate the time/temperature and mixing characteristics of practical industrial liquid and gas combustion system. Natural gas fuel, aqueous metal solutions, gas departs, and combustion air were introduced into the burner section through a moveable-block, variable-air, swirl burner.

→ The experimental system was composed of four parts, i.e. indirectly electrical heated furnace, pyrolysis reactor, on-line sample collected analyzer, and gas condenser & collector.

→ A high pressure chamber was used to investigate the fuel jet disintegration and the spray penetration under variable ambient pressure but constant ambient temperature conditions⋯ It was designed for the application of several measurement techniques, such as the schlieren and the shadow imaging, the 2D Mie scattering⋯.

下面的段落是另一個典型的例子。段落中第一句使用過去簡單式，說明是作者過去的行為。第二句與第三句則描述仍然存在、其他研究者還可以繼續使用的這個設備的原理及功能，因為這些原理及功能不受時間的影響，所以都使用了現在簡單式。

For experiments under conditions similar to those in a real engine, a rapid compression machine (RCM) was developed. This real scale RCM with a bore of 78.3 mm is based on a new driving concept. It offers optical access to the piston bowl from four directions, as shown in Fig. 3. The RCM simulates one compression stroke of an engine with a speed of up to 3,000 rpm.

在描述抽樣總體及樣本（研究對象）時，句子中時態的應用規則與上述原則相似。描述抽樣總體的句子內容是普遍、不受時間影響的事實，所以句子應該採用現在簡單式，而且句子常常出現typically、usually或generally等副詞。

→ Adults in these programs typically have six hours of instruction per week in English.

→ Enrollment in the course generally consists mainly of information science and engineering students.

然而，有時描述特定樣本（研究對象）句子的內容是指過去為了某個研究課題而專門選定的研究對象的事實。換句話說，關於樣本的許多事實只有在研究課題進行時才成立，一旦研究課題結束，這些事實就不再存在。例如當研究對象為人時，研究完成後，這些人年齡增大了，或有些人會調動工作。因此，這些句子中都得使用過去簡單式。例如：

→ The sample consisted of 270 senior engineers from three international companies in London.

→ All of the managers in the sample had at least five years of experience in their current job.

→ The average age of the first group of subjects was 25, and the average age of the second group was 45.

5.3 實驗程序的描述

◆ 5.3.1 時態的應用

對方法或實驗程序的描述，都用來反映作者過去的研究活動，所以這些描述通常需使用過去簡單式。讓我們看一個典型的實驗方法的介紹，請特別注意所用的時態。

例5-4

The experiments were performed on two different NMR spectrometers. Samples S03, S04, S06, and S10 were tested on a Bruker Avance DMX 200 NMR spectrometer, operating at 200-MHz proton resonance frequency using a 10-mm ^{13}C-NMR broadband probehead without proton decoupling. The bandwidth was set to 100 kHz using an acquisition time of 0.041s. The applied 90° pulse length was 8.0 μ s. The dead time was 7.14 μ s. The total number of transients (radiofrequency ［RF］ pulses) was first set to 1024 for samples S04, S06, and S10 and 3072 for samples S03 to compensate for the lower content of ethanol⋯ The spin-lattice relaxation time, T_1, was measured in each sample using a simple inversion recovery (180°- τ -90°)pulse sequence. The longer $T_1$of 189 ms was measured in sample S10, which contained the larger pore volume. The repetition time between RF pulses was set to 1 s⋯.

Samples S1 and S2 were tested on a Varian VXR 300S NMR spectrometer, operating at 300-MHz proton resonance frequency using an HR 5-mm probehead. Both[1]H and ^{13}C-NMR experiments were carried out. The^{13}C experiments were performed using a bandwidth of 20 kHz, with an acquisition time of 0.30 s and an RF pulse length of 8.2 μ s. The1H-NMR experiments were performed using a bandwidth of 25 kHz, with an acquisition time of 1.3 s, an RF pulse length of 0.2 μ s, and a dead time of 10 μ s. Good signal-to-noise ratio was achieved with only four accumulations. The pulse repetition time was set to 1 s for both[1]H and^{13}C-NMR acquisitions. The^{13}C-NMR spectra were accumulated using gated decoupling, i.e., decoupling of the protons during acquisition time only, to exclude differential nuclear Overhauser effects (NOE) ［8］. All NMR measurements were performed at room temperature of 25℃.

The experiments were carried out by immersing the samples of HCP in a reservoir of 10-ml 100% ethanol. The amount of ethanol entering the pore system of the sample as a function of time was measured by recording the proton and carbon NMR spectra at appropriate time intervals during the exchange process. Before each measurement, the samples were taken out of the ethanol, wiped dry with an absorbant tissue, weighed, and transferred to a 5-mm NMR tube. The samples were put back into the ethanol immediately after recording of the NMR spectra. During the initial stage of the process, the ethanol was changed between each experiment to avoid water concentration building up in the ethanol.

　　介紹實驗程序或方法的句子中，當作者敘述一般不受時間影響的事實或採用的標準程序時，可使用現在簡單式。

→ Typical enrollees in this course include information science and engineering students.

→ In this type of procedure, subjects are randomly assigned to one of several groups.

　　在理、工、醫等學科的研究論文中，實驗方法部分的多數句子都用來描述作者的實驗方法或程序，即作者過去的研究行為，所以這些句子都使用過去簡單式，只有少數的句子使用現在簡單式。

◆ 5.3.2 語態的使用

　　在敘述實驗方法或步驟中，實驗方法或步驟是介紹的焦點。而且毫無疑問採用這些實驗方法或步驟的主體是作者自己。因此，敘述實驗方法或步驟的句子通常使用被動語態，尤其在理、工、醫等領域中，絕大多數作者都比較習慣採用被動語態（見上面的例5-4）。

　　只有當作者想使讀者特別注意作者的角色，例如強調自己的假設或建議、解釋某種目的時，可能會把 "we" 當作句子的主詞。建議論文作者多閱讀一些擬投專業期刊上已刊登的一些文章，以便瞭解自己研究領域中一般學者是否常用 "we" 作為主詞的主動語態句子。

　　請注意下面的兩個段落。

We performed experiments on two different NMR spectrometers. We tested samples S03, S04, S06, and S10 on a Bruker Avance DMX 200 NMR spectrometer, operating at 200-MHz proton resonance frequency using a 10-cm ^{13}C-NMR broadband probehead without proton decoupling. We set the bandwidth to 100kHz using an acquisition time of 0.041s⋯

We carried out the experiments by immersing the samples of HCP in a reservoir of 10-ml 100% ethanol. We measured the amount of ethanol entering the pore system of the sample as a function of time by recording the proton and carbon NMR spectra at appropriate time intervals during the exchange process. Before each measurement, we took the samples out of the ethanol⋯.

在這兩個段落中,所有的句子都使用"We"為主詞的主動語態。從英語語法的角度看,這些句子沒有什麼錯誤,但是,讀者會感覺作者在過分地強調自己。合乎習慣的、比較自然的句子應該是使用被動語態的句子。因此,上面兩個段落可改寫為上面例5-4中原有的句子:

The experiments were performed on two different NMR spectrometers. Samples S03, S04, S06, and S10 on a Bruker Avance DMX 200 NMR spectrometer, operating at 200-MHz proton resonance frequency using a 10-cm^{13}C-NMR broadband probehead without proton decoupling. We set the bandwidth to 100 kHz using an acquisition time of 0.041s⋯.

The experiments were carried out by immersing the samples of HCP in a reservoir of 10-ml 100% ethanol. We measured the amount of ethanol entering the pore system of the sample as a function of time by recording the proton and carbon NMR spectra at appropriate time intervals during the exchange process. Before each measurement, we took the samples out of the ethanol⋯.

科技英文論文寫作實用指南 **Practical Guide to Scientific English Writing**

6 結果部分

研究論文的結論部分旨在介紹作者自己的研究成果，並對這些研究結果進行評論或作出總結。通常採用文字敘述和列出圖表兩種方式結合的方法來撰寫結論部分。文字敘述應該十分清楚及明確地表達最重要的結果和說明這些結果或依據這些結果而得出一些推論。圖表則應以資料或曲線等反映詳細、完整的研究結果，以便讀者能夠對結果的有效性作出評價。然而，資料及圖表應該簡明扼要以免讀者忽視了結果的要點。

6.1 基本內容及結構

一般而言，結果部分的內容包含下列三個主要項目：

①介紹研究結果，而且往往以一個句子指出反映完整研究結果的圖表。

②概述最重要的研究結果。

③對研究結果作出評論或概括由這些結果得到的推論。

在一個結果部分中，以上三個項目可能含在幾個段落中多次出現。而且每個段落通常由這三個項目組成，段落的第一句為第一個項目，第二個項目是段落的主要部分，第三個項目則是由段落的最後的一、兩個句子表達。請參閱下面兩例（均為結論部分中的一個段落）：

例6-1

Results

Table 1 shows that the measured drop ΔT_{exh} caused in the temperature of exhaust gases between the inlet to the heat exchanger (evaporator of the heat pipe) and the exit from it is considerably more than what was predicted by modeling studies.Thus ,referring to Table 1,it is observed that the ΔT_{exh} values measured on the actual setup are consistently above the predicted values .This occurrence is especially striking at the tower inlet temperatures. These observations signal that the modeling was on the conservative side.

Table 1. Temperature drop (ΔT_{exh}) of exhaust gases in the heat exchanger

Inlet temperature	ΔT_{exh} (measured)	ΔT_{exh} (predicted)	Ratio of recovery(%)
Ambient temperature =25℃			
378	154	131	71
361	140	117	70
212	106	53	93
274	46	12	88
Ambient temperature =30℃			
206	38	9	83
312	142	80	93
476	231	212	73
Ambient temperature =35℃			
155	30		not applicable
501	258	234	76

例6-2

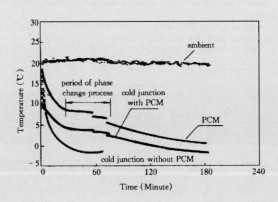

Fig.9　Variation of cold junction and PCM temperatures during the cooling process for the tests with and without PCM material.

Results

When a conventional heat sink is used on the cold side, the temperature of the cold junction drops rapidly until the maximum possible temperature difference across TEC is reached. When the PCM is used, most of the cooling energy is absorbed by the PCM, and therefore the cool side temperature drops more slowly than when PCM is not used, this is shown in Fig.9.With PCM, the temperature drops slowly at the beginning until the transient temperature is reached. During the phase change process, the temperature of the refrigeration system is almost constant until the phase change process is complete, as shown in Fig.9. This helps to keep the temperature difference across toe TEC to minimum, thus improving its performance.

值得注意的是，用文字敘述表格或圖中的資料時，作者不必列出全部資料，而只需要提出這些資料所反映的重要事實。作者應該避免在文字敘述中表達與圖表中提出的完全相同的內容，尤其是不能在文字敘述中重複圖表中的所有資料。圖表用於表示詳細的、完整的結果，而文字敘述則用來提出圖表中資料的重要特性或趨勢。文字敘述與圖表用途雖然有別，但它們相輔相成，通常不能缺少其中的一種方式。在介紹研究結果時，作者應注意為讀者解釋自己的研究結果。不能光在圖表中列出一大堆資料而需要讀者自己耗費時間來解讀這些資料。作者應該以文字敘述的方式直接告訴讀者這些資料出現何種趨勢、有什麼意義，並清楚地陳述根據圖表中的資料所能得出的推論和結論，以及說明這些資料如何能支持自己的推論。如果研究論文有獨立的討論部分，那麼對於研究結果的詳細討論應該留給討論部分。然而，在結果部分中還是有必要對研究結果提供一些基本的解釋，以便讀者能清楚、輕易地瞭解研究的結果。此外，如果作者覺得有必要說明自己的資料分析方法，那麼在結果部分也可以作這些說明。

還需注意，研究論文的圖表中宜包括足夠的資料，以便讓讀者在未看文字敘述的情況下還能大致瞭解研究的結果，尤其在學術會議上報告研究論文中將圖表單獨展示時，更是如此。另外，圖表應有清楚的標題與標記。

6.2 介紹研究結果

在結果部分的開始以及結果部分各段落的前面，通常出現介紹研究結果的句子，用於指出研究結果在哪個表格或圖形中給出。

→ Fig.5 shows the influences of secondary fragmentation on char loadings.

→ Data in Table 3 show that operating and capital costs of DiCTT technology are significantly lower.

→ The effect of having higher turbine inlet temperature on the cycle thermal efficiency is shown in Figure 4.

此類句子都使用現在簡單式，而且其動詞常用 show、present、display、summarize、depict及 illustrate。注意：當圖表用於作某種總結時，才可使用summarize；而depict和illustrate只有在指圖形時才可使用。

從上面的例子可以看出，介紹研究結果的句子可以採用被動語態或主動語態。前者把結果的內容作為主詞，後者則把圖表的名稱當作主詞。介紹研究結果的句子究竟採用被動語態還是主動語態，取決於句子強調的內容及主詞部分的長度。由於結果部分的焦點是結果本身，所以在介紹研究結果時，最好把名詞片語作為主詞，此時句子採用被動語態。但是，名詞片語作為主詞很長時，會使整個句子出現不平衡、不自然的結構，此時宜把圖表名稱作為主詞，句子採用主動語態。

　　還有一種常見的方法是直接陳述結果，並在句子中插入一個片語或括弧中的說明，以告訴讀者這些結果在哪個圖表中示出。下面是常用的句型：

→ At night the average hourly heat release from storage is massive (see Fig.3).

→ At night the average hourly heat release from storage is massive (Fig.3).

→ At night the average hourly heat release is massive, as shown in Fig.3.

→ At night the average hourly heat release is massive, as Fig.3 shows.

→ As shown in Fig.3, at night the average hourly heat release is massive.

→ As Fig.3 shows, at night the average hourly heat release is massive.

6.3 敘述研究結果

　　在敘述研究結果或對結果作總結時，因為所述的內容是過去事件的事實，所以通常採用過去簡單式。

The sensible and latent heat fluxes of Case 1 in daytime were greater than those of Case 2, but there was little difference in net longwave radiation.

The ionic conductivities of these membranes were either very close to or slightly lower than that of a Nafion 117 membrane.

Bubbles were hold between the two bottom electrodes at EHD voltages exceeding 10kV, and consequently heat transfer coefficients were adversely affected owing to the bubbles blanketing the heating surface.

上面的句子都採用過去簡單式，意指作者在這些研究過程中在某些特定情況下出現的結果。如果作者想要表達自己研究過程中所得到的是具有普遍有效性的結果，則可使用現在簡單式。一般而言，使用不同的時態表明了所得結果的不同有效範圍。但是，也有些期刊上的論文習慣統統用現在簡單式來陳述研究結果。建議撰寫研究論文的作者參閱擬投期刊上發表的論文，以確定自己在陳述研究結果時採用何種時態較妥。

此外，在許多學術領域中，作者在敘述自己實驗的結果時，常使用過去簡單式；而在描述由數學模型及理論分析得出的結果時，往往使用現在簡單式。

科技論文中，作者常常必須敘述的研究結果為：

①某個參數或變數在某段時間內的變化情況。

②不同試樣、方法或研究物件之間的比較。

③不同參數或變數之間的關係或影響。

下面介紹敘述上述三種研究結果的基本句型。

①某個參數或變數在某段時間內的變化。在這種句子中，被研究的參數或變數常作為主詞，而表達時間段的片語通常位於句末。見表6-1所示。

表6-1　表達參數或變數在某段時間內變化的基本句型

參數或變量	過去簡單式動詞	時間
The enhancement factor	increased decreased	when the applied voltage was 　from 0 kV to 20 kV.
The pressure	rose fell dropped	after more heat flux was added.

參數或變量	過去簡單式動詞	時間
The number of postgraduates in Management School	declined went up went down remained constant remained unchanged	from 1998 to 2000.
The pressure	peaked	after 20 seconds.
The number of postgraduates in Management School	reached a maximum reached a minimum	in 2001.

表6-2　不同試樣、方法或研究物件之間比較的基本句型

項目1	用於比較的動詞片語	項目2
The power throughput of the condenser	increased much slower than	that of the evaporator.
The NRP algorithm	has much higher packet dropping rate,	when compared to the PRP algorithm.
The PRP protocol	has a higher blocking probability	than the NRP algorithm.

　　②不同試樣、方法或研究物件之間的比較。在進行比較時，句子中常出現形容詞、副詞的比較級、最高級。

　　出現最高級形容詞或副詞的基本句型如下例所示：

→ The fastest algorithm was the genetic algorithm.

→ Samples 1 had the highest magnetic resistance.

→ The temperature difference between the cases with and without anthropogenic heat was smallest near dawn.

　　③不同參數或變數之間的關係或影響。常用的句型包括含有如 correlated、related等動詞的句子以及包含描述其中一個參數或變數變化的子句的複合句。見表6-3及表6-4。

表6-3　表達不同參數或變數之間關係或影響的基本句型（簡單句）

參數或變量1	關　係	參數或變數2
Pressure	was correlated with was negatively correlated with was dependent on was independent of was determined by was closely related to	the ambient temperature

6-4　表達參數或變數之間關係影響的基本句型（複合句）

參數或變量1	主句動詞	連接詞	參數或變量2	子句動詞
Pressure	increased decreased rose fellas	as when	temperature	increased. decreased. rose. fell.

表6-4中的複合句也可改寫為下列簡單句：

→ Pressure increased with an increase in temperature.

→ Pressure increased with temperature.

→ An increase in temperature led to an increase in pressure.

6.4 說明或評論研究結果

作者對他的研究結果的評論或說明通常包含下列內容之一：

①根據本人的研究結果作出推論。如：

These results suggest that untrained octopuses can learn a task more quickly by observing the behavior of another octopus than by reward-and-punishment methods.

②作者解釋研究結果或說明產生研究結果的原因。如：

These findings are understandable because the initial annealing temperature dictates the state of conformational structures.

③作者對此次研究結果與其他研究者曾發生的結果作比較，例如提出自己的結果是否與其他研究者的結果一致。

These results agree with Gerner's analysis, in that Qmax varies inversely with length and to the third power of the pipe width.

④作者對自己的研究方法或技術的性能與其他研究者的方法技術的性能進行比較，這種比較常出現在工程類研究論文中。例如：

The recognition rate of our system is significantly higher than that reported for Token's system.

⑤作者指出自己的理論模型是否與實驗資料符合。如：

The measured temperatures along the heat pipe were all highly consistent with the predictions of the theoretical model.

在評論或說明研究結果時，通常採用「個別評論」形式或「綜合評論」形式。

所謂「個別評論」形式，是先介紹一個結果，並立即對這個結果加以評論，然後再介紹另一個結果並加以評論，接著再對第三個進行介紹並評論，……。當作者認為有必要對幾個結果分別加以介紹評論時，適用這種形式。下面是這種形式的一個實例（例中的圖已省略）。在此實例中，作者敘述三個主要的結果，而且在介紹每個結果後即作簡短的評論。

Results

Figures 3 and 4 show the transient response of the power throughput and the temperatures for the disk-shaped heat pipe and the flat-plat heat pipe during the startup process, respectively .As shown in Figs. 3(a) and 4(a), the power throughput of the evaporator increases rapidly during the initial phase of the transient. Conversely, the power throughput of the condenser increases much slower and reaches the steady-state about 50s later than that of the evaporator. This is because the thermal capacity of the evaporator is smaller than that of the condenser due to the fact that the condenser area is seven times larger than the evaporator area for the disk-shaped heat pipe and nine times for the flat-plate heat pipe···.

The transient responses of the vapor temperature and the wall outer surface temperatures are shown in Fig.3 (b) and Fig.4 (b). The temperature difference across evaporator wall and wick is larger than that across condenser wall and wick. This is because the heat flux in the evaporator is larger than that in the condenser due to the smaller evaporator area···.

The vapor and wall outer surface temperatures along the heat pipe at different times during the starting transient are shown in Fig.6 and Fig.7. For both disk-shaped and flat-plate heat pipes, the bottom wick acts as a condenser. Therefore, the temperatures at the bottom wall outer surface are almost uniform. This indicates that neglecting heat conduction along the heat pipe is reasonable for the bottom wall and wick regions···.

所謂「綜合評論」形式，是先介紹數個研究結果，然後即對所有這些結果作一種綜合評論或說明。在下面的實例中，作者先敘述所有主要的結果，然後根據這些結果作出精簡的說明或評論。

The results are shown in Figure 4. The two tests of quenching from $153°C$ have identical creep curves, confirming the thermoreversibility of quenching and aging as well as the reliability of the apparatus. The quench from $153°C$ to $0°C$ produced the least dense structure and the highest creep, whereas the quench from $96°C$ to $0°C$ yielded the most dense structure, leading to the slowest creep behavior. These results are understandable because the initial annealing temperature (T_0) determines the state of conformational structures, from which the quenching takes place. For a higher T_0, greater excess free volume or molecular mobility is most likely to be frozen into the glassy matrix if quenching is performed properly. Thus molecular mobility is determined by the initial annealing temperature.

6.5 時態

在對結果進行評論或說明的句子中，正確的動詞時態應該依據評論或說明的內容而定。

當評論的內容為依據研究結果作出的推論時，句子的主要動詞通常使用現在簡單式，且常用appear、suggest、seem等推測動詞或情態助動詞may。

→ These findings suggest that the equivalence ratio is the strongest factor affecting the NOx emission levels through its influence on the combustion wave velocity and temperature.

→ The contact angles may have effect on the time required for the heat pipe to reach steady-state.

→ It appears that heat transfer coefficients are more dependent on heat flux in regions of lower quality $(x<0.5)$.

當評論的內容為對研究結果可能的證明時，句子的主要動詞之前通常加上may或can這些現在簡單式的情態助動詞。

→ The layer structural or some other mixed complex material may be the most suitable refrigerants for the Ericsson magnetic refrigerator.

→ The results can be explained by a giant magnetic entropy change.

→ One reason of this advantage may be that the Hank visual programming language can avoid some of the syntatic problems associated with textual programming languages.

常用的句型還有：

→ A possible explanation for this is that the Hank visual programming language can avoid some of the syntactic problems associated with textual programming languages.

→ This may have occurred because the calculation did not consider the initial cooling requirements to precool the semi-trailer body and the solar radiation load.

此外，在對結果提出可能的解釋和說明時，可使用現在簡單式的推測動詞，見表6-5所示。

表6-5　說明結果時採用推測動詞的句型

主詞	現在簡單式的推測動詞	說　　明
It	seens appears is likely is possible	that the Hank visual programming language can avoid some of the syntatic problems associated with textual programming languages.
These results These date	indicate suggest imply	

在上面所示的例句中，說明的具體內容往往出現在以that開頭的名詞性（主詞，形容詞，受詞）子句或以because開始的原因副詞子句中。根據情況的不同，子句中的動詞可能會使用現在簡單式、情態助動詞may加動詞原形或過去簡單式。具體來說，作者認為對結果的說明具有普遍有效性，則在子句中使用現在簡單式；若作者比較不確定此說明是否具有普遍有效性時，則使用may加動詞原形的形式；若作者認為說明的範圍只限在自己研究的特定情況，則使用過去簡單式。下面依次給出這三種情況的例句。

→ It seems that ash deposition of Coal P accelerates mainly through thermophoresis.

→ It seems that ash deposition of Coal P may accelerate mainly through thermophoresis.

→ It seems that ash deposition of Coal P accelerated mainly through thermophoresis.

注意：為了使句子更加簡潔，可以將先行主詞it開頭的句子改寫成簡單句。此時原複合句中子句的主詞變成簡單句中的主詞，而改寫句中的動詞用現在簡單式。例如，上例的句子可改寫為：

The ash deposition of Coal P seems to accelerate mainly through thermophoresis.

當評論的內容為比較作者的研究結果與其他學者的研究結果時，應該使用現在簡單式，因為不管兩組結果之間是不是一致，這個比較是一種不受時間影響的邏輯上的關係。此類句子中如果存在以that引起的子句，那麼，子句中的動詞也用現在簡單式。

例如：

→ These results agree well with the findings of Casadio, et al.

→ These data are consistent with earlier findings showing that the best alloying addition is trivalent Ga.

當評論的內容是對作者自身採用的方法或技術的性能與其他作者曾提出的方法或技術的性能進行比較時，可採用現在簡單式或過去簡單式。若在評論中使用現在簡單式，則意味著作者認定句子的內容具有普遍有效性，如：

The recognition rate of our system is significantly higher than that reported for Token's system.

若使用過去簡單式，則說明作者認為評論的範圍僅在特定情況下才有效，如：

The values predicted by our model had a smaller degree of error than the values generated by Baker's model did.

當作者指出由自己的理論模型所得到的預測與實驗資料之間的吻合程度時，通常得使用現在簡單式，說明模型預測與實驗資料是不是一致不受時間影響。若此類句子中出現以that開頭的子句，則子句中亦使用現在簡單式。如：

→ The data confirm closely to the prediction of the model.

→ The data indicate that the model is reliable and accurate.

→ The theoretical model fits the experimental data well.

→ The theoretical model agrees well with the experimental data.

→ The experimental measurements are very close to the predicted values.

→ There is a high level of agreement between the theoretical predictions and the experimental data.

但是，也有的作者把推測和實驗資料之間的比較視為一種過去的行為，因而在句中採用過去簡單式。

7

討論部分

　　研究論文的討論部分旨在闡明作者研究結果的意義。在討論部分中，作者需說明自己的結果和自己研究領域中其他學者的研究之間的關係。與導論部分一樣，作者需說明為什麼自己的研究工作很重要，以及對本領域的研究做出什麼樣的貢獻，例如：得到的結果能否支持或反駁重要的理論和假設，能否擴充或延伸此領域中的知識以及是否指出了新的研究題目或進一步研究的方向。換句話說，討論部分可以使讀者和專業期刊的審稿人從中看出作者研究工作的重要性與貢獻。

　　必須仔細而又充分地在討論部分中表達自己研究結果的內涵，如果不重視這一點，至少會被學術期刊的編輯退回論文初稿，正如Robert Day所指出的：即使論文所給的資料及結論很有價值，也令人感到興趣，但如果這些資料及結果的內涵寫得十分含糊，那麼還是會遭到排斥的。

　　為了讓讀者和專業期刊的審稿人易於瞭解研究論文的重要性，作者在討論部分中應該回答下面部分或全部的問題：

　　作者所得到的研究結果是否符合自己原來的期望？如果不是，為什麼不是？

　　根據這些結果，作者能做出什麼樣的結論或推論？如何解釋這些推論？

　　作者的試驗結果或理論分析結果是否和其他學者已提出的結果一致？如果不是，則能否說明不一致的原因？

　　是否能建議還有什麼樣的試驗或理論分析方法可以讓研究者來證實、反駁或擴展作者的研究結果？

這些結果能否支援或反駁作者領域中現有的理論？

根據這些結果，作者能否建議現有的理論應如何修正或擴充？

作者的結果是否有實際的應用價值？如果有，則有哪些應用價值？

討論部分是研究論文中很關鍵的部分，所以作者在討論自己的研究結果時應該直接表達自己對研究結果的解釋和說明，千萬不要過於含蓄。為了使自己的研究論文寫得成功，作者不僅需要得出一些有意義的研究結果，而且還需要清楚地闡明這些結果的重要性並說明這些結果值得其他學者注意的原因。

在大部分領域的研究論文中，討論（Discussion）作為獨立的部分常常位於結果部分（Results）後和結論部分（Conclusion）之前。然而，在一些領域之中，討論部分是研究報告的最後一部分；也有些研究論文將討論部分與結果部分合併在一起（Results and Discussion），還有些研究論文不出現單獨的討論部分，而是把討論的內容納入結論部分（Conclusion）內。建議論文作者參閱自己領域內幾種著名的期刊尤其要參考自己擬投學術期刊的數篇文章，以確定採用何種格式來適當地撰寫討論部分的內容。還要指出的是：討論部分的英文名稱為單數形式如 "Discussion"，不是其複數形式。

7.1 基本內容及結構

在撰寫討論部分時，作者通常首先闡述自己的研究工作並指出具體的研究結果，然後討論自己的研究結果的內涵以及這些研究結果對自己領域內的研究工作有無重要性與貢獻。典型的討論部分通常由以下六個項目構成：

①**研究目的** 再次概述自己研究的主要目的或假設。

②**研究結果** 簡述最重要的結果，並指出這些結果能否支援原先的假設或是否與其他研究者的結果相互一致。有時還會再次強調個別的重要結果。

③**對結果的說明** 對自己的研究結果提出說明、解釋或猜測。

④**推論或結論** 指出依據自己的研究結果所得出的結論或推論。

⑤**研究方法或結果的限制** 指出自己研究的限制以及這些限制對研究結果可能產生的影響。

⑥**研究結果的實際應用或建議新的研究題目** 指出自己研究結果可能的實際應用及其價值，對進一步的研究方向或新的課題提出建議。

從原則上講，研究論文的討論部分應該包含上述完整的六個項目。事實上，也有不少作者並沒有完全按照上面六個項目的排列順序，而是靈活地將上述項目②、③及④分散到各個段落中重複進行，還有些研究論文會省略其中的一、兩個項目。

例7-1是一個包含五個項目的結論，其中未包括的研究方法或結果的限制已在論文的其他部分涉及。

例7-1

Discussion

→ 研究目的

The studies reported in this paper have sought to determine the efficacy of the SHERPA and TAFEI as methods for human error identification for use in device evaluation. Both methods out-perform heuristic analysis, suggesting that there is merit to structured approaches.

→ 結果概述及說明

The results of experiment one show that SPERPA and TAFEI provide a better means of predicting errors than an heuristic approach, and demonstrates a respectable level of concurrent validity. These findings suggest that SPERPA and TAFEI enable analysts to structure their judgment. However, the results run counter to the literature in some areas (such as usability evaluation) which suggest the superiority of heuristic approaches[20]. The views of Lansdale and Ormerod[36] may help us to reconcile these findings. They suggest that, to be applied successfully, an heuristic approach needs the support of an explicit methodology to 'ensure that the evaluation is structured and thorough' (p257). The use of the error classification system in the heuristic group provided some structure, but a structured theory is not the same as a structured methodology. Heuristics are typically a set of 10-12 statements against which a device is evaluated. This strikes us as a poorly designed checklist, with little or no structure in the application of the method. SHEPRA and TAFEI, on the other hand, provided a semi-structured methodology which formed a framework for the judgment of the analyst without constraining it. It seems to succeed precisely because of its semi-structured nature which alleviates the burden otherwise placed on the analyst's memory while allowing them room to use their own heuristic judgment. Other researchers have found that the use of structured methods can help as part of the design process, such as idea generation activities.

The results of experiment two show that the test-retest reliability of SHERPA and TAFEI remains fairly consistent over time. However, the correlation coefficient for test-retest reliability was moderate (by analogy to psychometric test development) and it would have been desirable to have participants achieve higher levels of reliability. Reliability and validity are interdependent concepts, but the relationship is in one direction only. Whilst it is perfectly possible to have a highly reliable technique with little validity, it is impossible for a technique to be highly valid with poor reliability. As Aitken[18] notes 'reliability is a necessary condition but not a sufficient condition for validity' (p93). Consequently, establishing the validity of a HEI technique is of paramount importance. The current investigation is the first reported study of people learning to use a HEI technique; all previously reported studies have been with expert users. As a result, it is conceivable that the moderate reliability values (r.0.4-0.6) obtained here may simply be an artefact of lack of experience. With this in mind, it is important to note that Baber and Stanton[17] report much higher values when users are experts.

→ 結論或推論

→ 實際應用

The results are generally supportive of both SHERPA and TAFEI. They indicate that novices are able to acquire the approaches with relative ease and reach acceptable levels of performance within a reasonable amount of time. Comparable levels of sensitivity are achieved and both techniques look relatively stable over time. This is quite encouraging, and it shows that HEI techniques can be evaluated quantitatively. Both SHERPA and TAFEI would be respectable methods for designers to use in device design and evaluation. Any methods that enable the designers to anticipate the use of their device should be a welcome prospect. We would certainly recommend incorporating human error analysis as part of the design process, and this is certainty better practice than testing devices on the purchasers and waiting for complaints. The methodologies require something of a mind-shift in design, such that designers need to accept that 'designer-error' is the underlying cause of 'user-error'.

例7-2

Discussion

→ 主要結果及推論

Electric properties which may be of importance for the refrigeration industry were determined for five of the most widely used substitutes for CFC and HCFC refrigerants. The obtained values in this work characterize these fluids as fairly strong insulators even though CFCs are even stronger insulating media. The values on the other hand are comparable to what is known from R22 so that problems caused by unsuitable electric properties can be excluded for any of the five substances tested.

→ 某個結果及說明

The measured value of the a.c. resistivity for R134a is 38.5% lower than that given in [5] . As the resistivity is extremely dependant on water contents and other impurities of the tested substance as well as on the value of the applied field strength, such deviations are not unusual. All refrigerants tested in this work were taken from the regular production process and comply to the existing specifications. The maximum water content according to these specifications is 10 ppm. The uncertainties of the measurement are assumed to further contribute to the detected deviations.

→ 研究限制／研究方向

This paper only presents data for ambient temperatures and ambient pressures for gas phase measurements and saturation pressures for liquid phase measurements, respectively. Further works should be performed to establish temperature and pressure dependencies of the properties discussed, possibly over the full range in which the refrigerants are used. It was quoted that resistivity values as determined within this work strongly depend on water contents and other impurities. It would, therefore, be of value to established dependencies of resistivity data especially as a function of water content in order to gather information for systems operating under worst case conditions.

→ 應用前景

The properties, however, that are discussed in this work are receiving more and more attention from other fields such as manufacturers of control devices. Differences of these properties between liquid and vapor phase or pressure and temperature dependencies may be useful for various control means such as oil level or liquid level controls, measurements of oil contents.

7.2 常用句型與時態

下面介紹作者在表達上述基本內容的項目時常用的句型以及時態的用法。

◆ 7.2.1 回顧研究目的

在本書的第三章中曾經提到,研究論文在敘述研究目的時常採用兩種表達方式,即「論文導向」與「研究導向」。所謂「論文導向」,就是敘述研究目的的句子會強調研究論文本身。而「研究導向」則是指敘述研究目的的句子強調研究工作本身。

在討論部分中重述研究目的時,作者使用的時態是依據論文導論部分中所採用的「導向」而定的。如果作者在導論部分中採用「研究導向」以陳述研究目的,則在討論部分使用過去簡單式來回顧研究目的。請參閱下面的例句:

→ This research investigated the differences between the boiling behavior of surfactant and that of pure water.

→ The aim of this research was to propose a novel routing methodology which predicts the traffic load on each of the ISLs.

→ This study attempted to investigate whether there are differences in the evaluation cues that successful and unsuccessful salespeople use for classifying sales leads.

如果作者在導論部分中採用「論文導向」,則在討論部分常用現在完成式來重述研究目的,見下列例句:

→ This paper has proposed a detailed assessment of antecedent conditions preceding nocturnal heat islands in Regina.

→ This study has presented a unique method for measuring friction heat generated at ball bearings in vacuum and at LHe temperatures.

→ In this paper, we have reported the significant effect of the fuel additive on the soot formation.

　　顯然，上述六個例句都採用主動語態。主動語態的句子讀上去比較有力，而且作者可以將較長的名詞片語或子句放在動詞後面。有的作者在回顧研究目的時也採用被動語態的句子，此時作者把研究主題作為句子的主詞。如下列例句：

→ In this study, the differences between the boiling behavior of surfactant and that of pure water were investigated.

→ In this paper, the significant effect of the fuel additive on the soot formation has been reported.

　　若作者需要重述研究工作原來的假設，則通常也採用過去簡單式，而且在表示假設內容的主詞子句、形容詞子句或受詞子句中，往往也會使用情態助動詞would、could或might。

→ We originally assumed that the sputtering yield of a monoatomic target would be proportional to the energy deposited in nuclear collisions at the surface.

→ It was originally assumed that the sputtering yield of a monoatomic target would be proportional to the energy deposited in nuclear collisions at the surface.

→ Existing theories suggested that the sputtering yield of a monoatomic target would be proportional to the energy deposited in nuclear collisions at the surface.

→ The evidence led us to infer that yield could be improved by subsurface irrigation.

→ We originally hypothesized that successful salesmen would be more adept at organizing client evaluation cues.

→ We anticipated that tempo would have a clear effect on subjects' attitudes towards the music.

◆ 7.2.2 概述結果

在概述研究結果時，作者應該遵循本書第六章中已介紹的基本準則。這些基本準則是：若作者希望把結果的有效性限制在本次特定的研究範圍內，則使用過去簡單式概述結果。若作者以為自己的研究結果具有普遍的有效性，則可以使用現在簡單式。在心理學及經濟學等研究領域中，比較常用現在簡單式來概述結果。

→ In general, the losses of residue measured in our study were greater than those reported in previous research.

→ All perceptual dimensions seemed to be influences by the frequency response.

→ The programmers were able to recall and execute more of the semantically simple procedures than the semantically complex procedures.

在討論研究結果時，作者常會說明自己的研究結果是否與其他學者的結果或結論一致，或是否支援原來作的假設。此時通常採用現在簡單式，因為句子的內容反映作者目前對這些研究結果的評價。常用的句型如下所示：

→ These results are consistent with the original hypothesis.

→ These results provide substantial evidence for the original assumptions.

→ These experimental results support the original hypothesis that….

→ Our findings are in substantial agreement with those of Davis (1999).

→ The present results are consistent with those reported in our earlier work.

→ The experimental and theoretical values for the yields agree well.

→ The experimental values are all lower than the theoretical predictions.

→ These values are higher than would be expected according to the theory.

→ These results contradict the original hypothesis.

→ These results appear to refute the original assumptions.

　　然而，在指出自己的研究結果是否和原先作的假設或前人的研究工作結果一致時，有時候作者使用過去簡單式，以說明句子的內容為過去發生的事情，尤其當句中出現代表過去時間的詞或片語時，更是如此。

→ The reaction rates observed in our study were greater than those reported by Howell (1997).

→ In the first series of trials, the test values were all lower than the simulating results.

◆ 7.2.3 解釋結果

　　解釋結果的句子通常是主從複合句（形容詞子句、主詞子句或受詞子句）。主句中的動詞往往是表示可能性的、採用現在簡單式的動詞，而子句中的動詞常常使用過去簡單式或現在簡單式。在子句中，使用過去簡單式暗指對於自己研究結果的說明僅對此次研究結果起作用，使用現在簡單式則意指該說明具有普遍有效性。表7-1、表7-2示出了兩種解釋方式的句型。

表7-1 說明只對本次研究有效的句型

主句（現在簡單式）	That	說明（過去簡單式）
It is possible It may be It is likely It is unlikelyOne reason for this could be These results can be explained 　　　by assuming This inconsistency indicates	that	vibrating motion of heating wall enhanced melting rate and heat transfer. an erroneous value was attributed to one of quantities in Equation (5).

表7-2 說明為普遍有效

主句（現在簡單式）	That	說明（現在簡單式）
It is possible It may be It is likely It is unlikely One reason for this could be These results can be explained 　　　by assuming This finding seems to show	that	vibrating motion of heating wall enhances melting rate and heat transfer. the variety of options increases the complexity of the procurement decision.

　　上面的句型也可以把主詞子句、受詞子句或形容詞子句改成獨立、完整的句子，以代替原有的複合句。改寫時在動詞前加上情態助動詞，如may或could。在這類句型中，若要把說明的範圍限定為只有對此次研究才有效，則動詞應該使用現在完成式，而若要表示此說明具有普遍有效性，則動詞需用現在簡單式。例如：

→ Vibrating motion of heating wall may have enhanced melting rate and heat transfer.

→ An erroneous value may have been attributed to one of quantities in Equation (5).

→ Vibrating motion of heating wall may enhance melting rate and heat transfer.

→ The variety of options may increase the complexity of the procurement decision.

當作者對自己的說明正確性非常肯定時,還可以省略上面例句中的情態助動詞,而直接採用過去簡單式(表示說明只對這次研究有效)和現在簡單式(表示說明為普遍有效)。

→ Vibrating motion of heating wall enhanced melting rate and heat transfer.

→ An erroneous value was attributed to one of quantities in Equation (5).

→ Vibrating motion of heating wall enhances melting rate and heat transfer.

→ The variety of options increases the complexity of the procurement decision.

在作出說明的句子中其他常用的動詞片語還有:may be due to,can be attributed to和may be caused by。在包含這些片語的句子中,常把被說明的對象當作句子的主詞,並把說明的內容放在動詞片語的介係詞之後,如下例所示:

→ This inconsistency may be caused by an error in Equation (5).

→ The enhancement in melting rate and heat transfer may be due to vibrating motion of heating wall.

→ The rapid decrease in the secondary electron yield can be attributed to adsorbate sputtering followed by oxygen depletion.

◆ 7.2.4推論或結論

在表達自己研究結果的內涵時,作者應該使用現在簡單式。句子中的現在簡單式說明作者的推論或結論具有普遍有效性,而不是作者研究條件下的特定推論或結果。通常普遍認為研究結果與結論或推論之間的邏輯關係或依賴關係不受時間的影響,這也是採用現在簡單式的原因。

在討論推論或結論時，主句常用推測動詞（如appear，suggest，imply或seem）以及情態助動詞may。作為推論或結論的常用句型之一是把自己的研究結果或先行詞it當主詞，並利用以that開頭的受詞子句、主詞子句或同位語來陳述結論或推論的內容。若作者相當確定自己的結論或推論有效，則子句中採用現在簡單式；而若不太確定自己的結論或推論是否有效，則在子句的動詞前加上may。無論如何，主句的動詞應為現在簡單式的形式。表7-3給出了表達結論或推論時常用的句型。

表7-3　結論或推論的常用句型

主句（現在簡單式）	That	推論或結論（現在簡單式）
Our results indicate The data reported here suggest These findings confirm It appears	that	instructional design affects the outcome of education. （作者很確定結論或推論有效）
Our conclusion is These results imply These data show These findings support the hypothesis Our data provide evidence		instructional design may affect the outcome of education. （作者不太確定結論或推論是否有效）

與對結果的說明一樣，作者也可以將表7-3的句型中以that開頭的主詞子句、受詞子句或同位語子句改寫成獨立、完整的句子，並在句中的動詞前面加上may或把動詞換成推測動詞，而句子的動詞應採用現在簡單式。例如：

→ The energy deposited by the ions may rearrange the atomic structure of the damaged SiO_2 surface in the presence of oxygen.

→ Structural differences in the starting material also appear to strongly influence the sputtering yield.

當作者十分確定自己的結論或推論有效時，有時候省略上面句子中的may或推測動詞而直接使用現在簡單式。此時上面兩例子可寫成：

→ The energy deposited by the ions rearranges the atomic structure of the damaged SiO_2 surface in the presence of oxygen.

→ Structural differences in the starting material also strongly influence the sputtering yield.

◆ 7.2.5 研究方法或結果的限制

在指出自己研究方法或結果的限制時，作者應該視句子的內容來決定使用何種時態。若指出作者已完成的研究工作的受限，則句子應該使用過去簡單式。

→ The number of tourists surveyed was quite small.

→ Only three sets of samples were tested.

若作者需指出自己研究的方法、模型或分析的限制，則應該使用現在簡單式。

→ The proposed model is based on three simplifying assumptions.

→ Our analysis neglects several potentially important conditions.

→ The method presented here is accurate, but cannot be implemented in real time applications.

如果作者想表述其他可能的條件與情況會對研究總結果可能產生的何種影響，則在句中應該使用現在簡單式，且在句中動詞之前加上情態助動詞may或might。

→ Tests with other kinds of lubricates might yield different results.

→ Our findings may be valid only roe a wickless heat pipes.

→ An experiment using different absorber plate material and thickness might produce different results.

還有些作者會使用主詞We以及admit、recognize之類的動詞來直接表明自己研究方法的限制。

→ We recognize that the method adopted in this paper does not incorporate traffic re-shaping at intermediate nodes.

→ We readily admit that a single short test may not fully reflect the performance of the new type compressor.

◆ 7.2.6 指出實際應用或新的研究範圍

在指出自己研究結果的實際應用時，作者應該使用現在簡單式，且在句子動詞之前加上may、might或should等情態助動詞。若用should，則表示作者對自己研究的應用價值相當肯定。

→ Differences of these properties between liquid and vapor phase may be useful for various control means such as oil level or liquid level controls, measurements of oil contents.

→ The results of this study may lead to the development of effective methods for measuring the air velocity in various shapes of ducts.

→ The results of this research may help managers make more informed procurement decisions.

→ The technique presented in this paper should be useful in producing ethanol from corn kernels.

當作者對進一步的研究方向或新的研究題目做出建議時，常可在句中使用現在簡單式，並在動詞之前加上情態助動詞would、could或should。若用should，則表示比較強烈的建議。下面是常用的句型：

→ An important direction for further work might be to study the chunking process as it operates in programming tasks.

→ It would be interesting to learn why oxygen is depleted during this type of sputtering.

→ Another interesting topic would be to examine how learning outcomes are related to concept attainment.

→ The generality of the gender moderated affect could be assessed in studies using other types of music and different exposure durations.

→ Future research could explore the possibility to apply in chaos theory analysis.

→ A further experiment should be conducted with a more sophisticated measuring system.

→ A treatment of anthropogenic heat in the numerical model should be discussed in detail in the future.

→ Future research should focus on doubling or tripling the conversion efficiency of commercial plants, reducing costs further, and resolving issues related to biomass residual ash.

在提出自己的建議時，有時作者可以直接用第一人稱複數代名詞we作為主詞，並用suggest或recommend當作主句的動詞（動詞仍用現在簡單式）。要注意的是：在動詞suggest，recommend後為表達建議內容的受詞子句中，必須用動詞原形。見下例所示：

→ We suggest that similar studies be conducted with other algorithms, such as GA.

→ We recommend that these experiments be repeated using a wider range of working conditions.

還有些作者需在討論部分或結論中提到自己正在進行或打算開展的相關研究。此時，句子可以使用現在進行式或未來式，而且最好用We作為句子主詞，以強調這些正在進行打算開展的研究是作者本身的行為，否則讀者通常會不清楚這些行為的主體是誰。

→ The present authors are currently conducting experiments on a dry-expansion evaporator with R407C.

→ In the future, we will investigate the effect of using fuel cells for both transportation and electricity applications.

→ We are now conducting the numerical simulations of temperature distribution of all the surfaces of two urban blocks.

科技英文論文寫作實用指南 **Practical Guide to Scientific English Writing**

8 結論部分

　　科技論文的結論部分緊跟在論文的討論部分或結果與討論部分的後面，位於論文正文的最後。有不少讀者在準備閱讀論文全文時，首先快速地將結論看一遍，瞭解研究工作的主要成果，以便決定是否有必要認真地閱讀全文或其中的一部分。因此。論文作者應十分重視結論的寫作。在本章中，我們將扼要地介紹結論部分的內容組織、時態應用及撰寫結論時的注意事項。

8.1 基本內容及組織

　　論文的結論部分通常應包含以下內容：

　　①概述主要的研究工作（此項內容可有可無）。

　　②陳述研究的主要結論，包括簡略地重複最重要的發現或結果，指出這些發現或結論的重要內涵，對發現或結果提出可能的說明。

　　③本研究結果可能的應用前景以及進一步深入的研究方向或具體課題（此項內容可有可無）。

　　下面三個結論部分的例子分別摘自期刊*Energy and Buildings*、*Computer Networks*和*International Journal of Heat and Mass Transfer*。

例8-1

Conclusion

→ 主要結果及結論

→ 潛在的效益

Our analysis indicates that we can reduce the L. A. heat island by as much as 3℃. Cooler roof and paving surfaces and 11M more shade trees should reduce ozone exceedance by 12% in Los Angeles and by slightly less in other smoggy cities. This 12% improvement exceeds that estimated for clear-burning gasoline and dramatically exceeds our estimates for reductions from electric or hybrid vehicles. The combined direct and indirect effect of the cool communities strategies can potentially reduce air-conditioning use in a Los Angeles home by half and save about 10% of A/C use of a one-story office building. The total direct and indirect annual savings in the L.A. basin, including that attributable to smog reduction, is estimated at US$0.5B per year. The corresponding national A/C saving is about 10%.

例8-2

Conclusions and future work

While several events have occurred recently that have changed the landscape of satellite communications, satellite networks remain an important component of the network infrastructure for both developing and developed countries. Satellite networks are attractive to support data, audio and video streaming; bulk data transfer such as software update or dissemination of Web caches; and applications involving limited interactivity such as distance learning. In this paper, we have presented issues related to routing in a broadband LEO satellite network with an emphasis on delivering deterministic QoS to users. The traffic on the ISLs between the satellite nodes changes dynamically as the satellites move along their orbits. The routing algorithm has to consider these variations in traffic due to the mobility of satellites while delivering deterministic QoS grouting algorithm guarantees.

→ 主要結果及其可能的應用

We have proposed a predictive that exploits the deterministic nature of the LEO satellites topology in order to deliver QoS guarantees. It has been observed from a set of detailed simulation examples that the PRP can provide strict QoS guarantees without over-reserving capacity on the ISLs. An admission control curve has been obtained which may be used to ensure that the desired QoS metrics may be guaranteed.

→ 本研究下一步的具體課題

In the development of the paper we considered that links are either always up or always down. However, in several LEO satellite network designs we need to consider the connectivity among LEO satellites to change with time, e.g., links between cross-seam satellites and the links among satellites in the Polar Regions can be considered up for certain times. Time varying characteristics of the LEO satellite connectivity can be incorporated to our model easily. We may consider those links that are "down" at certain times as congested at those times. Our routing algorithm then determines routs avoiding these congested links at the down times.

→ 研究方向

The implementation of the algorithm is currently limited to point-to-point unicast connections. Future LEO satellite networks should be able to support efficient multicast connections as well. Supporting multicast connections with QoS guarantees is an interesting problem requiring further research. Our findings can also be extended for hybrid LEO-GEO, and LEO-wireless ad-hoc communication networks. To investigate issues in QoS routing in such hybrid environments is among our future research goals.

例8-3（一覽表形式）

Conclusions

Based on the analytical and experimental investigations presented in this paper, the following conclusions may be made:

1. The radially rotating miniature high-temperature heat pipe has a simple structure, low manufacturing cost, very high effective thermal conductance and large heat transfer capability. At the same time, the heat pipe can withstand strong vibrations and work in a high-temperature environment. Therefore, the turbine engine component cooling incorporating radially rotating miniature high-temperature heat pipes is a feasible and effective cooling method.

2. The non-condensable gases in the heat pipe have an adverse effect on the heat pipeperformance. It results in a large temperature gradient near the condenser end and reduces the effective thermal conductance and heat transfer capability of the heat pipe.

3. Eqs. (33) and (34) predict reasonably well the temperature distributions along the heat pipe length and are a useful analytical tool for heat pipe design and performance analysis.

8.2 時態

在這一節裡，我們將簡略地討論結論部分基本內容中所使用的動詞時態。由於基本內容中所使用的句型與時態和在上一章討論部分中所使用的都相同，因此下面只介紹一些基本規則。

◆ 8.2.1 概述研究活動

結論部分的第一個句子或前幾個句子常常是對研究目的或主要研究活動的概述（然而，也有不少作者不寫概述而直接敘述主要結論）。當文章使用「論文導向」時，研究活動的概述通常使用現在完成式，而當文章使用「研究導向」時，則常常使用過去簡單式。

論文導向

→ In this paper, we have presented issues related to routing in a broadband LEO satellite network with an emphasis on delivering deterministic QoS to users.

→ This paper has conducted the search for a practical magnetocaloric cooling configuration for the large near-room temperature refrigeration and air conditioning market.

研究導向

→ Overall energy balances for the various compressor elements were established to model the heat transfer between each of the compressor elements.

→ In this study, upsetting of A A 6082 was carried out for experimentally measuring friction areas ratios and normal pressure; five friction models were applied in finite element analysis in order to compare calibration curves of these models with the experimental results.

◆ 8.2.2 敘述主要結論

在結論中需要寫出其中一些重要的研究結果時，通常使用過去簡單式。

→ The effect of the structure on the free surface at the leading edge increased the total wave height by 6%.

→ The Gaussian arbor function developed center-surround RFs while the step arbor function enabled the development of multi-lobed RFs in addition to center-surround RFs.

在敘述自己研究工作的主要結論時，作者通常可使用現在式以及推測動詞（如appears、seems等）或情態助動詞（如may、could等）。使用現在式時，一般指作者陳述的結果不是在特定條件下的研究結果，而是具有普遍有效性的研究結果。

→ Calibration curves of the friction area ratio are more sensitive to friction at the tool /workpiece interface than those of normal pressure.

→ The lateral buckling capacity of beams with transverse loads are affected by the location of applied load as well as the fiber orientation.

→ This second-order sound feature cannot be described by existing sound parameters; even sharpness fails to be a good descriptor.

當作者對自己的研究結果做出說明時，認為說明的內容僅在此次特定情況下有效，那麼應該使用過去式。

→ The model presented here yielded a satisfactory consistence between the experimental data and numerical predictions.

→ Some amount of thinning near the bottom of the cup wall usually occurred.

如果認為自己的說明基本上具有普遍有效性，那麼可使用現在式。另外，作者也可常常使用情態助動詞（如may、could等）或推測動詞（如appear、seems等）。在大多數情況下，結論的內容旨在指出具有普遍有效性的結論，所以一般作者都會使用現在式、情態助動詞或推測動詞，而不用過去式。

→ This suggests that experimental measurements of the perturbed polymer volume in a nanocomposite or a polymeric thin film depend on the radiation wavelength used for probing.

→ As discussed, the particle size dependent reactivity may reflect as adsorbate induced and facilitated restructuring of the catalyst particle surface.

→ It seems that in the particulate phase homogeneous reaction may not be totally suppressed, but their rate is significantly reduced.

→ A damping layer between gypsum boards causes an increase in the sound reduction index curve.

◆ 8.2.3 指出研究方向或應用

在指出研究方向或下一步研究的題目，以及自己研究結果的應用或效益時，作者應使用現在簡單式及如may、should等情態助動詞。

→ The weakly reflecting case particularly merits further study.

→ Further research is needed to quantify the effect of the structure on the fluid accelerations.

→ Supporting multicast connections with QoS guarantees is an interesting problem requiring further research.

→ However, there are still some details missing in the diacetylene mechanism and more study (e.g., H and O atom measurements using atomic resonance absorption spectrometry) is needed to solve the issues.

→ For architectures there is the important task of adding sub-cortical structures, especially the thalamus and NRT, but also the cerebellum and the basal ganglia/prefrontal cortex are to be considered.

→ The combined direct and indirect effect of the cool communities strategies can potentially reduce air-conditioning use in a Los Angeles home by half and save about 10% of A/C use of a one-story office building.

→ Reducing runoff from the raised beds (e.g. by hoeing) in the middle of the rainy season is possibly a good measure to improve leaching efficiency of rainwater.

8.3注意事項

(1)在研究論文的結論中，作者應該以十分清楚、簡潔的方式敘述自己研究中所獲得的主要成果或發現。不要提到前文未涉及的新事實，也不要重複前文中關於研究動機與實驗程序的詳細描述。

(2)結論的功能與摘要的功能不同。結論部分的功能在於敘述研究工作最重要的結果、結果的內涵、結果的說明等結論，而不是概述論文的所有內容。摘要則是對整個論文的內容的概述，包括研究工作的目的、方法、主要結果及結論等資訊。此外，千萬不要在結論中直接重複論文正文中其他部分中的句子。結論部分不在於重複論文的內容，所以它並不是由論文的其他部分照抄下來的句子組成的。

(3)結論部分還常常描述作者的研究工作可能產生的應用或效益，或者指出本研究工作進一步深入的研究方向或具體的研究題目。然而，作者在書寫可能的應用與題目時，不要過於勉強，特別是要避免誇大對效益的描述。例如，假如自己的研究只有一兩種很明顯的應用或擴展的方向，那麼不要故意地提到其他不重要的或與自己研究工作沒有密切關聯的題目，以免使結論太長。

(4)在很多領域中，有些作者習慣在論文的討論部分表達所有的重要結論，而省略了結論部分。建議作者先參閱擬投期刊已刊登的研究論文，以確定在期刊上的一般研究論文是否包含獨立的結論部分。如果研究論文包含討論部分和結論部分兩者，則結論部分應該相當簡短，只需簡略、清楚地陳述作者研究工作的兩三個主要結論即可，不要再重複羅列論文的討論部分及其他部分已經表達清楚的一大堆資料。

(5)大部分研究論文的結論部分以"Conclusion"（單數形式）作為標題，但是也有些作者把該標題用"Conclusions"（複數形式）表示。還有的期刊用"Concluding remarks"或"Conclusions and future work"。原則上，如果結論部分是以一段文字來書寫，而且只陳述一兩個主要結論，則使用單數形式"Conclusion"比較普遍（如8.1中的例8-1）。如果結論部分包括好幾個個別的結論，則使用複數形"Conclusions"較為合適（見8.1中的例8-2），而且有些作者習慣用一覽表的方式列出數個結論，並在每個個別的結論前加上序號（如8.1中的例8-3）。還需提醒的是，作者最好查閱一下所投期刊發表的研究論文中關於結論部分標題的慣用表達方式，以確定使用"Conclusion"還是"Conclusions"，或是"Concluding remarks"等標題。

科技英文論文寫作實用指南 **Practical Guide to Scientific English Writing**

摘要（Abstract）通常是位於研究論文題目與研究論文正文之間對整個論文內容的概述。無論對專業讀者還是對非專業讀者而言，摘要都是一個非常重要的文件。有人把摘要喻為一個「篩選機」，因為一篇好的摘要能讓讀者迅速對論文的目的、方法、主要結果、結論及推論有一個概括的瞭解，讀者可依據摘要中提供的資訊來決定是否有必要詳細閱讀整篇論文，尤其在摘要與論文分開發表即摘要是獨立存在的情況下更是如此。

9.1 定義、作用及類型

摘要是一份濃縮的研究報告，即對整篇科技論文重要內容的簡短的概述。摘要不是論文的總結。總結是論文本身的一個重要組成部分，常放置在論文正文的末尾。論文摘要有可能獨立於論文全文，通常被收編在以學科分類的摘要檢索專刊之中，如Chemical Abstracts。

摘要的作用是很明顯的。首先，清楚和完整的摘要為讀者提供研究論文總體的概念，以便他們決定是否有必要閱讀論文全文。例如，在許多研究領域，單獨以電子資料庫或書面的形式發表摘要已成為一種越來越受到歡迎的做法。當研究者查閱這些資料庫時，他們會根據摘要內容獲知作者的主要研究活動、研究方法和主要結果及結論，然後決定是否詳讀論文全文。閱讀一篇論文很費時，而寫得好的、資訊足夠的摘要能使讀者省時省力。摘要的第二個重要作用是它們能以獨立形式加以利用。讀完摘要後，研究者可能會覺得論文的主題與自己目前的研究工作的關係不甚密切，因此不打算閱讀論文全文。然而，感覺到所讀摘要的研究資訊可能與自己未來的研究工作有用，此時讀者會把這篇摘要貯存在自己的電腦文件庫中。甚至也可能會直接利用摘要所含的一些局部資訊，而不需要閱讀論文全文。第三個重要作用是，當讀者確實需要進一步閱讀論文全文或論文的主要部分時，好的摘要可以為讀者提供一個有益的預覽，使讀者瞭解論文的主要觀點。摘要的最後一個重要作用是摘要有助於檢索。從家庭或研究所的小型圖書館到大型機構、公共設施，很多研究者會通過查尋作者姓名和輸入關鍵字來交叉檢索研究論文的摘要。研究論文的摘要寫得越好，那麼受到檢索的可能性就越大，這樣也增大了論文被閱讀的機會。

研究論文的摘要分成兩種類型：敘述性摘要（descriptive abstract或indicative abstract）和資訊性摘要（informative abstract）。

敘述性摘要只告訴讀者論文本身的細目，而很少或根本不涉及論文中這些細目的說明，不包括定性或定量的資料。敘述性摘要的優點是容易寫作，且其字數往往較少，但其突出的缺點是資訊量太少。下面給出了一個敘述性摘要的例子：

> Ten widespread diseases that are hazards in isolated construction camps can be prevented by removing or destroying the breeding places of flies, mosquitoes and rats, and by killing their adult forms.

資訊性摘要告訴讀者論文的要點或基本內容，包括論文最重要的資訊材料。資訊性摘要可視為一小型報告，它不僅僅講述細目，而且介紹這些細目下的內容。資訊性摘要的優點是比敘述性摘要能提供多得多的資訊，當然它可能比敘述性摘要長些，另外寫作起來也較費勁。然而，除非摘要的字數受到嚴格限制，毫無疑問應該首選資訊性摘要的形式。資訊性摘要見下例：

> Ten widespread diseases that are hazards in isolated construction camps can be prevented by removing or destroying the breeding places of flies, mosquitoes and rats, and by killing their adult forms. The breeding of flies is controlled by proper disposal of decaying organic matter, and of mosquitoes

by destroying or draining pools, or spraying them with oil. For rates, only the indirect methods of rat-resistant houses and protected food supplies are valuable. Control of adult forms of both insects and rodents requires use of poisons. Screens are used for insects. Minnows can be planted to eat mosquito larvae.

必須指出，大多數的摘要並不完全是資訊性的或敘述性的，而是兩者的結合。事實上，敘述性摘要的第一個句子往往非常接近資訊性的。在資訊性摘要中加入敘述性的陳述可解決摘要過長的問題。總之，需要在簡明和詳細之間尋求一種平衡，使摘要既能反映論文最重要的事實與概念，又能表達得簡短。

9.2 基本內容與時態、語態

因為從本質上講摘要是一份極為簡略、濃縮的研究報告，所以摘要的結構和研究論文本身的結構是對應的。摘要應包括下列項目：

①**研究背景** 這項目可有可無，尤其當作者認為摘要可能會過長時，這項目常被省略。

②**研究目的和研究題目**。

③**研究方法** 有時作者會把②和③項目合併在一個句子裡。

④**發現或結果**。

⑤**主要結論和推論** 如果作者無法敘述一、兩個很簡短、具體的結論，那麼有時可採用 "The results are discussed in comparison with earlier findings"、"A mechanism is proposed to explain the results" 或 "The implications of the data are discussed in detail" 等等句子來概述自己對研究結果的介紹。

還需要指出的是，近年來在一些高度專業化的學術期刊上，出現了一種摘要的特殊格式。在這種格式的摘要中，作者以研究結果作為主要內容，而把研究目的、研究方法或理論與實驗方面的簡介免除掉。這類摘要的閱讀對象通常是那些非常精通專業研究領域情況的老練的研究工作者。請參閱下面的例子：

This paper describes a new framework for the analysis and synthesis of control systems, which constitutes a genuine continuous-time extension of results that are only available in discrete time. In contrast to earlier results the proposed methods involve a specific transformation on the Lyapunov variables and a reciprocal variant of the projection lemma, in addition to the classical linearizing transformations on the controller data. For a wide range of problems including robust analysis and synthesis, multichannel H/sub 2/ state and out put-feedback syntheses, the approach leads to potentially less conservative liner matrix inequality (LMI) characterizations. This comes from the fact that the technical restriction of using a single Lyapunov function is to some extent ruled out in this new approach. Moreover, the approach offers new potentials for problems that cannot be handled using earlier techniques. An important instance is the eigenstructure assignment problem blended with Lyapunov-type constraints which is given a simple and tractable formulation.

　　摘要的內容應該是整篇論文的精華。例如，對於實驗研究論文，摘要應著重描述採用的方法、主要的結果和重要的結論。有時為便於非專業讀者閱讀理解，實驗研究論文的摘要中也有背景或目的的論述。通常實驗研究論文的摘要採用資訊性形式，其內容強調主要的發現與結論，參閱下例：

Neuropathic foot ulceration is a major medical and economic problem among diabetic patients, and the traditional treatment involves bed rest with complete freedom from weight bearing. We have investigated the use of walking plaster casts in the management of seven diabetic patients with long-standing, chronic foot ulcers. Although all ulcers healed in a median time of 6 weeks, this therapy was not without side effects. We conclude that casting is a useful therapy for neuropathic ulcers, although several clinic visits, including cast removal and foot inspection, are necessary to avoid potential side effects caused by the costing of insensitive feet.

注意上面摘要中句子的排列順序。第一句提供了背景資料，第二句概述了特定題目和研究方法，第三句指出了主要的結果，而第四句則引出了某些結論。這些句子的不同功能是由採用不同的時態來清楚表示的。第一句和第四句用現在簡單式，意指不局限於某個特定的時間框架的事實；第二句用現在完成式，把開頭的背景資料與正在報告的特定研究結合起來；第三句採用過去簡單式，敘述在一個特定的時間裡產生的特殊結果。

摘要各部分句子中動詞時態的使用規則和論文正文各章節中動詞時態的使用規則是相同的（語態的使用也是如此）。下面介紹這些使用規則。

①在介紹背景資料時，應該用現在簡單式來敘述不受時間影響的普遍事實。

→ Most alternative fuels for internal combustion engines have low cetane numbers.

→ This is particularly true of natural gas which has excellent clean burning characteristic and low greenhouse gas production.

→ In contrast to low power applications, long cavity lasers or laser bars are used in this field and mounting quality influences considerably laser performance and life time.

若介紹背景資料的句子內容是對某種研究動向的概述，則應該使用現在完成式。

→ The use of correlated coefficients of heat transfer from the experimental data has been the universal choice to analyze complex heat transfer processes.

→ Several laboratory studies have been conducted to determine actual decomposition rates of wheat and other small grain straws using $^{14}C'$ labeled plant material.

②在敘述研究目的、研究題目或活動時，若文章採用「研究導向」型，則句子的動詞使用過去簡單式（有少數作者會使用現在完成式，不過使用過去簡單式較恰當）。若文章採用「論文導向」型，則應該使用現在簡單式。關於「研究導向」與「論文導向」的定義，請作者參閱本書3.2節。

研究導向：

→ The objective of this research was to determine the variability of soil CO_2 temporally, spatially, and with depth in two acid soils in a mountainous, forested catchment.

→ In this study, we examined vertical nutrient mixing in late summer in a test area 15 kilometers off the coast.

論文導向：

→ This paper presents an auto-refrigerating cascade cycle that employs a rectifying column.

→ In this paper, we focus on the solder metallurgy and stress-induced laser behavior after mounting.

③在摘要的實驗部分的寫作中，實驗程序或方法通常使用過去簡單式來描述。

→ Experiments on high-enthalpy water blowdown through a short converging nozzle were performed to measure the critical discharge flowrate under different stagnation conditions.

→ The measurements were carried out in a high pressure chamber (HPC) and in a rapid compression machine (RCM).

如果論文的主要內容是介紹數學模型、演算法、分析方法或技術，則作者應該使用現在簡單式來描述這些研究方法。

→ The proposed rule is validated through numerical studies involving both analytic and numerical results form the frequency—and time—domain response of multiconductor transmission line circuits.

→ We use FASTCAP to compute the values of the capacitances, and a closed form formula to obtain the inductance values.

有的作者會用一個句子來同時表達研究目的或題目和研究方法。其中的一種寫作方法是使用主句來指出研究目的，片語用於描述研究方法。例如，在下列例句中，以斜體字標明的片語用來描述作者所使用的研究方法。

In the sensor part of the system, the quality of combustion inside the furnace is evaluated *by means of three parameters—the Combustion Center Point (CCP), the Refuse Mass Energy (RME) and the Air Balance in Future (ABF)*.

將研究目的和研究方法合併成一句的另一種方法是採用位於句首或句末的片語來表示研究目的，並使用主句以描述研究方法。在下例中，作者的研究目的是以斜體字標明的片語表達的。

Laboratory compaction and triaxial compression tests were performed *to assess the compaction characteristics and load deformation response of a sandy silt reinforced with randomly oriented recycled carpet fibers*.

在研究目的和研究方法合併的句子中，句子主要動詞的時態使用仍然需要遵循上述的基本規則，即用過去簡單式描述實驗方法和研究導向型的研究目的或研究活動；用現在簡單式介紹模型或數學分析和論文導向型的研究目的或研究活動。

④通常使用過去簡單式概述主要結果（也有一些作者用現在式）。

→ The properties of hot water dried products were very sensitive to process temperature.

→ The plant's thermal efficiency was increased from 17.6% to 21.3% for the single Rankine cycle by the adoption of the two-fluid cycle, using C_2H_6 as the working fluid under a constant condition of the topping steam temperature of 295℃.

但是，若作者認為自己的研究結果普遍有效，而不只是在本次研究的特定條件下才適用，則可以使用現在簡單式。

⑤使用現在簡單式、推測動詞或may、should、could等情態助動詞來敘述結論或推論。

→ These results suggest that an appropriate agreement of the elliptic tube enhance the heat transfer performance of the tube bank.

→ In general, dry compression is more favourable than wet compression.

→ The result can be expected to be of great technical interest as basic data for the use of the ball bearing in space cryogenic instrument.

至於文獻回顧性（或綜述性）的文章，摘要只是敘述文章的內容概要，而不包含一些特別的研究結果，因此通常都以現在式書寫，見下例：

This paper reviews the background to mechanical reliability from a design engineering viewpoint. It considers the way in which mechanical reliability is primarily dictated by design decisions and illustrates the reliability engineering models which can provide guidance during mechanical engineering design with some examples. Many modern technological systems involve the integration of multidisciplinary systems. These can be found in such diverse major industries as transportation, power generation, food production, chemical processing and advanced manufacturing. Clearly, the reliability of the mechanical system elements is a crucial consideration in all such highly integrated complex systems. Fortunately, after many years of research and application, the engineering approaches concerned with the reduction in uncertainty are sufficiently well understood to result in the existence of many examples of highly reliable mechanical system elements, although the particular problem of mechanical reliability prediction still exists. In particular, the engineering understanding resulting from an examination of potential failure modes, the messages resulting from a consideration of the load-strength interference theory, the load-chain model, environmental considerations and the complex equipment model are examined to identify the advantages of these approaches as a basis for mechanical design. Some of the many difficulties which still remain in dealing with mechanical reliability are also identified.

摘要中語態的使用規則也與論文正文中語態的使用規則相同。這個規則是：多使用主動語態。相對於被動語態，主動語態顯得更強有力、更直接，而且使用主動語態通常還可以使論文顯得較為簡潔且直截了當。多使用主動語態的規則並不等於不能用被動語態，在經驗豐富的作者撰寫的論文中，平均有25%的句子使用被動語態。見下例：

The conventional analog Adcock-Butler matrix (ABM) antenna array direction finder suffers from systemic errors, component matching problems, and bandwidth limitations. Three digital bearing estimators are developed as candidates to replace the analog signal processing portion of the ABM. Using the same antenna array, they perform all signal processing in the frequency domain, thereby benefiting from the computational efficiency of the fast Fourier transform (FFT) algorithm. The first estimator requires two analog-to-digital converters (A-D) and three antenna elements. It multiplies the difference between the discrete Fourier transforms (DFTs) of the output signals from two antenna elements with that from a third antenna element. At each frequency component, the phase of this product is a function of the bearing. A weighted least squares (LS) fit through all the phase components then gives a bearing estimate. The second estimator is similar to the first but uses three A-D and all four antenna elements. The output signal from the additional antenna element provides an independent estimate of the weights for the LS fit, giving an improvement in accuracy. The third estimator applies the physical constraint existing between the time-difference-of-arrival (TDOA) of a signal intercepted by two perpendicular sets of antenna elements. This yields a better estimator than simple averaging of the bearing from each set of antenna elements. The simulation studies used sinusoids and broadband signals to corroborate the theoretical treatment and demonstrate the accuracy achievable with these estimators. All three direction finders have superior performance in comparison with the analog ABM.

　　要記住的是只有因某種特定的理由時，才會使用被動語態。例如，使用被動語態比使用主動語態更能造出簡潔的句子，或作者想把某個詞作句子的主詞以便強調這個詞，或作者想描述某個標準化的過程而過程的執行者並不重要時，常使用被動語態。此外，在實驗方法的部分中，以被動語態來敘述實驗的程序也是一種約定俗成的寫法。撰寫摘要時不應該因為習慣就隨意使用被動語態，一定要根據語態的使用規則確定有必要使用被動語態時才可使用被動語態。有些學生在摘要中一律採用被動語態的作法是不恰當的。

9.3 摘要寫作的幾點建議

　　①摘要的長度要適宜。摘要的篇幅應該有多長，這並沒有確定的規則。有的專家認為一般最多不能超過200個詞；也有學者提出，摘要的篇

幅大約是文章長度的五分之一。不管怎樣，要儘量使摘要短而精是一個普遍的原則。有些學術期刊會規定摘要的篇幅不能超過一定的字數，所以作者在投稿前應查詢擬投稿的期刊是否有這種規定。假如期刊沒有規定摘要的篇幅應該有多長，那麼作者可以參閱該期刊上已發表的數篇文章，以便獲知一般摘要的長度。通常國際學術會議的通知中都會有摘要字數的限制，作者只要按規定進行摘要寫作就能符合要求。傳統上摘要是一段式的。但是兩段式、三段式的摘要也能見到，雖然它們的應用還不普遍。此外，摘要中不能省略冠詞，也不應該單獨使用研究論文中出現的名詞或片語的縮寫，還應極力避免採用那些對你研究工作不熟悉的讀者不明白的專門術語。

②摘要的句子不能重複論文中的句子。撰寫摘要時，作者應注意：不要直接抄錄論文主要部分中的句子，而對句子的結構與內容不作任何修改。因為摘要必須在篇幅很短的情況下概述很多資訊。摘要中句子的功能和論文主要部分中句子的功能稍有不同，所以論文主要部分中所使用的句子往往不適合直接在摘要中再次使用。有些學生在剛開始撰寫論文時，常常會在摘要、導論及結論中都重複同樣的句子，這是不妥當的。

③避免在摘要中列出一大堆資料。摘要的內容必須能讓讀者清楚地瞭解作者究竟進行了什麼樣的研究工作，為什麼要做這些研究，而且究竟得到了什麼樣的結果。在摘要中不必列出一大堆資料，因為這些資料對閱讀摘要的讀者來說可能沒有（或暫時沒有）什麼意義。應該用句子的方式來說明自己的研究，最多只引述幾個關鍵的資料供讀者參考。

④完成研究論文後再寫摘要。大部分情況中，作者是為自己的研究論文寫摘要；也有一些情況中，有的學者為別人的研究論文進行摘要寫作。無論哪種情況，都應該在完成研究論文之後撰寫摘要。一個可行的辦法是，先將論文通讀，再劃出論文中的關鍵句子和要點，然後將它們串聯起來，編寫成簡明而具綜合性的摘要。注意不要重複論文中的句子。

⑤撰寫「約定」摘要必須慎重。一般而言，在研究工作已完成和論文

已撰寫之後再寫摘要。但是有時需要你在論文完成之前寫摘要，有時甚至要求你在研究工作完成之前就要寫摘要。例如，你要在一個學術會議上發表論文，而且必須在會議前的8至12個月就要交論文摘要，那麼你要交的摘要就是「約定」的摘要。這種情況發生時，寫一個「約定」摘要並無不妥。然而，請牢記：寫「約定」摘要實際上牽涉到一個研究者的道德水準和學術可信性的問題。所寫的「約定」摘要必須是你最終要提交的論文的正確反映，兩者的內容應該保持一致。若「約定」摘要寫得言過其實，則很有可能會被認為有作「虛假廣告」之嫌。有經驗的研究者在撰寫「約定」摘要時常採用下列方法：十分正確地預見最終的研究結果；提出引人注意的觀點，但是不使用大量的實際資料；對於研究工作中有可能發生的意外結果，避免作正面描述。如果要寫一個「約定」摘要，初學者最聰明的做法是向那些資深的專家請教。

10

參考文獻目錄格式

　　參考文獻目錄通常位於科技論文的最後。參考文獻目錄的列出，一方面指出論文中借鑒的或用於比較的一些觀點或方法的出處，另一方面也有利於讀者在需要的時候進一步查閱有關參考文獻的原文。在本章中，我們將討論參考文獻目錄的標準格式及相關事項。

　　各種學術期刊或專業學會對參考文獻目錄的格式有各自的標準，包括所採用的資訊順序、縮寫詞以及標點符號都有不同的規定。例如，有些期刊依字母順序排列參考文獻而不加序號，而有些期刊則在每篇參考文獻前加上序號，並在論文正文中只使用序號來引述參考資料。有些期刊在參考文獻中文章的題目前後都加引號，而有些期刊則省略引號。在一般參考文獻目錄的格式中，若參考文獻是期刊上的文章，則參考文獻最後一項資訊是文章的頁碼，然而，也有些期刊把出版年份當作最後一項資訊。在某些參考文獻目錄中，在頁數前加上縮寫 "pp."（即"pages"）或 "p."（即page），但不少常用的格式則省去這些詞。在某些參考文獻目錄中，所有期刊的名稱均縮寫，然而也有很多參考文獻目錄格式將期刊的名稱全部寫出。綜上所述，作者在撰寫參考文獻目錄時，應先參考擬投稿的期刊上已發表的數篇論文，以瞭解該期刊採用的參考文獻目錄的格式。在查詢某個期刊所使用的參考文獻格式時，應該同時查閱論文正文中參考文獻引述的格式，並確定自己引述參考文獻的方式符合擬投期刊的標準格式的要求。

　　下面將概述三種常用的參考文獻目錄格式。第一種格式是被許多科技專業學術期刊採用的「序號格式」。第二種是不少科技學術期刊及社會科學專業期刊所使用的「APA格式」，這種格式源自美國心理學學會（American

Psychological Association）所推行的。第三種則是人文科學及部分社會科學期刊所使用的 "MLA" 格式，這種格式是美國現代語言協會（Modern Language Association）制定的。然而由於不少專業期刊所採用的參考文獻目錄格式是上述三種格式的變形格式，因此下面介紹的只是此三種格式的基本情況。

10.1 序號格式

當要求採用序號格式時，在論文正文中應使用阿拉伯數字來引述參考文獻，阿拉伯數字前後應該用括弧或方括號，或把數位當作上標。請參考下面的例子：

→ Various transient models for different heat pipe startup stages have been developed [7-10] .

→ This method of calculating net savings was checked experimentally by LBNL [8] and by the Florida Solar Energy Center [13] .

→ Table 3 also shows a peak demand saving of 0.6GW from white surfaces and trees[8].

→ Some technologies are already commercial, at least for some situations and applications (2).

在參考文獻目錄中，參考文獻的順序排列有兩種常用的方法。第一種方法中，參考文獻的排列順序是依文獻在論文正文中出現的順序，即在論文中所提到的第一個參考文獻為1，在論文中提到的第二個參考文獻為2等等。第二種方法中，參考文獻的排列順序則通常根據作者姓的第一個字母依字母順序排列（若有兩個或兩個以上作者，則按第一個作者的姓排列），而且在每一個參考文獻前面加上序號，即第一個參考文獻為1，第二個參考文獻為2等等。

下面就是以序號格式為基礎的典型的參考文獻目錄：

[1] J. V. Hall, Valuing the health benefits of Clean Air, *Science* 255 (1992)

812-817.

[2] C.A. Cardelino, W. L. Chameides, Natural hydrocarbons, urbanization, and urban ozone, *J. Geophys. Res.* 95 (D9) (1990) 3971-3979.

[3] M.T. Benjamin, M. Sudol, L. Bloch, A. Winer, Low emitting urban forests: a taxonomic methodology for assigning isoprene and monoterpene emission rates, *Atmos. Environ.* 30(9) (1996) 1437-1452.

[4] A.M. Winer, et al., Emission rates of organics from vegetation in California's Central Valley, *Atmos. Environ.* 26 (1992) 2627-2659.

[5] V. Meerovich, V. Sokolovsky, G. Shiter, and G. Gradef, "Testing of an inductive current-limiting device based on high-Tc superconductors," *IEEE Trans. Appl. Superconduct.*, vol.3, no. N3, pp. 3033-3036, Sept.1993.

[6] North, M. T. and Avedisian, C.T., Heat pipe for cooling high flux/high power semiconductor chips. *Journal of Electronic Packaging*, 1993, **115**, 112-117.

在此格式中，參考文獻的序號通常置於方括號之內。在序號後面的第一項是作者的姓名，按名在前、姓在後次序寫出，而且作者名只用名的第一個字母來縮寫。緊跟在作者姓名之後是文章的題目，題目通常用正體字書寫，文章題目往往不用引號。然後是期刊名稱，期刊名應使用斜體字表示，而且通常是縮寫形式。在期刊的名稱後應表示卷號及出版年代（出版年代通常放在括弧裡），有時候卷號使用斜體字或粗體字，見上面的例 [6]。最後是文章的頁數，而在頁數前不需要寫 "pp."。如果緊接在作者姓名後的是書的名稱，則書名需用斜體字表示，而且書名後應表示出出版城市、出版社以及出版年代。見下面的例7和例8。

7. Dunn, P.D. and Reay, D.A., *Heat Pipes*, 3rd edn. Pergamon Press, New York, 1982.

8. B. J. Punnett, D. A. Ricks, *International Business*, Bosten: PWS-KENT
   Publishing Company, 1992.

上面所列的不過是序號格式的一些典型例子。不同期刊所採用的格式
可能有各自的細目規定。例如參考文獻目錄中文獻的序號除了用如［５］
方式外，還可用無括弧的阿拉伯數字表示，只是記住阿拉伯數字後需加上
句點，如上面的例7和例8所示。上面例［６］、例7和例8還說明，有些期
刊把作者的姓放在縮寫的名之前。有些期刊還把出版年代放在最後（緊接
在頁數後面），或將卷、期號之前分別加上“vol.”及“no.”，或者在頁
數之前加上“pp.”見上面的例［５］。還有些期刊則甚至省略所有文章的
題目。綜上所述，作者在投稿之前，一定要仔細地查閱擬投期刊的有關規
定，使自己的論文的參考文獻目錄的格式符合要求（包括注意逗號、句
號、冒號等標點符號的用法）。

還有一些研究論文（尤其是回顧文獻性綜述性文章）需要在參考文獻
目錄中列出文章中引用到的條例、報告、決議、計劃、方案等文獻，則這
些文獻的目錄格式可按下述例子的方式書寫：

9. EPA, Guideline on Air Quality Models (Revised), US Environmental
   Protection Agency, EPA-450/2-78-027R, 1986.

10. D. S. Parker, S. F. Barkaszi, J. K. Sonne, Measured cooling energy
    savings from reflective roof coatings in Florida: Phase Ⅱ report,
    Florida Solar Energy Center, Cape Canaveral, FL. Contract Report
    FSECCR-699-95, 1994.

11. B. Fishman, H. Taha, J. Hanford, Albedo and Vegetation Mitigation
    Strategies in the South Coast Air Basin: Impacts on Total System Load
    for the LADWP and SCE, Lawrence Berkeley National Laboratory
    Report, LBL-35910, 1996.

12. CPUC Final Decision, California Public Utilities Commission, Decision

96-01-011, 1996.

13. BAAQMD, Promotion of the development and use of high-albedo (reflecting) materials for roofing and road surfaces, Control Measure CM F9, Bay Area Air Quality Management District, Draft Air Quality Management Plan, San Francisco, CA, 1997.

14. M. Trexler, P. Faeth, J. P. Kraemer, Forestry as a Presponse to Global Warming: An Analysis of a Guatemala Agroforestry Project, World Resources Institute, Washington, D. C., 1989.

專利引用的格式可見下面的例15所示：

15. V. V. Ivanov, V.I. Kirko, and V. I. Inanov, Rus. Pat. I2073736, C 22 C 9/00, 20.09.97.

在網際網路上查閱資料或通過電子郵件（E-mail）傳遞資訊已成為當前從事研究工作的重要手段之一。從網際網路上或電子郵件中獲取的文字資訊如何在論文的參考文獻目錄中以規範的格式表示，應當引起論文作者的充分關注。下面以美國通行的格式舉例說明。

[16] California Assembly Bill 1890, Public utilities: electrical restructuring, authored by Brutle and 46 Assemblymen and State Senators. 1996. Available on world-wide web: www.leginfo.ca.gov.

[17] Denning, P. J., "Business Designs for the New University.", Educom Review 31(1996). 23, June 1997 <http://educom.edu/wed/pubs/review/review Articles/31620.html>.

[18] Goodridge Stephen. E-mail to John Milford. 15 May 1999.

[19] Marius Anthony. "Advanced materials & process." E-mail to Wendy Paul. 28 October 2001.

由以上四例可以看出，網際網路上資訊條目與前文所列條目的格式有許多相同之處，其主要區別有：一是網際網路上資訊條目必須表明查閱並獲取該資訊資料的日期。如例［17］中的 "23 June 1997"。二是網際網路上資訊條目必須提供獲取該資訊資料的詳細網址。此外，對於已上網但未曾出版的文字資料，則只需表明該資料上網發表的年份（或主辦機構），如例［16］所示。若引用電子郵件中的文字資訊，則其順序首先是 E-mail 的作者，其次是 E-mail 的接收者，最後是 E-mail 的發送日期，見例［18］。若 E-mail 有標題，則該標題應在作者姓名之後標出並加上引號，如例［19］所示。

10.2 APA 的格式

應用 APA 的格式時，在論文正文中應該使用作者的姓及出版年代來引述參考文獻。這些資訊通常位於括弧內（有些期刊用方括號）。例如：

→ The sensible heat flux from a number of wooden and reinforced concrete building surfaces was calculated in our previous study (Iino and Hoyano, 1995) using an airborne scanner with lateral and downward orientation.

→ Some studies which mapped the anthropogenic heat in Tokyo have been published (Kimura and Takahashi, 1991; Narita and Maekawa, 1991; Saitoh et al., 1992).

如果文章的句中提到了某參考文獻的作者，那麼在括弧只需寫出出版年份。

Hiramatsu et al. (1992) estimated the amount of energy consumption in Tokyo in 1989 in each sector (household, commercial, manufacturing, and transportation) and for each kind of fuel with data from energy statistics.

若直接引述了所引文獻中的片語、整個句子或一段行文，則還需在括弧中加入引文的頁數。

According to Hawlader, the model based on Dreyer and Erens's correlation can be used for "the modeling of water droplets motion in cooling towers" (2000, pp.451).

在APA的格式的參考文獻的目錄中，所有的參考文獻都按照文獻作者的姓氏字母順序排列（不用序號）。若在目錄中列出同一作者的兩篇或兩篇以上著作，則這些著作應該依年代順序排列（由最早期到最近期）。若同一作者的兩篇或兩篇以上著作的出版年份相同，則應以字母順序排列，並在出版年份後加小寫字母，如1996a，1996b等等。請看下列APA的格式的例子：

Cleugh, H.A. Oke, T.R., (1986). Suburban-rural energy balance comparisons in summer for Vancouver B.C., *Boundary-Layer Meteorology*, 36, 351-369

Ellefsen, R. (1990/1991). Mapping and measuring buildings in the canopy boundary layer in ten U.S. cities, *Energy and Buildings*, 15-16, 1025-1049.

Patankar, S.V. (1980). Numerical heat transfer and fluid flow. New York: McGraw-Hill.

Rotach, M. (1993a). Turbulence close to a rough urban surface, Part I : Reynoids stress. *Boundary-Layer Metorology*, 65,1-28.

Rotach, M. (1993b). Turbulence close to a rough urban surface, Part II : Variances and gradients, *Boundary-Layer Metorology*, 66, 75-92.

在這種格式中，所有作者的姓都放在名之前，而且名都以字母縮寫形式表示。如果所列文獻有兩個以上作者，則在最後一個作者的姓之前用符號"&"以表示"and"的意思。但是，在論文正文中引述參考文獻時，則應該使用"and"而不用符號"&"。在參考文獻目錄中，應該列出每篇參考文獻所有作者的姓名，但是在論文正文中引述某個參考文獻時，若該文獻有六個或六個以上作者，則應寫第一個作者的姓並在其後加上et al.（不需要斜體或者逗號），如 "Hoyano et al."。如果某一參考文獻有兩個到五個作者，那麼在論文正文中第一次引述時應該列出所有作者的姓，但在第二、三次引述時只需寫第一作者的姓並加寫et al.。

在上面的例子中，請注意：出版年份都應該放在括弧中；在每個書名或文章的題目中，只有第一個詞的第一個字母需大寫，其他詞都小寫。書名及期刊名應該用斜體字來表示，但是文章的題目前後都不用括弧；與書名不同，期刊的刊名中每個詞的首字母都應該大寫（冠詞、介係詞除外）；期刊名應該使用斜體字，而且卷號應該使用斜體字或粗體字。此外，如果某個參考文獻的排行超過一行的話，則第二、三行必須縮進排印（縮進的距離大約五格）。請注意序號格式中不需縮進排印。

關於APA格式的詳細說明，請參閱*Publication Manual of the American Psychological Association*。

與序號格式的情況一樣，不同的學術期刊可能會採用APA格式的不同變形格式。如有的期刊使用APA格式時，在作者名之後加逗號，最後兩個作者姓名之間不用 "&" 而用 "and"，出版年份不用括弧，書名的所有詞（冠詞、介係詞除外）首字母均大寫，書名或期刊名及卷號不用斜體形式，在卷號與頁數之間加冒號，第二行起縮進，排印時縮進的距離為三格，在文章中第一次引述參考文獻時不全部寫出所有作者的姓而用第一個作者姓（或和第二個作者姓）加et al.表示等等。由此看來，某些期刊所使用的格式可能與上面的例子大致相同但有少許差別，因此建議作者在撰寫論文時一定要事先瞭解所投期刊採用APA格式的具體規定。

10.3 MLA的格式

在MLA格式中，論文正文引述參考文獻時通常只包括作者的姓氏及參考文獻的頁數。作者姓及頁數放在括弧內，並且括弧沒有任何標點符號，也不需要在頁數前加 "p."。如：

The genetic algorithm is a recent development (Rogers 34).

如果在論文的句子中提及作者的姓，則在引述參考文獻時只需在括弧內寫頁數。

Rogers describes the genetic algorithm as a recent development (34).

在參考文獻的目錄中，參考文獻根據作者姓氏依字母順序排列。第一作者或唯一作者的姓放在名之前，而從第二作者起，作者的姓放在名之後。在作者姓名後，應依次列出參考文獻的題目（放在引號內）、期刊名（用斜體字表示）、卷數、年份（放在括弧內）及頁數。若參考文獻為書籍，則在作者姓名之後列出書名、出版城市、出版社和出版年份。書名應以斜體字形式寫出。在下面的例子中，請注意標點符號及大小寫的用法。

→ Walton, Thomas F. *Technical Manual Writing and Administration*. New York: McGraw-Hill, 1968.

→ Gitman, Lawrence J., and Carl McDaniel. *The World of Business.* Cincinnati: South-Western Publishing Co., 1992.

→ Rockart, John and Michael S. Scott Morton. "Implications of Changes in Information Technology for Corporate Strategy." *Interfaces* 14 (1984): 84-95.

→ Wei, Julie, "Pure Mathematics: Problems and Prospects in Number Theory." The Research News 30(1979): 31.

關於其他各種參考文獻的引述方式，MLA都有詳細的規定。讀者可以參閱*The MLA Handbook for Writers of Research Papers*。仍要強調的是，與上述序號格式和APA格式一樣，有些期刊可能會使用基本MLA格式的變形格式。

10.4 其他注意事項

參考文獻目錄的英文標題的正確寫法是複數形式的"References"，而不是單數形式的"Reference"。若只列出一篇參考文獻，則有些作者用單數形式的"Reference"。另一個常用的英文標題是"Works Cited"。

在上面討論的序號格式、APA格式與MLA格式中，引述期刊上的文章時常省略卷、期及頁等的縮寫詞（即Vol.、No.、pp.或p.等）。然而有些期刊在參考文獻目錄中仍然寫出這些縮寫詞，例如本章介紹序號格式時所舉的例［5］。這裡再舉一例：

> ［18］C. Gabrielii and L. Vamling, Changes in optimal design of a dry-expansion evaporator when replacing R22 with R407C, *Int. J. Refrig.*, Vol.21, No.7, 1998, pp. 518-534.

在準備稿件時，作者應仔細核查自己論文中的參考文獻目錄的文字資訊有無錯誤，特別是不能將文獻作者的姓名拼錯。否則，一方面顯得對所引文獻的作者不尊重，另一方面也不利於讀者用文獻作者姓名查閱相應的摘要及全文。另外，應該不厭其煩地檢查參考文獻目錄中的標點符號是否符合擬投期刊的規定格式。

排印時請注意，不論是在論文正文中或在參考文獻目錄中，在左邊的括弧前都應有一個空格，而且，除非右邊的括弧後緊跟句號、逗號、分號或冒號等標點符號，否則在右邊的括弧後也需有一個空格。此外，在左邊的括弧後和右邊的括弧前都不應該加空格。

作者應該在參考文獻目錄中列出和此研究論文相關的自己的著作。但是，不宜過多地列出，以免參考文獻目錄看上去像過分展示自己的研究成果而忽略他人的研究工作。除非作者過去的研究論文等著作確實與本次發表的研究報告有密切關係，否則應該加以省略。此外，如果所引的參考文獻（不管是自己的著作還是別人的著作）是用中文發表的，則應該在參考文獻目錄的條目之後用"（in Chinese）"標示。

還要注意的是，在寫出參考文獻的頁數時，不能使用"～"符號來表示第幾頁到第幾頁，如"239～245"。在英文中，應該使用en-dash（－）以表示「從……到……」的意思。en-dash也可以用連字號（-）代替，如"239-245"。

　　最後要說明的是，“et al.”不需要用斜體字的形式表示。“et al.”是來自拉丁文的詞，傳統上需將這些外來語用斜體字排印。但是現今大多數詞典已將“et al.”視為一般英文縮寫詞（見牛津現代高級英漢雙解詞典，1996，p.1349），所以可用正體字排印。

科技英文論文寫作實用指南 **Practical Guide to Scientific English Writing**

11 科技論文寫作中常犯的錯誤

　　科技論文的英文必須正確、通順，而且英文句子應該簡潔、自然，以利於讀者瞭解並承認或接受論文的觀點。為滿足這個要求，論文的寫作應該遵循標準的英文規則，否則讀者會對論文感到迷惑不解，無法真正明瞭論文的意思。更嚴重的是，假如英文科技論文中出現過多的文法錯誤，那麼科技論文會遭到厭棄的命運，或者會使有些讀者懷疑論文作者的專業水準及論文內容的正確性。

　　本章將討論與分析撰寫英文科技論文時常犯的文法及造句上的錯誤。這裡，並不打算完整地復習所有的英文文法，而是把討論的內容集中在一般科技論文作者最感到困惑的英文文法上。希望本書的讀者仔細閱讀並掌握本章所強調的英文文法準則，以避免許多常犯錯誤的發生。

11.1 不完整的句子

　　句子必須表達一個完整的觀念。它含有比較完整意義的一組詞，一般至少包括主詞和述語這兩個主要成分。句子按其使用目的，可分為四種：直述句，疑問句，祈使句和感嘆句。按其結構又可分為三種：簡單句，並列複合句和主從複合句。每個句子以大寫字母開頭，最後一個字母之後緊跟句號（或問號、感嘆號）。所謂不完整的句子包括：單獨孤立的一個子句，兩個並列動詞述語分割使用，介係詞片語、動名詞片語、分詞片語、動詞不定詞片語、及同位語的孤立使用。不完整的句子應該和其他合併在一起，以構成一個至少包含一個主句的完整句子。

　　常見的一種不完整的句子是單獨孤立的一個子句。這些子句常以

after，although，because，before，if，since，when或while這些連詞開頭。改正這種不完整句子的方法通常是將它並入前後的主句中。

不完整：Although the problem is complicated. We can solve the problem in only two hours with an electronic computer.

修正句：Although the problem is complicated, we can solve it in only two hours with an electronic computer.

不完整：Given an input ρ . we can obtain the value of H using equation (6).

修正句：Given an input ρ , we can obtain the value of H using equation (6).

不完整：The amount of fluorine incorporated into the film on the substrate surface can be controlled. By reducing the amount of water added to the immersing solution.

修正句：The amount of fluorine incorporated into the film on the substrate surface can be controlled by reducing the amount of water added to the immersing solution.

另一種不完整句子是由把屬於同一主詞的兩個並列動詞述語分割開來造成的。改正的方法是將分割出來的動詞述語與前面的句子合併。

不完整：Researchers have doubled the previous efficiency of producing hydrogen from water. And have made major advances in carbon nanotube storage technology.

完　整：Researchers have doubled the previous efficiency of producing hydrogen from water and have made major advances in carbon nanotube storage technology.

其他經常產生不完整句子的原因還有介係詞片語、動名詞片語等的孤立使用。可以把這些不完整的句子通常併入前後的完整句子中。

不完整：To encourage the use of renewable energy electricity in the United States. Policy measures will be needed.

修正句：To encourage the use of renewable energy electricity in the United States, policy measures will be needed.

不完整：Within the broad variety of technologies that constitute renewable energy. Some are already making large inroads in the marketplace.

完　整：Within the broad variety of technologies that constitute renewable energy, some are already making large inroads in the marketplace.

　　注意，祈使句是完整的句子，不過其易被讀者理解的主詞已省略。

→ Analyze a set of tables or illustrations from either a professional journal or technical magazine.

→ Now let $NTU = \dfrac{U_c B_c L_c}{W_c}$.

→ Consider the situation in figure 4.2.

→ Note that the maximum heat exchanger effectiveness is limited to 0.5.

→ Assume $\Psi = 0$ in Eqs. (D.48) and (D.47).

11.2 散漫的句子

　　句子的結構能用來反映句子的內容。一個簡明、重要的觀點通常應該使用簡短有力的句子來表達，而一個詳細的說明則需要較長、較複雜的句子來陳述。簡短的句子可適用於提出新的題目、敘述重要論點，或表述段落或章節的結論；較長的句子則適用於詳細說明並支援段落的主要論點。科技論文的作者要學會採用多種不同結構和長度的句子，以強調需要表達的重要思想，並使句子的意義更加清晰。

　　經常閱讀英語國家的專家撰寫的論文，就會發現科技論文中句子結構與長度組織上的一些特點。在一個段落中，先有一個簡短有力的句子，其用意在於介紹新的論點，接著有一個或幾個較長的句子，其目的在於說明、發展或推廣這個論點，然後再寫一個較短的句子，目的在於敘述結論或提出另一個新論點。見下例：

> There are many problems of management to be solved. Some people try to solve them by considering changes in the structure of organizations and the locations of authority and responsibility. Others hope to do it by improve the quality of decisions by new technological ideas and the use of modern methods of data processing. Yet another group expects to solve the same problems by concentrating on human relations. The vital point to be considered is that the structural, technological and human aspects cannot be separated as they all interact. For example, if a firm changes from a functional to a product grouping, problems of interpersonal relations occur. This may in turn affect the techniques of control (i.e. new financial systems may be needed). A knowledge of the above facts should enable a manager to understand that it may not be easy to find a simple answer to a problem but, by acknowledging this fact and using available knowledge wisely, answers can be much more accurate and effective.

然而，任何句子都不應該過於冗長或表達太多的觀點，否則讀者在閱讀一遍後不得要領、難以理解。過於複雜和冗長的句子，或包含過多不同觀點的句子，稱為「散漫的句子」。散漫的句子通常可分為兩種：一種是雜亂的子句和主句所構成的複雜句子；另一種是一長串簡單句用and或but連接而成的冗長句子。

下面的例句是第一種散漫的句子。這個句子是一個以and連接的並列複合句，而且還有一個冗長的形容詞子句，而子句中還出現兩個用and、or連接起來的並列複合句，而在形容詞子句中還內含一個形容詞子句。這個句子太冗長、複雜，以至於無法表達一個清晰的概念，讀者必定難於閱讀和理解。

散漫句：A communication network can be modeled as a graph, and a net work under attack or with other sources of failure can be modeled as a random graph, regarding which, for the purpose of clarification, a graph, in the sense used here, consists of vertices (or points) and edges, of which each vertex corresponds to a command center or other node in a communication network and each edge represents a two-way communication link between two command centers-in a random graph, an edge may fail, leaving intact the vertices connected by the edge, or a vertex may fail, destroying all the edges connected to the vertex.

對這個散漫的句子進行修改，必須把句子分成幾個不同的句子，而每個句子能表達一個特定的清晰的概念。下面是其中的一種修改方法。

修正句：A communication network can be modeled as a graph, and a net work under attack or with other sources of failure can be modeled as a random graph. A graph, in the sense used here, consists of vertices (or points) and edges. Each vertex corresponds to a command center or other node in a communication network. Each edge represents a two-way communication link between two command centers. In a random graph, an edge may fail, leaving intact the vertices connected by the edge, or a vertex may fail, destroying all the edges connected to the vertex.

在上面的修正句中，把原來散漫的句子分成五個獨立的句子，每個句子陳述一至二個清晰的概念。修正句易於閱讀，而且段落的意思比較清楚。

下面給出第二種散漫句子的例句。這個散漫句子的特點是：結構不很複雜，句子的大部分都由一長串用and連接的句子。

Slime molds reproduce by means of spores, each of which is an independent, one-celled organism, however, the cells originating from spores divide repeatedly, and eventually the offspring swarm together in a heap to form a common amoeboid mass, and then the original cell boundaries sometimes disappear, and the once-independent cells take on specialized functions, somewhat like organs in a larger animal, and the creeping mass of protoplasm, in some cases as large as 30cm in diameter, is difficult to classify as plant or animal or, indeed, as either a collection of individuals or a larger, single organism, but at any rate, it is one of the most curious examples of self-organization in all biology.

可以把上面的散漫例句改成下面的一個含有五個句子的獨立段落，其中第一句陳述段落的主要觀點，其他的四句則進一步說明這個觀點。經過修改後的五個句子都能方便讀者閱讀並理解作者要表達的意思。

修正：Slime molds reproduce by means of spores, each of which is an independent, one-celled organism. However, the cells originating from spores divide repeatedly, and eventually the offspring swarm together in a heap to form a common amoeboid mass. The original cell boundaries sometimes disappear, and the once-independent cells take on specialized functions, somewhat like organs in a larger animal. The creeping mass of protoplasm, in some cases as large as 30cm in diameter, is difficult to classify as plant or animal, or, indeed, as either a collection of individuals or a larger, single organism. At any rate, it is one of the most curious examples of self-organization in all biology.

11.3 缺少連接詞

若英文句子中只有逗號來連接兩個獨立分句，而缺少任何連接詞，則這個英文句子在文法上是錯誤的。例如：

Heat transport occurs via evaporation and condensation, the heat transport fluid is recirculated by capillary forces which automatically develop as a consequence of the heat transport process.

　　缺乏連接詞的句子從表面上要表達一個完整的觀念，但實際上表達了不止一個的觀念，這樣易使讀者迷惑。

　　缺乏連接詞的句子可以用四種不同的方法來修正成正確的句子。下面將結合例子闡述修正的方法。

缺乏連接詞：

Assume that the wick thickness is small compared to the vapor space dimensions, then D_{hl1} and A_{l1}/A_{l2} are well represented by the Eqs. (E.8) and (E.9).

修正方法(1)｜把逗號改成句號。

Assume that the wick thickness is small compared to the vapor space dimensions. Then D_{hl1} and A_{l1}/A_{l2} are well represented by the Eqs. (E.8) and (E.9).

修正方法(2)｜把逗號改成分號。

Assume that the wick thickness is small compared to the vapor space dimensions; then D_{hl1} and A_{l1}/A_{l2} are well represented by the Eqs. (E.8) and (E.9).

修正方法(3)｜在逗號後加上適當的連接詞（and，but，for，or，nor，so，yet）。

Assume that the wick thickness is small compared to the vapor space dimensions, and then D_{hl1} and A_{l1}/A_{l2} are well represented by the Eqs. (E.8) and (E.9).

修正方法(4)｜把其中一個獨立分句改成子句或片語。

If we assume that the wick thickness is small compared to the vapor space dimensions, D_{hl1} and A_{l1}/A_{l2} are well represented by the Eqs. (E.8) and (E.9).

　　請注意：上例中 "then" 是連接副詞，而不是並列連接詞。

在連接副詞（also, consequently, furthermore, however, moreover, otherwise, then, therefore, thus）前面，或在連接兩個獨立分句的轉折插入語（for example, in contrast, in fact, on the other hand）前面，都必須加上句號或分號。這類連接副詞或轉折插入語後緊跟逗號，但是hence，otherwise，therefore及then之後常常不需放入逗號，尤其當之後的分句很短時，更是如此。

誤：Consider the circuit shown in Figure (3), then we can draw its Norton-equivalent circuit as shown in Figure (4).

正：Consider the circuit shown in Figure (3). Then we can draw its Norton-equivalent circuit as shown in Figure (4).

正：Consider the circuit shown in Figure (3); then its Norton-equivalent circuit can be drawn in Figure (4).

正：Consider the circuit shown in Figure (3); then we can draw its Norton-equivalent circuit as shown in Figure (4).

在修改缺乏連接詞的句子時，若省略兩個分句之間的所有標點符號，則會產生未經轉折的即仍然是錯誤的句子。

11.4 主謂不一致

在英文文法中，所謂「一致」是指句子成分之間或詞語之間在人稱、數、性等方面的一致關係，而主謂一致是其中的一種重要的關係。在處理主謂一致中，要遵循以下三條原則：①語法一致，即在語法形式上取得一致。例如主詞為單數形式，述語動詞也採用單數形式；主詞為複數形式，述語動詞也採用複數形式。②意義一致，即從意義著眼處理一致關係。例如，主詞形式雖為單數但意義為複數，述語動詞也採取複數形式；或者主詞形式雖為複數但意義上視為單數，述語動詞也採取單數形式。③就近原則，即述語動詞的單、複數形式取決於最靠近它的詞語。例如：

誤：The devices include pump sprays, Freon aerosols, pressurized rubber balloons, and hydrocarbon propellants. The last was initially considered most promising, but they are flammable and incompatible with food products.

正：The devices include pump sprays, Freon aerosols, pressurized rubber balloons, and hydrocarbon propellants. The last were initially considered most promising, but they are flammable and incompatible with food products.

下面我們將只討論撰寫科技論文時常使作者在主謂一致方面犯錯的幾個詞。

由every，each或no所引導的單數主詞必須配合單數述語動詞使用，即使以and連接數個這種主詞，其後也只能用單數述語動詞。不定代名詞another，each，either，neither及one後也用單數述語動詞。

→ Every paper, proposal, and report is stored in my computer.

→ Neither of the two generators is imported.

→ No substance is a perfect insulator.

→ Each of these lifestyles is associated with different goods and services.

若單數主詞後面緊跟以as well as，together with，along with，in addition to開頭的片語，即使片語中包含其他名詞，單數主詞還是配合單數動詞述語。

誤：The actual research as well as the company's industrial activities are supported by many skills and disciplines.

正：The actual research as well as the company's industrial activities is supported by many skills and disciplines.

誤：The administration building, with its dingy windows and deep gray paint, house the administrative offices, including the infamous "fishbowl".

正：The administration building, with its dingy windows and deep ray paint, houses the administrative offices, including the infamous "fishbowl".

名詞片語中心詞是「分數或百分數＋of＋名詞（或代名詞）」，述語動詞的單、複數形式就取決於of後名詞或代名詞的單、複數形式：若名詞或代名詞是單數形式，則述語動詞也用單數形式；若是複數形式，則述語動詞也用複數形式。例如：

→ Over three-quarters of the swampland has been reclaimed.

→ Two-thirds of the people present are against the plan.

→ Half of the units have been in service for ten months.

→ Half of the trouble is the fault of the drafting department.

對於一些表示總和、比率、測量和數量的詞語做主詞時，雖然它們往往以複數形式出現，但是句子的述語動詞通常用單數形式，見下面的例句：

→ Last year about forty hours was spent on that report.

→ About eight pounds of carbon is added to the mix.

注意，the number of後跟單數動詞，但是a number of後卻必須用複數動詞。

→ A number of samples were collected from a different geographical region to see whether the phenomenon occurred there as well.

→ The number of students in our university is great.

11.5 時態的誤用

英文中共有12種時態，在科技論文中常用的五種時態是現在簡單式、過去簡單式、現在完成式、現在進行式及未來式。

現在簡單式表達不受時間影響的普遍科學事實，以及論文作者的看法及建議。過去簡單式用於記錄過去發生的行動或存在的狀態，如實驗的步驟和電腦的模擬。未來式表示將要發生的行為或狀態。現在完成式用來敘述到目前為止已完成（或剛完成）的動作，而且其結果或影響保留到現在，其著重點是現在的情況而不管這種過去動作所發生的時間。現在進行式表示目前正在進行而尚未完成的行為。

撰寫科技論文時，在動詞時態使用上要特別注意以下三個要求。

①不要用現在完成式來敘述過去的事件。過去的事件應該用過去簡單式。例如，下面兩個句子的時態使用上都有錯誤：

誤：The graduate school of Business has been founded in 1925 at the urging of Herbert Hoover, a Stanford alumnus who was then serving as secretary of commerce in the Coolidge administration.

誤：At the ASHRAE Annual Meeting in Denver, Colorado, Mr. Patterson has delivered the inaugural address.

這兩個句子都提到一個特定的、過去的時間，即分別是 "in 1925" 和 "At the ASHRAE Annual Meeting"，因此，必須使用過去簡單式。

正：The graduate school of Business was founded in 1925 at the urging of Herbert Hoover, a Stanford alumnus who was then serving as secretary of commerce in the Coolidge administration.

正：At the ASHRAE Annual Meeting in Denver, Colorado, Mr. Patterson delivered the inaugural address.

②不要把現在完成式與過去完成式混淆起來。過去完成式用於表示在一個特定的、過去的事件或過去某一時刻以前已完成的行為。例如：

→ The reactor had worked twenty hours by ten o'clock yesterday evening.

→ They began their experiment after they had read the instruction.

動詞的過去完成式很少出現在科技寫作中。

③靜態動詞不能使用進行式，只有動態動詞（也稱動作動詞）才能使用表示動作目前正在進行的現在進行式。所謂靜態動詞是指用來描述主詞狀態的動詞，也稱狀態動詞，包括appear，afford，be，believe，concern，consist of，constitute，contain，correspond，exist，feel，forget，know，suppose，involve，mean，mind，need，own，posses，remember，represent，result in，satisfy，seem，smell，understand及yield等動詞。下面的句子使用了靜態動詞的進行時態，是錯誤的。

誤：Breadth is also important, because students are needing to appreciate the interplay among the functional areas of business.

正：Breadth is also important, because students need to appreciate the interplay among the functional areas of business.

誤：Considerable uncertainty is existing about climate change responses to greenhouse gas emissions.

正：Considerable uncertainty exists about climate change responses to greenhouse gas emissions.

11.6 不正確的動詞補語

動詞補語是指用來補充說明動詞意思的詞或片語，通常以形容詞、直接受詞或間接受詞的形式出現。科技論文中，大多數是用動詞不定詞或that開頭的子句作為補語，如下面的例句：

→ The purpose of this paper is to propose a new simulation method that dramatically reduces the time needed to conduct the simulation.

→ The numerical results show that the pattern of distribution and magnitude of the radiative heat flux agree with the experimental data.

但是在科技寫作時要注意一些動詞不能帶不定詞結構做受詞，而只能帶-ing結構做受詞。這些動詞常用的有admit，acknowledge，anticipate，appreciate，avoid，cannot help，cannot resist，cannot stand，consider， contemplate，defer，delay，detest，ensure，escape，evade，facilitate，finish，imagine，include，keep (on)，mind，miss，postpone，practise，put off，resent，resist，risk，stop，suggest等。例如：

→ We appreciate your inviting us to visit your laboratory.

→ I hope that by posting the final six pages now at midday I shall ensure your receiving them before the week-end proper.

請注意，有一些動詞後既能帶-ing結構做受詞，又能帶不定詞結構作受詞，而意義無甚區別或相差不大，如begin，continue，neglect，prefer，propose，start，require，attempt，intend，plan，permit，allow，recommend，advise，encourage等。另一些動詞之後用-ing結構或不定詞結構作受詞，意義上卻有很大差別，這些動詞如try，mean，remember，forget，stop，leave off，go on。以try為例：

→ If you want to improve the simulation, try using GA.（try作「試、試用」解）

→ Smith tried to answer each question by himself.（try作「努力、設法」解）

此外，在有些動詞let，make，see，have，watch，observe，feel等之後，不定詞作為受詞補語時，要省掉符號to，如：

→ Let N represent the number of customers in the system.

→ A force is needed to make a body move.

→ Suppose half of the customers exit the system at the same time.

11.7 被動語態的誤用

在英文中，當強調行為的承受者或給予行為的承受者較大的關注時，使用被動語態；當行為的執行者是物而不是人時，往往使用被動語態；當行為的執行者已被大家熟知而沒有必要寫出來或不知道行為的執行者時，我們也使用被動語態。被動語態的句子常出現在科技論文中，尤其是當作者描述某種方法、過程或因果關係時。

為了不過度使用或錯誤使用被動語態，撰寫科技論文的作者在使用被動語態時，務必遵循下述的規定。

(1)若使用被動語態來指出自己的行為，一定要清楚表明自己是這個行為的執行者

當論文作者使用被動語態來陳述自己的研究目的及工作，或提出某些建議或主張時，一定要確定讀者已瞭解論文的作者就是這些行為的執行者。例如，在論文的方法部分中，讀者自己可以從上下文清楚地知道所描述的行為的執行者是作者，因此方法部分中常使用被動語態。但是，若科技論文導論的文獻回顧部分中出現下列句子：

It is believed that the annealing treatment improved the electrical characteristics of the film.

則這個句子未能清楚地指出作者表達的是自己的看法或其他人的看法（句子原意是作者自己提出此看法），改正後的句子如下：

清楚：We believe that the annealing treatment improved the electrical characteristics of the film.

清楚：The annealing treatment appears to have improved the electrical characteristics of the film.

清楚：It appears that the annealing treatment improved the electrical characteristics of the film.

上面後兩個修正句省略了動詞believe，然後再使用試探性的動詞appear，以表示作者的看法。當作者根據自己研究結果提出看法時，不要使用如believe這類動詞的被動語態。

一般說來，以英語為母語的人把believe之類的動詞寫成被動語態，而又不明確這些動詞的執行者時，他們的用意並不是表達「我們認為」或

「我個人認為」，而是想表示所指的信念是普遍的或幾乎普遍的信念。例如：

→ Legionnaires' disease is believed to be caused by bacteria.

→ Effective illustrations are believed to transcend the text in the scientific and technical writing.

在這些句子中，is (are) believed並不表示「我們認為」或「我個人認為」，而意味著「絕大多數專家都認為」。上面第一句的意思應理解為「絕大多數的醫生、醫學科研人員等專家都認為，軍團病是由細菌感染引起的」；上面第二句的意思則是「絕大多數資深的科研工作者或專業人士普遍認為，在科技寫作中有效的插圖比文字更能說明問題。」

要注意，動詞argue，assume，believe，desire，modify，present，propose，recommend，suggest，suppose常出現在不自然、不清楚的被動結構中。例如：

Now that the method has been modified, it is used to analyze the chemical heat pump dryer.

當論文讀者看到這個句子時，會提問modify和use的執行者是誰，是其他研究者還是論文作者自己？其實，作者想表達的是作者本身修改了這個方案，且作者將它用在化學熱泵乾燥器的分析中，但是論文的讀者理解這點是不容易的。應該將此句修改為：

Now that we have modified the method, we can use it to analyze the chemical heat pump dryer.

特別要注意desire這個動詞，見下例：

It is desired that the region's economy improve quickly.

在這個例句中，It is desired顯得既生硬又不自然。下面是修改句：

→ It would be desirable for the region's economy to improve quickly.

→ The region needs to improve its economy quickly.

→ We hope the region's economy will improve quickly.

假如句子本身已指明行為發生的地點，那麼可以使用被動語態，因為讀者已明白行為的執行者是誰。這是一個重要的規則。下面用例子加以說明。

不清楚：Two examples are employed to illustrate the urban heat island effect.

我們將此例句改寫成下列句子，會使句子顯得自然、清楚。

清楚：Two examples will be employed below to illustrate the urban heat island effect.

清楚：Two examples will be employed here to illustrate the urban heat island effect.

清楚：The following examples illustrate the urban heat island effect.

清楚：In section 3, two examples are employed to illustrate the urban heat island effect.

清楚：In this paper, two examples are employed to illustrate the urban heat island effect.

清楚：In Rosenfeld's paper, two examples were employed to illustrate the urban heat island effect.

然而，若子句子的上下文中可以明顯地瞭解行為執行者或行為發生的地點，則可以用被動語態，如：

This paper presents a new method to predict the heat island potential using remote sensing and GIS data. This method is illustrated by means of two examples.

在該例中，若只看第二個句子則並沒有清楚地表明句子行為的執行者。然而第一個句子已清楚地說明論文的作者將會提出一種新方法，且緊跟的第二個句子表示作者會進一步用二個例子加以說明，所以第二個句子使用被動語態是妥當的。

總而言之，採用被動語態時，必須確定論文的讀者能夠很清楚句子中行為的執行者是誰，否則，需更改句子。

(2)被動語態的句子所陳述的事情必須與事實相符

在撰寫科技論文時，經驗豐富的作者常在句子中使用現在簡單式、被動語態的動詞。由於這些句子所陳述的事情與事實相符，即它們能正確地描述屬於標準做法或程式的某些行為，所以句子中的描述不受作者寫作時的特定情況影響。請看下例：

→ In industry metals are often used in the form of alloys.

→ Energy is neither created nor destroyed, but it may be transformed from one form into another.

當我們使用現在簡單式、被動語態的動詞來做某種觀察或指出某件事情，被動語態的句子應該表達一個普遍的事實。下面的句子並沒有表達一個普遍的事實：

不自然：From these data it is seen that the self-phase modulation and the self-frequency shift are enhanced by forward pumping.

這個英文句子很不自然，因為用 "it is seen" 意味著 "it is seen by everyone"，即表達普遍事實之意，然而事實並非如此。因為不是所有的人都看到句子陳述的資料，所以並不是每個人都知道句子後面所表達的情況。為了使句子合乎事實，可以通過加上情態助動詞來加以修正。

自　然：From these data it can be seen that the self-phase modulation and the self-frequency shift are enhanced by forward pumping.

或者把原句改寫成主動語態，用data做主詞：

修正句：These data show that forward pumping enhances the self-phase modulation and the self-frequency shift.

讓我們再參考下面的例子：

Now these values are substituted into the equations of motion and the solution is obtained.

如果在作者從事的研究領域中，把數值代入運動方程式並得到解答是很標準的做法，那麼使用被動語態是恰當的。但該作者似乎並不真正地要描述某種標準的作法，只是指出自己的求解方法，因此用現在簡單式、被動語態的動詞就不妥當了。如果作者真的要指出他自己的求解方法，那麼可以把原句修改成：

→ These values can now be substituted into the equations of motion to obtain solution.

→ We can now substitute these values into the equations of motion to obtain the solution.

(3)在確定動詞不定詞主詞的基礎上使用正確的語態

在決定動詞不定詞採用主動語態還是被動語態時，先要確定不定詞中動詞所暗指的主詞（邏輯主詞）。若這個主詞是動詞不定詞所指行為的執行者，則動詞不定詞通常使用主動語態；若這個主詞是動詞不定詞所指行為的承受者，則通常使用被動語態。例如：

→ He is the first to solve this problem.

→ The prototype design is expected to be completed by September.

→ Some molecules are large enough to be seen in the electronic microscope.

→ The book seems to have been translated into many languages already.

但是，在某些英文句子結構中，雖然動詞不定詞和所說明的人和事物是動詞和承受者（受語）的關係，但仍然用主動語態的不定詞，而不用被動語態的不定詞。

→ They gave me some books to read.

→ We found the report hard to understand.

上面兩句不定詞所表示的行為的邏輯主詞從意義上看分別是me和we。沒有採用被動語態的動詞不定詞，看來與不定詞邏輯主詞已出現有關。

此外，還有句中動詞不定詞邏輯主詞沒有出現而仍用主動語態的不定詞。這樣用的不定詞都是跟在形容詞後，語法稱之為方面副詞。例如：

→ This question is easy to answer.

→ This kind absorber is difficult to install.

這兩個例句中的不定詞沒有使用被動語態，可以理解為泛指不定詞的邏輯主詞或省略「for＋不定詞的邏輯主詞」結構。若需強調不定詞的邏輯主詞，這個例句可以改寫成在主動語態不定詞前加「for＋不定詞的邏輯主詞」結構的形式：

→ This question is easy for everyone to answer.

→ This kind absorber is difficult for us to install.

請注意：下列兩個句子的含義是有差別的。

→ We wanted the letter to type at once.

→ We wanted the letter to be typed at once.

上述第一句的意思是我們希望我們自己立即將信打好字，第二句的意思是我們希望請別人立即將信打好字。

(4)確定行為的執行者，以免混用主動語態與被動語態

很多科技論文的作者在描述實驗方法或陳述實驗結果時，會混用主動語態與被動語態。在這兩種情況中，被動語態表示某行為是由研究者某個動作所產生，主動語態則表示某個行為或事件是自己發生，或是另外一個行為或事件的結果，而不是由研究者的某個直接動作所致。請參閱下列句子：

→ When the A value goes beyond 0.02m², the measured temperature does not decrease any more.

→ After the polymer was placed in a tank, the temperature was increased gradually.

在上面第一個例句中，主動態動詞does not decrease表示測量到的溫度不自行降低，反映了測出的溫度與方法A之間的變化規律，溫度不降低並非是研究者某個動作產生的結果。在第二個例句中，被動態動詞was increased表示所描述的行為是由研究者的操作產生的，即研究者將聚合物放在槽內，然後逐漸提高槽內的溫度。

(5)不及物動詞不可以使用被動語態

不及物動詞後面沒有受詞，因此不及物動詞沒有被動語態。在科技論文中常用到的不及物動詞有appear，arise，be，become，come，consist of，correspond，depend on，exist，happen，have，let，occur，proceed，remain，result in，rise，seem，tend，work，yield等。也有些動詞既可作及物動詞，又可作不及物動詞，如develop，change。例如"proceed"這個動詞無法使用被動語態，所以下面的例句在文法上是錯誤的。

誤：The calculation was proceeded by the student.

正：The calculation was performed by the student.

正：The calculation was carried out by the student.

(6)避免過度使用被動語態

　　雖然被動語態有很多用途，但是在撰寫科技論文時不要養成隨意使用被動語態的習慣。過多地使用被動語態，會使論文變得笨拙和失去主觀意義，每個讀者會排斥這種沈悶的、公文性的寫作風格。此外，被動語態的濫用也導致句子出現垂懸修飾詞語，這也是英文科技寫作常犯的錯誤之一。一個訓練有素的英文科技論文作者只有在必要的時候才使用被動語態，如在論述實驗方法和分析計算的部分中。

11.8 主詞、語態的隨意更換

　　在英文科技寫作中，應該避免將句子中的主詞或語態做不必要的更換，不必要的主詞更換，或不必要的主動語態和被動語態之間的更換，會使句子顯得生硬、笨拙，同時還會給讀者的理解帶來麻煩。請看下列的句子。

If we attempt to solve the equation in this form, several difficulties are encountered.

雖然這個句子在文法上沒有錯誤，但是其副詞子句中的主詞、語態和主句中的主詞、語態不同，整個句子顯得不夠自然。子句中的主詞是we，主句中的主詞是difficulties；子句中的動詞用的是主動語態，而主句中的動詞使用被動語態。若將上面的子句和主句都改用同一個主詞和語態，那麼整個句子會變得比較通順。

If we attempt to solve the equation in this form, we shall encounter several difficulties.

上面改寫的句子用於強調研究者的行為。若作者想要強調遇到的困難，則還可以將原句的子句與主句都改成被動語態：

If the problem in this form is to be solved, several difficulties are encountered.

在改寫的句子中，主詞由problem轉到difficulties是正確的，因為這兩者是句子的主要概念，而且把這兩個名詞當作子句與主句的主詞，使得我們能一致地使用被動語態來寫出整個句子。我們還可以用比較簡短的-ing片語來取代上面句子中的子句。

Attempting to solve the equation in this form leads to several difficulties.

有時，根據文章上下文的結構或句子的意思，主句與子句中動詞的語態互不相同，這種用法也是正確的。例如：

When the system was tested, it performed well.

或：

When it was tested, the system provided excellent performance.

在這兩個句子中，子句中的動詞採用被動語態，主句中的動詞採用主動語態，這種主、子句語態的轉換是正確的，因為作者希望把句子的焦點集中在「系統」這個名詞上，而「系統」這個名詞剛好都是主、子句的主詞。

11.9 垂懸的修飾詞語

垂懸的修飾詞語，亦稱為孤立的修飾詞語或邊垂的修飾詞語。它是指句子中在語法上或邏輯上沒有任何修飾對象的修飾詞語，或者指似乎在修飾一個詞但實際上不能合理修飾這個詞的詞語。在科技寫作中，常常會出現垂懸的修飾詞語，其原因主要是以被動語態來描述行為是難於掌握的。另外，也許因為這些垂懸的修飾詞語對專業讀者的理解往往不會引起麻煩，所以許多論文作者對句子中出現垂懸的修飾詞語採取容忍的態度。不過，在撰寫正式的科技論文時，作者應該特別小心，要避免垂懸的修飾詞語。例如，在下面的句子中，After connecting this lead to pin1 of the second tube就是一個垂懸的修飾詞語。

After connecting this lead to pin1 of the second tube, the other lead is connected to pin2.

在英文中，像after connecting this lead to…的修飾詞語，若處在句首的位置，則通常應該修飾句子的主詞。但是，在上面的例句中，after connecting this lead to…這個修飾詞語並不能合理的修飾句子的主詞the other lead，因此，它是個垂懸修飾詞語。這個垂懸修飾詞語產生的原因是在主句中用被動語態代替了主動語態。原句可修改成下面的句子：

After this lead has been connected to pin1 of the second tube, the other lead is connected to pin2.

或：After connecting this lead to pin1 of the second tube, the technician connects the other lead to pin2.

在上面第二個修改句中，我們提供了一個能讓after connecting this lead to…這個片語合理地修飾的主詞the technician。而在第一個修改句中，我們把主動性的connecting片語改成被動語態的子句，這樣可與主句的語態一致。

學生在撰寫論文時，常出現的垂懸修飾詞語的種類有垂懸的分詞片語、動名詞片語、不定詞片語和省略的子句。下面分別進行介紹。

(1)垂懸的分詞片語

分詞片語作副詞時，其邏輯主詞必須是句子的主詞，否則必須給出其邏輯主詞，這種帶有自身邏輯主詞的分詞片語，稱為獨立分詞結構。分詞片語包含一個分詞（現在分詞或過去分詞）、分詞的受詞以及修飾分詞及其受詞的詞。位於句首的分詞片語應該用來修飾句子的主詞，若不能修飾句子的主詞，則該分詞片語就是垂懸的分詞片語，必須對句子進行修改。

誤：Comparing Huckin's method with ours, the difference between them is that we don't use external forces to join the panels in the model together.

正：Unlike Huckin's method, our method does not use external forces to join the panels in the model together.

誤：Examining this problem, the following fact can be observed.

正：Examining this problem, we observe the following fact.

誤：Starting the machine, an unusual problem occurred.

正：When the machine is started, an unusual problem occurred.

在上面三個例句中，分詞片語似乎都修飾句子的主詞，但是主詞無法合理地產生分詞片語所表示的行為。在第一個例句的修正句中，我們用一個介係詞片語來代替垂懸的分詞片語。第二個例句的修正句中，我們提供了分詞片語能夠合理修飾的另一個主詞（"we"）。而在修改第三句時，我們用一個子句取代了原句中的垂懸的分詞片語。

請注意，在英文中，有一些介係詞（如concerning，according to，regarding，owing to，excepting，failing，considering）和從屬連接詞（如supposing，providing，seeing，considering），本身常有-ing詞尾。以這類詞或片語開始的片語或子句不存在垂懸修飾語的問題。

(2)包含垂懸動名詞的垂懸片語

在一個帶有垂懸動名詞的垂懸片語中，動名詞通常當作介係詞的受語使用。

誤：After determining the mapping of A_i from L_1 to L_p, the next array dimension can be processed in the same way.

嚴格說來，after引導的介係詞片語應該修飾句子的主詞，但是在上面的例句中，主詞dimension是無法執行determining這個行為的。原句可以用下列兩種方式進行修改：

第一種方式是加入一個主詞，該主詞是after determining修飾的合理對象：

正：After determining the mapping of A_i from L_1 to L_p, we can process the next array dimension in the same way.

　　第二種方法是把垂懸的介係詞片語改成子句，主、子句均用被動語態或均用主動語態：

正：After the mapping of A_i from L_1 to L_p is determined, the next array dimension can be processed in the same way.

正：After we determine the mapping of A_i from L_1 to L_p, we can process the next array dimension in the same way.

　　第三個修改方法則是省略after這個介係詞，並直接用動名詞determining作為句子的主詞，且整個句子使用主動語態。

正：Determining the mapping of A_i from L_1 to L_p makes us process the next array dimension in the same way.

　　有時，若句首出現包含動名詞的介係詞片語，則這個介係詞片語可以合理地修飾句子的動詞。例如：

原　句：By focusing the scene to be imaged on the photo cathode of the tube, the image is intensified.

　　By focusing…可以被認為不是一個垂懸的介係詞片語，因為它合理地說明了如何增強影像的明暗度。但是，如果將這個片語移到句尾，句子就會變得通順多了，讀者也會瞭解這個片語是用來修飾動詞的。

修正句：The image is intensified by focusing the scene to be imaged on the photo cathode of the tube.

請注意，不要像原句那樣完全按照中文的表達順序硬譯成英文。相較之下，修正句的結構顯得較為自然。

(3)垂懸的不定詞片語

動詞不定詞片語包括不定詞符號to、動詞原形、動詞受語以及其他修飾動詞或受語的詞。一般說來，位於句首的不定詞片語應該修飾句子的主詞，否則就很可能是垂懸的修飾語。

差：To write effective software programs for banks, training in both computer science and finance is necessary.

佳：To write effective software programs for banks, software developers need training in both computer science and finance is necessary.

差：To develop a high-performance air conditioner, it is important to use an intelligent control system.

佳：To develop a high-performance air conditioner, designers use an intelligent control system.

在上述錯誤例句的修改中，我們都插入了適當的主詞，使動詞不定詞片語有了對應的修飾對象。

在撰寫科技論文中，位於句首的不定詞片語如果不能修飾句子的主詞，只要句子不會因此變得生硬或毫無意義，也許能被編輯和專業作者所接受。此外，有時候不定詞片語不能合理地修飾主詞，卻可以修飾句子的動詞述語。下面句子中的不定詞片語或許因為可以合理地修飾句子的動詞，所以顯得比較自然。

To meet this requirement, an optimization technique for implicit-form problems must be developed.

但是，經驗豐富的作者和大多數專業編輯會覺得，下面的句子會比原句還通順：

To meet this requirement, we must develop an optimization technique for implicit-form problems.

對於這種類型的句子，撰寫科技論文的作者要認真思考寫出來的以動詞不定詞開頭的句子是否能被人接受，如果不被接受，那麼應該改寫句子。

(4)垂懸的省略子句

所謂省略子句是指一個省略主詞（有時還有be）的子句，而且被省略的主詞與主句的主詞相同。然而，如果子句中被省略的主詞與主句的主詞不相同，那麼省略子句就成了一個垂懸的修飾片語。修改垂懸的省略子句有兩種方法，即在省略子句中加入合適的主詞，或改寫這個省略子句，以便子句能合理地修飾主句的主詞。

誤：When applying Kaviany's method in our simulations, the modeled objects had an unrealistic shape.

正：When we applied Kaviany's method in our simulations, the modeled objects had an unrealistic shape.

誤：When simple, we can solve this type of problem quickly using the direct method.

正：When simple, this type of problem can be solved quickly using the direct method.

11.10 誤置的修飾詞

在英文句子中，詞或片語的位置反映了詞或片語與句子中其他組成成分之間的關係。具有修飾功能的詞或片語的位置一定要正確，否則句子的意思變得不清晰，使讀者感到迷惑不解。

(1)程度副詞

程度副詞多數用來修飾形容詞或副詞，有少數也可用來修飾動詞或介係詞片語。在英文科技論文中，常見的程度副詞有：much，(a) little，very，enough，quite，fairly，extremely，considerably，entirely，completely，definitely，nearly，almost，hardly，approximately，partly， slightly，half，only，even等。程度副詞通常都放在它所修飾的詞之前。在撰寫英文科技論文時，要特別注意這些副詞在句子中的正確位置，它們往往與中文句子中的位置不同。

誤置：The United States only installed 420 MW of additional wind capacity in 1998.

修正：The United States installed only 420 MW of additional wind capacity in 1998.

誤置：The experiment took three hours approximately.

修正：The experiment took approximately three hours.

上面第一個例句中，only不是用來修飾動詞installed，而是修飾420。在第二個例句中，approximately應放置在three之前。

注意下面兩個句子意思之間的差別：

→ The tests are nearly all completed.

→ The tests are all nearly completed.

在第一個句子中，nearly用於修飾all，於是句子的意思是「大多數的測試都已完成，但還有少量的測試尚未做完」。在第二個句子中，nearly修飾的是completed，句子的意思就變成了「沒有任何一個測試已經完成，不過所有的測試都會很快完成」。所以，在同一個句子中，若程度副詞的位置變化，則句子的意思也會隨之改變，下面的例句雖然很簡單，但頗能說明問題。

Only George said that he displaced his computer.（只有喬治說了，沒有其他人這麼說。）

George only said that he displaced his computer.（他只說了這件事，除此之外，他沒有做其他的事。）

George said only that he displaced his computer.（除此之外，他沒說其他的事。）

George said that only he displaced his computer.（他是唯一搬動電腦的人）

George said that he only displaced his computer.（他只搬動了電腦，除此之外，沒有做其他的事）

George said that he displaced only his computer.（他沒有搬別的東西，也沒有搬別人的電腦）

George said that he displaced his only computer.（他只有一台電腦，而且它把這台電腦搬動了）

George said that he displaced his computer only.（他只搬動了自己的電腦，並沒有搬自己的其他東西，也沒有搬別人的東西。）

(2)副詞修飾動詞時的位置

副詞修飾動詞時，多數的副詞都可以放在動詞後面，如果修飾的是及物動詞，那麼副詞一般位於受詞後面。然而，當動詞述語中出現情態助動詞且使用被動語態（如can be＋過去分詞）時，要特別注意修飾動詞的副詞的位置，請參閱下面的句子：

The results can be easily obtained by using three following methods.

這個句子是正確的。但是，很多以英語為母語的人會認為，若將easily這個副詞放在情態助動詞can和be之間，則會使句子比較自然。

The results can easily be obtained by using three following methods.

當作者有意強調一個副詞，或副詞片語較長時，可以將副詞或副詞片語放在句末，而不放在它所修飾的動詞的前面或後面。這也符合上述，修飾及物動詞時副詞一般放在受詞後面的規則。請比較下面兩個句子中副詞的位置：

不通順：The student quickly and accurately answered the question.

修正句：The student answered the question quickly and accurately.

　　第一個句子在文法上沒有錯誤，卻沒有第二個句子通順。第二個句子中，動詞直接跟在主詞後面，使句子比較容易閱讀，副詞放在句末，也有表示強調副詞的意思。

(3)明確修飾詞

　　撰寫英文科技論文時應該明確修飾詞所修飾的特定詞。若修飾詞的位置不恰當，則讀者會對所修飾的詞感到困惑。請注意下面句子中often這個副詞的位置。

不清楚：The professor required his graduate students often to read references.

　　讀者不禁要問：often究竟是修飾required還是read？答案是不明確的。為了使答案清晰，可以根據作者要表達的意思把原句改成下列句子。其中第一句中，often用於修飾句子的動詞required，第二句中，often則用於修飾不定詞動詞read。

修正句：The professor often required his graduate student to read references.

修正句：The professor required his graduate student to read references often.

(4)介係詞片語的位置

　　介係詞是英語中最活躍的詞類之一。介係詞用在名詞或代名詞等的前面，以介係詞片語的形式表示它們與句中其他成分之間的各種關係（所屬、時間、地點、方式、原因等）。

　　介係詞片語作形容詞修飾名詞時，通常位於它所修飾的名詞之後，否則整個句子的意思會含糊不清。在下面的例子中，介係詞片語in chemistry似乎用來修飾students這個名詞，但實際上它應該修飾experiment，因為句子要表達的是「學生將做化學實驗」。

誤置的：The students in chemistry will conduct the experiment.

修正句：The students will conduct the experiment in chemistry.

　　介係詞片語做副詞時，一般用來修飾動詞或形容詞，其位置比較靈活，可以直接放在被修飾的詞之後，也可以放在句首、句尾。然而，當選擇這類介係詞片語的位置時，需要考慮句子的意思是否能表達清楚。在下面誤置的句子中，in Appendix 1這個片語是用來修飾theorem的，但是，作者的原意是告訴讀者：上述定理的證明見附錄1。

誤置的：The above theorem in Appendix 1 is proved.

修正句：The above theorem is proved in Appendix 1.

　　再看下面的例子，介係詞片語of great complexity應該是用來說明problem，而不是用於修飾classical physics。

誤置的：This is a problem in classical physics of great complexity.

修正句：This is a problem of great complexity in classical physics.

(5)形容詞子句的位置

　　形容詞子句通常應該緊接它所修飾的詞。下列所謂「誤置的」句子，因為句中形容詞子句的位置是錯誤的，所以會使讀者產生疑惑。在第一個誤置句中，形容詞子句應該說明名詞device；第二個誤置句中，形容詞子句應該修飾名詞information，而不是memory。

誤置的：A laser disk drive is used in the CD-ROM device that is the same size as a traditional 5.25-inch drive.

修正句：A laser disk that is the same size as a traditional 5.25-inch drive is used in the CD-ROM device.

修正句：The CD-ROM device has a laser disk drive that is the same size as a traditional 5.25-inch drive.

誤置的：Information can be loaded into memory that is stored on ACD-ROM and then displayed or printed.

修正句：Information that is stored on ACD-ROM can be loaded into memory and then displayed or printed.

　　請注意，如果形容詞子句太長，而使得形容詞子句直接放在它所修飾的名詞之後，會引起句子笨拙而不平衡，那麼就應該把形容詞子句移到比較恰當的位置（如放在句尾）。例如，下面的句子中，如果形容詞子句放在動詞述語之後，那麼句子就會比較通順。

不通順：In section 4, experiments in which the proposed method is applied to control a standard industrial robot manipulator are described.

修正句：In section 4, experiments are described in which the proposed method is applied to control a standard industrial robot manipulator.

修正句：In section 4, we describe experiments in which the proposed method is applied to control a standard industrial robot manipulator.

誤置的：In this report, an efficient algorithm that employs the concept of static equilibrium to determine the stability of clamping is developed.

修正句：In this report, an efficient algorithm is developed that employs the concept of static equilibrium to determine the stability of clamping.

修正句：In this report, we develop an efficient algorithm that employs the concept of static equilibrium to determine the stability of clamping.

　　在科技論文中，許多形容詞子句是由「介係詞+關係代名詞which」引出的，關係代名詞在形容詞子句中作介係詞的受詞。如果用that，那麼介係詞應放在子句的句末。例：

→ The motor is a machine in which electricity is changed into mechanical energy.

→ High-speed steel is a material the cutter is made of.

　　關係代名詞作形容詞子句中的及物動詞或介係詞的受詞時，經常可以省略。但關係代名詞作介係詞受詞時，如果省略，則介係詞要放在子句的末尾。例：

→ Most of the things (which, that) we use are taken from the surface of the earth.

→ Air will completely fill any container (that) it may be placed in.

　　當關係代名詞後面緊跟聯繫動詞to be時，關係代名詞及聯繫動詞有時可以省略，使句子顯得簡明。參閱下例：

The results that were obtained are shown in Figure 2.

其省略句為：

The results obtained are shown in Figure 2.

由於obtained在此表示一個縮短的形容詞子句，所以把obtained放在它所修飾的results後面。若顛倒名詞和修飾詞的順序，如：

The obtained results are shown in figure 2.

雖然這個句子在語法上無錯（有人會理解成過去分詞obtained作形容詞），但是相較而言，the results obtained這種寫法較自然。此外，如果不是用在一個句子裡，而是用在如圖名這樣的場合，那麼如The computed flow field of middle section in width direction 中computed放在flow field之前也是常見的。

(6)副詞子句的位置

　　以although，because，since，until及after等連詞開頭的副詞子句，可以放在被修飾的詞之後，也可放在句首或句尾。作者一定要在明確句子意思能表達清楚的基礎上，確定副詞子句的位置。若副詞子句的位置不正確，則會使句子變的模糊或生硬。

誤置的：The sensors were used in the test systems after they were calibrated.

修正句：After they were calibrated, the sensors were used in the test systems.

上面句子中，將副詞子句放在句首，就很明確的表達了作者的意思，即感測器已被校準過；而若將副詞子句放在句尾，則有可能被誤認為測試系統被校準過。

還要說明的是：應注意代名詞在主從複合句中的位置。請參閱下兩個例句：

→ When they are combined with natural-gas-fired turbines, parabolic-trough systems can produce electricity for about 94 kWh.

→ When parabolic-trough systems are combined with natural-gas-fired turbines, they can produce electricity for about 94 kWh.

這兩個句子在英文文法上都是正確的，但是在中文中，對應的第二句的結構較自然（先提systems這個名詞，然後再使用代名詞they）。當然，上面的句子可以改寫成下面較簡單的形式：

When combined with natural-gas-fired turbines, parabolic-trough systems can produce electricity for about 94 kWh.

11.11 冠詞的誤用

冠詞位於名詞之前，用來幫助說明名詞的含義。冠詞是最典型的限定詞，它分成定冠詞、不定冠詞及零冠詞（即不需任何冠詞）。冠詞的表達功能可以歸納為三種，即類指、特指和獨指。類指是表示類別，也就是泛指一類人或物。定冠詞與單數可數名詞搭配，或與某些形容詞或分詞連用，或零冠詞與複數可數名詞或不可數名詞搭配，不定冠詞與單數可數名詞搭配都屬於類指。特指不同於類指，它不是泛指一類人或物，而是特指一類人或物中的具體對象，它包括使用定冠詞、零冠詞與抽象名詞的搭配的有定特指，以及使用不定冠詞的不定特指。獨指是指獨一無二的人或物，定冠詞常作這種用法。

即使上述使用規則很容易被記住，但對非英語國家的人來說仍然是最難掌握的詞類之一。為了正確地使用冠詞，一定要判斷句子中某個名詞是指一個種類中的任何一個，還是指一類中的具體對象或一個特定的人或物。

使用英文冠詞中常出現的錯誤之一，就是當使用不定冠詞與單數可數名詞搭配來說明一個總類的任一個例時，卻忘了不定冠詞a（或an）。

The function of bus is to transfer information in the form of electric signals between the different parts of electronic system.

上面例子的作者是想介紹a bus（資訊通道）的功能。句子中，bus和electronic system都是單數可數名詞，各是bus和electronic system總類中任一個例，因此，它們之前的不定冠詞是必要的，不能忽略。改正的句子見下面段落中的第一個句子。

The function of a bus is to transfer information in the form of electric signals between the different parts of an electronic system. The generic term for system components connected by a bus is devices. A group of devices is connected to control the bus segment. Only one device, the bus master, is allowed to control the bus and initiate data transfers at any onetime. Several masters may be present on a bus, so contention between them must be resolved using arbitration rules.

另一個常犯的錯誤是當有必要使用定冠詞the時，卻沒有使用定冠詞。還有的作者不分青紅皂白地在每個名詞之前一律加上定冠詞，不管是確實需要使用定冠詞還是應該使用不定冠詞或使用零冠詞。請讀者結合本節開始時介紹的使用冠詞的規則，認真閱讀上面的段落例子，仔細體會段落中不同的地方分別採用不定冠詞、定冠詞或零冠詞的原因。

11.12 不正確的複數名詞

英文中，可數名詞通常有單複數形式，不可數名詞一般沒有單複數名詞之分，但有時也以複數形式以表示不同的意義。有些名詞的數在用法上確實不易掌握，它們是某些以-s結尾的名詞、抽象名詞和專用名詞的數。

英文中有一些以-s結尾的名詞並不是可數名詞，它們當中有的作單數用，有的作複數用，有的既可作單數用又可作複數用。常作單數用的以-s結尾的名稱包括某些疾病的名稱、學科名稱及某些地理名稱等。見下例：

→ Arthritis is a disease causing pain and swelling in the joints of the body.

→ Acoustics is the science of sound and is a factor which must be considered when building a theatre or a cinema.

物質名詞一般是不可數名詞，沒有複數形式。可是有些物質名詞有時也以複數形式出現，但表示的意義不同。下例第一句中的water指水，第二句中的waters是領海。

→ They were given some bread and water.

→ They were not allowed to fish in our territorial waters.

一般來說，抽象名詞是不可數的，因而沒有複數形式，例如"Knowledge is strength."。專用名詞通常以單數形式出現，但有時也可以複數形式出現，例如"Have you invited the Browns?"（指姓布朗的一家人）。

科技論文的作者在撰寫時，一定要留意複數形式的用法。若名詞應該用複數形式，則切勿寫成單數形式。此外，千萬不要把單數形式寫成複數形式，尤其不能將不可數名詞寫成複數形式。記住，不要把下面的不可數名詞寫成複數形式：

literature	equipment	notation
research	work	terminology
information	software	hardware
knowledge	engineering	pollution
combustion	magnetism	business
proximity	orientation	degradation

　　科技論文還常出現以every、each、no、another、either、neither及one這些詞後加名詞的片語。這些片語中的名詞不能寫成複數形式，如下例所示：

→ Every substance is constantly emitting radiant heat.

→ Either answer is correct.

→ No substance is a perfect insulator.

　　還要注意的是：若一個計量單位之前有一個數字，則除非這個數字剛好是1，否則單位應該是複數形式，而不管數字是大於1還是小於1。例如：

The overall heat pipe length remains 40 inches (1.016 meters) and the heat pipe outer radius is 0.310 inches (0.0787 meters).

或

The overall heat pipe length remains 40 in. (1.016 m) and the heat pipe outer radius is 0.310 in. (0.0787 m).

　　關於計量單位的單、複數用法請讀者參閱本書12.6節的詳細介紹。

11.13 不明確的先行詞

　　在英文中，每一個代名詞必須有一個先前已提到的明確的它所替代的名詞，這裡稱之為先行詞。如果一個代名詞的出現使讀者不能清楚地看出它的先行詞，那麼就可能引起讀者的困惑。這一點對那些對論文內容不太熟悉的讀者更是如此，請看下面的例句：

不清楚：Gallium arsenide, as well as silicon, is studied in Philips, mainly in our French laboratories. We are particularly interested in its qualities that make it so suitable for ICs and FETs that are either extremely fast or have a very low power consumption.

在上例的第二句中，代名詞it和its指砷化鎵（的）還是矽（的），可能會對一般讀者產生困擾。應該改寫句子，以便讀者能清楚地看出代名詞的先行詞，或者用名詞代替這個代名詞，修正的句子如下所示：

修正句：Gallium arsenide, as well as silicon, is studied in Philips, mainly in our French laboratories. We are particularly interested in the qualities of this material that make it so suitable for ICs and FETs that are either extremely fast or have a very low power consumption.

另外一個句子見下面所示。 在該例子中，讀者會很難判斷出it是指formal financing system還是指pre-selling system。

不清楚：When a formal financing system does not exist, a preselling system is established to make the market more effective. It can be found in a number of areas.

修正句：When a formal financing system does not exist, a preselling system is established to make the market more effective. The latter can be found in a number of areas.

it可作為形式主詞出現在句子中，如it is sometimes necessary to change the horsepower to watts or kilowatts.。但是，應避免在同一個句子中使用代名詞it來表達兩個或三個不同的意思。例如，當句子中使形式主詞it時，就不應該在同一句子中再使用it代替某個特定的先行詞。請參閱下面的例句：

不清楚：Since you cannot be sure in advance where the table will be placed, it is necessary to refer to it by saying "see Table 1" or "Table 1" or "the accompanying table" rather than "the table above" or "the table below".

清　楚：Since you cannot be sure in advance where the table will be placed, refer to it by saying "see Table 1" or "Table 1" or "the accompanying table" rather than "the table above" or "the table below".

清　楚：Since you cannot be sure in advance where the table will be placed, you must refer to it by saying "see Table 1" or "Table 1" or "the accompanying table" rather than "the table above" or "the table below".

不清楚：When it is important for a system to handle complex data, it is difficult to design it so that it also provides solutions quickly.

清　楚：It is difficult to design a system that both handles complex data and provides solutions quickly.

再如下面的不清楚的句子中，it被用來表示不同的意思。

不清楚：The solar water heater used in the experiment is shown in figure 3. At its top left is a cold-water inlet, where water flows into it. Its main portion consists of many coils of plastic pipe connected together in an accordion fashion and covered with a sheet of heat-absorbing plastic. The water flows through them, absorbing heat from the sun, and then exists the heating apparatus through the outlet at the lower right of the heater. From the outlet it flows into an insulated storage tank in the basement of the house, from which hot water is drawn when needed.

清　楚：The solar water heater used in the experiment is shown in figure 3. At the top left of the water heater is a cold-water inlet, where water flows in to it. The main portion of the heater consists of many coils of plastic pipe connected together in an accordion fashion and covered with a sheet of heat-absorbing plastic. The water flows through the pipes, absorbing heat from the sun, and then exists the heating apparatus through the outlet at the lower right of the heater. From the outlet the water flows into an insulated storage tank in the basement of the house, from which hot water is drawn when needed.

若使用一個代名詞來表達或代替前面整個句子或整段的意思，則不可以使用代名詞it，而必須用指示代名詞this。

誤：After the initial investments have been made, the economics of renewable energy technologies improve in comparison with conventional technologies because operating and maintenance costs are low compared with those incurred using conventional fuels. It is especially high, and will be especially true in the future as fuel prices increase.

正：After the initial investments have been made, the economics of renewable energy technologies improve in comparison with conventional technologies because operating and maintenance costs are low compared with those incurred using conventional fuels. This is especially high, and will be especially true in the future as fuel prices increase.

但是，只有在this等指示代名詞表達的意思十分明確的前提下，才可以使用。若表達的意思不夠清晰，則需加入能清楚反映句子意思的名詞，或者取消代名詞，再把句子重寫。例如：

原句：Panels should be exposed at more than one test station on exterior racks and regular inspections should be made. This will require trained personnel.

上面的原句中，this是指exposing the panels，或making inspections，還是它們兩者？this表達的意思很不清楚，必須取消代名詞this，再改寫句子。若作者想說明inspections要求受過訓練的人去做，則原句可改寫成：

Panels should be exposed at more than one test station on exterior racks and regular inspections should be made. Inspections will require trained personnel.

若作者想說明exposing the panels要求受過訓練的人去做，則原句可改成為：

Panels should be exposed at more than one test station on exterior racks and regular inspections should be made. Exposing panels will require trained personnel.

再例如：

原　句：With respect to global warming, the burning of fossil fuels contributes three-fourth of the carbon dioxide emissions in the United States today. And the public health implications of energy-related pollution present a serious problem. Meeting the rapidly growing demand for energy, while also maintaining a clean global environment, requires clean energy to power the economy. This will eventually prompt the transition from oil-based fuels to renewables-based fuels and fuel cells.

修正句：With respect to global warming, the burning of fossil fuels contributes three-fourth of the carbon dioxide emissions in the United States today. And the public health implications of energy-related pollution present a serious problem. Meeting the rapidly growing demand for energy, while also maintaining a clean global environment, requires clean energy to power the economy. This challenge will eventually prompt the transition from oil-based fuels to renewables-based fuels and fuel cells.

此外，學生在撰寫英文文章時，不應該使用不必要的代名詞。

誤：Oxygen is a gas that we obtain it from the air.

正：Oxygen is a gas that we obtain from the air.

誤：For a program with n iterations, there are n iterations in its corresponding DFG.

正：For a program with n iterations, there are n iterations in the corresponding DFG.

正：A program with n iterations has n iterations in its DFG.

在上面第一個錯誤的例句中，形容詞子句中的代名詞it是多餘的，因為已經有關係代名詞that來代替oxygen這個名詞。如果我們將這個例句改為Oxygen is a gas and we obtain it from the air.，即原句中的子句改成一個並列獨立分句，那麼代名詞it出現在obtain的後面是必要的。然而，在形容詞子句中，關係代名詞that就取代了代名詞it，因此應該在形容詞子句中去除不必要的代名詞it。

11.14 不一致的代名詞與先行詞

代名詞必須有明確的先行詞。除此之外，代名詞的數也必須與其先行詞保持一致。下列規則必須注意：當代名詞代替不定先行詞any、each、either、neither及person和以-one、-body及-thing（如everyone，anybody，something）結尾的詞時，就必須使用單數代名詞。若兩個或兩個以上的單數先行詞用and相連接時，則應使用複數代名詞。若兩個或兩個以上單數先行詞以or或nor相連接時，則應使用單數代名詞。若一個複數先行詞與一個單數先行詞以or或nor相連接時，則應該使代名詞的數和與它最靠近的先行詞的數保持一致。英文中傳統的作法是，陽性代名詞he、him和his都可以用來代表男性或女性的單數先述名詞，如someone、everyone、person、student、user、author及reader這些詞。但是，目前有許多讀者認為陽性代名詞同時指稱兩種性別是不明智的作法。為了避免這種做法，可以採用一些調和的辦法。請看下例：

原　句：Any author who wishes to present a paper at the conference should submit an English abstract of his paper before December 31, 2001.

修正句：Any author who wishes to present a paper at the conference should submit an English abstract of his or her paper before December 31, 2001.

修正句中用his or her來取代原句中的his。這個修改方式一般只用於代名詞在句中只出現一次的情況。若代名詞在句子中出現兩次或兩次以上，則不採用此方法，因為過多的his or her或he or she會使句子冗長且笨拙。

另一個調和的方法是將句子中的單數代名詞與其相對應的先行詞都改寫成複數形式。

Authors who wish to present papers at the conference should submit the English abstracts of their papers before December 31, 2001.

還有一種改寫的方法是將原句中所有代名詞全部除去。

Any author who wishes to present a paper at the conference should submit an English abstract of the paper before December 31, 2001.

在正式的英文中，複數代名詞they、them和their不能用來作為單數先行詞的代名詞。也不應該以his/her或he/she這種書寫形式來表達兩個代名詞的合併使用。

誤：Any author who wishes to present a paper at the conference should submit an English abstract of their paper before December 31, 2001.

差：Any author who wishes to present a paper at the conference should submit an English abstract of his/her paper before December 31, 2001.

指示形容詞（this, that, these, those）的數必須與其所修飾的名詞的數一致。特別是指示形容詞後面跟著kind of或type of這類片語時，應該與kind of或type of之後緊跟的名詞的數相符。

誤：This type of pens

誤：These kinds of circuit

正：This type of switch

正：These types of switches

正：This kind of solvent

正：These kinds of solvents

11.15 不正確或不自然的複合名詞

複合名詞是由兩個或兩個以上的名詞有機地組合成的名詞片語，如

electronics engineer，figure caption，research team，government report，computer science，metal part等。複合名詞中最右邊的名詞稱為首詞（head noun），首詞前面的所有名詞則是作為修飾詞。下面例句有四個複合名詞，每一個複合名詞都由兩個名詞組成：

> The author provided an overview of the research program and described the research objectives, the potential research opportunities, and the impact of some past research accomplishments.

複合名詞的意思可以簡單地把它從右至左展開並插入適當的介係詞這種方法表達出來。例如，例句中的research program即是program of research。再例如，a water purification system實際上是a system for the purification of water。複合名詞可以用來簡潔地表達某些複雜的概念，但是，應該注意千萬不要造出不自然的或不正確的複合名詞。為了確保所寫的複合名詞是讀者易於理解的正確、清楚的表達形式，學生在撰寫科技論文時，應該記住複合名詞使用的三個規則：只用規範的、結構合理的複合名詞；複合名詞要簡短；不使用名詞的所有格。

複合名詞需規範且搭配合理，要使得論文讀者能迅速理解，特別要注意複合名詞複數的正確用法。一般來說，只有複合名詞的首詞才可以寫成複數。用來修飾首詞的名詞通常寫成單數形式，即使這個名詞可能表達複數的意思，也是如此。例如，an electron beam這個複合名詞的意思是a beam of electrons，即使許多電子形成的電子束，beam的形式還必須是單數。再例如a passenger ship也是如此。

但是，這個規則有許多例外，即非首詞具有複數的形式，如weapons system，communications satellite，teachers college，emissions sampling，parts shortage，materials science。讀到這些例外的複合詞時，除了死記硬背，別無他法。

使用複合名詞時，最重要的是不要使複合名詞太長。一個複合名詞最多出現三個或四個名詞。一般而言若一個複合名詞的組合超過三個名詞，複合名詞中各名詞之間的關係會不易弄清楚，可能導致讀者的困惑。例如，當讀者見到the lift arm front bearing cup retainer這個複合名詞時，他們很可能不明白作者的真正意思。遇到類似情況時，建議作者把這樣的複合名詞分成幾個較小的部分，然後再用介係詞將這幾部分連接起來。The lift arm front bearing cup retainer可以改寫成the retainer for the front bearing cup of the lift arm，這樣就能使讀者清楚作者要表達的意思了。參閱下面的例句。

差：In this paper we introduce a new actuator location selection method.

佳：In this paper we introduce a new method for selecting the location of actuators.

差：Existing network bandwidth assignment methods are not suitable for this case.

佳：Existing methods for assigning bandwidth in networks are not suitable for this case.

誤：This document is a government research institute technology development guidance model proposal.

正：This document proposes a model for guiding the development of technology at research institute operated by the government.

在中文中，「的」這個字常用來類比於英文中的介係詞of。中文中，「的」也可以用來表示名詞的所有格，而在英文中所有格用's來表示，因此有些科技論文的作者誤認為's可用於所有中文的「的」。例如，有些學生常將's用在複合名詞之中，如將emergency brakes、a screw jack、an auto entertainment center及a coal liquefaction process誤寫成emergency's brakes、a screw's jack、an auto's entertainment center及a coal's liquefaction process。實際上，複合名詞首詞之前的名詞是修飾詞而非所有格。

然而，「不使用名詞的所有格」這項規則也有例外的情況，人們常見到的user's guide就是一個典型的例子。user's guide這種形式雖然與規則不符，但是它已經成為一個默認的標準用法。對於這種情況，只能強記。

要強調的是，複合名詞中的首詞可以由它之前的一個或更多的名詞加以修飾，但是，建議在撰寫科技論文時，儘量用恰當的形容詞來修飾名詞。例如，應該用experimental result來代替experiment result，用technological development取代technology development。

11.16 不合理的比較

科技論文中常用到兩個項目的比較，但是要注意，兩個項目之間的比較一定要合理且完整，而且兩個項目本身是可以比較的相同類型的名詞。此外，必須把比較的項目陳述清楚，以免讀者不知所云。在下面表明「不合理」的例句中，用於比較的兩個項目不屬於相同種類。

不合理：The accuracy of the new robot arm is greater than the conventional one.

合　理：The accuracy of the new robot arm is greater than that of the conventional one.

合　理：The new robot arm is more accurate than the conventional one.

不合理：These results are consistent with Smith et al.(1989).

合　理：These results are consistent with those of Smith et al.(1989).

不合理：The alignment problem is simpler in imperative languages than the functional language Alpha.

合　理：The alignment problem is simpler in imperative languages than in the functional language Alpha.

不完整的比較常出現在有similar這個詞的句子中。請看下面例句：

誤：The cost function and alignment algorithm are also similar as ﹝15﹞.

對於這個句子，讀者無法理解比較的對象，因此這個句子是不合理的。而且similar所接的介係詞應該是to，而不是as，所以這個句子文法上也有錯誤。修改的句子如下所示：

修正句：The cost function and alignment algorithm are also similar to those in ［15］.

在Sound travels much more slowly than light句子中，light後面does已被省略。這類句子省略了does之類的動詞，不會影響讀者對句子意思的正確理解。然而，也有一些句子如果省略了助動詞、介係詞或其他的詞，那麼句子中的比較對象會變得模棱兩可。

不清楚：Compare the voltage drop between node 1 and node 2 and node 3 and node 4.

清　楚：Compare the voltage drop between node 1 and node 2 with that between node 3 and node 4.

不清楚：Low-frequency noise is filtered out more effectively by the AGC than the limiter.

清　楚：The AGC filtered out low-frequency noise more effectively than the limiter does.

清　楚：Low-frequency noise is filtered out more effectively by the AGC than by the limiter.

11.17 「主題與評論」句型

一般說來，一篇說明文或者一個結構完整的段落，通常都有一個概括全篇或全段中心思想的主題句。主題句通常出現在篇首或段落的前部。主題句一般有關鍵字，並通過關鍵字在結構形式上和意義上與輔助句緊密相連，從而體現出全篇或整個段落意義的連貫性和統一性。主題句的結構形式也有人稱之為「主題與評論」的句型。

英文科技論文的作者經常按照中文的習慣，利用句首的包含關鍵字的片語來強調句子的主題，然後在其後寫一個對主題進行評論或描述的句子。例如：

在應用方面，已有許多模糊神經網路應用的報告。

關於這個問題，採用了下面的解決方法。

如果我們完全按照中文的表述方法直接地把它們翻譯成英文：

不自然：In application aspects, many applications of fuzzy neural networks have been reported.

不自然：Concerning this problem, the following approach was adopted to solve it.

那麼，雖然這些英文句子的文法上無錯誤，但是顯得不自然。修改的方法可以是省略句首的片語，直接直述句子中心意思。具體的作法是將原句首片語的意思並入句子的主詞或受語之中。按此方法，我們可將上面兩句不自然的句子改寫為：

修正句：Many applications of fuzzy neural networks have been reported.

修正句：This problem was solved by adopting the following approach. The following approach was adopted to solve this problem.

學生撰寫英文科技論文時，往往喜歡用as far、as to、concerning、considering、for、in respect to、in the area of、regarding等詞作為開頭的句子。但是，應該注意這些詞開頭的句子可能是不自然的「主題與評論」型的句子。針對這種情況，可以去除這類句子的句首片語，直接直述句子的重點，使句子顯得通順、自然。請參閱下列的修改例子：

不自然：Regarding the effect of Rayleigh number on the wall temperature of the inner cylinder, it is illustrated in Figure 5.

修正句：Figure 5 illustrates the effect of Rayleigh number on the wall temperature of the inner cylinder.

修正句：The effect of Rayleigh number on the wall temperature of the inner cylinder is illustrated in Figure 5.

不自然：Comparing the differences between Robert's approach and our approach, the main difference between them is that our method is much simpler to use.

修正句：The main difference between Robert's approach and ours is that our method is much simpler to use.

修正句：Our method is much simpler than Robert's approach.

不自然：For each character image, it is identified as belonging to a set of m candidate characters.

修正句：Each character image is identified as belonging to a set of m candidate characters.

科技英文論文寫作實用指南 **Practical Guide to Scientific English Writing**

12

標點符號

標點符號是作者用來闡明句子結構和意義的重要工具。在英文中，標點符號的正確用法是有相當一致的約定的。學生有必要瞭解英文標點符號的基本使用規則，並加以正確使用。

本章主要介紹英文標點符號和數字的基本使用規則，並指出在撰寫英文科技論文時常犯的標點符號和數字方面使用上的錯誤。

12.1 句尾標點符號

句尾標點符號表示英文句子的結束，包括句號、問號及驚嘆號。這三種句尾標點符號中，僅句號常用於科技寫作。

◆ 12.1.1 句號（Period）

英語的句號是一個圓點，而不是中文句號那樣的圓圈。

①句號常用於表示直述句、祈使句或間接問句的結束。

→ Everything in the world is made of matter.

→ Let him measure the temperature and the pressure.

→ They investigated whether a lower temperature would decrease the rate of the action.

②句號常用於名字的縮寫字母及縮寫字的小寫字母後面。

Z.G.　　Wang　　J.A. Barclay　　Dr.　　Ms.　　etc.　　et al.

③由大寫字母所構成的縮寫字或機構組織名稱的縮寫中，句號可被省略。

GSP　　GDP　　CPU　　UN　　WTO　　CIA

句號常用於學位的縮寫中。注意，學位的縮寫字母間不需要空格。

Ph.D.　　M.S.　　B.A.　　M.D.

句號也可用於由二個以上的字所構成的國家名稱縮寫中，但這些縮寫字後面通常不需標點。

USA或U.S.A.　　UK或U.K.

④句號常用於英里、分、秒等測量單位縮寫字母之後。但其他測量單位的縮寫字母後面通常不用句號。

10mi.　　20min.　　15sec.　　37km　　12m　　4cm

⑤若句子的最後一個字是帶有句號的縮寫字，則此句句尾不需再標上句號，即一個句子的句尾不能出現兩個句號。

誤：The author of that paper is Gustav Foster, P.E..

正：The author of that paper is Gustav Foster, P.E.

⑥句號標於用來表示大綱或豎式一覽表的字母、羅馬數字或阿拉伯數字的後面。請不要在這種目錄式標點中將句號與括弧合用。

Do

1.Operational definitions

2.Logical definitions

3.Examples

4.Comparisons

5.Contrasts

如果將上例中的阿拉伯數字標示成(1.)或(1).等都是錯誤的。

⑦在標準的美式用法中，句號即使不是用來標示引號內的資料，也總是位於引號內。而在英國，句號只有在被看作引號內事物的一部分時，才置於引號內。下例是美式用法。

His paper is entitled "Representative Operating Problems of Commercial Ground-Source and Groundwater-Source Heat Pumps."

⑧一個和前後句子相互獨立、但被置於括弧內的句子，其句號應該標於右括弧內側。但若括弧內的句子、分句或片語為前後句子的一部分，則必須省略括弧內的句號。

→ The Siberian tiger still has a good chance of survival. (In contrast, the south china tiger may already be doomed.) Several strategies for saving this tiger have been adopted. （注：本句括弧內的句子是獨立的句子）

→ The first of Hunt's articles was published in 1974 (the others were published soon afterward). Yamamoto's work, on the other hand, was not published until five years later. （注：本句括弧內的句子是第一句的一部分）

⑨目前大部分作者在使用電腦進行文字處理時，句子句號後面都只加一個空格。縮寫字中間的內在句號後面不需要空格。

e.g.　i.e.　a.m.　p.m.　Ph.D.

傳統上名字字首之後的句號後面要加一個空格。然而，許多作者在使用具有自動邊界線的文書處理軟體時，為了使名字的兩個字首均能位於文章的同一行，所以省略了兩個名字字首間的空格（但名字字首和姓之間必須有一空格）。

正：Mr. X. Z. Gao

Mr. X. Z. Gao

劣：Among those at the conference is Dr. H.

S. Zhang, who will meet you to discuss your paper tomorrow.

佳：Among those at the conference is Dr. H.S. Zhang, who will meet you to discuss your paper tomorrow.

請記住，英文文章中的句子句號前面不允許有空格。

◆ 12.1.2 問號（Question Mark）

①問號位於直接疑問句的後面。

→ Are you reading the operating instructions?

→ Why is heat a form of energy?

→ What device is this?

正式的科技論文中很少出現直接疑問句，而間接疑問句則常常使用。間接疑問句並不直接詢問問題，而是一種隱含或指涉問題的陳述。英文中，間接疑問句後面不使用問號。

→ Another important problem is how to improve the reliability of the machine.

→ The purpose of the experiment was to determine whether the material would be harmful to human being.

②當問號所標示的是整個句子時，問號應位於引號之外。當所標示的只是引號內的內容而非整個句子時，問號應位於引號之內。

→ Can you explain to me why this pipe is called "heat pipe"?
（問號標示整個句子）

→ The professor asked, "What dictionary have you? "

（問號標示教授的問題）

　③同句號一樣，在使用電腦進行文字處理時，句子問號後面都只加一個空格。

◆ 12.1.3 感嘆號（Exclamation point）

　①感嘆號用於感嘆語句或表示驚嘆的直述句後面。

　　　　Help!　　Fire!　　Follow me!　　How fast light travels!

　②感嘆號的使用規則基本上同問號的相同。但請注意，在正式的英文中，感嘆語詞或表示驚嘆的直述句後面不能使用兩個或兩個以上的感嘆號。

誤：What a high speed it is!!!

正：What a high speed it is!

　③感嘆號幾乎不會出現在正式的英文科技寫作中。

12.2 句內標點符號

　句內標點符號用來表示句子中各組成部分之間的關係，共有五種，即逗號、分號、冒號、破折號與括弧。

◆ 12.2.1 逗號（Comma）

　英文中的逗號的使用必須遵循下述的特定規則。

　①逗號用來區分以並列連接詞（and，but，or，nor，for，so或yet）所連接的主要分句。

→ Air has weight, but it is very light.

→ The quantitative interpretation of heat capacity data for ferromagnetics is still very rudimentary, and experiment of this type may serve as a guide for further modification of theory.

　　在有三個及三個以上分句的句子中，可以使用逗號或分號來區分分句。若分句很短或沒有句內標點符號（如逗號），則通常使用逗號；若分句很長或有句內標點符號，則一般使用分號。

→ The economy is shrinking, the unemployment rate is up, and a major political shake-up seems likely.

→ The economy is shrinking, with no prospects for growth in sight; unemployment is up, as foreign manufacturers close their doors and the largest domestic employers continue to lay off workers; and a major political shake-up seems likely, if only to placate the armed force.

　　逗號通常不用於區分分享同一主詞的兩個動詞。例如，下列句子並不需要任何逗號。

→ Low carbon steels can be formed and shaped easily by forging.

→ They examined the vacuum pump but failed to discover the source of the malfunction.

　　若分享同一主詞的兩個動詞都很長，則可用逗號來加以區分，即在連接詞and，but，or等前面加上逗號。此外，當作者需強調連接詞but前後兩個對比的部分時，有些作者會在but前面加逗號。

→ We planned to collect some new results, but did not expect to refute the conclusion.

　　②位於複合句主句和簡單句前面的子句或片語，其後通常都會標示逗號。

→ Since electricity can change into other forms of energy, it is widely used in industry.

→ In order to test the theory, more experiments must be carried out.

→ In the third experiment, they used a kind of new refrigerant to replace R12 in the system.

　　當引介性的子句或片語很短時，在不影響句意明確性的前提下，可以省略逗號。

→ In 2001 her family moved to Shanghai.

→ After school he went home to play the piano immediately.

　　③逗號應該用來把句子中的非限定修飾詞區隔出來，但不能用於限定修飾詞。限定修飾詞可以是子句、片語或詞，用於定義或限定被修飾詞句的意義。若限定修飾詞被省略，則句子的基本意義即隨之改變，因此是不可以省略的。但是非限定修飾詞提供的只是補充性的資訊，因此可省略而不會改變句子的基本意義。例如：

限 定 的：The material which allows electrical current to flow easily is called a conductor.

非限定的：Silver is a conductor, which allows electrical current to flow easily.

在第一個例句中，若省略形容詞子句which allows electrical current to flow easily，則整個句子在意義上和原句完全不同。原句中的子句which allows electrical current to flow easily是限定修飾詞（此例中是限定的形容詞子句），所以此子句不使用逗號。在第二個例句中，若省略形容詞子句which allows electrical current to flow easily，則整個句子所表達的主要概念仍與原句相同。原句中的子句是非限定形容詞子句，需要以逗號將它子句子中區隔出來。請注意，除非非限制子句位於句首或句尾，否則需要兩個逗號區隔，一個在非限定子句之前，一個在其後。

　　同樣的逗號使用規則適用於同位語。限定同位語不需要逗號，而非限定同位語應用逗號將其與句子的其餘部分區隔開來。非限定同位語可以省略而不影響句子的基本意義。

　　在下述例句中的or boiling point是非限定同位語，因此以逗號將其與句中的其餘部分區隔開來。它的省略並不影響整個句子的基本意義。

非限定的：The boiling temperature, or boiling point, is the temperature at which a liquid boils under ordinary pressure.

作為比較，下述例句中的that things must move to do work是限定同位語，因此不能用逗號區隔開來，它的省略會使整個句子變得無意義。

限定的：The fact that things must move to do work is known to all.

④若位於主詞後面的子句或片語提供的是限定的資訊，則不使用逗號；若提供的是非限定的或補充性的資訊，則使用逗號。

→ We will accept this paper for publication if you make the following minor revisions.

→ This is an excellent paper, although I don't completely agree with the conclusions.

上述第一個例句中的子句提供了限定的資訊，即論文接受出版的必要條件。第二個例句中的子句提供了附加、非限定的資訊，即與主句相對照願意讓步之意。

對於具有限定或非限定意義的片語as follows（以及as shown below），若as follows是非限定的，它不是句子主要意義的必要部分，原則上可以省略，因此需用逗號將句子中的as follows和句子的其餘部分區隔開來。若as follows有限定的意義，不能省略，否則句子會變得不完整、不自然，因此句子中的as follows不能用逗號。

非限定的：By using the state equation of the refrigerant, T and h can be calculated as a function of the other two thermodynamic properties, as follows.

限定的：The initial assumptions are as follows.

⑤獨立片語與主句之間總是以逗號區隔開來。獨立片語是由「主格名

詞（或代名詞）＋分詞（或分詞片語）」構成，整個片語用作副詞，修飾整個句子。

→ The experiment having been completed, the students began their discussion.

→ Other conditions being equal, the pressure remains constant.

　　⑥插入語應以逗號和句子的其餘部分區隔開來。插入語包括轉折、反意關係的詞或片語（如moreover，in contrast，indeed，finally等），引出例句的詞或片語（如for example，e.g.，that is，i.e.，namely等），以及respectively。

→ Water, for example, is a compound.

→ Drag, in general term, is the force which opposes the forward motion of the airplane.

→ ΔT_{corr} and ΔT_{app} correspond to the correct or erroneous value of the adiabatic temperature change, respectively.

　　連接副詞hence，otherwise，then，therefore以及thus後面有時並不加逗號，尤其是副詞後面所接的句子很短時。

　　Failure to control such a plant effectively could be disastrous. Hence an accurate and reliable control algorithm is needed.

　　請注意，像indeed或finally這樣的詞不作為轉換用途時，則不需加逗號。

→ Our homework was finally finished.

→ We predicted that conductivity could be improved by boron doping, and the experimental results show that this is indeed true.

　　若插入語不位於句首或句尾，則必須用一前一後兩個逗號區隔開來。

誤：Kerosene molecules, however have longer carbon chains than gasoline molecules.

正：Kerosene molecules, however, have longer carbon chains than gasoline molecules.

⑦逗號用來分開三個或三個以上相連的並列詞、片語或子句的幾個項目，其形式如a，b，and c或a，b，or c。

→ High energy efficiency, specific productivity, and selectivity may be achieved in plasmas for a wide range of chemical processes.

→ Therefore, the development of alternative compounds is earnestly desired in the field of refrigerants, form blowing agents, and cleaning solvents.

在上述形式中，詞and或or前面的逗號稱為「系列逗號」。省略系列逗號是報紙或新聞雜誌的標準慣例。然而，由於系列逗號對明確某些句子的意義非常必要，所以為了達到清晰與一致性，論文作者應養成使用系列逗號的習慣。請參閱下列例句：

The new building in our university will include many classrooms, a laboratory with complete testing equipment and offices.

因為缺少系列逗號，讀者無法判斷辦公室究竟是實驗室的一部分，還是整個建築物的一部分，在使用系列逗號後，整個句子就清楚多了。

The new building in our university will include many classrooms, a laboratory with complete testing equipment, and offices.

⑧逗號可用來區分兩個及兩個以上的並列形容詞。對等形容詞是指對同一個名詞作個別修飾的不同形容詞。

They have to develop a rapid, inexpensive, efficient method.

相較之下，累積形容詞各自修飾接於其後的整個觀念。在下面的例句中，first則修飾direct numerical method，direct修飾numerical method，而numerical修飾method。

Theirs is not the first direct numerical method to be introduced.

在確定形容詞是對等形容詞還是累積形容詞時，作者可以審視一下是否能將and置於這些形容詞之間。例如，在上面第一個例句中，若用and取代逗點，則所得句子仍是合理的，所以此例句中的形容詞是對等形容詞。在第二個例句中，若將and插入形容詞之間，則句子變得無意義，所以此例句中的形容詞是累積形容詞。

⑨逗號用作區分直接引語和指示說話者的片語或子句。

→ "You will find this project challenging," said Professor Reindl.

→ Professor Reindl said, "You will find this project challenging."

當句子中的引言是此句子意義的一部分，引言的前後不需要任何標點。

"Creative and excellent" was the reviewer's response to Smith's paper.

當所引述的片語或句子有限定的意義時，不需逗號加以區隔。下面第一個例句中的引述詞具有限定片語的功能；第二個例句中的引述詞則為非限定片語。

→ Enclosed is a paper entitled "Reciprocating Compressor Performance Simulation."

→ Did you read the book Anne Eisenberg published last summer, *Effective Technical Communication*"?

⑩逗號用於引導直接問句，即使這個問句不在引號內或問句的第一個字母不是大寫，也需要用逗號。

The question is, how do we measure the voltage?

⑪逗號用於劃分句子中的對比詞語。

→ The students talked to professor Zhang, not Professor Meng.

→ This interesting, although unpersuasive, argument out to be developed further.

→ They expected the engine output to increase, but only by about 5%.

使用兩個以or或but連接的形容詞來修飾同一個名詞時，or或but前後不需要加逗號。

> These significant but incomplete results should be supplemented by further research.

⑫對資訊作對照或較長的長對稱分句必須以逗號區分。

> The more you practice, the more you know.

⑬當相鄰兩個詞可以用兩種方式解讀時，逗號用來防止發生錯誤的理解。

> To Sophia, Frederick was the brother she had never had.

（若省略句子的逗號，則讀者可能會將 "Sophia Frederick" 誤解為一個人的名字。）在句中只列出兩個項目時，第一個項目後面通常不用逗號。

> There are two types of plasmas used for chemical applications: thermal plasma and non-thermal one.

然而，為防止理解錯誤，可以加逗號。在下列句子中，若省略 "clauses" 後面的逗號，則可能使句意混亂。

> Rambling sentences may be divided into two types: excessively complex sentences with many subordinate clauses and independent clauses, and sentences formed of a long string of simple independent clauses joined

together by coordinating conjunctions.

⑭若日期以月、日、年的順序書寫，則需要在日與年之間加逗號。若這種記載形式的日期出現在句子中，則通常在年的後面也會加逗號。

→ October 20, 2001

→ They arrived in London on March 16, 1999, and began their study the next week.

若日期書寫順序是日、月、年，則不需要加逗點。

4 June 1968

若僅僅標示月、年，則月與年之間或年的後面都不用逗號。

He graduated from the university in August 1989 and was promoted less than two years later.

⑮逗號用於區分姓名和頭銜。

→ The professor who delivered the lecture on Heat Pump was Bruce Garetz, Ph.D.

→ Robert Jones, Ph.D., will show us the new electronic expansion valve he has developed tomorrow.

⑯逗點用於區分地址的組成或地理名詞。

→ His address is 400 Main Street, East Hartford, Connecticut.

→ She visited her daughter in Vancouver, Canada, for 6 weeks.

以信封格式書寫的各行地址結尾處不需要逗號。

Professor S. H. Chen

Department of radiology

University of Pittsburgh

200 Lothrop Street

Pittsburgh, PA

USA

⑰在大數目中使用逗號以顯示千位元，但表示年份的數字中不應用逗號。

148,000　　25,000　　1,105　　1,895,673

⑱當所提到的項目只有兩項時，逗號不能用來表示 "and" 的意思。

誤：For cases 1, 2 we apply equation (8).

正：For cases 1 and 2 we apply equation (8).

誤：Substituting these values for p, q , we obtain the following solution.

正：Substituting these values for p and q , we obtain the following solution.

⑲逗號後面要加一個空格（表示數目的逗號例外，即在數字標示中，逗號後面不用空格）。請記住，在逗號前面任何時候都不要加空格。

⑳英文中沒有頓號（、）。當列出數學項目時，切忌以頓號代替逗號。

誤：The results of the tests A、B and C are shown in Table 4.

正：The results of the tests A, B, and C are shown in Table 4.

◆ 12.2.2 分號（Semicolon）

①分號用於區分未經並列連接詞（and，but，or，nor，for，so，yet 等）相連但意義緊密相關的兩個句子。這種關係可以是一種原因或對比的關係，如下例所示。

→ It is getting late; she must start back for the village.

→ Some of these methods scan the rows from top to bottom; others scan from right to left.

作者可以使用分號而不使用逗號去區分以並列連接詞相連的長獨立句子，但這種情況不多見。

> To prevent the occurrence of suppuration, with its attendant risks, was an object manifestly desirable; but till lately apparently unattainable, since it seemed hopeless to attempt to exclude the oxygen, which was universally regarded as the agent by which putrefaction was effected.

②分號用以區分由連接副詞相連的句子。連接副詞包括consequently，for example，further more，however，in contrast，indeed，moreover，nevertheless，on the other hand以及otherwise等詞。

> Electronic expansion valves are generally more reliable and functional than thermostatic expansion valves; however, they are also more expensive.

③當一連串的項目本身包含有內在的標點符號時，應用分號將這些項目區分。

> At the meeting were John Derek, the general manager; Ronald Huang, the senior advisor; Chris Pearce, the technical director; Robert Strader, from Global Strategy Development Division.

分號使讀者能較容易認清序列項目中的各項。若以逗號取代上述例句中的分號，則讀者可能無法說出作者所提到的是四個人還是七個人。

④列印稿中，分號後面要有一個空格，分號前面則不應加空格。

◆ 12.2.3 冒號（Colon）

①冒號用於區分主句與那些用來說明、闡述、強調或重述主句主題的子句、片語、詞或記號詞組。

→ Management activities are focused in four key areas: planning, organizing, directing, and controlling.

→ Most of these problems are briefly mentioned here: changes are needed in job content; key workers should be involved early and retrained if necessary; fewer staff being needed may affect promotion chances.

②冒號可用於將片語或詞as follows或the following引介的連續數個項目區隔開來。

> Professor Carl McDaniel asked the students many questions including the following: Do you think business ethics can be taught? Is it in the stockholders' interest for major corporations to spend time and money on community and public-affairs activities? What are the limits to the social responsibilities of a business?

請注意，冒號前面應是完整的句子。另外，在句子中的詞或片語such as，including後面不需要冒號。

誤：In this chapter, we shall describe several common types of the throttling devices, such as: manual expansion valves, thermostatic expansion valves, electronic expansion valves, capillary tubes, and float-ball regulating valves.

正：In this chapter, we shall describe several common types of the throttling devices, such as manual expansion valves, thermostatic expansion valves, electronic expansion valves, capillary tubes, and float-ball regulating valves.

③冒號可用於把方程式和例子區隔開來，但冒號前面必須是完整的句子。

正：The same approximation is utilized in the present study:

$$k = k_{\text{cont}} + k_{rad} = k_{cond} + 16n^2\sigma T^3/3$$

誤：The governing equations can be written as:

正：The governing equations can be written as

正：The governing equations can be written as follows:

④在書名的指稱上，冒號可用來區分書名的主標題與次標題（即使書封面上的書名沒有冒號）。

His newest book is Information Systems: A Management Perspective.

⑤商務信件的稱述語後面應使用冒號。

Professor Alter:　　Dear Ms. Appleby:

⑥在使用電腦文字處理時，只在冒號後面加一個空格。英文中的冒號前面絕對不可加空格，此外，數學比例中兩個數字之間的冒號後面也不需加空格（如1:20）。

◆ 12.2.4 破折號（Dash）

破折號用於句子的主要意思中劃分出插入的詞、說明、例子或其他插入詞句。括弧也有相同的功能，但破折號強調它所劃分出來的插入詞句。另外，逗號也用於劃分非限定子句之類的插入詞句，但逗號通常只用來劃分和句子主旨有密切關係的插入字句。

位於句子中間的插入詞句必須使用位於一前一後的兩個破折號。當插入詞句為句子末端時，只需一個破折號。

→ Human biology—which combined biological, medical, and behavioral sciences—was the first program of its kind to be offered by any university.

→ The ad was legal—but irresponsible.

請注意。破折號（dash）與連字號（hyphen）不同。連字號是較短的橫線（"-"），而破折號是較長的橫線（"—"）。破折號是電腦鍵盤上找不到的符號，目前的文字處理設備均有特殊的 "em-dash" 符號（"—"），但可以通過軟體將這個符號打入文件。該符號之所以稱為 "em-dash"，是因為傳統上它的長度與小寫字母 "m" 的相同。若所使用的文字處理設備中找不到破折號，則可以用兩個中間及兩邊的皆沒有空格的連字號（"--"）代替破折號。

①破折號用於表示句子結構中的突然轉變或中斷。

Our new digital camera—as well as several other attraction advanced product—is scheduled to be introduced in September.

②破折號用於劃分非限定同位語或其他具有強調功能的插入詞句。若插入詞句位於句子的中間，則必須使用兩個破折號一前一後地將其區隔開來。

On November 14, 1885—a year and eight months after their son's death and eight months after Leland Stanford began his first term as a U.S. senator—the couple formalized their plans to found a university.

◆ 12.2.5 括弧（Parentheses）

①括弧用於將對句子主旨而言並非必要的插入資訊、說明或評論區隔開來。

→ The red fluorescence was recorded by a 0.85 meter double monochrometer (SPEX model 1404).

→ In this case, the bifilar coil would be used nor only for increasing the floor fiability but also for accomplishing a "basic" heating (when the water circulates through only one pipe) completed with a "peak" one (when the water circulates through the two pipes).

②括弧用於包含句子中標示項目的數字或字母。

The transition mechanisms are roughly devoted into three categories: (1) he focusing of a precursor shock-wave; (2) local explosions resulting from re-ignition of partially quenched volumes (hot-get ignition); and (3) the exceeding of a critical flame speed due to a turbulent flame-acceleration.

請注意，應同時使用左括弧與右括弧，而不能只使用右括弧。

③括弧和其包含的資訊或標於其後的標點符號之間不能有空格。位於句子中間的括弧，其左括弧前面需加一個空格；若右括弧後面沒有標點符號，則其後也需加一個空格。下述例句中左括弧前面少了一個空格，所以是錯誤的。

誤：Active(gas regenerated) desiccant cooling systems are often used for these passive recovery applications.

左括弧後面不能有空格，右括弧前面也不需要空格，例如下列的第一個句子中的括弧空格是錯誤設置的。

誤：Active (gas regenerated) desiccant cooling systems are often used for these passive recovery applications.

正：Active (gas regenerated) desiccant cooling systems are often used for these passive recovery applications.

④在某些編輯格式中，括弧用於標示如下例所示的所引的參考作品或參考頁碼：

→ Dr. Steven Alter (1884, p. 127) described the types of information systems.

→ Several authors (Lin et al. 1998, Pohorecki et al. 1999) found no dependence on temperature and pressure.

◆ 12.2.6 引號（Quotation Mark）

在美式英文中，雙引號（ "…" ）用於劃分引言。英式的用法則通常使用單引號（ '…' ）。

①引言之前的說明詞後面通常會有逗號，但若引言很短或說明詞和引言中的詞密切相關，則常會省略此逗號。

→ The professor said, "He is one of the best students I have had in twenty years of teaching."

→ He shouted "be quick!" and began to run toward the house.

→ Smith's professor said that he was "one of the best students ever to graduate from this university."

②引號用於區分文章的標題或較長著作中部分文章的標題（即它們不是獨立的書或出版物）。引號也用於區分演講稿、詩詞、短篇故事、書中章節、歌曲以及收音機、電視節目的標題。

→ Their paper was entitled "Nature in Management."

→ Chan and Elphick's recently published article, "Critical Two-Phase Flow in a short Converging Nozzle," has received much attention in the readers.

③逗號用於區分開啟式引言與句子的其他部分，但若引言是以問號或驚嘆號結尾，則省略逗號。

→ "The time is up," the teacher said.

→ "When shall we start the experiment?" asked the students.

④美式用法中，逗號和句號位於引號內；分號和冒號則位於引號外；問號和驚嘆號只有在是引言的一部分時，才位於引號內，否則位於引號外。在英式用法中，逗號和句號除非是引言的一部分，才位於引號內，否則位於引號外。

→ The teacher said, "The time is up."

→ The students asked, "When shall are start the experiment?"

→ What is "brainstorm"?

當一個詞不是以意義而是以名稱來使用時（主要發生在邏輯和哲學中），上述規則有一例外，即引用詞後面的句號和逗號應放在引號外。

→ The boy knows how to spell "apple".

→ There are six letters in the name "Gitman".

上述兩個例句中引用的apple和Gitman皆非字義的使用，而是純當名稱使用。第一例句中，引號內的詞不是指真正的蘋果，而是指apple這個名稱，說話者說這個孩子知道如何拼出apple這個詞，而不是如何拼出蘋果這種水果。第二個例句中，引號內的詞並非指Gitman這個人，而是指Gitman這個詞（Gitman這個人並非由六個字母組成，但名稱Gitman是）。

請注意，上述兩例句中的引號可以去除而以斜體字代替，同時，斜體字的應用也消除了句號究竟應該置於引號內或引號外的疑問。

→ The boy knows how to spell *apple*.

→ There are six letters in the name *Gitman*.

請注意，如上面例句中所示，使用斜體字時，不應同時使用引號：

誤：There are six letters in the name "*Gitman*".

⑤引言之中的引言應用單引號來表示。

　　Smith said, "I know why Kun Ming is called 'the Spring City'."

◆ 12.2.7 方括號（Brackets）

①方括號 "〔 … 〕" 用於說明評論、校正或其他插入文章的資訊，尤

其是指插入引言中的資料。

> Mr. Peterson said, "I fully support his ［President Clinton's］ Clean Air Act."

在上述例句中,作者插入"President Clinton's"以說明"his"所指的是誰。

②在數學方程式或化學公式中,方括號和括弧常被合用。

$$Q_w = q_w D/[k_e(T_{sat} - T_0)]$$

③在某些編輯格式中,方括號用於論文參考文獻資料的引用。在下述例句中,方括號內的數位是指列於論文末尾處的參考文獻中的第二、第三篇及第四篇論文或書籍。

> Banks of fin-tube elements were studied experimentally in ［2, 3］, and numerically in ［4］.

請注意,不同的學術期刊使用不同的引文格式,投稿之前需閱讀所投期刊的有關規定,以確定符合要求的引文格式。

◆ 12.2.8 省略號（Ellipsis Points）

①省略號是以三個中間有空格的句號來表示,用於反映引用資料的省略。在科技論文中及其他學術著作中,若自某位作者的作品處引用某段文字,但又想省略原作的部分文字,則應插入省略號以表示省略的部分。英文句子中的省略,可以三個句號（只能是三個句號）表示,每個句號的前後均需加一個空格。若省略部分位於句末,則使用四個句號,其中第一個句號標示句子結束,後三個才是省略號。若句末的省略號後面接有括了號的頁碼,則需在頁碼前放置省略號,並將句子的句號放在閉括弧之後。

> Two types of technology . . . to have a huge impact on business are computers and communication. Over the next ten years, the amount of

information we can put on an electronic chip will increase . . . . This advance will drive down the cost personal computers . . . (P.6).

②省略號也可用於方程式或數學式的表達中，以顯示一系列的項目。

$$Dj，where \quad j=1, 2, 3, . . . , n$$

$$C (t1) = C (t2) = . . . = C (tn)$$

省略號通常位於本文字行行底，與句號或逗號在同一水平線上，如上述第一例所示。然而，當省略號的前面或後面接有像加號（"＋"）或等號（"＝"）等數學運算符號時，如上述第二例所示，則常常會將省略號提升到和其前後符號同一高度的位置。

省略號的前面與後面必須是對等的標點符號或數學符號：

正：$x_1, x_2, . . . , x_n$

誤：$x_1, x_2, . . . x_n$

誤：$x_1, x_2 . . . , x_n$

12.3 大寫字母、斜體字和詞的標點符號

在英文寫作中，大寫字母、斜體字、粗體字、所有格符號以及連字號都被用來表達句子中詞的特殊用法及功能。本節將介紹大寫字母、斜體字、粗體字以及詞標點符號的使用規則。

◆ 12.3.1 大寫字母（Capital or Uppercase Letters）

這裡，將一個詞大寫是指將此詞的第一個字母用大寫字母書寫，而此詞的其他字母仍然用小寫字母。

①凡是句子，句首的第一個字母必須大寫。

There is a water tower about the laboratory.

句子結構部分的直接引言或包含於括弧或方括號之內的完整句子，其

第一個字母必須大寫。

→ After answering the students' questions, the professor said, "We shall discuss the other topics next Tuesday."

→ The experimental apparatus consists of a multi-phase heat transfer unit, electrodes, and a DC-power supply unit. (See Figure 2.)

包含句子中的直接問句，其第一個字母應該大寫。

The question we now need to consider is, When shall we begin this project?

②若接在冒號後面的獨立分句，其作用不僅僅是強調或說明冒號前面的子句，還陳述新資訊，則有些作者會將此獨立分句句首的第一個字母大寫。

Our main reason for rejecting the proposal is simple: The idea of the proposal is not advanced.

冒號後面的獨立分句若只是重複或說明冒號前面的分句，則通常不大寫。

The other companies' products have become popular because of their low price and high quality: they offer quality comparable to that of our product at only half its price.

③專有名詞必須大寫。

人名、族名、國家名、語言名稱及地名都必須大寫。

Machael Jordan	Massoud Kaviany	Akira Sekiya
Chinese	African	Turkish
Thai	French	Germany
Cantonese	Shanghai	Hong Kong
Vancourer	New York	Sydney

以顏色為基礎的名稱通常不大寫。請注意，美國指稱黑人的通用語辭這些年來已逐漸改變。近幾年，"African-American" 和 "black" 已成為新聞媒體及政府演說與刊物中指稱黑人的最常用語辭。同樣，"Asian-American" 或 "Chinese-American" 通常用於指稱生於美國或現居於美國的亞洲人或中國人。白種人則通常被稱為 "white" 及 "Caucasian"。

組織、歷史事件與時代，以及歷史文件的名稱均大寫。

the Energy Department	the United Nations
the Civil War	World War II
the Treaty of Versailles	the Magna Charta

一星期的七天、月份和假日都需要大寫。

Saturday　November　Independence Day　Valentine's Day

書本、戲劇、影片、電視節目、報紙、雜誌、文章的標題，以及所有的版權、商標名稱或產品，全應大寫。第一個詞以及除了冠詞、連接詞、不定詞to和少於五個字母的介係詞以外的詞都要大寫。標題中長度五個字母以上的介係詞需大寫（例如，About，Before，Between）。另外，出現於刊物標題冒號後面的第一個詞也要大寫。

Electronics	Pearl Harbor	Journal of Heat transfer
People's Daily	The Mirror	Philips

專有名詞前面的職稱為大寫。接在專有名詞後面的學位縮寫和專業證明也是大寫。

President Bush	Dr. Kunio Kuwahara
Professor Wang	X. Z. Meng, Ph.D.
Vice President Byrnes	James Hou, M.D.

任職於法人團體、大學或政府的人員的職稱，若是接於人名之後的說明片語的一部分，則不應大寫。

A. A. Naville, professor of chemistry

F. Richard, director of marketing

R. J. Thompson, general manager

Raymond Chen, director of Strategy and Technology

普通名詞附加於專有名詞之後而形成專有名詞時，其第一個字母必須大寫。這些普通名詞如road，street，park，river，lake，ocean，sea，island等。

Central Park	Stanford University	Springs Road
the Suez Canal	Yellow River	the Riukiu Islands
Silver Lake	Oxford Street	the Red Sea

然而，普通名詞為複數時，其第一個字母不需大寫。

→ He has been to Green and Hyde parks.

→ The policemen were cruising up and down Main and South streets.

④作為科學定律和原理及方法使用的專有名詞必須大寫，但接其後的普通名詞則不需大寫。地質學時期的術語必須大寫，但接於其後的普通名詞則不用大寫。此外，化學元素與化合物的名稱不應大寫。

Newton's laws	Ohm's law	Gibbs equation
the Jurassic era	Euler equation	carbon dioxide

⑤當所指的是同一本書或論文各節的通用標題，如序言（Preface）、導論（Introduction）或附錄（Appendix）時，這些通用標題必須大寫。

→ The explanation for using GA is given in the Appendix.

→ The background of our research was mentioned in the Introduction.

⑥當詞chapter，section和其後的數字合用以說明書或論文中的某章時，並沒有關於chapter，section等詞的大寫通則。許多作者將這些詞看作是專有名詞，因而使用大寫，但某些著名的寫作格式指導手冊則建議這些詞不可大寫。

→ The results and discussion are described in Section 3.

→ The results and discussion are described in section 3.

⑦圖、表格及方程式的名稱通常為大寫，但某些作者喜歡用小寫表示。請作者參閱所投期刊的格式規定，以確定這些名稱是否用大寫。

→ The results of the experiments are shown in Table 2 and Figure 3.

→ The results of the experiments are shown in table 2 and figure 3.

→ The variation of density with temperature is represented by Equation (6).

→ The variation of density with temperature is represented by equation (6).

⑧各方向或季節的名稱不需要大寫。但當東、南、西、北所指為地理區域時，需大寫。

east   north   spring   winter

→ She has lived in the South for ten years.

→ Have you been to the Middle East?

→ The president believes in using a Western management method.

⑨用於替代專有名詞及形容詞的普通名詞及形容詞不用大寫。

→ He graduated from the Ohio State University.

→ He graduated from university.

→ S. F. Li is a graduate student in the EE Department at UBC.

→ Blake is studying Electrical Engineering in graduate school.

⑩撰寫英文文章時，不要隨意使用大寫字母。除了書寫頭字語、字首語、縮寫，以及某些特形容詞詞如某些電腦程式語言的名稱外，不能以大寫的形式書寫所有的字母。頭字語和字首語是由幾個單詞字首組成的縮寫字。頭字語（acronym）在拼音時以縮寫後組成的單字發音，例如Disc Operation System的縮寫是DOS，即發單詞dos的音。字首語（initialism）雖然也是數個單詞的縮寫，但在拼音上是以縮寫字母發音，如Domain Name Server的縮寫是DNS，其發音即字母"D"、"N"、"S"的連續音。

ROM　　COM　　WHO　　ISBN　　GRE　　ISO　　DVD

上述這些頭字語和字首語是由數個單詞的縮寫字組成，每個縮寫字母代表一個詞，所以全都用大寫字母書寫。請注意下面的書寫形式：

FAX　　MODEM　　CROSS Writing Instruments

這種縮寫和名稱因其大寫字母未代表任何詞，所以是錯誤的。它們的正確書寫形式如下：

fax　　modem　　Cross Writing Instruments

在英語文件中，公司名稱應用大寫，但不應全以大寫字母書寫：

誤：The CROSS guarantee extends assurance of a lifetime of writing pleasure to every owner of a CROSS Writing Instrument.

正：The Cross guarantee extends assurance of a lifetime of writing pleasure to every owner of a Cross Writing Instrument.

⑪英語科技論文中圖表大寫詞的用法，存在各種不同的習慣。但不管怎樣，圖表標題第一個詞和表格內每一項目的第一個詞都需大寫。某些期刊的規定中，圖表標題和表格中的每一個詞全都加以大寫（除介係詞、連接詞與冠詞以外）。關於圖表詞的大寫，請參閱所投學術期刊所列的有關規定。

◆ 12.3.2 斜體字（Italics）

①斜體字常用於書籍、雜誌、學術期刊和其他以單行本發行的刊物的題目或名稱（科技論文後面的參考文獻中通常採用此方法），但不用於刊物中的文章或書中的某個章節之類的標題。

American Scientist IEEE Spectrum

The Chicago Manual of Style

A Practical Guide for Advanced Writers in English as a Second Language

Proceedings of Symposium on Energy Engineering in the 21st Century.

Journal of Fluorine Chemistry

②用斜體字標示詞、字母或數字。

→ The first letter in unpermeability is *u*.

→ The secretary often think my 5s look like 6s.

③斜體字用於第一次在文中出現或界定的特殊詞。然而，再次使用這些特殊詞時，不必再以斜體字書寫。

The *renewable energy* is the term used to represent self-renewing energy sources such as sunlight, wind, flowing water, the earth's internal heat, and biomass such as energy crops, agricultural and industrial waste, and municipal waste. The renewable energy can be used to produce electricity for all economic sectors, fuels for transportation, and heat for buildings and industrial processes.

④斜體字用於尚未成為英語一部分的外國詞，如下例中的*Taijiquan*（太極拳）。

The information on the different styles of *Taijiquan* is described in the book.

若一個外來詞（如ad hoc）已列於標準英語詞典中，而且在字典中不以斜體字列出，則不需使用斜體字。

The research center will hold an ad hoc meeting on Monday, July 15.

⑤拉丁文縮寫，如e.g.，et al.，i.e.，cf.，ibid.，及etc.等，傳統上已設定為斜體字。然而，這些拉丁文縮寫，目前多數作者和刊物都使用正體字。

⑥斜體字有時用於強調特殊的詞和片語。

By *December* 31, 2001, the author should submit an English abstract of no more than 150 words, together with paper title, author's name, organization, address, telephone and fax number, and E-mail.

事實上，一些編輯認為，即使上述例句也不需使用斜體字，以避免過度使用斜體字以強調某些詞。在科技論文寫作中，很少需要使用斜體字作強調。

⑦在專業科技期刊和書籍中，數學符號（除向量外）與數學公式通常都使用斜體字表示。其細節要求請按照有關科技期刊和出版社的規定執行。

◆ 12.3.3 粗體字（Bold Print）

粗體字只宜用於科技論文的標題或小標題。一般說來，粗體字不宜用於論文中詞的強調。

粗體字也於標示向量、矩陣等形式的數學符號。

◆ 12.3.4 所有格符號（Apostrophe）

①所有格符號和字母s用於構成單數名詞（無論名詞的末位字母是否為

s）、不定代名詞以及字尾不是s的複數名詞的所有格。

Jane's comb　　　　the women's team　　　everyone's suggestion

Frances's book　　　the dog's plate　　　　Louis's camera

②字尾為s的複數名詞，只需在字尾加上所有格符號即成所有格。

The students' question　　　　the competitors' products

③當具有某物的人和物是由兩個以上的名詞相連組成時，只把最後一個名詞變為所有格形式。當具有某物的人或物在對某物的擁有上是個別擁有時，每一個名詞都必須變為所有格形式。

The director read Albert and Jack's proposal yesterday.

The director read Albert's and Jack's proposal yesterday.

上述第一例句中，只有一份由Albert和John一起寫的計劃書，而在第二例句中，Albert和John各寫了一份計劃書，共有兩份計劃書。

④所有格符號用於表示被省略字母或數字的位置。

do not→ don't　　　　　1999→ '99

it is→ it's　　　　　　I am→ I'm

請注意，日期縮寫（如"October 10, 1998"）的正確形式是"10/10/98"，而不是"10/10/'98"。

⑤所有格符號常用於構成小寫字母（這些小寫字母常以斜體字形式出現）的複數。

x's and y's　　　m's and n's　　　four λ's

所有格符號常用於大寫字母的複數形式，儘管有時會省略所有格符號。

　　　　　five P's　　　　two Ts

　　在片語或複合名詞加標點的縮寫中，所有格符號用於顯示其複數形式。

　　　　　Ph.D.'s　　　　Ms.'s

　　在片語或複合名詞未加標點的縮寫中，其複數形式通常不用所有格符號。

　　　　　CFCs　　LCDs　　two XJ-100s　　five CCDs　　the 1990s

　　不同的英文格式指導書對複數的所有格符號用法上有不同的規則。作者在投稿時，應事先查閱所投期刊的有關規定。

　　⑥若科學定律、理論或數學方程式的名稱中含有人名，則只在未用定冠詞the的情況下，才使用's的所有格形式。若使用了定冠詞the，則不使用所有格符號及緊跟其後的s。

誤：the Ohm's law

正：Ohm's law

正：the Ohm law

誤：the Euler's equation

正：the Euler equation

正：Euler's equation

◆ 12.3.5 斜線號（Virgule或Slash）

　　①斜線號代表用比例的詞per或to，或計量單位合用。斜線號有時也用來取代如at，for或with等詞。

　　　　　a 25/75 split　　8 g/m^3　　　　a price/performance tradeoff

HIV/AIDS   CAD/CAM   U.C./Berkaley

CaO/Ca(OH)$_2$ reaction   Executive Assistant/Finance

②當有兩種選擇並列時，斜線號有時也用於代表詞and或or。

input/output   LCD/FLC   LDV/PIV method

March/April 1979   the research of 1987/88

在英文文章中，有時候以斜線號表示and或or會導致文意模糊不明，此時用and或or代替斜線號，反而會使文章確切清楚。所以作者在撰寫文章時，應注意勿使用斜線號作不必要或不清楚的縮寫，以免嚴重影響文意的清晰性。

③斜線號有時還用作某些縮寫的標點。

c/o (care of)   w/ (with)   w/o (without)

④斜線號有時也用於標點日期和分數。

7/3/98   5/10/99   1/3   △F/F

請注意：在美國，日期的縮寫通常按月、日、年的順序，例如"12/17/88"。但在英國和歐洲大陸，日期的縮寫順序是日、月、年，例如"31/5/89"。

◆ 12.3.6 連字號（Hyphen）

連字號用於構成複合詞或用於表示位於上下行的一個詞的連續性。連字號與破折號不同，連字號（"-"）是較短的橫線，而破折號（"—"）則是較長的線（參閱12.2.4節）。連字號也不同於底線符號，連字號位於字高的中間，而底線符號則位於字行行底。通常在電腦鍵盤上能找到連字號的鍵。連字號直接打在所接字母後面，連字號前後均不需空格。

①連字號用於連接兩個以上的詞，以作為位於名詞前面的形容詞。由

兩個以上詞所組成的形容詞組，若未直接置於所修飾名詞之前，則通常不應使用連字號。

His main contribution was the setting up of a well-measured task for a worker, thus giving him a goal to achieve.

Einstein's theory of relativity is very well known.

有ly字尾的副詞和其他詞之間不應使用連字號。

誤：a rapidly-growing high education

正：a rapidly growing high education

　　②用連字號可以避免字母產生意思混淆或奇怪的組合，例如，recover詞意是重新獲得本身的力量，即康復之意，但re-cover意為再次覆蓋某物。再如，recollect指的是回憶、追想，而re-collect具有重新收集的含義。若對一詞是否需要連字號有疑問時，可查閱字典。

　　③連字號用於構成21到99的複合數字。當分數修飾名詞時，應使用連字號連接分數中的詞。

thirty-five　　　　eighty-eight　　　　three fifth　　　　one half

Brown was elected by a three-fifth majority.

The baby can drink one-half bottle of milk once.

two thirds of the solvent　　　　a three-inch copper plate

④連字號常與某些字首或字尾合用，如self-、ex-及pre-。

anti-G suit　　　　　　　　socio-technical system

self-monitoring function　　ex-president

pre-dection　　　　　　　　passer-by　　　　fore-topsail

◆ 12.3.7 連字號與分節法

當一個詞只有部分可書寫在文章某行的行尾時，此詞可能被分隔成兩部分，後一部分將位於下一行的行首。請注意：詞只能在音節之間分隔，並且必須在被分割的詞中插入連字號以表示中斷的位置；連字號必須放在被分割詞的第一部分後面的行尾，而不是此詞第二部分所在行的行首。

目前大多數文書處理軟體可以自動對詞分音節並插入連字號。若作者需要親手對詞進行分割，請查詢詞典以決定詞的分隔位置。詞典（例如鄭易裡等人修訂的《英華大詞典》，1984）通常利用點將詞分成數個音節，如ob·ser·va·tion，sim·u·la·tion，prob·a·bil·i·ty，kil·o·me·ter等

此外，請記住關於斷詞方法的下述兩條規則：千萬不要分割僅有一個音節的詞；勿分隔只有一個字母會留在某行的詞。

誤：de-al   pea-rl   sp-eed   hea-th

正：deal   pearl   speed   heath

誤：a-gency   o-mit   creak-y

正：agency   omit   creaky

12.4 方程式的標點符號

當數學方程式或公式和句子其餘部分分隔開來，並單獨列為一行時，若句子的結構需要標點，則有些期刊規定方程式或公式後面應加句號或逗號。請參考下述兩個例子。

The partical devolatilization is modeled by considering a pair of parallel first order reactions:

$$(\text{raw coal}) \xrightarrow{k_1} (1-Y_1)(\text{char})+Y_1(\text{volatiles})$$

$$(\text{raw coal}) \xrightarrow{k_2} (1-Y_2)(\text{char})+Y_2(\text{volatiles}).$$

這個例子的第二個公式位於句尾，因此 "Y_2(volatiles)" 之後有句號似

乎符合要求。下面是第二個例子。

For pulverized coal, the total energy balance equation can be expressed as

$$\frac{\mathrm{d}}{\mathrm{d}t}(M_p C_p T_p) = C_p T_p \frac{\mathrm{d}M_p}{\mathrm{d}t} + Q_{pc} + Q_{pr} + Q_{pb} \ ,$$

where Q_{pc}, Q_{pr} and Q_{pb} represent heat transfer by conduction, thermal radiation, and chemical reaction.

在這個例子中，詞where…reaction是修飾方程式的非限定關係子句，所以在文法上，Q_{pb}後面應有一個逗號。

對於和句子其他部分區隔開來的方程式或公式而言，標點符號的使用並沒有硬性的統一規定。有些學者認為在方程式與公式後面應使用標點符號，他們覺得標點符號有助於釐清句子的文法結構，可增強文章的可讀性。此外，為防止讀者有誤解，某些例子需要標點符號。另一些學者認為含有方程式和公式的句子對於讀者來說不難理解，而且在含有大量數學式的文章中太多標點符號的使用會使頁面擁擠，故他們往往省略方程式或公式後的標點符號。建議論文作者先查閱所投期刊的有關格式規定，再確定論文中是否應在方程式或公式之後加注標點符號。

未和句子其餘部分區隔開來的方程式或公式，若所在句子的結構有所要求，則應使用標點符號，否則不用。

→ The last term $G_E = -K \sum\limits_k n_k m_k$ is the production term due to mass change of coal particles.

→ However, the data from the different nozzles lie well along the line $S_t = 0.0037L^* - 0.004b$.

→ The Ntu, or number of transfer unt, is defined as $Ntu = UA/C_{min}$, where U is obtained from Eq.(3), whilst A is the heat exchange area of heat exchanger.

介紹方程式時要用完整的句子。如下例中，詞then不是完整的句子，應加以改寫。

誤：When designing an attenuator, we already know R_1, R_2, and P_1/P_2. Then：
（下接方程式）

正：When designing an attenuator, we already know R_1, R_2, and P_1/P_2. Thus we have the following equation:

另外，在研究論文中，方程式的號碼常常位於和方程式同一行、靠近右邊界的括弧內。方程式與方程式號碼之間的空格應為空白，勿在方程式及其號碼之間放置虛線或一連串的連字號。

12.5 數字

英文數字和阿拉伯數字的使用規則隨文章屬性的不同而有所變化。如適用於報紙的規則與適用於出版社的規則有所不同，而這兩種規則也可能都和應用於科技期刊的規則不一樣。但是，科技論文的作者應當遵循下述關於英文數字和阿拉伯數字的一般規則。

①科技論文中，十以下的整數通常應用詞表示，如one，two，three等。

佳：In 25 years of continuing development in chip-processing technology the number of transistors on the chip has at least doubled every two years.

差：The department has received 5 applications.

本規則的例外是：在物理量前面通常使用阿拉伯數字，而且若物理量是用縮寫或符號方式表示，則必須使用阿拉伯數字。

差：The two samples were both one m long and each weighed about three kg.

佳：The two samples were both 1 m long and each weighed about 3 kg.

若在同一個句子中或段落中出現兩個以上有比較性質的數字，則數字的表達形式應一致，而且其表達形式通常以最大數字的形式為准。

佳：In this class, 3 of the 24 students failed in an examination in geography.

差：In this class, three of the 24 students failed in an examination in geography.

　　②切勿以阿拉伯數字作為句子的開端。若句子必須以數字開始，則要使用英文數字；否則需改寫句子，使阿拉伯數字處在除句首之外的其他位置。

差：12 academicians attended the conference.

佳：Twelve academicians attended the conference.

佳：There were 12 academicians at the conference.

　　③阿拉伯數字可用於表示時間、金額、計量值、以及小數或百分比。

　　7：30 p.m.　　3：16　　68% 或 68 percent

　　£ 10.99　　3 mm　　7.87　　3.1415

　　請注意，o'clock（點鍾）之前的數字只能是英文數字，如 "eight o' clock"，不能寫成 "8 o'clock"。另外，百分比符號之前不需空格。

　　④論文中大於十的序數詞可以縮寫，小於十的序數詞不能縮寫。

誤：1st, 2nd, 3rd

正：first, second, third

正：21st, 42nd, 96th

　　⑤小於一的分數必須用詞表示。

　　One-half litre of wine　　　　one third of the voters

　　⑥一百萬以上的數字應同時使用阿拉伯數字和英文數字。

→ The company produced 2 million cameras in 1996.

→ The 32nd ExCom Meeting approved US $13.5 million for UNDP projects that will phase out 2,163 ODP tones/year.

　　⑦書籍中的章節和頁碼通常用阿拉伯數字書寫。文章中的圖號和表號

也常用阿拉伯數字書寫。

See chapter 5　　　　in Figure 9

The result is discussed on page 5 in section 4.

⑧在表示單位的符號或縮寫之前的數字應用阿拉伯數字，且在阿拉伯數字與符號或縮寫之間通常需一個空格。

a 2 MB cache memory

7 MHz

273 K

注意，上述最後一個例子中的"K"是"Kelvin"（絕對溫標）的縮寫，它不需像華氏溫標（℉）或攝氏溫標（℃）中的度（"°"）的符號。

⑨書寫複合數字形容詞時，其中第一個數字應用英文詞，第二個數字應以阿拉伯數字表示。

誤：12 256 K SRAMS

正：twelve 256 K SRAMS

⑩不可以在英文數字後面加上括弧重複書寫數字。但在法律或商業性的文件中有例外。

誤：He selected five (5) samples.

正：He selected five samples.

例外：On September 19, we sent you an order for seven (7) sensor amplifiers.

（在某些法律或商業性的特殊文件才可使用）

⑪使用阿拉伯數字書寫日期時，只能是基數形式，雖然日期必須讀成

序數。

誤：David Starr Jordan, Stanford's first president, addressed the crowd at the university's opening ceremonies on October 1st, 1891.

正：David Starr Jordan, Stanford's first president, addressed the crowd at the university's opening ceremonies on October 1, 1891.

12.6 複數

大多數英文名詞的複數是由名詞的單數形式加上s構成。字尾為s，x，z，sh或ch的名詞，是在其單數名詞詞尾加上es以構成複數，原因是這些名詞需要一個額外的音節以方便複數名詞的發音。字尾為y而y之前是輔音的名詞，其複數是將y改成i並加上es而構成。以f或fe結尾的名詞，多數先把f變為v，再加es（如half→halves，life→lives，shelf→shelves）；少數不發生音變（如foot→feet，tooth→teeth，woman→women）。有的名詞單、複數形式一致，沒有變化（如means，series）。還有些名詞無單數形式（如scales，pliers，shears，scissors），若要用作單數時，需在這些名詞前加a pair of等量詞。

要獲知特殊名詞的正確複數形式，需查詢字典。若名詞有不規則或變化的複數，詞典會列出其複數形式。若詞典上未列出所查名詞的複數形式，則該名詞的複數形式複合上述規則。本節介紹一些關於複數構成的特殊規則，對這些規則的掌握有助於科技論文的寫作。

①外來語的複數形式通常保留其在外語中的複數形式。但不少此類名詞的複數也可寫成單數名詞加s或es的形式。

antenna→antennas或antennae

formula→formulae

datum→data

index→indices（指數），indexes（索引）

helix→helices

basis→bases

phenomenon→phenomena

thesis→theses

medium→media

radius→radii

appendix→appendices或appendixes

②英文字母斜體字及片語的複數通常是由加上's構成

a series of *x*'s and *y*'s　　　six *M*'s and *N*'s in the matrix

three *yes*'s and five *no*'s

③雖然有些編輯選擇用's來表示數字的複數形式，但通常是在單數形式的後面只加上s。此外，英文數字的複數形式通常只在字尾加s，而不加所有格符號。

the 1980s　　　　　　　an order for ten XJ-100s

two 2s and three 3s　　He threw three sevens in a row.

④字尾為句號的單一詞縮寫，在句號前面加s即構成複數。

fig.→figs.　　tab.→tabs.　　sec.→secs.

⑤片語或複合語詞標了點的縮寫，在其最後句點後面加上's即構成複數。片語或複合語詞未標點的縮寫，其複數形式則是直接在縮寫後面加上s。

Ph.D.→ Ph.D.'s　　DRAM→ DRAMs

⑥非測量單位的小寫單一字母的縮寫，其複數是重複該字母而構成。

　　pp. (pages)　　　cc. (copies)

而測量單位的小寫單一字母的縮寫，其複數形式與單數形式相同。

　　10cc　　30min.　　55mm　　40sec.

⑦以非意義使用的詞，其複數形式通常是在單數字尾加上's。

change the effect's to affect's

replace all of these &'s with and's

⑧一個接有複數受詞的of介係詞片語所修飾的名詞，可能是單數也可能是複數，完全視句子的意義和強調點而定。

→ The value of t, p, m, H, and M should be recorded in the experiment.

→ The values of t, p, m, H, and M should be recorded in the experiment.

這兩個句子都是正確的。第一句中，實驗中需記錄的是 "The value of t, that of p, that of m, etc."。第二句中，需記錄的是 "The value of all of these parameters: t, p, m, etc."。兩者的含義都很明確，而且是一致的。

⑨若一個符號作為某個名詞的限定同位語，則不可同時以複數表示此名詞和符號。

誤：From the analysis we obtain the error signals δ 's.

正：From the analysis we obtain the values of the error signal δ .

正：From the analysis we obtain the values of δ .

⑩當某一數字後面接有物理量單位時，除非前面的數字正好是一，否則該物理量單位通常應以複數形式寫出。

　　6.3 inches　　　0.5 microns

0.7 degrees   0.35 liters

物理量單位只有在單獨使用時，才以複數形式表示。若物理量單位後面接有名詞，則寫成單數，且此物理量單位需以連字號與其前面的數字連結起來。

a 0.5-micron manufacturing process

an 8-inch silicon wafer

⑪當the number of用於表示"how many"的含義時，不可寫成複數。見下面第一句例句。當the number of用於表示某一特定的數目時，則可寫成複數形式，見下面的第二個例句。

→ They wish to determine the number of the students who will visit Seoul National University in the summer vacation.

→ What are the numbers of those three candidates?

12.7 專業術語的縮寫

科技論文中採用專業術語的縮寫形式時，應將首次出現在論文中的專業術語完整地拼寫出來，並在其後接以帶括弧的縮寫。此後，相同的專業術語可只以縮寫表示。

Both the Ozone Depletion Potential (ODP) and the energy efficiency of substitutes and alternative technologies are determining factors in the selection of replacement refrigerants. Compared to the direct Global Warming Potential (GWP) of the replacement chemicals, the global warming of the carbon dioxide emitted in operating the stationary refrigeration and air conditioning equipment is greater by at least one order of magnitude. In domestic refrigeration the direct GWP will be in the order of some percent of the Total Equivalent Warming Impact (TEWI).

經過對 "ODP"、"GWP" 及 "TEWI" 縮寫的清晰定義，作者可在其後只使用這些縮寫，因為讀者已明白這些縮寫的含義。

12.8 其他

在正式的英文中，請勿以and的記號 "&" 來代替and。而在某些期刊的列出的格式規定中允許使用 "&" 記號。請作者查閱所投期刊的有關規定。

在英文中，請勿使用 "～" 這個符號來表示to的意思，因為這個符號不是標準的英文標點符號。需要代表to的時候，必須使用en-dash（"－"）。en-dash是短橫線，它比破折號（em-dash）（"—"）稍短，單比連字號 "-" 長些。也可使用減號或連字號代替en-dash，或把英文字to拼寫出來。

誤：the 2001～2002 academic year

正：the 2001－2002 academic year

注意在下列例句中應將冒號置於括弧陳述內容之後。

誤：The contents of this register are shown below: (for RGB mode and 24-bit YC_bC_r mode)

正：The contents of this register are shown below (for RGB mode and 24-bit YC_bC_r mode) :

13 常見詞及片語的用法

本章主要討論在英文科技論文中一些常見的、也容易誤用的詞和片語的正確用法。在使用這些常見詞和片語時，既要顧及到文法的正確性，又要注意寫作風格的適宜性。

◆ A, an

一個名詞前使用不定冠詞a還是an，取決於其後跟著的名詞的第一個音是否為母音，並非取決於名詞的第一個字母是否為母音字母。若名詞的第一個音是子音，則使用不定冠詞a，若名詞的第一個音是母音，則應用不定冠詞an。

→ A capacitor   a unified appro   ach a student
→ An X-ray   an hour   an electronic computer

◆ A lot of

A lot of 是口語表達形式，在正式論文中應避免使用，而應改用many，much或a great deal of 等表達「許多」的意思。

◆ Above

Above可用於指稱前面提到的資料，不過應以一個段落或前幾個句子中曾出現過的資料為限。Above不能用來說明前幾個段落甚至前幾頁中曾經出現的資料，因為讀者會感到迷惑，不清楚above所指資料是什麼。

→ The above explanation will help answer this question.

若剛提及該解釋，則這是正確的寫法，否則就應該用下列寫法

→ We can adopt the explanation introduced earlier to answer this question.

→ We can apply the explanation introduced in Section 2 to answer this question.

◆ Adopt, adapt

Adopt與adapt這兩個詞容易被混淆在一起。Adopt具有「採用」或「沿用」的意思，然而adapt卻是「適應」、「修改」等之意。

→ We shall adopt Howard's method, but we must adapt it slightly so that the experiment will be conducted at a higher pressure.

◆ Affect

不要把affect與effect兩個詞混淆在一起。Affect是及物動詞，其意思是「影響」、「對……起作用」。然而effect可以是動詞，也可以作名詞。當effect作動詞時，其意思是「實現」、「達到」、「引起」、「產生」。當effect作名詞時，其意思是「效果」、「操作」。在科技論文中，effect常被用作名詞。

→ Changing the concentration of the solution affected the reaction rate.

→ Changing the concentration of the solution had effect on the reaction rate.

◆ Aforementioned

在撰寫科技論文時，應該避免如aforementioned或hereinafter之類的古語。在當代英文中，這類古語僅出現在某些正式的法律文件中。

生硬：They will now apply the aforementioned algorithm to carry out the calculation.

自然：They will now apply the algorithm described above to carry out the calculation.

自然：They will now apply the proposed algorithm to carry out the calculation.

生硬：This set will hereinafter be referred to as set S.

自然：This set will be referred to below as set S.

自然：We will refer to this set as set S.

◆ Alternate, alternative

Alternate具有「輪流」、「交替發生或出現」之意；而alternative卻表示「二者中擇一」或「數種可能之一」。Alternately是「先取其一，然後再另取一個」之意；而alternatively卻是「另作選擇」之意。在提出另一個可能的選擇時，通常使用alternative或alternatively，而不使用alternate。

→ You have the alternative of working hard and being successful or if not working hard and being unsuccessful.

→ Alternatively, we can adopt the following algorithm.

◆ Although

Although將讓步副詞子句與主句連接起來時，不能在句子中同時出現although和but兩個連接詞，必須在這兩個連接詞中選擇一個使用，並把另一個刪除。

誤：Although the new process has many advantages, but there are some weak points in it.

正：Although the new process has many advantages, there are some weak points in it.

正：The new process has many advantages, but there are some weak points in it.

◆ Among, between

Among這個介係詞表示三者以上之間的關係，或表示某事物和其他許多事物之間的關係。Between則是指某種相對或一對一的關係，而不論關係者的數目，尤其是當有三方發生關係而每兩方之間需分別考慮時。所以不要以為只要說三個以上事物之間的關係，就必須使用among。在科技論文中，between和among常用。

→ Among all the metals iron is the most widely used engineering metal.

→ What is the difference between a mixture and a compound?

→ Early man did not know how to explain the difference between gases, solids and liquids.

一般說來，想表示「從幾個可能的選擇中選出其中一個」，應該使用 from among。

→ Choose a book from among this.

→ This algorithm selects the optimal solution from among all possible dynamic alignment patterns.

◆ Amount, number

A large amount of 後接不可數名詞，而a large number of 後接可數名詞。

→ A large amount of oxygen was added to the system.

→ A large number of samples are used for our experiments.

◆ And

英文句子通常不應以and開頭。不過，有些資深的作者會違反這個規則，以便產生某種特殊效果。儘管如此，科技論文中還是不要把and放在句首。

差：And the purpose of decision making is to direct human behavior towards a future goal. If there were no alternatives, there would be no need for a decision.

佳：Moreover, the purpose of decision making is to direct human behavior towards a future goal. If there were no alternatives, there would be no need for a decision.

◆ And /or

And /or是意義含混不清的表達方式。要麼兩者擇一，要麼採用or⋯or both的形式。

模糊：The application of this new refrigerant may improve the EER and/or reliability of the air conditioner.

清楚：The application of this new refrigerant may improve the EER and reliability of the air conditioner.

清楚：The application of this new refrigerant may improve the EER or reliability of the air conditioner.

◆ Anymore

在科技論文中，含有anymore及否定動詞的句子，應該改寫成no longer 與肯定動詞組合的句子。

差：The humidifier does not work anymore.

佳：The humidifier no longer works.

◆ Apparently

這個詞的意思是「顯然」、「宛然」、「儼然」，但往往暗指「似乎（但不確定）」、「似乎（但未必）為真」。為避免模糊起見，科技論文中，不要用apparently來表示clearly或obviously之意。

模糊：Apparently, different fuel cell operation temperatures correspond to different optimal cycle configurations.

清楚：Clearly, different fuel cell operation temperatures correspond to different optimal cycle configurations.

清楚：Obviously, different fuel cell operation temperatures correspond to different optimal cycle configurations.

◆ Appendix

　　若著作、論文或研究報告只有一個附錄，則在文章中應該使用the Appendix（Appendix之前有定冠詞）。若有兩個以上的附錄，則該用 Appendix A，Appendix B等（或Appendix Ⅰ，Appendix Ⅱ等）來指稱這些附錄，而且Appendix前可不加定冠詞。

誤：The properties of various materials used in the design and analysis of heat pipes are presented in the Appendix C.

正：The properties of various materials used in the design and analysis of heat pipes are presented in Appendix C.

◆ Approach

　　Approach作為及物動詞使用時，其後千萬別緊接介係詞to。

誤：When x increased, the value of the function approaches to zero.

正：When x increased, the value of the function approaches zero.

　　Approach作為名詞使用時，後面常緊跟介係詞to及另一個名詞或動名詞。該名詞或動名詞片語是用來修飾名詞approach的。例如：

→ Dr. Kasten proposed a new approach to solving this problem.

句子中to solving this problem這個介係詞片語用來修飾approach。若將此片語改成to solve this problem，則此動詞不定詞片語是用來修飾動詞propose。兩者的作用不同，句子的意思自然也有區別。

◆ As

　　單個as引出的子句有：時間子句，原因子句，讓步子句，比較子句，方式副詞子句和形容詞子句。As引出的原因子句，它與主句一般有明顯的因果關係。利用這一點，就可以把as引導的原因子句和時間子句區別開來，請看下面兩例。

→ We cannot see sound waves as they travel through air.

→ As heat energy makes things move, it is a form of energy.

第一個例句中，as引出的是時間副詞子句；第二個例句中，as引導的是原因副詞子句，因為子句與主句有明顯的因果關係。不過，建議在英文科技論文中應儘量避免使用as表示「因為」、「由於」的意思，以免模稜兩可。

◆ As follows

As follows，the following，as shown below都是正確的形式，而"as followings"，"as the followings"，"as below"等都是不正確的形式。

正：Solutions for equation (1) and (2) can be derived as follows：

正：This results in the following expression：

正：Commonly used methods include the following：

As follows作為非限定的修飾詞使用時，前面需加逗號。As follows和the following後面通常緊跟一個冒號。然而，在某些情況下，也可以使用句號。一般說來，若as follows或the following所介紹的內容很少，如一個或數個數學式，則後面就需加冒號。若他們所介紹的東西很長，如很長的例子或演算方法，則應緊跟一個句號。

通常不使用as follows來介紹論文中新的小節。在結束一個小節、開始新的小節之前，常用"We will discuss this problem below"或"We will discuss this problem in the next section"之類的句子結束，而不會以"We will discuss this problem as follows"結尾。

◆ As mentioned above, as mentioned previously

這兩個片語的用法有些不同。As mentioned previously（或as mentioned earlier）通常用來指幾個段落或幾頁前所提到的內容。而as mentioned above通常用來指前一、二段中剛敘述的內容。另外，作者想指明前幾個句子所提到的內容時，也可使用as just mentioned。

建議撰寫科技論文的作者盡可能使用較準確的詞來代替as mentioned above或as mentioned earlier。例如，若作者指的是上一節中的內容，則可用 "as mentioned in the preceding section" 來表達，而不用as mentioned above。

◆ As you know, as we know

不管句子的內容如何，這兩個插入片語肯定是累贅的，因此，在科技論文中，千萬不要使用它們。

◆ As well as

這個並列連詞的意思與and不盡相同。用as well as連接兩個並列成分時，重點在前面一項，即其用意在於強調其前面的名詞。We can turn electric energy into light energy as well as into heat energy.（我們能把電能轉化為熱能，也能轉化為光能。）

He can operate a grinder as well as a lathe.（他不僅能開車床，而且也能開磨床。）上面二個例子中，強調分別是「轉化為光能」及「開磨床」。

◆ Aspect

在英文科技論文中，aspect及area之類的詞，常常是累贅的而應該加以省略的詞。

累贅：Regarding the application aspect of Genetic Algorithm, many approaches have been proposed.

累贅：In the area of application of Genetic Algorithm, many approaches have been proposed.

簡潔：Many approaches to application of Genetic Algorithm have been proposed.

簡潔：Many applications of Genetic Algorithm have been proposed.

◆ Assume

Assume這個動詞後面不應該緊跟as。正確的書寫形式應該是assume to be。

誤：The main steam pressure is assumed as 3 MPa owing to the limit of the steam quality at the turbine exit.

正：The main steam pressure is assumed to be 3 MPa owing to the limit of the steam quality at the turbine exit.

正：We assume that the main steam pressure is 3 MPa owing to the limit of the steam quality at the turbine exit.

◆ Assure

請參閱ensure。

◆ At

科技論文中，下列片語中at的用法都是不正確的：at Table 2，at Figure 4，at row y in the matrix。正確的方法是使用介係詞in，如in Table 2，in Figure 4，in row y in the matrix。

◆ At first

At first和first的意思完全不同。At first之意為「起初」，表示句子所表述的情形已因時間而改變；而first則是指一系列項目、事件或步驟中的第一個行為或事物。

→ At first he planned to discuss the first paper with Dr. Smith, but later he decided to discuss the second paper with Mr. Huxley.

◆ At last

不要把at last和last混淆在一起。At last之意為「終於」，然而last卻是指一系列項目、事件或步驟中的最後一個行為或事物。

→ At last they reached the last building on the street.

◆ Based on

若句首出現以based on開頭的過去分詞片語，則必須注意過去分詞表示的被動行為對象是句子中的主詞。然而，在絕大多數以based on開頭的句子中，based on開頭的過去分詞片語卻不能合理地修飾句子的主詞。由此看來，還是應該用on the basis of, by, from, according to或其他詞來替代based on，否則就需要重寫句子，以便使讀者清楚地瞭解是什麼的「基礎」。

誤：Based on Eq. (6), it is obtained that⋯.

正：From Eq. (6), it is obtained that⋯.

正：Eq. (8) entails that⋯.

差：Based on the experimental results, we conclude that⋯.

佳：On the basis of the experimental results, we conclude that⋯.

佳：From the experimental results, we conclude that⋯.

佳：The experimental results show that⋯.

差：Based on the conventional method using Lagrange multipliers, the closed form solution can be written as follows.

佳：According to the conventional method using Lagrange multipliers, the closed form solution can be written as follows.

佳：If we apply the conventional method using Lagrange multipliers, we can write the closed form solution as follows.

若以based on開頭的分詞片語確實可以修飾句子的主詞，則把based on開頭的片語放在句首是正確的做法（不過這種情況很少見）。例如，在下列例句中，以based on開頭的片語就可以正確地修飾句子的主詞。這個句子的含意是Nikon Cool Pix 995照相機是以"advanced digital technology"為基礎的。

→ Based on advanced digital technology, the Nikon Cool Pix 995 camera provides the excellent performances.

此外，-based之類的詞尾，有時可用於縮短很長的名詞片語，如"a computer system that is based on an 8084b microprocessor"縮短成"an 8084b-based computer system"。請注意，第一次使用這個名詞片語時，應將其完整的形式寫出，而且，在實際應用時，要儘量避免使用如-based這種字尾的詞，而應該使用更清楚精確的詞。

◆ Basically

在大多數英文句子中，basically這個詞是個模糊的修飾詞，而且是個應加以省略的詞。千萬不要濫用。

累贅：There are basically two types of new simulation method.

簡潔：There are two types of new simulation method.

簡潔：There are two basic types of new simulation method.

◆ Because of the fact that

Because of the fact that是個冗長、累贅的片語。其中of the fact that應省略，僅寫because即可。

冗長：Because of the fact that electricity can change into other forms of energy, it is widely used in industry.

簡潔：Because electricity can change into other forms of energy, it is widely used in industry.

◆ Because that

Because後面緊跟that，是不符合英文文法的用法

誤：Because that no machine ever runs without some friction, overcoming that friction wastes energy.

正：Because no machine ever runs without some friction, overcoming that friction wastes energy.

誤：This is because that the direct current flows in a wire always in one direction.

正：This is because the direct current flows in a wire always in one direction.

◆ Because … so

在一個句子中，不能同時使用because和so。應該在兩者中選擇一個，並把另一個去除。

誤：Because our home market was too small to support economic lamp production, so we have had to export our products from our earliest days.

正：Because our home market was too small to support economic lamp production, we have had to export our products from our earliest days.

正：Our home market was too small to support economic lamp production, so we have had to export our products from our earliest days.

◆ Become

英文中的become這個詞的用法與中文的「成為」不完全相同，撰寫英文科技論文時要特別對此加以注意。當描述某種改變時，可用become這個動詞。若只陳述某個普遍的事實，並非強調某種變化，則不應使用become，而應使用to be。

差：A three dimensional CFD code, TASCflow developed by AEA technology becomes the effective tool in the present study.

佳：A three dimensional CFD code, TASCflow developed by AEA technology is the effective tool in the present study.

　　若需用become來描述從過去到現在的某種改變，則應該採用現在完成式，即to have become。然而，在反映事實或過程的一般規律時，也可以用現在簡單式。

誤：Air conditioners become more widely used in families in recent years.

正：Air conditioners have become more widely used in families in recent years.

正：Before they can become law, proposal for legislation must be approved by both Houses of Parliament-the elected House of Commons and the House of Lords.

◆ Belong

　　在英文中，belong通常表示屬某人的財產（後加to）和應歸入某部類（後加to, among, in, under, with）和適合的意思。但在科技論文中，想要表示某個項目屬於某種類型時，通常不使用"belong"，改用"to fall into the category of"，"to be a form of"或"to be classified as"。

→ The building belongs to the college.

→ The house belongs to Mr. Benson.

→ This problem can be classified as a nonlinear programming problem.

→ This problem is a type of nonlinear programming problem.

◆ Besides

　　在正式的英文文章中，不宜用連接副詞besides來表達「此外」之意，應該使用in addition，moreover或furthermore。

差：Besides, sending these messages electronically eliminates the need for 100 pieces of paper that people glance at and throw away.

佳：In addition, sending these messages electronically eliminates the need for 100 pieces of paper that people glance at and throw away.

佳：Moreover, sending these messages electronically eliminates the need for 100 pieces of paper that people glance at and throw away.

◆ Better

在英文科技論文中，當我們比較兩個事物的時候，最好不要告訴讀者其中一個比另一個「更好」（"better"），而應該使用更精確的詞。

模糊：The gas turbine is better than the steam engine.

精確：The gas turbine is more efficient than the steam engine.

模糊：Our algorithm is better than the conventional one.

精確：Our algorithm is faster than the conventional one.

◆ Build

在大多數科技論文中，使用construct比使用build更恰當，因為construct的意思也是「建造」，但是它另外有按照一定的而且往往是比較複雜的計劃進行建造的意思，如construct a bridge，construct a theory。

差：Architects, engineers, and carpenters are needed to build a skyscraper.

佳：Architects, engineers, and carpenters are needed to construct a skyscraper.

◆ But

通常英文句子不應以but開頭。不過，與and一樣，為了產生某種特殊效果，有些資深的作者偶爾會違反這個規則。在科技論文中，若需在句首表示「然而」或「但是」之意，則應該使用however。

不恰當：Among many engineers and the general public, ammonia is notorious for its toxicity and flammability. But these problems can be overcome in commercial air conditioning application.

恰　當：Among many engineers and the general public, ammonia is notorious for its toxicity and flammability. However, these problems can be overcome in commercial air conditioning application.

◆ Call

在call後面不能加as，但refer to後面必須用as。

誤：They will call this installation as Heat Pump Dryer (HPD).

正：They will call this installation Heat Pump Dryer (HPD).

正：They will refer to this installation as Heat Pump Dryer (HPD).

◆ Called

科技論文的作者常常用called來介紹新的術語或某個事物的別稱。但是，此時called有時候卻可以加以省略。

原　句：An increase in the natural greenhouse effect, called global warming, refers to the physical phenomenon that may lead to heating of the earth.

修正句：An increase in the natural greenhouse effect, global warming, refers to the physical phenomenon that may lead to heating of the earth.

◆ Can

可以用「可以」來造出通順的中文句子。但是在某些情況下，為簡潔起見，英文句子中can常常可以被省略。

累贅：The finite element formulations can be expressed in the non-dimensional form as follows.

簡潔：The finite element formulations are expressed in the non-dimensional form as follows.

在正式的英文文章中，can作「能、會」解，表示能力之意；否定為

cannot。如下列第一、二例句。而may則表示可能性或允許之意，見下列第三、四例句。兩者不能混用。

→ Electricity can drive motor.

→ He cannot operate the computer.

→ It may take too much time to solve the problem.

→ May I use this instrument to measure?

◆ Case

Case作「情況」、「事例」等解時，緊跟在名詞case後面的關係代名詞或關係副詞，必須使用in which的形式或when，而不能使用that。有些資深作者也會用關係副詞where，但非常少見。

誤：Let us now examine the case that the mass flow rate of air is smaller than 3 kg/s.

正：Let us now examine the case in which the mass flow rate of air is smaller than 3 kg/s.

◆ Change

若change用於描述某物或某現象在一段長時間內的變化，則change後面的介係詞應該是in，而不是of。

差：The changes of the liquid pressure in the cylinder were measured every two minutes.

佳：The changes in the liquid pressure in the cylinder were measured every two minutes.

◆ Choose … as

注意使用choose … as或select … as的正確方法。

誤：We choose the fan diameter of the prototype heat exchanger as six inches.

正：We choose six inches as the fan diameter of the prototype heat exchanger.

除此之外，下列寫法也是正確的。

→ We specify the fan diameter of the prototype heat exchanger as six inches.

→ The fan diameter of the prototype heat exchanger is specified as six inches.

→ The fan diameter of the prototype heat exchanger is set to be six inches.

◆ Classical, traditional, conventional

這些形容詞的用法在某些情況下大同小異，但三個詞的意思有些差異。Classical這個詞強調所指的理論或方法是經過時間的考驗而證明為有價值的，被學者廣為承認的。Traditional是指「傳統」或「慣例」，通常表示某個理論或方法使用已久，目前仍有人在使用，不過或許有人已提出更新的理論與方法。Conventional則表示時下最流行的理論與方法，而不反映這個理論與方法已存在多長時間。一個學者使用"conventional"這個詞來形容某種方法，就意味著此學者知道（或自己打算提出）更先進的方法。

原　句：The proposed architecture is more efficient than the traditional design, which was originally developed by researchers at IBM in 1993.

修正句：The proposed architecture is more efficient than the conventional design, which was originally developed by researchers at IBM in 1993.

◆ Compare

Compare…to是指兩個根本不同的事物的相同之處（如功能）。而compare …with則用於比較兩個相同事物的相異之處。在科技論文中，compare …with應比compare …to常用，尤其是作者在比較不同的資料和結果時。

→ The flow pattern around the tip clearance is compared with smoke　wire flow visualization by Goldstein.

◆ Compensate

Compensate後面加直接受詞時，直接受詞應是受到補償的人或事物。若compensate表達「補充」或「抵消」的意思，則其後通常需加上介係詞for，而不能加直接受詞。

誤：This mechanism compensates the slower speed of the genetic algorithm.

正：This mechanism compensates for the slower speed of the genetic algorithm.

正：The boss compensated the staff for their extra efforts by paying a bonus at the end of the year.

◆ Complete

Complete是及物動詞，可以有被動語態。

→ The students completed a circuit experiment on Friday.

→ The numerical simulation for the system performance was completed three weeks ago.

◆ Comprise

Comprise有「包含」、「包括」、「由……組成」之意。它是個及物動詞，後面應跟直接受詞。英文中，沒有is comprised of這樣的形式。

誤：A refrigeration system is comprised of four main components.

正：A refrigeration system comprises four main components.

正：A refrigeration system consists of four main components.

正：A refrigeration system is composed of four main components.

正：Four main components constitute a refrigeration system.

◆ Conclusion

科技論文中，常用state conclusion或present conclusions這樣的動詞受詞搭配，而不用make conclusions或give conclusions這樣的搭配形式。有時

候，作者只需使用conclude這個動詞，即可避免一些不自然的表達方式。

差：Finally, we make a conclusion in section 5.

佳：Finally, we state a conclusion in section 5.

差：The final section of the paper gives the conclusion.

佳：The final section states the conclusion of the paper.

佳：Section 5 concludes the paper.

◆ Consider

Consider有兩個不同的含意。一個是表示「相信」、「視為」之意，另一個表示「評價」、「討論」或「考慮」之意。表示這兩種意思的方式是有區別的。

若consider的含意是「相信」或「視為」，則其後不應加as，有些作者會用consider to be這樣的寫法。然而，regard as及view as都是正確的形式。

誤：For practical purpose, the wall temperature may be considered as a constant.

正：For practical purpose, the wall temperature may be considered a constant.

正：For practical purpose, the wall temperature may be regarded as a constant.

若consider表示「評價」、「討論」或「考慮」之意，則其後可加as。

→ The committee considered the student as one of the candidates for joining the co-operative research.

◆ Contrary

請參閱on the contrary。

◆ Currently

請參閱recently。

◆ Criteria

Criteria是複數形式，其單數形式為criterion。"criterions" 是不正確的複數形式。

→ These criteria are only a starting point for evaluating software. Many other points about organization and software development will be covered in part IV.

→ The applicability of the Laminar-transitional criterion for liquids was investigated.

◆ Data

Data是datum的複數形式。

→ The data have been received using ScnsaDyne PC500-LV Surface Tensionmeter System.

◆ Decide

Decide常用於作「選擇」或「判斷」之意。若要表示「確定」、「辨識」、「定義」之意，則用determine較為恰當。

→ They decided to use this instrument to measure pressure.

→ They determine a date for a meeting to discuss the project.

→ The expert system, called the Packaging Advisor, helps determine the quantities required to meet performance requirement.

◆ Defect

Defect不僅具有「缺陷」的意思，而且可以指「瑕疵」或「毛病」。在科技論文中，defect用於指出某方法或系統的缺點有點不夠自然，因為即使該方法或系統不很理想，但它未必有明顯的毛病。此時可用shortcoming，disadvantage或drawback以表示「缺點」之意。

原　句：Stanley's method of analysis of market trends has two major defects.

修正句：Stanley's method of analysis of market trends has two major shortcomings.

修正句：Stanley's method of analysis of market trends has two major drawbacks.

◆ Defined

被動語態to be defined的句子中，若其後緊跟定義的具體內容，則應使用介係詞as。然而，若其後緊跟表示方式等副詞介係詞片語，則應該使用介係詞in或by，請參閱下例。

誤：The variable θ is defined as equation (4).

正：The variable θ is defined in equation (4).

正：The variable θ is defined by equation (4).

若作者想說明前面已定義過的變數或名詞，則可以使用下面的句型。

→ The solution is 3θ, where θ is as defined in equation(4).

→ The solution is 3θ, where θ is defined as in equation(4).

此外，definition之後的介係詞是of。

→ The definition of chromatogram was stated on chapter 2.

◆ Demonstrate

Demonstrate與illustrates, depicts或 presents的含義不同，不能混用。Demonstrate是表示「清楚示範」之意，即向他人示範如何做某件事情。另外，demonstrate也有「證明」之意。

差：Figure 10.7 demonstrates the natural irrational frequencies for trucks.

佳：Figure 10.7 illustrates the natural irrational frequencies for trucks.

差：Figure 11.2 demonstrates the relationship between relative fluorescence intensity and time.

佳：Figure 11.2 depicts the relationship between relative fluorescence intensity and time.

差：This book demonstrates the method for effective technical communication.

佳：This book presents the method for effective technical communication.

正：Now let me demonstrate how the refrigerant cycles in the heat pump system.

正：We have demonstrated over 40% of the Carnot efficiency in such a device.

◆ Denote

Denote作「代表」、「指」用，並出現在被動語態句子中，其後必須加上by，而不是as。Represent也可以當作denote的同義詞使用。注意，referred to之後卻要加上as。

誤：In Table 2, the heat flux in each subsection is denoted as q_i.

正：In Table 2, the heat flux in each subsection is denoted by q_i.

正：In Table 2, the heat flux in each subsection is represented by q_i.

正：In Table 2, qi denotes the heat flux in each subsection.

誤：A domain name sever is denoted below as a DNS.

正：A domain name sever is referred to below as a DNS.

◆ Depict

Depict通常具有「用圖畫表示」的意思。在科技論文中，常用describe表示「描述」之意。

差：Here, we depicted some new and innovative uses of porous media in combustion.

佳：Here, we describe some new and innovative uses of porous media in combustion.

◆ Desire

Desire表示「需求」之意時，不要既用desire，又用被動語態。應該使用need或must，而且使用主動語態。

誤：The heat transfer of horizontal cylinder by ultrasound is desired to be improved.

正：The heat transfer of horizontal cylinder by ultrasound needs to be improved.

正：The heat transfer of horizontal cylinder by ultrasound must be improved.

◆ Detail

Describe in detail是「詳細描述」之意。「一個詳細的描述」可以寫成a detailed description。Detailly和detailedly是不正確的寫法。此外，detail也用作動詞，不過常用describe代替detail作動詞來表示「描述」或「說明」之意。

→ The characteristics of the machine are fully detailed in our brochure.

→ The characteristics of the machine are fully described in our brochure.

◆ Details

有些作者撰寫科技論文時，常在介紹了一項技術或程序之後，接著寫 The details will be described in the next section，以說明「下一節中將對這些技術進行詳細的描述」。但是這樣的句子並沒有清楚的指出要詳細描述什麼事物。建議將這個句子改成下述三個句子之一。

→ The hybrid acoustic stirling engine will be described in detail in the next section.

→ The details of the hybrid acoustic stirling engine will be described in the next section.

→ A detailed description of the hybrid acoustic stirling engine will be given in the next section.

◆ Difference

名詞difference用於比較兩個項目或事物時，應該使用介係詞between（有時候也使用in），如 "the difference between A and B"。

→ What is the difference between a mixture and a compound?

→ The agreement between experiments and calculations is strikingly good.

→ This risk is reflected in the difference between the price of real estate in the pre sales market and that in the finished housing market.

→ This risk is reflected in the difference in the price of real estate in the pre sales market and that in the finished housing market.

關於介係詞between的用法見本章 "Among, between" 一節。

◆ Different

Different後緊跟介係詞from。Different than, different to或different between的寫法都是錯誤的。

誤：It is a matter of common observation that mixtures are different than compounds.

正：It is a matter of common observation that mixtures are different from compounds.

誤：The definition is different between P and P*.

正：The definition of P is different from that of P*.

正：There is a difference between the definition of P and that of P*.

注意，句子不應該以different from放在句首。請參閱unlike。

◆ Display

Display、show和exhibit作為動詞都可用來表示「呈現」，「顯示」之意，但表示「提出」時，應該用present。例如：

差：Today scientists typically display the results of their investigations in the form of research papers.

差：Today scientists typically exhibit the results of their investigations in the form of research papers.

佳：Today scientists typically present the results of their investigations in the form of research papers.

正：The computing results display an increasing trend.

此外，「以圖表表示」所對應的動詞通常為show或display，其中show的使用較普遍。若用exhibit表達「以圖表表示」之意，則嫌不自然。例如：

正：The relationship of Nu_m and C_d for the various values of A and P_l is shown in Fig.6.

正：The relationship of Nu_m and C_d for the various values of A and P_l is displayed in Fig.6.

差：The relationship of Nu_m and C_d for the various values of A and P_l is exhibited in Fig.6.

◆ Dramatic, drastic

Dramatic通常表示「驚人」、「奇蹟般」、「引人注目」的意思。而drastic是指行為、方法、藥品的「猛烈」、「激烈」。Dramatic既可以是正面的，又可以是負面的；drastic則通常是負面的。Drastic通常在下列這種方式使用：Drastic measures to cure inflation, e.g. a steep increase in the bank rate。在科技論文中，通常應該使用a dramatic來表示「大幅增加」之意。

◆ Due to

在標準的英文中，due to只能用於修飾名詞，以指出事情的原因。不要把due to當作介係詞引出原因副詞並放在句首，此時應該使用owing to或because of。

→ The accident was due to careless driving.

→ Owing to his careless driving, we had a bad accident.

→ Because of his careless driving, we had a bad accident.

Due to the fact that是個冗長的詞語，應該用because代替。

冗長：Combine figure when possible if the combination will convey the same information due to the fact that space is at a premium in most publications.

簡潔：Combine figure when possible if the combination will convey the same information because space is at a premium in most publications.

◆ Effect

請參見affect。

◆ e.g.

e.g.是拉丁文片語exempli gratia的縮寫，其意思是「例如」。由於它是非限定片語，所以務必要用逗號將它和句子分開來。"e. g."這個縮寫中，兩個字母後都必須加句號。

◆ Ensure

Ensure和insure都有「確保」之意，但用ensure比較好。Insure常用於特指「防止財務上的損失」，如保險、投保等。此外，不要把assure和ensure混淆起來。Assured的意思是「承諾」或「保證」，而不是「確保」。Assure和insure很少出現在科技寫作中，科技論文中卻常出現ensure這個詞。

→ She tried to assure the nervous old lady that flying was safe.

→ You should ensure yourself against loss of heat by having double glazing.

→ Insurance companies will insure ships and their cargoes against loss at sea.

◆ Equal

Equal為動詞時，其後不能緊跟介係詞。Equal為形容詞時，其後必須加上介係詞to。

誤：A kilometer equals to 1000 meters.

正：A kilometer is equal to 1000 meters.

正：The depth of corrosion pits at 2000h equals 40-60 μ m for 15CrMo.

◆ Especially

把especially或particularly放在句首或分句的開頭，以表示「尤其」、「特別」之意，是不常用的，而常用in particular。

→ Graphs are effective if you want to show a trend －particularly if you want the reader to extrapolate.

→ Graphs are effective if you want to show a trend－in particular, if you want the reader to extrapolate.

especially用來修飾形容詞是正確的用法。

→ All of the measurements are fast, but the temperature measurement is especially fast.

◆ et al.

et al.是拉丁文片語et alii的縮寫，其意思是「以及其他人」。et al.用於引述書籍或論文時，若該書籍或論文的作者超過了3個人，就可以只列出第一位作者的姓名或姓，並在之後寫上et al.，以說明所有作者姓名已提及

（例如，"S. Eisen et al."）。請注意，這個縮寫的正確寫法是"et al."。此外，在論文的引文中，在第一位作者的姓名和et al.之間通常不加逗號。但在論文末列出參考文獻時，則必須在第一位作者的姓名和et al.之間加上逗號。

◆ etc.

etc.是拉丁文片語et cetera的縮寫，意思是「以及其他事物」。在英文中，etc.的意思與中文的「等等」較為接近。然而，在科技論文中，卻不常用etc.。etc.尤其不應用在以such as, including, for example或e.g.開頭的一系列事物的結尾。另外，若作者事實上已經不可能再提及任何事物或讀者並不瞭解作者所指的「其他事物」是什麼，都不應使用etc.。在科技論文中，and so on 或and so forth可能比etc.的使用更妥當。

差：A moderately long laboratory report has a variety of contents, such as introduction, description of experiment, results, analysis of result, and conclusions, etc.

佳：A moderately long laboratory report has a variety of contents, including introduction, description of experiment, results, analysis of result, and conclusions.

佳：There are many ways to use information systems to improve work practices, including eliminating unproductive uses of time, streamlining processing, eliminating unnecessary paper, and reusing work.

正：The samples in the series will be denoted by s1, s2, s3, etc.

◆ Exhibit

參見display。

◆ Exist

Exist用於表示「有」、「在內」或「包含」之意時，會顯得不太自然。建議作者在撰寫科技論文時用其他詞來表示「有」、「在內」或「包含」。

差：Large natural changes exist in ozone concentration in the stratosphere; for example, between summer and winter there is a change of about 25% at mid-latitude.

佳：Large natural changes are present in ozone concentration in the stratosphere; for example, between summer and winter there is a change of about 25% at mid-latitude.

佳：There are large natural changes in ozone concentration in the stratosphere; for example, between summer and winter there is a change of about 25% at mid-latitude.

誤：Many factors exist in designing an expert system for fixing computer disk drives.

正：Many factors must be considered in the design of an expert system for fixing computer disk drives.

正：Many factors must be considered in order to design of an expert system for fixing computer disk drives.

正：Many factors are involved in the design of an expert system for fixing computer disk drives.

◆ Fact

若句子中不用the fact that這種表達形式，則句子會顯得較為簡潔。

冗長：The fact that the pressure rose caused the power consumption of the system to increase.

簡潔：The rise in pressure caused the power consumption of the system to increase.

簡潔：Because the pressure rose, the power consumption of the system increased.

◆ Famous

在科技論文中，使用well-known通常比famous恰當。

不自然：A famous approach to constructing and maintaining information systems is introduced in the book "Information Systems: A Management Perspective" by Steven Alter.

自　然：A well-known approach to constructing and maintaining information systems is introduced in the book "Information Systems: A Management Perspective" by Steven Alter.

◆ Farther, further

Farther主要指距離上的「更遠」，而further主要指時間或數量上的「更多」、「更近一步」。

→ Tokyo is farther from Shanghai than Seoul.

→ We will now modify the product further to improve its reliability.

◆ Feedback

Feedback是名詞的形式，而feed back可當作動詞使用。

誤：Each output neuron is feedback to the corresponding node in the input layer.

正：Each output neuron is fed back to the corresponding node in the input layer.

◆ Fewer, less

Fewer修飾可數名詞，而less修飾不可數名詞。

→ No fewer than twenty students were absent through illness.

→ The output power of a machine is less than the input.

◆ Finalize

參見-ize

◆ Firstly, secondly

與firstly，secondly等詞相比，first，second等詞顯得文雅、簡潔。

差：Secondly, avoid circular definition and definitions that are too general or wordy.

佳：Second, avoid circular definition and definitions that are too general or wordy.

注意，下述錯誤例句中的firstly的用法是不正確的。

誤：For the sake of convenience, the dimensionless variables are firstly explained.

正：For the sake of convenience, we first explain the dimensionless variables.

正：First, we will explain the dimensionless variables for the sake of convenience.

◆ The following

參見as follows。

◆ For example

For example是正確的英文用法，而for examples則是不正確的用法。要強調的是：for example是連接副詞，因此只能用來表示兩個分句、句子或段落之間的關係。

→ The regulations require vehicles, beginning in 2004, to meet CARB emission standards for their first 120,000 miles. Emission standards will be relaxed somewhat after 50,000 miles. For example, a vehicle certified as a LEV will have to meet a 0.075 g/mile NMOG standard for its first 50,000 miles, and then 0.090 g/mile standard until it attains 120,000 miles.

For example之後不能羅列一系列的例子，如下面第一個例句所示。

誤：The lungs of the average Californian are regularly exposed to significant levels of pollutant substances, for example, ozone, hydrocarbons and other volatile organic compounds, oxides of nitrogen, and a bewildering variety of microscopic particles.

正：The lungs of the average Californian are regularly exposed to significant levels of pollutant substances, such as ozone, hydrocarbons and other volatile organic compounds, oxides of nitrogen, and a bewildering variety of microscopic particles.

正：The lungs of the average Californian are regularly exposed to significant levels of pollutant substances, including ozone, hydrocarbons and other volatile organic compounds, oxides of nitrogen, and a bewildering variety of microscopic particles.

◆ For ＋動名詞

參見to do …。

◆ Form, formulate

作動詞用時form是及物動詞，也是不及物動詞，意指「形成」、「製作」、「作成」、「組成」。Formulate是及物動詞，是「用公式表示」、「明確表達」、「規劃」、「正式提出」之意。

→ Atoms with the outer layer filled do not form compounds.

→ When water boils, steam forms.

→ The present study attempts to formulate a geometry independent turbulence model for incompressible heat transfer problems.

◆ Functionality

表達「功能」之意時使用function，而不要使用functionality。

差：The controlling system has several functionalities.

佳：The controlling system has several advanced functions.

模糊：The functionality of the TV set has been expanded.

清楚：The TV set has several new functions.

◆ Get

在科技論文中，get這個詞不夠正式，應換用obtain, have, derive或其他詞來表達「獲得」之意。

差：By using equation (5) at nodes P and E, we get⋯.

佳：By using equation (5) at nodes P and E, we obtain⋯.

佳：By using equation (5) at nodes P and E, we have⋯.

◆ Give

Give是個意思不精確的詞，要防止在撰寫英文科技論文中濫用give。在大多數情況下，要表達「提出」、「給出」之意，使用state，present或propose這些意思較為精確的詞要比使用give好得多。

模糊：The concept of "Sequential Combustion" developed by ABB is given in this paper.

精確：The concept of "Sequential Combustion" developed by ABB is presented in this paper.

精確：The concept of "Sequential Combustion" developed by ABB is described in this paper.

精確：The concept of "Sequential Combustion" developed by ABB is stated in this paper.

模糊：First we will give the governing equations in the Cartesian coordinates.

精確：First we will state the governing equations in the Cartesian coordinates.

精確：First we will write the governing equations in the Cartesian coordinates.

在許多學生撰寫的研究論文的導論中，常常可以見到"The final section gives the conclusions"這樣不自然的句子。此句可以改寫成：

佳：The final section states the conclusions of the paper.

佳：Section 5 concludes the paper.

佳：The conclusions of the paper are stated in section 5.

◆ Given

Given引導的短句不是一個完整的句子，其後必須緊跟一個主句。

誤：Given that M_2 $Cp\triangle T$=0. M_2 must be zero.

正：Given that M_2 $C_p\triangle T$=0, M_2 must be zero.

正：Assume that M_2 $C_p\triangle T$=0, M_2 must be zero.

正：If M_2 $C_p\triangle T$=0, then M_2 must be zero.

◆ Given as

Given as用來表示「從某處得到」或「表達」之意時，會顯得非常不自然。

差：The solution is given as⋯.

佳：The solution is given by the following equation.

差：The frictional pressure drop of two-phase flow is given as the following relationship.

佳：The frictional pressure drop of two-phase flow is expressed by the following relationship.

◆ Good

參見better。

◆ Happen

在科技論文中，使用occur常常比使用happen更恰當。

原　句：They did not observe what happened as the experiment proceeded.

更恰當：They did not observe what occurred as the experiment proceeded.

◆ Her

不要用she和her這些代名詞來指稱機關、學校或公司，而應用it或its。

誤：The company agrees to modify her design promptly.

正：The company agrees to modify its design promptly.

◆ Herein

要表達「在這裡」之意時，避免使用如herein之類古英文詞。

差：We herein use CCD cameras in order that the path of the suspended tracer particles can be visualized.

佳：Here we use CCD cameras in order that the path of the suspended tracer particles can be visualized.

◆ However

使用however表示「可是」、「然而」之意時，必須用逗號把它與句子分開。若however表示「無論如何」之意，則在其後不需加逗號。

→ However, today's petroleum prices (especially in the United States) have been the lowest in 20 years-presenting difficult challenges for alternative transportation fuels.

→ However hard he tries, he will never succeed.

◆ i.e.

i.e.是拉丁文片語id est的縮寫，其意思是「即是」。i.e.是非限定片語，所以必須使用逗號將其與句子分開。

◆ The idea of

The idea of的意思與中文的「這個概念」或「這個主意」類似。在撰寫科技論文時，當作者想解釋提出的方法或理論背後的基本概念時，不宜用the idea of，而應使用the idea behind 或the idea underlying。

差：The main idea of the proposed method is to use an iterative algorithm to eliminate the effect of the under-relaxation factor.

佳：The main idea behind the proposed method is to use an iterative algorithm to eli minate the effect of the under-relaxation factor.

佳：The main idea underlying the proposed method is to use an iterative algorithm to eliminate the effect of the under-relaxation factor.

◆ Illustrate

Illustrate的意思是「舉例或以圖表等說明」。因此其受語（對象）應該是一個論點或方法。 "to illustrate an example" 這種表達方式是不正確的。

誤：Figure 3 illustrates different examples of pore-level and system-level chemical non-equilibrium.

正：Figure 3 shows different examples of pore-level and system-level chemical non-equilibrium.

不要把illustrate和example混淆在一起。

誤：An experimental illustration will show how LDV can be applied to measure velocity.

正：An experimental example will show how LDV can be applied to measure velocity.

◆ Impact

不要把impact當作動詞來表示「影響」的意思。

誤：The climate impacted his health, injured it.

正：The climate affected his health, injured it.

◆ In this case

In this case或者in that case是正確的英文片語，表示「若是這樣（那樣）的話」之意。In such case是錯誤的表達方式。

◆ Indicate

Indicate意指「表示」、「指出」。不要把它和denote，represent或stand for（代表）混用起來。

差：D indicates the diameter of the cylinder and K the thermal conductivity of air.

佳：D denotes the diameter of the cylinder and K the thermal conductivity of air.

佳：D represents the diameter of the cylinder and K the thermal conductivity of air.

佳：D stands for the diameter of the cylinder and K the thermal conductivity of air.

◆ In other words

In other words是正確的寫法，意指「換言之」（換句話說），而in another word或in the other words都是不正確的。請注意in a word或in one word意指「簡言之」（簡單地說），它的意思是與in other word的意思不相同的。

◆ In order to

在英文科技論文的句子中，in order to中的in order盡可能地加以省略。

原句：She decided to study harder in order to catch up with the others.

簡潔：She decided to study harder to catch up with the others.

◆ Insure

參見ensure。

◆ It should be noted that

It should be noted that是個冗長的表達方式，通常可省略或用note that這個簡化的方式。此外，it is noted that這種不恰當的表達方式也應該用note that取代。

冗長：It should be noted that oral presentations are increasingly important for working scientists and engineers.

簡潔：Note that oral presentations are increasingly important for working scientists and engineers.

◆ Interesting, interested

Interesting用於修飾某人覺得有趣或有意思的主題觀點、或事物。而interested則用於描述某人對有趣或有意思的主題、觀點或事物的感覺。千萬不要混用interesting和interested這兩個詞。

→ Many students find theoretical analysis interesting, but I am more interested in experimental work.

◆ Introduce

科技論文中，儘量用explain，describe或state來代替introduce。

差：We will introduce the advantage of an informational abstract later.

佳：We will describe the advantage of an informational abstract later.

佳：We will state the advantage of an informational abstract later.

◆ Its, it's

Its是所有格形式，意思是「它的」。至於it's則是表示"it is"。

誤：It's advantage is that it provides much more information than does a descriptive abstract.

正：Its advantage is that it provides much more information than does a descriptive abstract.

◆ -ize

查詢詞典以確定可以有-ize詞尾的單詞，不能用-ize字尾來杜撰單詞。應避免使用如finalize及prioritize這種意思不清楚的單詞。

模糊：We have not yet finalized the squelch circulate design.

清楚：We have not yet put the squelch circulate design into final form.

清楚：We have not yet finished the squelch circulate design.

◆ Know

英文中的know是靜態動詞，不能用來指從「不知道」到「知道」的轉變，所以know的意思與中文中「可以知道」的「知道」不同。英文中的know通常不用於表示「學習」、「看出」、「發現」或「得知」的意思，而只能表示靜態的「知道某件事情」的事實。

誤：According to the experimental data, we can know that the grading filtration efficiency is a function of particle size.

正：According to the experimental data, we can see that the grading filtration efficiency is a function of particle size.

正：The experimental data show that the grading filtration efficiency is a function of particle size.

◆ Latter, former

Latter用於指稱前面曾經提到的兩個項目中的第二個項目，former則用於指稱兩個專案中的第一個項目。它的意思（後者及前者）和first與last的意思不同。First指連續多個項目的第一個項目，即使只有兩個項目也是如此，last是指連續的三個以上項目的最後一個項目。不要把latter寫成later，later的意思是「在一段時間以後」。

◆ Less

參見fewer。

◆ Less than

嚴格說來，含有less than的片語的正確寫法應該是with a size of less than 1及has a value of less than a。

誤：They then obtained a result with error less than the size of the cell.

正：They then obtained a result with an error of less than the size of the cell.

◆ Let

Let是動詞，因此以它開頭的句子或分句應該接著句號或分號，而不是逗號，否則會形成缺乏連接詞的複合句。此外，在科技論文中，最好不要使用let's來代替let us。

誤：Let X be the Cartesian product of these sets, A is their union.

正：Let X be the Cartesian product of these sets, and let A be their union.

正：Let X be the Cartesian product of these sets and A be their union.

誤：Let k=1, the solution can be obtained using equation (4).

正：Let k=1; the solution can be obtained using equation (4).

正：Let k=1. The solution can be obtained using equation (4).

◆ List

只有在確實列出幾個不同的項目時，才可能使用動詞list，否則應該使用describe, state或其他詞。

正：The differences between a technical business report and a journal report are listed in the accompanying table.

差：The calculation procedure is listed in Appendix B.

佳：The calculation procedure is stated in Appendix B.

佳：The calculation procedure is given in Appendix B.

佳：The calculation procedure is described in Appendix B.

◆ Make

Make是弱動詞，它有很多用途。然而，除一些固定的動詞受詞搭配或片語外，為避免它的詞義模糊，在科技論文中應儘量使用較特定的、具體的動詞取代make。

模糊：Form the results of the experiment, the following conclusions can be made.

清楚：Form the results of the experiment, the following conclusions can be drawn.

清楚：The experimental results support the following conclusions.

模糊：A detailed analysis of the proposed control algorithm is made in section 3.

清楚：A detailed analysis of the proposed control algorithm is presented in section 3.

在上面兩個標明「模糊」的例句中，make的使用顯得很不自然。以英語為母語的讀者決不會使用如 "make a conclusion" 或 "make an analysis" 之類的表達方式。

◆ Match

在對不同的資料進行比較時，使用agree或其他詞表示「一致」之意，通常比使用match恰當。

原　句：The computed lift coefficients m　atch the experimental data.

更恰當：The computed lift coefficients agree with the experimental data.

更恰當：The computed lift coefficients are in good agreement with the experimental data.

更恰當：The computed lift coefficients are consistent with the experimental data.

更恰當：The experimental data confirm the accuracy of the computed lift coefficients.

◆ May

請參閱can。

◆ Meanwhile

在中文中，「同時」可用來表達「此外」、「也」和「而且」的意思。但是，在英文中的meanwhile只能用於表示「在同一段時間」的含義（the time between, in or during）。若用meanwhile表示「同時」，則會產生不自然的句子。

差：The use of ethanol blended with gasoline can reduce motor vehicle emissions of carbon monoxide by 25% to 30% and also reduce ozone levels that contribute to urban smog. Meanwhile, the combustion of ethanol produces 90% less dioxide than gasoline.

佳：The use of ethanol blended with gasoline can reduce motor vehicle emissions of carbon monoxide by 25% to 30% and also reduce ozone levels that contribute to urban smog. In addition, the combustion of ethanol produces 90% less dioxide than gasoline.

佳：The use of ethanol blended with gasoline can reduce motor vehicle emissions of carbon monoxide by 25% to 30% and also reduce ozone levels that contribute to urban smog. Moreover, the combustion of ethanol produces 90% less dioxide than gasoline.

◆ Method for

Method後面常緊跟介係詞for或of及其後的動名詞。這種搭配形式比使用動詞不定詞要顯得自然些。

差：We selected the method to solve this problem.

佳：We selected the method for solving this problem.

佳：We selected the method of solving this problem.

關於用for＋動名詞與動詞不定詞來解釋事物或行為的功能與目標時的使用規則，可進一步參閱後面的to do…和for doing…。

◆ Modern

Modern的意思比較複雜，它可以指of the present or recent times（如歐洲近代史，自1475年迄今），也可以指modern inventions and discoveries（即現代的發明與發現）。因此，在一些句子中，使用modern這個詞不能清楚的表明作者所指的究竟是什麼時代。在科技論文中,若提到「現代技術」,使用contemporary這個詞要比modern會使意思更加清楚。

模糊:The modern digital video interactive (DVI) technology offers another kinds of compression, edit-level video, done on the developer's DVI system in real time.

清楚:The contemporary digital video interactive (DVI) technology offers another kinds of compression, edit-level video, done on the developer's DVI system in real time.

◆ More than one

More than one作主詞時,後面必須接單數動詞。

→ More than one student is interested in the experiment.

◆ Most, most of

Most和most of表示不同的普遍程度。Most是指一個總類中的大多數個別項目,緊隨其後的複數名詞不加任何冠詞。Most of則是指特定的一組事物中的大多數,其後必須接定冠詞the。使用most of the時,所指的事物不是前文已經提及或讀者可以方便理解的,就是句子中有指定的範圍。請參閱下述例句。

不清楚:Most of the engineers are co-operative.

清　楚:Most of the engineers in our group are co-operative.

誤:Most of graduate students are creative.

正:Most graduate students are creative.

上述most的使用規則也適用於some。

誤:Some of students are absent.

正:Some students are absent.

不清楚:Some of the students are absent.

清　楚：Some of the students in this class are absent.

◆ Namely

Namely這個詞在很多句子中是不必要的，可以省略。

累贅：Reports on experimental findings prepared for journals, namely, journal reports, follow the pattern of abstract statement of the problem, related literature, materials and methods, results, and conclusions.

簡潔：Reports on experimental findings prepared for journals, journal reports, follow the pattern of abstract statement of the problem, related literature, materials and methods, results, and conclusions.

◆ Notation

Notation常用於表達「符號」、「標誌」之意。當notation所指的是一整組符號時，應該把它當作不可數名詞使用，當所指的是一個特定的符號時，它有時可當作可數名詞使用，並寫成複數形式。但是，此時使用types of notation或symbols更恰當。

正：The notation used in this book is presented in Table 1.3.

差：The author of this paper applied two different notations to represent temperature.

佳：The author of this paper applied two different symbols to represent temperature.

佳：The author of this paper applied two different types of notation to represent temperature.

◆ Obvious, obviously

形容詞obvious具有「清楚」、「顯而易見的」之意，與clear同義。副詞obviously的主要意思是「顯然」，但是有時不宜用來作為clearly的同義字。從下面的例句可以看出，obviously的使用不自然，宜用clearly或

significantly。

差：The temporal temperature response of the flat-plate heat pipe increases obviously as the time increases.

佳：The temporal temperature response of the flat-plate heat pipe clearly increases as the time increases.

佳：The temporal temperature response of the flat-plate heat pipe increases significantly as the time increases.

正：Obviously, the time affects the temporal temperature response of the flat-plate heat pipe in some way.

◆ Occur

參閱happen。

◆ Of

撰寫科技論文時，不能把文中的「的」這個字統統翻譯成英文的of，例如有些人把of和in混淆使用。

誤：A heat flux is applied to the liquid-vapor interface of the condenser section as a result of vapor condensation.

正：A heat flux is applied to the liquid-vapor interface in the condenser section as a result of vapor condensation.

誤：The use of reformulated gasoline has helped vehicle manufacturers to meet CARB standards without a costly investment of infrastructure for alternative fuels.

正：The use of reformulated gasoline has helped vehicle manufacturers to meet CARB standards without a costly investment in infrastructure for alternative fuels.

　　文中的「的」有時實指「關於」、「針對」的意思，此時應使用 about、on、concerning或regarding，而不能用of。

誤：Professor Robinson has done some interesting research of fuzzy logic control.

正：Professor Robinson has done some interesting research on fuzzy logic control.

誤：This is a book of the design of rapid access memory.

正：This is a book about the design of rapid access memory.

　　還要注意，不要把of和for混用在一起。

誤：The vapor velocity profile and pressure distribution of the disk-shaped heat pipe are as follows.

正：The vapor velocity profile and pressure distribution for the disk-shaped heat pipe are as follows.

誤：Applying boundary conditions given by equations (53) and (62) to equation (47) yields the temperature distribution of the wick region.

正：Applying boundary conditions given by equations (53) and (62) to equation (47) yields the temperature distribution for the wick region.On the contrary,

◆ on the other hand, in contrast, in comparison

　　這四個片語的意思不同，因此用途也不同。On the contrary是用於否定或反駁前一個句子或分句所提出的論點，例如：

→ He argues that this strategy has increased sales. On the contrary, sales revenue has dropped 20% since the strategy was adopted.

　　不要把on the contrary與in contrast（或by contrast）混用。In contrast（或

by contrast）用於介紹一個與前一句所陳述的觀點強烈對照的新觀點。例如：

→ Approach A provides high speed at the cost of increased memory requirement. In contrast, approach B is slower but requires much less memory.

On the other hand和in comparison（或by comparison）是用來提出新的資訊並與前一個句子或子句所提到的資訊作比較或對照。

→ The serial design is still the most common design. On the other hand, the parallel design is becoming increasingly popular.

→ The parallel design is quite complex. In comparison, the serial design is much simpler.

On the other hand, in comparison和in contrast的意思近似，其用途亦類似，使讀者較注意下文的內容在於引導新觀念。不過與on the other hand或in comparison相比，in contrast更強調句子內容與前文的對照。On the contrary的意思與上述三者截然不同，它使讀者暫時較注意前文提出的論點，其功能在於強調對前文內容的否定。

On the other hand這個片語只有在其所引導的句子的主題是前文曾經提過或與前幾句的主題有明顯的對照關係時，才可適用。否則就會使其使用不自然，請看下例。

→ Fuzzy set theory has been the focus of much research in the last decade, because it can be used to model ambiguous data or uncertain information. On the other hand, neural networks have also attracted a great deal of attention in the last ten years.

在上面這個例子中，所討論的兩個項目 "fuzzy set theory" 和 "neural networks" 既沒有形成明顯的對照，而且前文也未提到過。修改方式有兩種，一種時乾脆將該例中第二個句子的on the other hand省略。第二種方式是將該例改寫成：

→ Fuzzy set theory has been the focus of much research in the last decade, because it can be used to model ambiguous data or uncertain information. Neural networks are another area of research that has attracted a great deal of attention in the last ten years.

◆ Otherwise

除非所指的事物非常清楚（例如：Do you have been told, otherwise you will be punished），否則不要使用otherwise來說明某個狀態或情況，以免句子的含意模棱兩可。下面的例句含糊不清，因為看不出otherwise所指的情況究竟是bit 2不設為0，數據傳不到pin R0, 還是其他情況。因此應該使用更精確的陳述方式來代替otherwise。

含糊：If bit 2 is 0, the data will be transmitted to pin R0. Otherwise the data will be transmitted to pin R1.

精確：If bit 2 is 0, the data will be transmitted to pin R0. If bit 2 is set to 1, the data will be transmitted to pin R1.

◆ Owing to the fact that

應該使用because或since代替owing to the fact that 這個冗長的表達方式。

冗長：Electric energy is used most widely owing to the fact that it can be easily produced, controlled, and transmitted.

簡潔：Electric energy is used most widely because it can be easily produced, controlled, and transmitted.

◆ Particularly

請參閱especially。

◆ Performance

在許多科技論文中，作者常用“performance”（性能）這個詞對某個系統、裝置或方法進行評價。但是除非讀者對「性能」的含義早就瞭解或文中對之已有定義，否則 "performance" 的意思太籠統。建議考慮使用其他比較精確、清楚、具體的表達方法。

模糊：When this technique is adopted, system performance is improved greatly.

清楚：When this technique is adopted, the accuracy of the system increases greatly.

清楚：The technique increases the accuracy of the system by 15%.

誤：Parallel computing is a popular technique for enhancing the performance of scientific calculation.

正：Parallel computing is a popular technique for enhancing the speed of scientific calculation.

◆ Phenomena

Phenomena是複數形式，其單數形式為phenomenon。Phenomenon的意思是「現象」，常用在中文中，但在英文中較少使用。一般說來，英文句子中的phenomenon可以省略，最好使用比較具體的文字來描述所指的對象。

累贅：We must also consider the phenomenon of the radiation effect.

簡潔：We must also consider the radiation effect.

◆ Precise, accurate

Precise的意思是「精確」、「精密」，如at the precise moment, precise casting by the lost wax process指分毫無差。Accurate 的意思是「準確」或「正確」，指符合某一種公認的標準，如quick and accurate calculation, accurate scales等。

→ The test began at ten o'clock precisely.

→ Clocks in railway stations should be accurate.

◆ Present, propose

　　Present和propose這兩個動詞都是「提出」的意思，但它們的意思稍有區別。"present"是指提出來給他人參考之用，而"propose"還有「建議」或「推薦」之意。科技論文的作者可以"present"某個自己不完全贊同的論點或方法。相反，"propose"一個論點或方法，等於建議或推薦別人也應該接受。科技論文中常用到的"the proposed method"或"the proposed technique"等片語是用來指論文中所推薦的方法或技術，此時使用"presented"是不合適的。

誤：In addition, the transcribability from the surface nature of mold to the surface of polymer by the presented method was experimentally confirmed.

正：In addition, the transcribability from the surface nature of mold to the surface of polymer by the proposed method was experimentally confirmed.

　　Present作為形容詞時，可用於指論文作者所提出的理論或方法。在這種情況下，"the present method"就代表"the method proposed in this paper"或"the method we are now proposing"。

→ The present theory successfully explains how….

◆ Principal, principle

　　Principal的意思是「主要的」、「首要的」，principle的意思則是「原理」、「原則」。

→ The principal algorithm applied is GA.
→ Later papers and patents discussed the use of the principle for engines.

◆ Propose

　　只有說明一個真正的提議時，才可以使用propose這個詞。

誤：Brown has proposed theoretical aspects of heat pumps.

正：Brown has studied theoretical aspects of heat pumps.

正：Brown has discussed theoretical aspects of heat pumps.

◆ Prove

　　除非指的是數學的證明，否則使用prove似乎顯得過於強烈。應改用 confirm, verify或其他詞。

→ Recent achievements in near room temperature magnetic refrigeration prove the effectiveness of the AMR cycle.

→ Recent achievements in near room temperature magnetic refrigeration confirm the effectiveness of the AMR cycle.

◆ Purpose

　　在許多英文句子中，purpose是累贅而可以省略的詞。

累贅：An ammeter is used for measuring current purpose.

累贅：An ammeter is used for the purpose of measuring current.

簡潔：An ammeter is used for measuring current.

◆ Reason … is because, reason why

　　在the reason … is because和the reason why這兩個詞語中，because和why 這兩個詞是累贅而應該省略的。

冗長：The reason never to send out a proposal without an abstract is because it is essential for reviewers to have a nutshell description of the proposal before they begin reading.

冗長：The reason why never to send out a proposal without an abstract is that it is essential for reviewers to have a nutshell description of the proposal before they begin reading.

簡潔：The reason never to send out a proposal without an abstract is that it is essential for reviewers to have a nutshell description of the proposal before they begin reading.

簡潔：Never send out a proposal without an abstract because it is essential for reviewers to have a nutshell description of the proposal before they begin reading.

◆ Reason is that

要對某個現象或某事物說明原因時，使用the reason is that這個詞是不夠精確的。The reason for this is that雖然較為清楚，但較為冗長。推薦使用this is because這個簡短、直接的詞語。

冗長：Take the time to check and double-check references. The reason for this is that they will typically be copied and recopied three or four times in the transition from original notes to typed manuscript, it is easy to garble information.

簡潔：Take the time to check and double-check references. This is because they will typically be copied and recopied three or four times in the transition from original notes to typed manuscript, it is easy to garble information.

◆ Recently

在中文中，作者習慣把表示時間的副詞放在句首，如「目前」、「近年來」、「近幾年」等。但是在撰寫英文文章時，請不要按照中文的習慣來書寫。把表示時間的單一副詞如recently或currently放在句首，語法上沒有錯誤，但使英文句子顯得不夠自然，如下列兩句所示。

→ Recently, many researchers have investigated Magnetocaloric effect (MCE).

→ Currently, Magnetocaloric effect (MCE) is attracting a great deal of attention.

若將recently等副詞置於動詞旁邊或移至句尾，則這些句子較為通順自然。

→ Many researchers have investigated Magnetocaloric effect (MCE) recently.

→ Magnetocaloric effect is currently attracting a great deal of attention.

此外，recently這個字的意思比較模糊。建議科技論文的作者使用更加明確的詞語來表示時間，如in the past decade或in the last three years。

◆ Refer

論文中引述參考文獻時，不要使用refer的被動語態，應該寫成主動態的祈使句。

誤：Detailed descriptions of the elastohydrodynamic lubrication (EHL) are referred to (Tanaka, 2000).

誤：Detailed descriptions of the elastohydrodynamic lubrication (EHL) can be referred to (Tanaka, 2000).

正：For a detailed description of the elastohydrodynamic lubrication (EHL), refer to (Tanaka, 2000).

正：For a detailed description of the elastohydrodynamic lubrication (EHL), see (Tanaka, 2000).

正：A detailed description of the elastohydrodynamic lubrication (EHL) can be found in (Tanaka, 2000).

此外，refer表示「稱為」時，其正確的用法是 "refer to … as" （主動式）或 "… is referred to as …" （被動式）。

→ In 1964, Grover, Cotter, and Erickson of Los Alamos National Laboratory described heat transfer experiments with three structures of unique internal construction, which they referred to as "heat pipes".

◆ Reference

絕大多數情形中，reference作為名詞使用。有時候reference可當成動詞使用，其意為「核對位置」、「清楚資料來源」。記住，應該避免把reference當成動詞，而應該使用refer, retrieve, read, recall或use等詞代替。

誤：For the details of the calculation, reference Appendix B.

正：For the details of the calculation, refer to Appendix B.

正：For the details of the calculation, see Appendix B.

差：The CPU then references the data in memory.

佳：The CPU then reads the data in memory.

佳：The CPU then retrieves the data in memory.

◆ Represent

　　Represent（代表）和indicate（表示，指出）兩者的意思是有區別的，不能換用。

差：The experimental data represent that temperature dependence from equivalence ratio is well approximated as a linear function.

佳：The experimental data indicate that temperature dependence from equivalence ratio is well approximated as a linear function.

佳：The experimental data show that temperature dependence from equivalence ratio is well approximated as a linear function.

◆ Request, require

　　Request是指請求某人做某事，實現讀者的願望，但被請求者不受約束，可以不答應請求者的要求。Require則是要求某人辦某事，同時不允許對方不答應，被請求者有責任必須滿足這個要求。

→ I request them to stop making such a noise.

→ All passengers are required to show their tickets.

◆ Research

　　表示某方面或某題目的研究，使用research on這個組合，不能使用

research of。另外，在當代英語中，research是不可數名詞，因此只能用單數形式。

→ Management is a process, which is constantly changing, as the results of continuous research are made available and incorporated in management knowledge.

→ Much research on urban heat island has been published.

◆ Respectively

在科技論文中常用到respectively這個字。在一些句子中，respectively可省略。在某些其他的句子中，若省略respectively，則句子會更加直接，更易於理解。值得注意的是，若respectively的句子提到多種項目，則易使讀者感到迷惑。

不清楚：The initial values of H, δ , S, X,Y, L, B, and the total amount of passage at the air and refrigerant sides are 9.5, 0.2, 1.7, 1.5, 9.3, 110, 215, 19, and 20, respectively.

若確需表達這麼多的數值，則應該考慮使用表格列出。

注意：必須用逗號把respectively這個詞與句子的其他部分分隔開來。

◆ Restated

及物動詞restated有「重新陳述」之意。但不要將它當作介紹某種結論或解釋的插入詞。當需重新表達某個觀點或結論時，應該使用in other words，that is，thus，in summary或其他詞，以使句子自然、清楚。

差：Restated, modern business is a complex system of production, distribution, consumption, services, and regulations.

佳：In other words, modern business is a complex system of production, distribution, consumption, services, and regulations.

佳：In summary, modern business is a complex system of production, distribution, consumption, services, and regulations.

◆ Resultant

Resultant作形容詞時，是指某個過程或方法產生的結果。但通常在大多數句子中使用resulting而不用resultant，這樣可使句子顯得自然。

原　句：We now substitute the resultant value for y in equation (4).

更恰當：We now substitute the resulting value for y in equation (4).

◆ Results of

緊跟在the results of後的名詞應該指產生這些結果的過程，若該名詞指結果的題目，則應寫成the results on或the results concerning。參閱of。

正：The results of the test are listed in Table 2.

誤：The results of the performance of the thermoacoustic effect are described in section 4.

正：The results on the performance of the thermoacoustic effect are described in section 4.

正：The results concerning the performance of the thermoacoustic effect are described in section 4.

◆ Reveal

Reveal可用於表示「揭示」之意。在科技論文中，若使用show或indicate比較自然、恰當，則不要用reveal。

差：The experimental results are revealed in Table 7.

佳：The experimental results are shown in Table 7.

◆ Right-hand

請注意，書寫right-hand和left-hand這些形容詞時，應該用連字號將其中兩個字連起來。

→ The first and second terms of the right-hand side of Equation (2) indicate performance degradation.

◆ Same

表示兩者相同之意，正確的用法是A is the same as B，而不是A is the same with B。

◆ Search

He searched his suitcase.這個句子的意思是他在手提箱裡尋找什麼東西。而He searched for his suitcase是指他遺失了他的手提箱，而且要找回這個手提箱。因此to search和to search for兩者的含意是不同的。在科技論文中，不能寫We searched the solution，而應該寫成We searched for the solution。

◆ Show

不要使用"show"表示「提出」的意思。

誤：The paper shows the experimental results on directional distribution of reflectance ρ.

正：The paper presents the experimental results on directional distribution of reflectance ρ.

誤：Simulation results are shown in section 3 of the paper.

正：Simulation results are presented in section 3 of the paper.

在介紹數字方程式時不要使用show表示「表示」或「寫出」的意思。

誤：The total heat removal rate can then be shown as follows.

正：The total heat removal rate can then be expressed as follows.

正：The total heat removal rate can then be written as follows.

若能用使句子比較清楚、簡潔的動詞，則不要使用show。

誤：Section 5 shows the summary of the computing results.

正：Section 5 summarizes the computing results.

誤：Table C.4 shows a list of the properties of liquid potassium, cesium, and water.

正：Table C.4 lists the properties of liquid potassium, cesium, and water.

Show的另一個意思是「證明」，此時show的使用帶有強烈的語氣。在撰寫科技論文時，有時使用語氣較弱的詞比較恰當。

非常強：Brown (1989) showed that the temperature of refrigerant rises steeply in the compression process and falls suddenly in the expansion process.

較不強：Brown (1989) found that the temperature of refrigerant rises steeply in the compression process and falls suddenly in the expansion process.

弱：Brown (1989) suggested that the temperature of refrigerant rises steeply in the compression process and falls suddenly in the expansion process.

◆ Significant

Significant、obvious和apparent這些詞在意義上互不相同。Obvious與apparent的詞意差異見Apparently。Significant意指「重要的」、「重大的」、「有特殊意義的」，例如a significant change是指在特定情況中被看作在性質或數量上具有重要性的變化。

在下面的例句中，obvious或significant都可用來修飾decrease這個詞。若是使用obvious，則例句的意思是「這種減少是可以清楚觀察得到的」，若是使用significant，則是指「這種減少在這個特定條件下是相當重要的」。除非作者想暗示「減少僅僅是表面現象，並沒有真正發生」之意，否則不能使用apparent。

→ When the annealing temperature was increased, an obvious decrease in the C-H bond absorption peaks was observed.

→ When the annealing temperature was increased, a significant decrease in the C-H bond absorption peaks was observed.

◆ Similar

Similar to是表示「與……相似」、「與……類似」的正確表達形式，similar後面緊跟介係詞to，而不是as。此外，不能把一個名詞放在similar和to之間。參見下例：

差：The second sensor has a similar reliability to the first.

修正句：The second sensor has reliability similar to the first.

佳：The second sensor has reliability similar to that of the first.

◆ Similarly

Similarly是用於指出兩個觀點或事物之間相似的地方。當所涉及的關係不是相似關係，而是對照關係或相對關係時，則不應該用similarly，而應該用in contrast, by contrast或conversely。

差：Method A provides high speed at the cost of increased memory requirement. Similarly, method B is slower but requires much less memory.

佳：Method A provides high speed at the cost of increased memory requirement. Conversely, method B is slower but requires much less memory.

◆ Simply

Simply有時可用來表達一個簡單的動作與一個複雜的動作之前的對照。但在許多句子中，simply是可以省略的。

正：Instead of completing this complex measurement procedure, we simply obtain the value from the effective simulation.

累贅：Whenever the operators restarted the circulation pumps and closed the block valve on the pressurizer, a new trouble simply developed.

簡潔：Whenever the operators restarted the circulation pumps and closed the block valve on the pressurizer, a new trouble developed.

◆ Since

由since這個連接詞引導原因副詞子句時，since之後不應緊跟that。在以since開頭的主從複合句中，主句句首不能放then。

誤：Since that electricity can change into other forms of energy, it is widely used in industry.

誤：Since that electricity can change into other forms of energy, then it is widely used in industry.

正：Since electricity can change into other forms of energy, it is widely used in industry.

◆ So

在口語用法中，so代替very，具有感嘆和加強語氣的作用。但在書面英語中，so不應該用來表示very的意思。

劣：These results are so interesting.

佳：These results are very interesting.

一般說來，英文的句子不宜用so開頭。在科技論文中，若需在句首表示「所以」或「因此」的意思，則通常用thus或hence。此外，由於對等連接詞後面不需加逗號，所以萬一在句首放置so，切勿在so後面加上逗號。

差：The results of the first trial were surprising. So, we repeated the experiment using a new set of data.

佳：The results of the first trial were surprising. Thus we repeated the experiment using a new set of data.

正：The results of the first trial were surprising, so we repeated the experiment using a new set of data.

◆ So-called

表示「所謂」、「號稱」之意的這個複合形容詞的兩個字，必須使用連字號連接起來。

◆ So far

在科技論文的文獻回顧部分中，不要使用so far或until now來表達「到目前為止」的意思，應該使用to date。然而，當句子採用現在完成式時，可省略to date，因為現在完成式本身就表明「從過去到目前為止」的意思。

差：So far, little research has been done on this ferromagnetic material.

佳：To date, little research has been done on this ferromagnetic material.

佳：Little research has been done on this ferromagnetic material.

◆ So that

在表示目的或結果的子句前，使用so that比so較適合。此外，一般而言so that連接目的副詞子句時，主子句之間往往不用逗號分開，子句中的述語常常用may（或might），shall（或should），can（或could），will（或would）等情態助動詞，而連接結果副詞子句時，主子句之間往往用逗號分開，通常不用may等情態助動詞。

→ The temperature is lowered so that water may be turned into ice.

→ The changes of nucleus and electrons are equal, so that the atom is electrically neutral.

在表示因果關係時，because要比so更精確些。

不精確：The cache memory was not cleared, so that the result was affected by stale data.

精　確：Because the cache memory was not cleared, the result was affected by stale data.So that, such that

So that用來引導表達目的或結果的子句，such that則是用於陳述某種條件，such that通常用於修飾其前面的名詞，如下例所示。

→ There are two objects p and q such that p does not equal q and p and q are members of the set S.

此外，so… that和such … that這兩個連接詞都用來連接結果副詞子句，它們所表達的意思相似，其區別是：so一般與形容詞或副詞連用（如so fast that），而such則常常與名詞連用（如such an important part that）。

◆ Solution

The solution to the problem (or equation) 意指某個問題或方程式的解答。注意，此時solution後應跟介係詞to。然而，當涉及某個方程式（如E）中的某一變數（如x）的值時，應該採用the solution for x in equation E這樣的表達形式。

另外，在科技論文中solution不能用於表達 "system"、"package"、"kit"、"design" 等詞的意思。

◆ Solve

在對某個問題或方程式求解時，應該寫成solve the problem或solve the equation。在求出某方程式中變數y的值或運算式時，應該使用solve for y。

→ Solving the above equation, we obtain the following value for the vapor velocity.

→ Solving for y in Equation (5), we obtain the following expression for the vapor velocity.

　　請注意：只有當確實需要解決某個問題時，才可使用solve這個動詞，否則應該使用handle、treat等此類較為精確的動詞。

差：A simple and efficient method is proposed for solving the effect of the under-relaxation factor.

佳：A simple and efficient method is proposed for handling the effect of the under-relaxation factor.

◆ Some

　　在英文科技論文中，為使句意明確、清晰，應該避免使用some，quite, rather, very之類的修飾詞。可考慮用several, a number of或many來替代some。Some有時也表示「某一組」的意思，則可改用specific或certain。

模糊：In recent years, some scientists have proposed quite a few theories for explaining this rather challenging climate phenomenon.

清楚：In recent years, scientists have proposed many theories for explaining this challenging climate phenomenon.

◆ Suffer

　　若使用動詞suffer來指出某方法的缺點，則其後必須緊跟介係詞from，否則不僅語法錯誤，而且由於suffer也有「忍受」的意思，所以句子的意思會和作者要表達的意思正好相反。

誤：This method suffers several problems.

正：This method suffers from several problems.

正：There are several problems with this method.

正：This method has several problems.

正：This method is subject to several problems.

◆ Support

從事工業和商業的人往往喜歡用support這個詞來描述兩個項目之間的關係（如兩個軟體或硬體）。應避免使用support，而應該用provided，include, can be used with, is compatible with或其他較精確的詞或片語來表達。

模糊：The computer supports many popular software applications.

清楚：The computer can run many popular software applications.

模糊：The company supports customers with a variety of services.

清楚：The company provides customers with a variety of services.

模糊：The system supports two operating modes.

清楚：The system has two operating modes.

模糊：The program supports both Windows and DOS.

清楚：The program is compatible with either Windows or DOS.

清楚：The program can be used with either Windows or DOS.

◆ Suppose

Suppose用作表達「假定」時，切勿將它與if加以混淆。Suppose是動詞，而if是從屬連接詞。以if開頭的句子是子句，不是一個完整的句子。以suppose開頭的句子後面應接句號或分號。若接逗號，則除非逗號後再接一個對等連接詞（and, but等），否則是不允許的。

誤：Suppose that emissions from the gasoline are higher than from methanol or ethanol, then the widespread use of methanol or ethanol might require modifications to that infrastructure.

正：Suppose that emissions from the gasoline are higher than from methanol or ethanol. Then the widespread use of methanol or ethanol might require modifications to that infrastructure.

正：Suppose that emissions from the gasoline are higher than from methanol or ethanol; then the widespread use of methanol or ethanol might require modifications to that infrastructure.

正：If emissions from the use of gasoline are higher than from methanol or ethanol, then the widespread use of methanol or ethanol might require modifications to that infrastructure.

◆ That

要注意形容詞子句中關係代名詞that和which的區別。Which表示「物」，that可以表示「人」或「物」。在指物時，which與that均可以用，沒有什麼區別。That較多地用於限制性形容詞子句中，而which既可用於限制性形容詞子句中，也可用於非限制性形容詞子句中。但下列情況均用that：先行詞為all, much, little, none, everything, everyone, nothing, nobody, anything等不定代名詞時；先行詞為形容詞的最高級或序數詞所修飾時。

原　句：This is the book which I bought yesterday.

更恰當：This is the book that I bought yesterday.

正：That is all (that) I know.

正：Silver is the best conductor that is found in nature.

但是，若限制性形容詞子句以介係詞開頭，則關係代名詞必須使用which。

→ High-speed steel is a material which the cutter is made of.

→ The temperature at which water changes to ice is 0℃.

當使用that引導名詞性子句時，that後面不加逗號。

誤：A simple experiment shows that, air has weight.

正：A simple experiment shows that air has weight.

當that出現在名詞子句或形容詞子句前面時，若that後面緊跟名詞片語或代名詞，則只要句子的意思仍然清楚，就可以省略that。但是，若省略that使句子不自然並使讀者迷惑，則不能省略that。為使句意清晰通順，在科技論文中一般需保留that。

不清楚：The climate phenomenon the theory must explain is very complex.

清　楚：The climate phenomenon that the theory must explain is very complex.

That引出主詞子句，不能省略。

錯　誤：It has been reported the flow resistance of the circular cylinder is remarkable larger than that of a streamline one.

正　確：It has been reported that the flow resistance of the circular cylinder is remarkable larger than that of a streamline one.

◆ Then

Then通常不用作並列連接詞，而是副詞。應該在then前面加上並列連接詞，如and或but，或是把then前面的逗號改成句號或分號。

誤：Bar charts are useful for data that can be separated into clear-cut division, then these divisions may be shown on the chart by heavy lines or bars in lengths that correspond to the quantities.

正：Bar charts are useful for data that can be separated into clear-cut division, and then these divisions may be shown on the chart by heavy lines or bars in lengths that correspond to the quantities.

正：Bar charts are useful for data that can be separated into clear-cut division. Then these divisions may be shown on the chart by heavy lines or bars in lengths that correspond to the quantities.

◆ There exists

不要隨意把there is 寫成there exists的形式以表示「有」或「存在著」的

意思。在討論邏輯或數學時，可以用there exists表示存在量詞（ㄅ），此外，使用there is通常較為恰當。

差：There exist two variables in this equation.

佳：There are two variables in this equation.

◆ They

不可以用they來指稱前述的單數代名詞，如each person, everyone等等。例如在某種情況下，用he或she不恰當的話，那麼應該修改句子。修改的方法是要麼把前後的名詞及代名詞一致地改為複數形式，要麼就省略代名詞。

誤：When each person arrives, they must register.

正：When each person arrives, he must register.

正：When the attendants arrive, they must register.

正：Upon arriving each attendant must register.

◆ This

在使用this來表達整個句子的內容時，最好在this後面加一個名詞，以指出this所指對象。

差：If the audience were solely peers, there might be no problem. But this rarely arises outside the readership of specialized journals.

佳：If the audience were solely peers, there might be no problem. But this situation rarely arises outside the readership of specialized journals.

◆ Those

在科技論文中，若在名詞前面加上指示代名詞those，則會使句子顯得生硬、不自然。應該用the替代those，或把those刪去。

差：The Walgreen drugstore chain was telecommunications to ensure the availability of prescription refills for those customers who are out of town.

佳：The Walgreen drugstore chain was telecommunications to ensure the availability of prescription refills for the customers who are out of town.

◆ Thus

只有第二個分句或子句所表達的意思是第一個分句或子句所表達的論點所蘊含的結果時，才可以使用thus或therefore來連接句子或子句。

◆ To do…, for doing…

在說明某個事物或行為的目的或功能時，若被修飾的物件是名詞，則通常使用介係詞（一般是for）加上動名詞片語來修飾，若被修飾的物件為動詞，則較常使用不定詞片語來修飾。在下列例句中，使用不定詞片語很自然，因為它修飾句子中的動詞，說明採用拉普拉斯轉換的目的。

→ Laplace transform is applied to write the previous system in a quadripole form.

在下面的例句中，for measuring high temperature這個介係詞片語修飾名詞instrument，說明該儀錶的功能。因為被修飾的是名詞，所以使用for doing這種動名詞片語形式較自然。

→ This is an instrument for measuring high temperature.

英語語法中，動名詞片語和動詞不定詞片語均可作為句子的主詞，動名詞作主詞表示一般情況，不定詞表示具體情況。但是，當他們位於句首時，動名詞片語比動詞不定詞片語通常要自然些。

差：To represent knowledge and create ways for computers to use knowledge remains a major research topic.

佳：Representing knowledge and creating ways for computers to use knowledge remains a major research topic.

◆ Totally

副詞totally是entirely, wholly和completely的同義詞，表達「完全」、「統統」、「一概」之意。若需表示「總共」的意思，則應該使用a total of和altogether。

誤：There are three types of transient porous burners totally.

誤：There are totally three types of transient porous burners.

正：There are a total of three types of transient porous burners.

正：There are three types of transient porous burners altogether.

◆ Type of

Type of, form of及kind of中type, form及kind的數和接在介係詞of後面的名詞的數必須相互一致。此外，在科技論文中，用type of通常比用kind of恰當。

→ We adopt a new type of sensor for measuring pressure.

→ There are three types of methods used in business data processing.

◆ Unlike

Unlike放在句首以表達「與x不同」或「不同於x」之意。若把"different from"或"differing from"放在句首，則使句子很不自然。

差：Differing from previous works, this book emphasizes applications of information systems and issues facing managers and users.

差：Different from previous works, this book emphasizes applications of information systems and issues facing managers and users.

佳：Unlike previous works, this book emphasizes applications of information systems and issues facing managers and users.

正：Unlike the direct MCE measurements, the indirect experiments allow the calculation of both $\Delta T_{ad}(T)_{\Delta H}$ and $\Delta S_m(T)_{\Delta H}$.

◆ Until now

在科技論文的文獻回顧中，應該用to date來表示「到目前為止」的意思。比較而言until now和so far在大部分情況下都不恰當。

差：Until now, most of the researchers have focused on the thermal performance of a specific type of latent heat thermal energy storage (LHTES).

佳：To date, most of the researchers have focused on the thermal performance of a specific type of latent heat thermal energy storage (LHTES).

◆ Utilize

撰寫科技論文時，要避免使用utilize這個詞，而應該使用use, adopt, apply, employ等字，這樣句子顯得簡單、直接。

原　句：Local area networks (LANS) can be utilized to share personal files and send messages.

更恰當：Local area networks (LANS) can be used to share personal files and send messages.

◆ Versus

Versus的正確縮寫形式是vs.，不能寫成"v.s."。

◆ Whether or not

在大多數使用whether or not的情況中，可省略其中的or not，以使句子更簡潔。只有當作者需要強調兩種可能的情形或要表達的意思是「無論如何」時，才有必要完整地寫whether or not三個字。

累贅：It is still a question whether or not the materials could stand the test.

簡潔：It is still a question whether the materials could stand the test.

正：Whether or not excess oxygen is available, the fuel will still burn.

◆ Which

請參閱that。

◆ While, when

While和when都可作「在……時」解，但是，when可以指一個時刻或一段時間，而while只能指一段時間。以while引導的副詞子句中，常使用進行式，有時可用現在簡單式與過去簡單式。

→ When the magnetic field is applied isothermally, the MCE can be also expressed by means of the isothermal magnetic entropy change.
→ While an electric current is passing through a conductor, heat occurs.
→ While an electric current passes through a conductor, heat occurs.

◆ Without loss of generality

這個片語的正確形式是without loss of generality。下面前三個例句中，這個片語的寫法都是不正確的。

誤：Without the loss of the generality, we can assume that …

誤：Without losing of the generality, we can assume that ….

誤：Without lost the generality, we can assume that ….

正：Without loss of generality, we can assume that ….

附錄1 投稿信函

在給專業重要期刊投稿時，為禮貌起見，作者應該附上投稿信函，以表明自己的用意。在英語中，投稿信函稱作"cover letter"。

投稿信函應簡短。但是，它必須包含下列五個基本要素：

①信頭（Heading）包括系、所名稱，研究所或大學的名稱，發信人的地址，還有發信人的電話號碼、傳真號碼及E-mail地址及發信日期，信頭一般位於右上側。若採用大學研究所或研究機構的正式信紙，而且正式信紙上已有上述通訊地址，可僅加上發信日期。注意，美國的州名後放郵遞區號（Zip code）。

②信內地址（Inside address）包括收信人的全名、地址（與信封上的人名、地址一致），學術期刊名稱（通常以斜體表示）。收信人姓名之前加上Dr.、Prof.等學銜、職稱或Mr.與Ms.。收信人姓名的拼寫應正確無誤，也不要隨意縮寫收信人的姓名或期刊名稱。信內位址與信頭之間應有兩行空格。

③稱呼（Salutation）與信內地址之間空兩行。稱呼後用冒號。如果不知道收信人（期刊編輯）的具體姓名，可用"Dear Sir"、"Dear Madam"（複數形式為"Dear Gentlemen"或"Dear Ladies"）。在不知道對方姓名及性別時可用"Dear Sir or Madam"。稱呼後不用逗號，因為逗號通常用在私信的稱呼後。

④信函正文（Body of the letter）投稿信函的正文通常只包括論文的題目、稿件份數以及投稿的意圖。通常只以一個段落出現。它與稱呼之間應空一行或二行。一般論文題目應加上引號，而學術期刊名用斜體字表示。正文的最後用"Thank you"加以結束。

⑤禮貌套語（Complimentary Close）禮貌語是信函結束的信號。標準的用語有以下幾種：Sincerely，Yours sincerely或Sincerely yours，Yours truly或Truly yours, Your respectfully或Respectfully yours，以及Cordially yours（在彼此相識時才適用）。這些套語一般位於右側並在其後需緊接逗號。禮貌套語後與信函正文之間空二行。

⑥簽名（Signature）簽名緊接在禮貌套語下面，應留有足夠空白處（4-6行）用於手寫簽名。手寫簽名空白部分的下面列印發信人的姓名，列印姓名的下面或另旁邊列印發信人的職稱、職務或學銜。

除了上面的五個基本要求之外，還可在信紙的左下方列印縮寫"Enc."或"Encl."，以表示信函有附件。"Encl.(3)"則表示有3份附件（論文拷貝）。另外，如果要將稿件分發給其他人，則可用"Copies to"或縮寫"cc"例如"cc：Joseph Smith"。

應當指出，商用信函的任何標準格式都適用於投稿信函。下面是兩封典型的投稿信函。第一封是作者在初次投稿時可能採用的信函，第二封則是可以在投修改稿時採用。

Department of HVAC

School of Energy and Power Engineering

Xi'an Jiaotong University

28 Xianning West Road

Xi'an 710049

P R China

March 11,2002

Professor A A M Sayigh

Editor in Chief

Renewable Energy

147 Hilmanton

Lower Earley

Reading RG6 4HN

UK

Dear Professor A A M Sayigh:

Enclosed are three copies of a manuscript entitled "Experimental study on a horizontal tube falling film evaporation and closed circulation desalination system." Please consider this paper for publication in *Renewable Energy*.

Thank you.

Sincerely,

(Signature)

Liangfeng Huang

Professor

Department of HVAC

School of Energy and Power Engineering

Xi'an Jiaotong University

28 Xianning West Road

Xi'an 710049

P R China

August 23,2002

Professor A A M Sayigh

Editor in Chief

Renewable Energy

147 Hilmanton

Lower Earley

Reading RG6 4HN

UK

Dear Professor A A M Sayigh:

Enclosed are two copies of a revised version of our paper entitled "Experimental study on a horizontal tube falling film evaporation and closed circulation desali-`nation system." We have revised the paper according to your directions and the suggestions of the reviewers and are resubmitting it for publication in *Renewable Energy*.

Thank you

Yours sincerely,

(Signature)

Liangfeng Huang

Professor

　　注意：投稿信函應簡短、明確，內容直接點明主題。要仔細核對發信人及收信人的姓名、地址、號碼和論文名稱及期刊名稱，確保所有資訊正確無誤。此外，應避免咬文嚼字，信函正文部分中不要使用那些不常用的片語或詞。如 "Attached please find"、"attached herewith"、"hereto" 應改寫為 "Attached"；"Endeavor to ascertain" 改為 "Try to find out"； "In compliance with your request" 改為 "As requested"；"In view of the fact that" 應換用 "As"；"utilize" 改為 "use" 等等。

科技英文論文寫作實用指南 **Practical Guide to Scientific English Writing**

附錄2 致謝

　　眾所周知，絕大多數的研究工作是得到了資助和協作才得以完成的。這些資助可能包括政府部門、機構、公司、學校等的資金或計劃的資助，而協作人員或單位可能指對研究工作和研究論文的初稿作過指導與建議的專家、提供試驗樣品或數據資料的單位、提供試驗或計算條件的實驗室或計算中心、建造試驗台架的技術人員、參與實驗或計算的學生或同事、提出研究計劃專案的資深人士，以及在計算軟體使用上作過幫助的工程師。這些協作人員的姓名一般不列在論文作者的名單中，但他們所做的工作對研究工作完成來說是很重要的，甚至是必不可少的。

　　目前，越來越多的論文作者願意藉論文發表的機會來表達對基金資助和協作人員或單位的謝意。這樣做的目的一方面是表示作者肯定基金資助和協作人員或單位對自己研究工作所作出的貢獻，另一方面也使讀者能更多地瞭解作者研究工作的相關背景資料。

　　致謝的英文名稱是"Acknowledgement"。它通常位於論文正文之後及參考文獻目錄之前。大多數論文用"Acknowledgement"作為致謝內容的標題。致謝通常為一個段落。下面列出一些常用的句型，請注意這些句型中不同形式的表達方法。另外，句子可採用主動語態或被動語態，所用時態則可以是現在簡單式、現在完成式或過去簡單式。

Funding for this work was provided by the Ministry of Energy and Resources.

The work was supported by National Natural Science Foundation of China through grants No.59676011 and No.59836220. The authors would like to thank Dr. A.B. Murphy for his providing the property data of the argon-air mixture.

This work has been supported by National Science Foundation under grant (SGER# 9810784); the corporate support of Texaco, Kodac and Dupont are gratefully acknowledged.

This work was sponsored by King Abdulaziz City for Science and Technology, Riyadh, through grant No.AR-12-39.

This project has been supported by Trans-Century Training Programme Foundation for the Talents by the State Education Commission, China.

This project was supported by National Natural Science Foundation of China and cooperated with Shanghai Boiler Works and Harbin Boiler Works.

This work has been sponsored by Sumitomo Heavy Industries, Inc., with additional support from the David Taylor Research Center.

The authors are thankful to the "Deutscher Akademischer Austauschdienst (DAAD)" for its financial support in form of a scholarship to enable to perform the present study.

The author would like to acknowledge the support of University of Kansas (under Award No.3578-20-0003-1101) and the National Science Foundation (under Grant No.CTS-9803364).

It is gratefully acknowledged that the work presented in this paper has been supported by the German Ministry of Economics and Technology (BMWi) and the European Commission.

The support provided by the North Carolina Supercomputing Center (NCSC) under an Advanced Computing Resources Grant and by the AvHumboldt Foundation is greatly appreciated.

The present research is financially supported by the Monbusho's Grant-in Aid for JSPS Fellows. One of the authors, Mr. Ziping Feng, his studying is also supported by the JSPS.

The authors gratefully acknowledge the financial support provided under the National and Technology Board, Singapore Grant No. JT/ARC 5/96 for the development of the experimental facility described in this paper.

Support of this work by Hong Kong Research Grant Council Grant (No. HKUST 6045/97E) is gratefully acknowledged.

The financial support received from the China National Petroleum & Natural Gas Corporation and National Natural Science Foundation of China are gratefully acknowledged.

The support of this work under the NASA Microgravity Fluid Physics Program is gratefully acknowledged.

We are grateful to Federal German Ministry of Science, Education, Research and Technology, DLR for support of this research (project 6-036-0041) as well as to Russian Foundation for Basic Research (grant 96-02-17546). Also, we would like to thank the entire working Group of LITP, IVTAN, especially, R.G. Muchnik, A.B. Andrianov, A. V. Zuev, I. A. Orlova, V. P. Baev, and M. N. Makeev.

This study was supported by the Computational Mechanics Research Chanllenge grant sponsored by the Ohio Board of Regents.

The authors wish to acknowledge the financial support provided by the

Cooperative Research Center for Black Coal Utilization, which is funded in part by the Cooperative Research Centers Program of the Commonwealth Government of Australia. The authors thank Dr. Alan Wang from UNSW, Mr. David Murphy and Mr. Naranjin Sharma from Pacific Power for their invaluable efforts in construction, assembly, commissioning and operation of the facility.

This work was partially supported by the Research Committee of The Hong Kong Polytechnic University under Grant No.A.63.

The part of this work was sponsored by Creative Research Initiatives Program funded by the Ministry of Science and Technology, Korea.

The collaborative support of the Australian Research Council and Fuel & Combustion Technology Pty Ltd is gratefully acknowledged. Thanks also go to Dr. G. Newbold and Mr. S.J. Hill for their helpful comments.

The authors gratefully acknowledge the support of this work by the Department of Energy (DE-PS02-98EE504493) and thank D.D. Macdonald for helpful discussions during the course of this study.

It is a pleasure to acknowledge the financial support of the Natural Science and Engineering Research Council of Canada, Centra Gas Inc., and the University of Victoria. As with any overview paper, there are references that I have neglected to cite or have missed in my literature search. This was not done intentionally and should not be an inference that uncitied works are not important. Discussions with many colleagues were stimulating and helpful.

The authors acknowledge the support of the students, K. Nagaya, J. Higurashi, T. Sano, S. Tsuchiya and M. Tsuchiya for their assistance in the experiments and measurements.

Mr. Jay P. Weaver, of Thermacore, provided technician supports to prototype heat transfer fabrication and testing. He also provided supports to transition of the heat exchanger design to production.

We are indebeted to Prof. M. Shiga for valuable discussions. We also thank Prof. T. Kanomata of Tohoku Gakuin University for his advice on sample preparation.

This work is supported by NASA grant NAG8-1335. The authors would like to thank Dr. Wang Jing for her excellent job preparing our camera-ready manuscript.

The experiments were performed in the Thermo-Fluids Laboratory in Ontario Hydro Research Division.

We are grateful to professors Even Ma, Efstathios Meletis, and Aravamudhan Raman for many helpful discussions. In addition, we thank Professor Ma for initiating our interest in this work, and Professors Raman and Kurt Schulz for their comments on the manuscript. Acknowledgement is made to the Donors of The Petroleum Research Fund, administered by the American Chemical Society (PRF#34049-G5to HW) and to the Louisiana Board of Regents (Research Competitiveness Subprogram, LEQSF 1999-02-RD-A-21 to HW) for support of this research.

The present study is supported by U.S. Department of Energy through the Advanced Gas Turbine System Research (AGTSR) program. The authors would like to thank AEA technology for providing TASCflow, and Dr. C. Camci for providing information on the turbine passage geometry. All the computations in this work were performed in Scientific Development and Visualization Laboratory (SDVL) at the University of Minnesota Supercomputing Institute.

This paper was prepared with the support from DOE Office of Advanced

Automotive Technologies under cooperative agreement No. DE-FC02-98CH10954, Sandia National Laboratories under Contract No. BF-6597, Commonwealth of Pennsylvania, and Penn State University. The author is also grateful to his research associates and students, Z. H. Wang, Sukkee Um, W.B. Gu, and X. O. Chen for their help.

This work was performed with the financial support from the foundation of Shizuoka Institute of Science &Technology, for which the authors are very grateful. The authors also express sincere thanks to undergraduate students N. Nagoji and T. Sugimoto for their efforts in doing this experiment.

Ames Laboratory is operated for the U.S. Department of Energy (DOE) by Iowa State University under Contract No. w-7405-ENG-82. The work was supported by the Advanced Energy Projects and Technology Research Division, Office of Computational and Technology Research of DOE. This work also benefited from the expert contributions of T.A. Henning, J.F. Laarsch, J.W. Johnson, and L.M. Lawton, Jr.Dr. Alom Lloyd, former chief scientist, and Henry Hogo, Julia Lester, and Joe Cassmassi at South Coast Air Quality Management District, have over the years provided data for our meteorological and urban airshed modeling, along with advice and helpful criticism.

In order to assemble the data presented in this paper, many investigators were asked to diligently search their files for the required tabulated data. They are too many to list here; they have my thanks.

Astronautics engineering staff contributing to the design of the Hydrogen Liquefier at the Technology Center include: Alex Jastrab, Jerry Kalisze-wski, Rich Lubasz, and Kurt Echroth. Their contributions are greatly appreciated. Major funding for this effort has been supplied by the Department of Energy and Astronautics Corporation. The vision of both organizations has made it possible for this development to proceed.

The author would like to express their sincere thanks to Dr. Itsushi uno of National Institute for Environmental Studies for advice on the modification of CSUMM. The authors would also like to thank the Bureau of Urban Planning and the Bureau of Sewerage, both of the Tokyo Metropolitan Government, for access to their digital geographic land use data set for Tokyo.

The Bureau of Environmental Preservation of the Tokyo Metropolitan Government is acknowledged for providing hourly data on the atmospheric environment of Tokyo and the Japan Meteorological Agency for providing the hourly AMeDAS data for Tokyo.The author would like to thank the Department of Geography and the Faculty of Graduate Studies and Research at the University of Regina for their financial support. Special recognition also goes to the following people: Ron Hopkinson of Environment Canada (Prairie and Northern Region, Regina) for the timely provision of meteorological data; Dr. A.H. Paul (Department of Geography, University of Regina) for his guidance and encouragement; and the field assistants for their show of patience and enthusiasm while collecting data at inconvenient times. Finally, sincere appreciation is extended to the reviewers of this paper for their helpful recommendations.

科技英文論文寫作實用指南 **Practical Guide to Scientific English Writing**

附錄3 學術演講

對於科技工作者來說，作學術演講這樣的口頭交流與專業期刊上發表論文這樣的書面交流同等重要，所不同的是，在大多數情況下學術演講是一種與同行專家面對面的交流。作學術演講是研究人員專業生涯中的常事，各種專業大會、專題討論會、報告會、座談會、甚至工業界的交流會，都為科技工作者提供了宣讀研究論文或學術報告的機會。為了達到交流的目的，必須十分重視學術演講的質量。

學術演講的成敗往往不在於演講內容的正確與否，而在於技術問題。例如，初次進行學術演講的人常常不知道事先如何去準備，他們會神情緊張地站在觀眾前面，不知採用何種恰當的語調，甚至出現古怪的目光接觸、變化無常的陳述方法、數量過多的幻燈片等問題。他們錯誤地估計現場聽眾的興趣與背景，也不瞭解自己能提供的資訊量與現場聽眾所能吸收的資訊量之間的差距。

事實上，一個成功的學術演講取決於三個重要的環節：充分而又仔細的準備，認真而又適當的練習，以及精力充沛、熱情洋溢的演講。下面將分別討論這三個基本的環節。

(1)準備

在作學術演講的準備時，應該牢記：演講的目的不僅在於發表某些資訊，而且要把這些資訊傳達給現場聽眾，達到交流的目的。另一方面，所有現場聽眾對學術演講的注意時間是有限的，他們不會從頭到尾注意演講的每一句話，即使演講時間只有短短的十分鐘。也就是說，聽眾會有選擇地來注意演講內容。為了儘量確保現場聽眾能清楚瞭解學術演講所表達的資訊，必須在準備階段很好地組織演講內容（包括話語及所使用的視覺教具），要突出重點，使聽眾能清楚地領會這些要點。另外，如果準備工作既充分又細緻，那麼演講者在演講時就會少緊張，會更加自信，能比較順利地把演講內容有效地傳達給現場聽眾。

在學術演講的準備工作中，演講者應該按下列步驟進行。

①**分析現場聽眾的性質，然後確定合適的演講內容**。在準備任何講演與報告時，第一個步驟就是對現場聽眾進行分析，然後根據現場聽眾的性質來確定合適的演講或報告的內容。如聽眾對演講的題目究竟熟悉多少？他們需要或想要瞭解有關這個題目的什麼資訊？他們能接受多少新的資訊？他們需要比較詳細專業的報告，還是只需要演講人概要地介紹自己研究的要點？以同領域研究人員為對象的演講（宣讀論文）內容和以一般技術人員為對象的演講（科學講座）內容是不一樣的。即使在專業學術會議上宣讀論文時，同專業但不同研究方向的聽眾也會有不同的興趣和要求。如果演講者告訴聽眾的是聽眾早已知道的內容，那麼他們會感到厭煩 。與之相反，如果演講太多太快地「傾倒」所有的資訊，則聽眾會無法接受或消化，甚至會將演講內容「短路」。所以，演講者必須根據現場聽眾的性質，確保自己能告訴他們目前缺少的新的資訊。

②**明確演講的目的**。演講者在準備階段的第二個步驟是需要明確自己演講的目的，例如是否有些要點要傳達給現場聽眾？是否要聽眾相信這些要點？是否要教他們如何做某件事情？初次演講者想在演講中包羅與題目相關的所有資訊，企圖表達覆蓋整個領域的內容，似乎只有這樣才能使聽眾理解。事實上，閱讀書面的資訊與吸收演講的資訊之間有很大的差異。對於出版物上的文章，讀者在閱讀時可以返回重讀一些圖表或重新考慮一些難點，而且時間上也允許這樣做。然而，在聽講時聽眾是無法做到這些的。因此，演講者需明確自己演講的目的是要將1至2個重要的論點集中地介紹給聽眾。一些比較複雜的資訊可以同時以列印資料的形式發放給現場

聽眾。

③**確定自己想要表達的要點**。在瞭解了聽眾的性質和明確了演講目的之後，演講者就能確定演講的要點，並以此作為整個演講內容的基礎。這些要點主要指一些新的資訊及其論證，用於說服聽眾並讓他們接受。在確定要點時，需要考慮會議規定的演講時間。如果規定的時間為15分鐘，那麼最好選擇1至2個要點；如果允許演講者用1小時作報告，那麼也只能把自己演講的要點限制在4至5個。否則，無論演講者演講的時間有多長，現場聽眾能記得的資訊總是有限的。在宣讀自己的研究論文時，至少有四個要項要清楚地傳達給現場聽眾，即研究目的或動機，研究方法，研究結果，以及研究結果的意義。通常，學術會議上會發放學術會議的論文集，演講者的論文自然列於其中，因此只需在演講時概要地介紹上述四個要項。例如，簡略地描述實驗方法，而不必詳細解釋自己實驗方法的細節；不需列出所有的詳細資料只要提供足夠的資料支援自己的結論，而且，儘量利用使讀者一目了然的圖形來代替複雜的表格。

④**選擇有效支援要點的資料**。在準備階段第四個步驟中需考慮的問題是：什麼樣的資料最能支援要表達的要點？什麼樣的資料能有效地吸引聽眾的注意力？一般而言，選擇二至四項主要的支援資料，且每項支援資料只能最多包含二至三個細節。切記不要提供過多的詳細資料，以免現場聽眾無法認出或記住演講的要點。

⑤**選取適當的組織形式整理演講內容**。準備演講的下一個步驟是選取適當的組織形式，並利用此組織形式來架構演講的要點及相關資料。組織形式有許多種，一定要根據演講的主題、主要目的及聽眾的性質來選取合適的組織形式。例如，如果演講者企圖告訴聽眾如何做一件事情，則可以將要表達的資訊組成一個指引列表。另一方面，如果要介紹實驗研究方面的成果，那麼可以採用標準的陳述格式，即依次介紹研究背景及目的、實驗材料及方法、研究結果及對研究結果的討論。如果需要比較兩種不同的方法或技術，則可以採用比較與對照的組織形式。在確定了適當的組織形式並初步整理了演講內容之後，應該再次對演講的內容進行篩選，將必要

的內容留下，把不必要的內容刪除。千萬不要在演講內容中提供過多的資料。不是要點、不能直接支援要點的資料都應加以省略。

⑥**準備演講內容的大綱**。第六個步驟是撰寫一份演講內容的大綱，以作為練習與演講的依據。切記：大綱應簡略，通常包括要點、主要的支援資料，並把這些要點和支援資料按照步驟⑤中選定的組織形式進行安排。當然，大綱的寫法因報告人的需求而異。英語能力很強而且經常演講的人可能只需要非常簡略的大綱，而其他人則可能喜歡有一個較完整的大綱。較完整的大綱通常包含報告主題、要點、支援要點的資料（如實驗程式，材料及主要結果）及結論或總結。在絕大多數的國際學術會議上（不管是全體會議還是分會場），大家都會期望宣讀論文的演講者能面對現場聽眾說話，而不只是向聽眾朗讀一篇準備好的研究報告。況且，會議規定的時間也不允許演講者將一整篇研究報告念完。所以演講者應該準備依據筆記或投影片的內容而演講，不要直接朗讀研究報告，也不要把演講內容一字一句地背下來。演講者正確的準備方法是先以大綱方式寫下要點，然後熟悉這些要點及其支援資料，接著多練習以自然、口語化的方式表達這些內容並在不同要點之間作順暢轉接。

⑦**利用適當的視覺教具**。視覺教具包括：投影片，幻燈片，翻轉圖表，黑板，印製文件，立體實物，電腦螢幕投影等種類。視覺教具是學術演講不可缺少的重要組成部分。它們具有以下重要的作用：首先，視覺教具可以作為整個演講內容的提示，以幫助演講者記得所要表達的要點。視覺教具甚至可以完全取代演講者的大綱或筆記。其次，視覺教具能使現場聽眾的注意力集中在演講者所表達的資訊上。當演講者需要強調某個要點時，最好能利用視覺教具來支援該要點。研究表明，聽眾對演講中視覺教具上內容的記憶要比對口頭內容的記憶更加有效。最後，視覺教具能幫助演講者清楚、有效地把複雜的資訊傳達聽眾。有些資訊（如某種電子線路，某些物質的分子結構，某個試驗系統）難於用口語表達，而且口語表達也常會令聽眾感到混淆，但只要利用視覺教具來表達，則比較容易使聽眾領會。關於視覺圖表的設計原則，請參閱本書附錄4。

⑧ **選擇能提供具體資訊的標題**。要認真細心地選擇適當的標題，標題應能清楚反映出演講的內容。

⑨ **準備合適的導論**。學術演講開始時應該有一個清楚的能提供具體資訊的導論。演講者需在導論中介紹足夠的背景資料，以使聽眾瞭解演講的內容並看出它的價值。導論中的背景資料包括將要討論的題目或問題，問題或題目的重要性以及整個演講的要點。如果需提出並解決某個問題，則要在導論中明白地敘述這個問題，以便聽眾能正確無誤地知道問題的實質並能評價你提出的解答。如果打算批評某個不正確的理論或觀點，則應該在導論中直接告訴聽眾。如果準備介紹比現有技術更好更準確的技術，則也應該在導論中加以說明。此外，在較長的學術報告中，每次轉接到新的部分或次題目時，應該再做一個簡短的小導論，以幫助聽眾瞭解報告的結構並對下面將要介紹的資訊有心理準備。

在演講開始之前，會議主持人通常會向聽眾簡要介紹演講者的基本資料，之後，演講者只需以 "Good morning" 或 "Good afternoon" 開始直接演講。不管主持人是否介紹演講者，演講者可在第一張投影片上列出自己的演講題目和自己的姓名、學校與職位。若有必要的話，演講者通常可採用下列其中一種句型來介紹自己：

Good morning /afternoon. My name is _____, and today I will be describing the results of research on _____ conducted at Xi'an Jiaotong University, in China.

Good morning /afternoon. 或 Thank you . It's an honor to be here.

Today I would like to report on _____.

Today I will be reporting on _____.

This afternoon I will report some of our findings concerning _____.

In my report today, I'd like to present a new method for _____.

My topic today is   .

Today I will be discussing   .

⑩**準備簡明的總結**。一般而言，聽眾比較重視演講的開頭和結尾。換句話說，聽眾對演講最後的內容比較感興趣，希望從中抓住演講者總結性的評論或建議。所以演講者在報告結束前，應以非常簡潔的方式重述自己的最重要的結論或建議，以及支援這些要點的主要理由，以便給聽眾對這些論點留下深刻的印象。

述結論之後，演講者還可自己利用下列句子來鼓勵聽眾提問：

If there are any questions, I'd be happy to take them now.

If there are any questions, I'd be happy to answer.

如果沒有時間讓聽眾提問，則演講者在作了總結之後，可以用"Thank you"或"This concludes my report. Thank you."來結束演講。

(2)練習

在準備妥當了演講內容之後，接下來演講者必須練習自己的演講技巧。對於一個成功的演講而言，勤於練習演講的技巧是最有效的手段。即使是一個非常善於作學術演講的學者，他（她）也需要以自己慣用的方式進行練習，以期獲得最佳的演講效果。練習使演講者能找出演講中可能出現的瑕疵並消除它們，練習使演講者能自然、流暢地進行各部分內容之間的轉接，而不會出現不自然的停頓和開始；練習還能使演講者確定準備的演講內容需要多長時間才能完成，進而決定是否有必要增刪一些內容，以便演講者最終能以一個令人滿意的節奏表達自己的內容。所有以上這些練習的作用可以使演講者對自己的演講能力充滿自信，而且進一步以最有效、最有說服力的方式來作演講。

練習演講的最好辦法是請同事或朋友來聽你的試講。要求他們聽完你的整個演講，聽講過程中儘量做筆記，但不要中途提任何問題。試講結束後，請他們「解剖」你的演講。你需要記下他們在聽試講時感到不恰當的地方和感到效果很強的地方。對於前者，你可以立即換用一種其他方式加以陳述，看是否使內容表達得很清楚。對於後者，也許值得你在其他部分內容的表達中加以採用。如果覺得召集同事或朋友來聽你試講這種方法不便實現的話，你也可以利用錄影機將你的試講錄下來，然後觀看錄影帶，點評你自己的表現。或者使用錄音機錄下你的講話，然後再重播錄音帶，這種方法特別適用於採用讀手稿的演講方式。不管是看錄影還是聽錄音帶，都應該注意是否有些地方暫停得太久，是否存在不自然的各部分的轉接，是否出現因為神情緊張而引起的急促語調、無意義的聲音、重複呆板的手勢等等。

在練習自己的演講時，應該注意下列事項：

①**找到適當重複要點的方法**。適當地重提演講內容的要點，特別是在演講的總結中重複要點，對於加深聽眾的印象是必要的。然而，用一模一樣的詞句重複要點會使演講顯得呆板、單調，所以建議在第三次或第四次重提要點時改換恰當的詞句。

②**想出各部分之間的自然轉接的方式**。練習時應記下演講過程中哪些地方會出現停頓，然後確定是否能插入一、二個片語或語句作為轉接的橋樑。如果發現無法找到合適的片語或語句用於轉接，則可能是整個演講內容的結構不合理造成的，遇到這種情況，必須對演講內容重新組織。實際上，最好的轉接方式是自然地介紹新的次題目。在轉接時，演講者可利用如 "Now let me describe…" 或 "Next, let's look at…" 等語句，以使聽眾在這些句子的引導下注意下面要介紹的內容。另一種方式是直接地說明下面要講的內容，如把投影片打到螢幕上，直接說 "Here are the results of our experiment." 以介紹實驗結果。

③**使自己熟悉演講時所用的設備**。演講時常使用的設備有幻燈機、投影機、電腦螢幕、麥克風等，想像一下，如果在演講過程中，演講者張皇失措地操作某個設備，結果浪費了聽眾寶貴的時間，而且使他們感到煩

擾，這是個多麼令人難堪的景象，尤其是你的演講必須依賴某個設備，而你根本就不會操作它，情況就更糟。所以，演講者如果打算在演講時使用某個設備，必須事先要確認所有設備無任何障礙，而且要學會如何操作。如果在報告中必須做某種演示或需用動態模型，則應確定自己熟練地掌握了演示方法，還要確保模型沒有任何問題。此外，必要時準備好備用系統，以防萬一。

④**應事先自己準備聽眾可能提出的問題**。聽眾會針對演講的任何一點內容提出問題，演講者需要回答問題並使他們感到滿意。如果做不到這一點，那麼作為一個演講者，你的可信度可能會受到質疑。因此，演講者務必要對自己演講的題目瞭解得十分透徹。練習時，演講者可以先猜測聽眾可能會提出什麼樣的問題，並對這些問題先準備好精簡的答案。也可以請幾位同學或朋友聽你試講，然後故意對你提出一些棘手的問題，然後，你可以針對這些問題進行更充分的思考並做出解答。對於聽眾可能提出的每一個問題都給出一個明確的答案是不必要的。因為有些問題是任何人都沒有答案的。但是，如果你的研究工作很深入，並且掌握最新的研究進展，你一定有能力、有信心回答大部分問題。當聽眾提出了演講者無法回答的問題，應該直接表示自己不知道或不確定應該如何回答，如可以坦白地說

"We don't have the answer to that yet."、"We aren't sure about that yet." 或 "We're still working on that question."。事實上，解決這些不能給出答案的問題正好應該是演講者今後進一步開展研究工作的任務。

⑤**通過練習改進自己的演講風格**。應該訓練自己用清楚、專業的演講方式。在演講時，要抬頭挺胸，不要駝背或斜靠在講臺上。聲音不要由喉嚨或胸部上方發出，而應該讓喉嚨與胸部放鬆。既不要大聲吼叫，也不要喃喃自語，音量要適中。儘量利用生動、自然的手勢。要適當變化語調及講話的速度。總之，使自己的演講富有表現力，充滿激情。此外，還要在練習時記下可能出現的一些令人生厭的毛病，如咬手指甲、玩弄鉛筆、不斷地重複呆板的動作如經常出現 "you know" 或 "and-uh" 這種口頭語等，然後採取措施控制自己，在正式演講時避免這些不良習慣。重要的

是，要自然地、放鬆地進行演講。

如果應邀在重要的國際會議上作大會報告，則建議演講者請一位以英語為母語的人或多次參加國際會議的資深人士試聽自己的演講，聽取他們有關演講技巧及內容方面的意見。

在練習演講時，還要注意儘量用簡單的詞語與表達方式，而且應該又慢又清晰地發音。那種認為只有用複雜的語句和快速的發音才能贏得聽眾，使聽眾承認自己研究價值的想法是不正確的。只要自己的研究工作本身有一定的水準，演講風格良好，則自然會取得聽眾的信任。此外，演講中應避免生硬不自然的句子構造。如在介紹某個圖表中的資料時，應該用"This figure shows that…"或"From this figure, we can see that…"，而避免採用"It is shown in this figure that…"或"It can be seen from this figure that…"這樣不恰當的被動態句子。

⑥**宣讀手稿時應練習生動的語調**。有些演講者採用宣讀預先準備好的手稿來作演講。越來越多的事實證明，以呆板大聲宣讀手稿容易使聽眾感到厭倦。所以在練習時應注意在大聲朗讀時變化自己的聲調，如讀到非常重要的詞語時提高音量，而對於不太重要的詞語時降低音量；在恰當之處作一次暫停；要強調形成顯著對比的詞語等等。另外，注意要間或與聽眾進行目光接觸。

(3)演講

演講的方式可分成即席演講和直接朗讀手稿兩種。無論採用哪一種演講方式，均需作好充分的準備和認真的練習。上一節「練習」的內容基本上都是針對即席演講而展開討論的。

即席演講是絕大多數演講者採用的演講方式，也是大部分聽眾樂於接受的演講方式。它不要求演講者逐字逐句地記住整個演講的內容，而是緊緊圍繞演講的要點展開陳述。演講者的手中只有一份大綱（附關鍵字與幻燈片清單）以及一些必要的數據資料。與朗讀手稿相比，演講者說話的音調與快慢非常接近自然，可以保持演講者與聽眾的目光交流，以便在發現聽眾感到迷惑時增添一些解釋或重新組織資訊；還有，可根據聽眾的反應及時調整嗓音、語調和強調語氣。反之，朗讀手稿方式對聽眾來說難於接受。朗讀手稿時演講者由於盯著手稿很少與聽眾目光交流，因而無法依據聽眾的反應來變化自己的節奏與聲調。如果必須採用朗讀手稿的方式，記住要定期地把自己的眼光自然地投向聽眾，還要注意採用生動的語調和適當的暫停。

大多數的專業人士都有這樣的體會：越是臨近演講，越是感到神經緊張。想想自己將要在幾十個甚至數百個研究人員面前作學術報告，況且還必須用英語演講，感到緊張確實是難免的。對一般演講者來論，在國際學術會議上克服怯場是擺在面前的一個挑戰。

如何才能控制住自己的緊張情緒呢？首先，確信自己已經精心地準備好演講，包括已將所有的視覺教具和大綱紙條已準備妥當，同時自己在心理上和身體上也作好了準備。記住，學術演講是一個體力活動。與其他所有體力活動一樣，講演之前要用餐，還應該做一些暖身運動。因為運動對緩解緊張情緒特別有效。還要注意自己穿著是否適當，是否已經過修飾。服裝須與自己的身份一致，表示自己是專業研究人員。演講者個人的外表本身是他（她）強有力的「視覺教具」，聽眾會在整個聽講過程中看著演講者，他們會部分參考他們所看到的來判斷演講者的專業可信度。如果自己深信自己看上去非常好，那麼演講者在演講時更會有自信。

其次，演講者需在自己演講之前與聽眾見面和聊天，看看他們對什麼內容興趣。儘量地瞭解聽眾可以幫助演講者更多地思考聽眾的意願，也有助於演講者避免陷入自我麻痺狀態，而且還會促使自己採用更加自然的、口語化的風格作演講。

第三，當演講者站起來去作演講時，要果敢地、信心百倍地邁到講臺上。可以先應要求適當地表達謝意。有些有經驗的演講者在開始時還會說些笑話、典故或軼事，以活躍一下會場的氣氛。如果自己喜歡講笑話或故事，而且還很擅長的話，那麼儘管去做。但是，千萬不要勉強。如果覺得自己在這方面不在行，甚至連試一下都不需要。

第四，在進行正式的演講時，務必使自己全神貫注在所演講的內容上。手裡攥著包含所有要點及其支援資料的大綱。使聽眾明白所演講的題目是十分重要的，在演講過程中顯示每一張幻燈片以使聽眾能理解和評價它。保持節奏，不要浪費時間。如果你的演講內容是經過精心組織的、令人感興趣的，那麼聽眾會注意你、支援你，否則，他們會失去興趣。不必擔心自己的英語表達能力不夠好，只要已經準備好了清楚的、內容充實的、有意義的演講，即使英語表達上有些小毛病，仍然能得到聽眾的肯定。

第五，注意自己的演講姿態。應該讓自己適度地走動，並利用恰當、生動的手勢來強調演講內容。不要僵直地站在一個地方不動，也不要一直躲在講臺後面。要抬頭挺胸，精神抖擻。要常常看著聽眾，並注意聽眾對演講內容的反應，以便及時調整演講的內容和表達的方式。說話的速度要慢，發音要清晰。要放鬆，順其自然，使聽眾覺得你對自己的研究工作很感興趣，並樂意和大家分享研究成果。切記，千萬不要做出那些令聽眾感到不適的動作，在身上某處搔癢，撫摸某件東西，輕咬指甲等。

最後，要鼓勵聽眾提問。如果你對聽眾提出的問題一時想不出一個簡短的回答，可以禮貌地告訴提問者你會以後再與他討論。最重要的是不要出現與提問者產生對抗的狀態。事實上，這種對抗的狀態不僅使提問者感到不適，而且，即使提問者頗為不公正、不友好，那麼作為演講者還是會被認為是產生不愉快局面的主要責任者。因此，解決這個問題的最佳方法是當眾平息任何對立的局面，然後私下再進行調解。

(4)作英語演講時需格外注意的事項

多採用以簡單的詞所組成的簡短的句子，避免使用冗長、生硬的句子。

演講時發音要清晰，聲音要宏亮。

控制說話的速度，儘量要慢些。

一定要把英語單詞中的母音發出來。

確保每一個英語單詞的最後一個音節都發音清楚，尤其是字尾是子音時。

所說的每一個句子必須是完整的句子。

掌握自己專業領域中常用英語單字的正確發音方法，對於自己不知道重讀音節的詞，應該先閱讀詞典加以確定。有條件時，可請英語為母語的外國教授、同事或朋友指教。

應將演講內容中所有的關鍵字都包含在視覺教具中，以便使聽眾能從口頭及教具上都可理解我們演講中提出的某個詞。

不要過分擔心演講中出現些小小的語法錯誤。聽眾知道英語不是我們的母語，他們會原諒一些語法上的小毛病。他們並不特別注意我們的英語表達是否完美，而是特別關心我們能否以清楚的方式對他們提供一些有價值的資訊。

附錄4 圖表的設計及應用

　　圖表是科技論文或會議簡報的重要組成部分。在很多的情形中，圖表是論文作者或演講人把複雜的資訊傳達給讀者或聽眾的最直接和最有效的方式。

　　心理學家指出，只要簡單地用重複的方法就能提高記憶資訊的能力和強度，特別是在更換另一種重複的方法時更是如此。圖表與文字敘述的結合能產生更加強烈、易於記憶的資訊，而且圖表能表達文字敘述部分要點的總結。所以，設計優良的圖表能使讀者或聽眾對圖表內容的印象特別深刻，以便幫助他們較容易記住這些內容。對於學術演講，由於聽眾可能沒有書面的資料供參考，因此設計精良的圖表所扮演的角色更加重要。

　　當單獨的文字敘述不可能或十分無效地表達一個概念或物體時，當需要清楚地強調一個要點，特別是總結時，當需規範或方便地表達資料時，就需要使用圖表。

　　在設計圖表之前，必須瞭解讀者的閱讀習慣及圖表表達重點的慣例。讀者期望資料的排列順序是從左到右和從上到下。例如，圖中我們應該使用橫坐標以表示自變數，且自變數的數值應該從圖的左邊開始，並向右逐漸增加。縱坐標則應該代表因變數。表中最右邊的列通常列出獨立變數（時間、項目序號等），右邊的列給出非獨立變數，表中最上面一行應給出各非獨立變數的名稱（或符號）及單位。圖內表達重點的慣例為：中心位置比周圍更重要；前部的比背景上的更重要；大的比小的重要；厚粗的比細薄的更重要；具有相同的尺寸、形狀、位置或顏色的東西之間有關係；包含很多資訊的面積內的是指最重要的資訊，與背景成強烈對比的東西更突出。

本附錄將簡略地介紹科技論文中圖表的設計與應用的原則，以及會議演講中使用圖表等視覺教具的方法與注意事項。

(1)科技論文中圖表的設計與應用

在向專業學術期刊投稿前，作者務必先參考所投期刊上已刊登的若干篇文章，以查詢該期刊標準的圖表格式，尤其是圖表標題與標記的格式以及標點符號的用法。在自己製作圖表時，應該完全使用該期刊的標準格式。

為了提高圖表的可讀性，圖表中的標題與標記應以大小寫書寫。使用全部小寫是錯誤的，而使用全部大寫則會降低圖表的可讀性，並佔用過多的空間。

與英文報紙上的標題一樣，圖表標題中的冠詞the或a常被省略。同時要注意，圖表的標題應該既精確又能提供具體的資訊。

圖表的標點符號的用法，不同期刊或許會有不同的規定。如有的用"Figure 1"或"Figure 1.1"或"Figure 1-1"，而有的則用"figure 1"或"Fig .1"等。有些刊物習慣在圖表的序號與標題之間加上句號及一個空格，還有些期刊則加冒號及一個空格。因此作者在製作圖表時應仔細查詢和遵循所投期刊的標準格式，千萬不要隨意使用不符合要求的標點方式。

圖表的序號與標題可位於圖的上面或下面，序號一般位於標題的左側。圖上的尺規說明應該易於理解，尺規旁一定要標出單位。尺規數值需水平書寫。若引用他人的圖表，則應在圖表下方註明出處文獻。出處文獻的寫法與參考文獻的寫法一樣，但在不使讀者迷惑的前提下，為節省空間，可以採用更多的縮寫。

一般情況下可用座標紙畫出曲線圖，以便提供較精確的資訊。如果自己畫出圖中的格線，則可使矩形網格的長、短邊之比約為1.5：1，即其精確值為$\sqrt{2}$：1。有時為了在眾多的格線提供的精確性和較少格線使用時的清晰性與表現力之間取得折衷，則可在橫坐標上方加上細線以進一步區分。

圖表中的資料應該清楚且完整，以便在必要時圖表和文字敘述部分分開而單獨使用。圖表的標題及標記應該十分清晰明確，以便某些讀者在沒有閱讀論文全文的情況下，還能夠理解圖表中的資訊及領會這些資訊的重點。

在科技論文中，常用的圖表可以分為九類：線圖（line charts），直條圖（bar charts），層面圖（surface strata charts），圓形圖（pie or circle charts），流程圖與組織圖（flow sheets and organization charts），地圖（map charts），繪圖（drawings and diagrams），照片（photographs），以及表格（tables）。下面將引述這些不同種類圖表的應用場合和設計方法。

線圖

線圖分為折線圖和曲線圖。它們是科技論文中最常用的、製作及閱讀較簡便的圖形，最適用於展示連續性數據的變化趨勢以及最高點或最低點的重要性，也能清楚地比較不同數據或變數在某段時間內的變動（參見圖1）。但是，線圖不適用於進行量之間的明顯的比較，而且不能比較清楚表示精確的數據或個別數據的重要性（除了最高點與最低點以外）。為表示連續過程的比較，可以在同一圖上用幾根曲線，然而若圖上包含4條以上並且相交的線，則圖的內容會變得複雜而難於理解。在多線圖上，必須在線側加上標記，標記無邊框（見圖1）。線條相交時，應該用符號、顏色或圖例標記配合使用（見圖2）。不同的圖進行比較時，應使兩圖的座標一致。

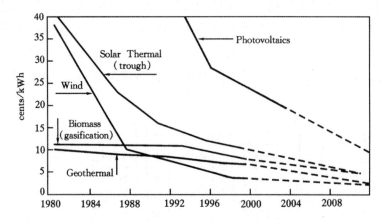

Fig.1　Renewable Electricity Cost Trends and Projections

圖1　線旁有標記的折線圖

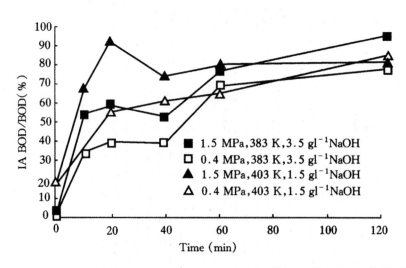

Figure 4.　Influence of oxygen partial pressure on ratio of Immediately Available BOD (LA BOD) to BOD for temperatures of 383 and 403 K and sodium hydroxide concentration of 1.5 and 3.5gl-1 for 120 min of the oxidation process.

圖2　用不同符號並有標記的折線圖

線圖的一個重要問題是：繪製時是將代表不同數值的點連接成折線狀還是需經平滑處理？若要顯示連續過程的趨勢，則用平滑曲線；若過程或變化是非連續的，平滑曲線會引起誤解。在精確度必要時，通常可在圖上保留數值點，且同時用平滑曲線反映過程變化的內在規律，見圖3所示。

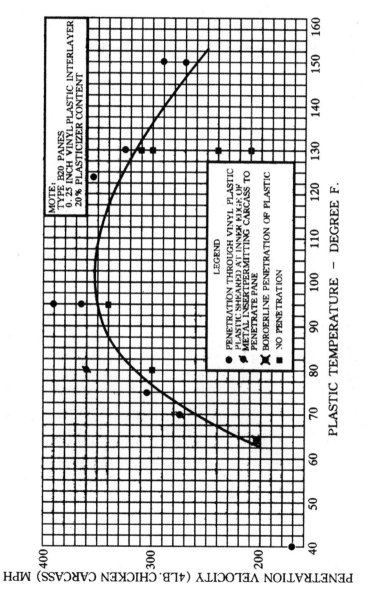

Figure 3. Single-line chart with faired curve; the effect of plastic temperature on the velocity at which the carcass of a bird penetrates an aircraft win dow, *Soutce*; CAA Tehnical Development Report No. 105, Fig, 11.

圖3 平滑曲線圖

直條圖

以尺規表明長度的直條代表數值,適用於表示不同時期的數量和大小,或同一時期內某物的大小或相對值,或整個量中各部分之間的相對大小。直條圖能清楚地展示幾個不同項目之間的關係、數量的對比,以及不同數量之間相近或相差關係。它比線圖更能表達引人注目的比較。但是,與線圖相比,直條圖不能很清楚地反映連續性的趨勢或變化動向,而且,直條圖也不能比較清楚表示精確的數量,除非在每個直條上加上表示精確數量的標記。

若表示不同時期的自變數的數值,則用豎直條較為有效(見圖4);若表示同一時期一些項目的不同量,則用橫直條較為妥當,見圖5所示。直條的寬度及直條間的間隙都應該相等。

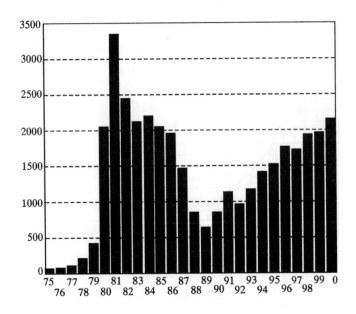

Fig.1: Heating-Only Heat Pump Sales in Austria

圖4　豎直條圖

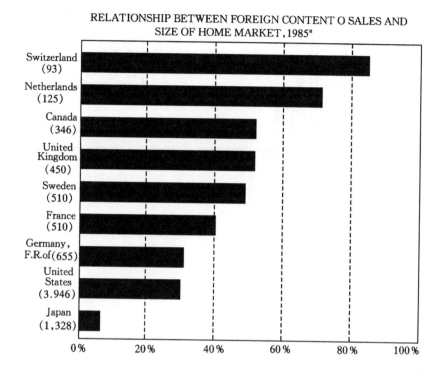

RELATIONSHIP BETWEEN FOREIGN CONTENT O SALES AND
SIZE OF HOME MARKET, 1985[a]

ions in World Development Trends and Prospects (*New York: United Nations*, 1988).

圖5　橫直條圖

　　直條之間間隙的大小既要使直條間儘量靠近以便易於比較，也要能使直條間相互分開以防混淆，直條圖中的直條可以結合在一起，這樣可以在同一圖上進行不同分項的比較，且使圖面緊湊，但是，結合在一起的各直條應該以不同深淺的陰影或不同圖案的陰影加以區別。見圖6所示。

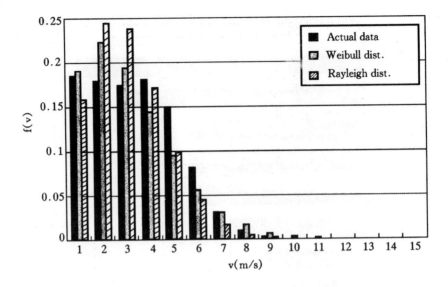

a The amounts given in parenthesis are the figures in billions of U.S. dollars for the country's GDP in 1985.

Source: United Nations Centre on Transnational Corporations, Transnational Corporat-

Figure 5.　Weibull and Rayleigh approximations of the actual probability distribution of wind speeds.

圖6　結合直條圖

　　一獨立直條又分成幾個部分，而每一部分代表分量或百分比，這種直條被稱作百分數直條。百分數直條的各部分應以不同深淺的陰影或不同圖案的陰影加以區分，並加以標記。對於橫直條，深色的陰影通常置於橫直條的左邊，淡色的陰影則排在右邊（見圖7）。對於豎直條圖，深色的陰影放在底部，且自下面上陰影由深到淺排列。在演講用的投影片上，也可以用不同的顏色以示區分。

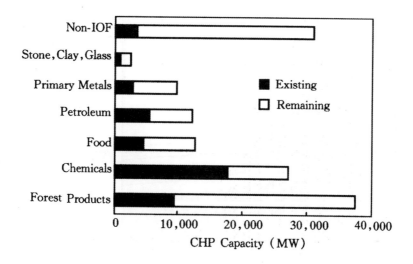

Figure 8.   Existing and Remaining CHP Potential Sorted by Industry

圖7　百分數直條圖

層面圖

　　層面圖亦稱片狀圖、條狀圖或帶狀圖（圖8）。層面圖與多線圖類似，線下面面積用不同的陰影或顏色以給出量的概念。然而，對於同樣的數據，當量值較比例或變化趨勢更重要時，層面圖比線圖更能滿意地表示要強調的內容。其缺點是，讀者無法從層面圖上獲得精確的信息，而且，當層面圖高度不規則或所繪曲線交叉時，層面圖將不適用。只有對於平緩的，有規則的過程或變化，層面圖才適用。

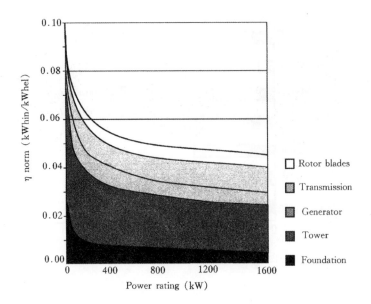

Fig.2.　Contributions to ηnorm of five WT component groups as a function of power rat-ing (derived from [21,22,30,35]). 'Transmission' includes hub. shaft and gear box.

圖8　層面圖

圓形圖

　　圓形圖的優點是能清楚顯示幾個不同項目之間量的百分比、大的百分數和小的百分數之間的對比以及相近百分數之間的相似性（參見圖9）。但是，除非加上標記，否則圓形圖不能清楚地表示任何精確的數量或兩個相近百分數之間的差別。圓形圖適用於份量不多（最多5～6個）的場合。若所示項目過多時，圓形圖會變得繁雜而造成讀者了解內容的不便。記住，在圓頂部作為起點按順時針方向計量。圖10則是另一種形式的圓形圖。

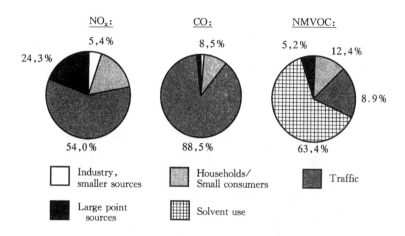

district of Augsburg in 1998 according to emission estimates 2.

圖9　平面圓形圖

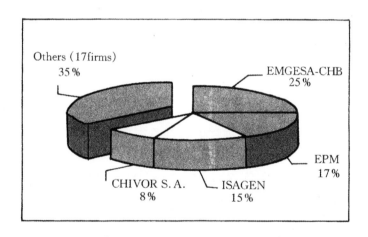

Figure 1.　NO*x*, CO and NMVOC source apportionment of the annual emissions of the
　　　　　Fig.1.　Capacity ownership.

圖10　立體圓形圖

流程圖與組織圖

　　流程圖採用符號或幾何圖形與連接線來表示一個過程的步驟和運行

（見圖11）。組織圖與流程圖相似，但不表達一個實際的過程而代表一個組織內部的行政關係（見圖12）。

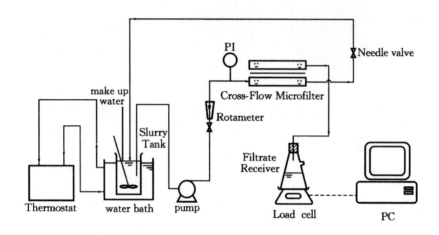

Figure 2.　A schematic diagram of the cross-flow microfiltration system.

圖11　流程圖

　　流程圖通常從左至右佈置，連接線應該加箭頭以示流動方向。零組件或設備可以用幾何圖形或符號表示，但必須使用專業領域中公認的或標準規定的符號，幾何圖形上必須有標記說明。為便於讀者讀懂流程圖，通常要求按頁面的長度方向佈置圖形，雖然可能需要讀者轉90°才能閱讀，但總比擠在狹窄紙面上的圖好些，有必要時還需用大張紙且將圖形折疊起來。圖的符號及標題一般位於圖的底部且居中對齊。組織圖中矩形框內的內容代表組織內的一個單位。利用連接線和相對位置指出單位之間的相互關係。框內的字要足夠大，而框與框之間要離得夠遠，頁面上不要顯得過擠。閱讀組織圖通常按從上到下的順序進行。在演講時，為產生強烈的視覺效果，投影片上可採用彩色的流程圖與組織圖。

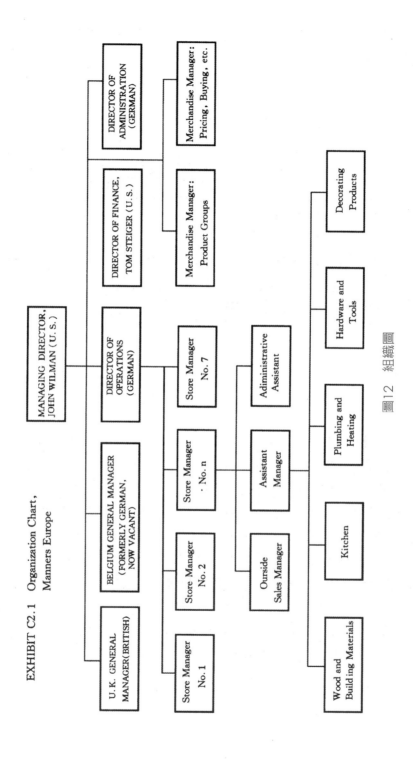

EXHIBIT C2.1   Organization Chart,
Manners Europe

圖12　組織圖

地圖

地圖適用於圖示地理的或空間的分佈。地圖上的符號及文字必須清楚易讀。參見圖13。

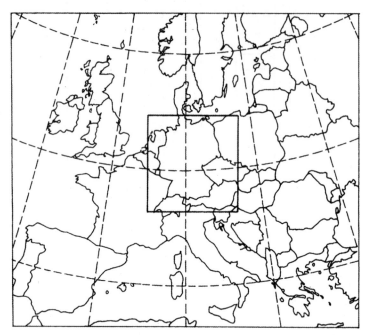

Figure 1.　　Total model domain and German subarea.

圖13　　地圖

繪圖

繪圖在顯示工作原理和不同零組件功能上的關係方面特別有效（見圖14）。繪圖也能清楚地展示某個物體的內部結構（見圖15），製圖時，通常可省略一些不重要的細節，所以繪圖能使讀者或聽眾的注意力集中在複雜物體的少數重要部分。繪圖的缺點是不如照片那樣具有具體性和真實性，而且需要特殊的技能或設備才能製作，有時候製圖也很費時。

繪圖包括電子線路圖到複雜機械裝置的藍圖。繪圖的各部分應該加上標記，使其清晰且有意義。若展示的為一含有少數零組件的裝置，零組件名稱

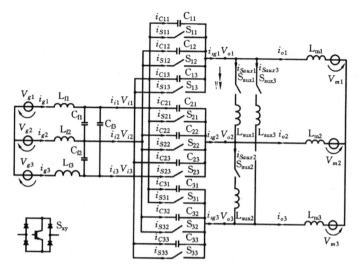

Fig.3.　AC/AC ARCP-MC II [6]

圖14　繪圖一

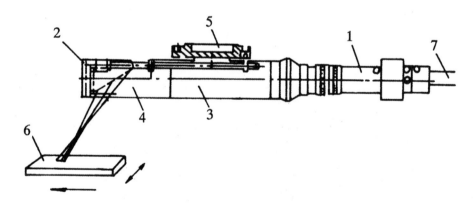

Fig.1　Experimental setup for laser processing: (1) Collimator, (2) Integrating mirror, (3) Body, (4) Mirror head, (5) Mounting flange, (6) Coating/substrate, (7) Optical fiber

圖15　繪圖二

可直接標記在繪圖上，且用箭頭指示相應零組件。若顯示包括許多零組件的複雜裝置，則應採用文字符號或數字。繪圖的序號、標題應在底部居中位置。如出處文獻有寫出的必要，則將出處文獻寫在較低的右下角。

照片

照片是展示某物體外表的一種很有用的工具，具有真實性與具體性（見圖16）。然而，照片強調物體的外觀而不是內部結構或剖面，所以可能會失去很多細節。選擇照片時要格外注意需要展示的主要部分能夠顯著地表達出來。為了提升印刷時的品質，宜採用高對比度、有光澤的、背景無干擾的8×10英吋的黑白原版照片。建議採用數位相機拍攝實物。

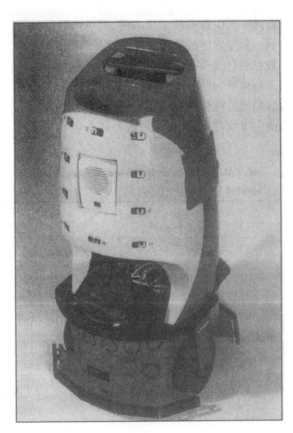

Figure 4.   CARL from the Universidade de Aveiro in Portugal.

圖16　照片

表格

　　表格可用來方便地列出大量的資料或精確的資料，而且表格的出現不會使論文失去連貫性。但是，表格不能清楚地表示變化的趨勢與方向，而且表格需要讀者自己去尋找和領會數據或資料之間的關係。因此只有在有必要提供大量精確資料或資料，或在難於表達資料變化趨勢時才採用表格這種形式。

　　為使表格易於閱讀，應該在表內外留出足夠的空間。如果表格出現在有文字敘述的頁面上，那麼通常應該在表的上方及下方各留出2-3行空白。各列之間和每列中各項之間均應留出足夠的空間。表格的序號、標題一般置於表格頂部。若表格中各列之間分開或各行水平方向需隔開各部分，大部分情況下可用單實線。若需特別強調某一列或某一行，也可用雙實線或粗實線。如果各列之間與各行之間留有足夠空白，那麼除了表頭上下的兩根橫線及表底一根橫線外，可以不用其他任何橫線及豎線，如圖17所示。表格中每一列上有表頭，表頭中水平方向寫出項目或參數名稱，項目或參數第一個字母通常為大寫。表頭中還需要寫出項目或參數的單位。若同一列中資料的單位不同，則應將資料轉化為同一單位列出。同一列中數字的排列應以小數點為準上下對齊。若表格中的某個資料引自他人文獻，則可以用英文字母或*號等符號在該資料右上角標示，並在表格底線下用註腳示出出處。若需對表中自己的資料或某些特殊項目進行說明，應採用與標示他人文獻資料不同的字母或符號，其註腳的位置應在表底線與文獻註腳之間。

(2)會議演講中圖表的設計和應用

　　在學術會議演講時常用到的視覺教具有：投影片、幻燈片、立體模型或實物、海報、講義、錄影帶、黑板。目前最通用的、效果最佳的是利用電腦及多媒體投影機放映的投影幻燈片，這種投影幻燈片通常用微軟公司的Powerpoint 2000辦公軟體製作。相比之下，這種投影幻燈片較易製作，容易控制聽眾的注意力，無論聽眾人數多少都很適用，不會浪費聽眾的時間，而且對演講人而言是非常有用的提示工具。

Table 3　Nd：YAG Laser Parameters Used in Laser Remelting of HVOF Sprayed Coating

Power, W	Traverse Speed, mm/min	Beam Width, mm	specific Energy, Theoretical(J/mm²)
Mirror 1			
4000	1100	10	21.8
4000	1400	10	17.1
4000	1700	10	14.1
4000	2000	10	12.0
Mirror 2			
4000	400	20	30.0
4000	500	20	24.0
4000	600	20	20.0
4000	700	20	17.1

圖17　典型表格

會議演講中圖表的設計與應用的原則和科技論文中的相同。然而，由於應用場合的不同，會議演講中圖表的設計與應用應注意下列事項。

在國際學術會議作演講時，演講者的語句應儘量符合英語語法，即使有些語法上的不妥，仍然不會使演講的成功受到影響。但是，投影幻燈片上的圖表及文字內容則不應該出現任何文法上的錯誤，否則可能會影響演講者的專業形象。為避免這種情況出現，建議演講者無論如何要事先仔細核查投影幻燈片上的英文文法，防止由於各種原因引起的問題。若不是很有把握，則可請求他人幫助。

圖表等設計應該盡量簡化，以便聽眾能快速而又輕易地理解其內容。若有可能，應該盡量避免使用表格而應多採用各種圖形。若有必要使用表格，則表格的設計與內容應盡量簡單，只要提供足夠的資料以支援自己的論點即可。論文中很適用的表格，可能因其複雜而不適用於會議演講，因此，應該在投影幻燈片上設計一些較大的、較簡單的表格。

投影幻燈片上都應該使用大小寫字母。千萬不要用全部大寫，因為全部大寫字母會降低可讀性並浪費頁面空間。另外，投影幻燈片上的字型要足夠大，以便讓會議廳最後一排的聽眾也都能看清楚。

在設計投影幻燈片時，應使所有的頁面都具有統一的標準格式，如在每一頁面上，在同一地方標明頁數，下端標明演講的題目與日期，上下左右邊都應留有很寬的空白邊，應該採用同一種字型，而且字體大小應該大致相同。此外，也可以考慮在每一頁面的同一位置上放上自己大學的校徽或研究機構的徽記。這樣可使演講內容顯得連貫、專業。

對僅有文字的投影幻燈片，則要注意以下幾點。首先，每個頁面上的資料最多只應該有五個不同的要點。如果需要表達六個以上的不同要點，則應將其分成兩個頁面。若有可能，每個頁面上應有不同的副標題。其次，文字投影幻燈片上每個資料項目最好不要超過兩行，而且千萬不要超過三行。最後，應該使用大小寫的英文字母，即句子或項目的第一個字及名稱應以大寫字母開頭，其他的字母應該均小寫。全部大寫的字或句子的可讀性較差。另外，應該使用Times New Roman字體。

還要說明的是：投影幻燈片上所使用的色彩應盡量柔和，以免使聽眾感到刺眼。頁面上的圖可使用不同顏色的線條，以示區別。文字部分也可用不同的顏色和正、斜體，以作對比或強調。

科技英文論文寫作實用指南 **Practical Guide to Scientific English Writing**

附錄 參考文獻

1. Huckin T N, Olsen L A. Technical Writing and Professional Communication for Nonnative Speakers of English. 2nd ed. New York: McGraw-Hill, Inc., 1991

2. Mills G H, Walter J A. Technical Writing. 5th ed. New York: Holt Rinehart and Winston, 1986

3. Eisenberg A. Effective Technical Communication. New York: McGraw-Hill, Inc., 1982

4. Fraser C J.英文科技寫作：文法與修辭原則（English Scientific and Technical Writing）。新竹：方克濤，1995

5. Fraser C J.英文科技論文與會議簡報（English Scientific Reports and Presentation）。新竹：方克濤，1996

6. Punnett B J, Ricks D A. International Business. Boston: PWS-KENT Publishing Company, 1992

7. Gitman L J, McDaniel C. The World of Business. Cincinnati: South-Western Publishing Co., 1992

8. Appleby R C. Modern Business Administration. 6th ed. London: Pitman Publishing, 1994

9. Alter S. Information Systems: A Management Perspective. Reading: Addison-Wesley Publishing Company, Inc., 1992

10. AFEAS Administrative Organization. Alternative Fluorocarbons Environmental Acceptability Study. Washington: AFEAS Program Office, 1997

11. Michaud F, Gustafson. The Hors d'Oeuvres Event at the AAAI-2001 Mobile Robot Competition. AI Magazine, 2002, 23(1): 31-36

12. Huang K J, Lin K P. Cross-Flow Micro Filtration of Dual-Sized Submicron Particles. Separation Science and Technology, 2002, 37(10): 2231-2249

13. Kim K H, Hong J. A Mass Transfer Model for Super and Near-Critical CO2 Extraction of Spearmint Leaf Oil. Separation Science and Technology, 2002, 37(10):

2271-2288

14. Garcia A, Arbeláez L E. Market Power Analysis for the Colombian Electricity Market. Energy Economics, 2002, 24: 217-229

15. Lenzen M, Munksgaard J. Energy and CO2 Life-Cycle Analysis of Wind Turbines-Review and Applications. Renewable Energy, 2002, 26(3): 339-362

16. Nelson S A C, Soranno P A, Qi J. Land-Cover Change in Upper Barataria Basin Estuary, Louisiana, 1972-1992: Increase in Wetland Area. Environmental Management, 2002, 29(5): 716-727

17. Slemr F, Baumbach G, Blank P, et al. Evaluation of Modeled Spatially and Temporarily Highly Resolved Emission Inventories of Photosmong Precursors for the City of Augsburg: The Experiment EVA and It's Major Results. Journal of Atmospheric Chemistry, 2002, 42(1-3): 207-233

18. Ulgen K, Hepbasli A. Determination of Weibull Parameters for Wind Energy Analysis of Izmir, Turkey. Energy Research, 2002, 26: 495-506

19. Langmann B, Bauer S. On the Importance of Reliable Background Concentrations of Ozone for Regional Scale Photochemical Modelling. Journal of Atmospheric Chemistry, 2002,42(1-3): 71-90

20. Tuominen J, Vuoristo P, Mäntylä T, et al. Corrision Behavior of HVOF-Sprayed and Nd-YAG Laser-Remelted High-Chromium, Nickel-Chromium Coatings. Journal of Thermal Spray Technology, 2002, 11(2): 233-243

21. Verenich S, KALLAS J. Biodegradability Enhancement by Wet Oxidation in Alkaline Media: Delignification as a Case Study. Environmental Technology, 2002, 23(6): 655-661

22. Bi T, Ni Y, Shen C M, et al. An On-line Distributed Intelligent Fault Section Estimation System for Large-scale Power Networks. Electric Power Systems Research, 2002, 62: 173-182

23. Mohn F W, Zambroni de Souza A C. On Fast Decoupled Continuation Power Flows. Electric Power System Research, 2002, 63: 105-111

24. Brar Y S, Dhillon J S, Kothari D P. Multiobjective Load Dispatch by Fuzzy Logic Based Searching Weightage Pattern. Electric Power Systems Research, 2002, 63: 149-160

25. Haese P M, Teubner M D. Heat Exchange in an Attic Space. International Journal of Heat and Mass Transfer, 2002, 45: 4925-4936

26. Riffat S B, Holt A. A Novel Heat Pipe/Ejector Cooler. Applied Thermal Engineering, 1998, 18: 93-101

27. Short G J, Guild F J, Pavier M J. Delaminations in Flat and Curved Composite

Laminates Subjected to Compressive Load. Composite Structures, 2002, 58: 249-258

28.Schäfer R, Merten C, Eigenberger G. Bubble Size Distributions in a Bubble Column Reactor under Industrial Conditions. Experimental Thermal and Fluid Science, 2002, 26: 595-604

29.Schoenmakers J G M, Heemink A W, Ponnambalam K, et al. Variance Reduction for Monte Carlo Simulation of Stochastic Environmental Models. Applied Mathematical Modelling, 2002, 26: 785-795

30.Guet S, Ooms G, Oliemans R V A. Influence of Bubble Size on the Transition from Low-Re Bubbly Flow to Slug Flow in a Vertical Pipe. Experimental Thermal and Fluid Science, 2002, 26: 635-641

31.Jönsson H, Söderberg B. An Information-based Neural Approach to generic Constraint Satisfaction. Artificial Intelligence, 2002, 142: 1-17

32.Satpathy P K, Das D, Dutta Gupta P B. A Novel Fuzzy for Steady State Voltage Stability Analysis and Identification of Critical Busbars. Electric Power System Research, 2002, 63: 127-140

33.OIT Report, On-site Power Generation Opportunities for U.S. Industry. Cogeneration and Competitive Power Journal, 2002, 17: 6-28

34.Ludwig W, Seppälä A, Lampinen M J. Experimental Study of the Osmotic Behaviour of Reverse Osmosis Membranes for Different NaCl Solutions and Hydrostatic Pressure Differences. Experimental Thermal and Fluid Science, 2002, 26: 963-969

35.Akyurt M, Al-Rabghi O M. Curtailing noncondensables in Steel Heat Pipes Using a NaCr Solution. Energy Conversion & Management, 1999, 40: 281-286

36.Miyara A, Nonaka K, Taniquchi M. Condensation Heat Transfer and Flow Pattern Inside a Herringbone-type Micro-fin Tube. International Journal of Refrigeration, 2002, 23: 141-152

37.Lü X. Modelling of Heat and Moisture Transfer in Building I. Model Program. Energy and Buildings, 2002, 34: 1033-1043

38.Thorn S, Forsman M, Zhang Q, et al. Low-threshold Motor Unit Activity During a 1-h Static Contraction in the Trapezius Muscle. International Journal of Industrial Ergonomics, 2002, 30: 225-236

39.Kim Y, Kim K R, Kang Y S, et al. On the Critical Behavior of Phase Changes of a Forward-scattered Light in an Isotropic Chiral Fluid. Chemical Physics, 2002, 283: 455-461

40.Yu W, Hodges D H, Volovoi V V. Asymptotic Construction of Reissner-like Composite Plate Theory with Accurate Strain Recovery. International Journal of Solids and Structures, 2002, 39: 5185-5203

41. Jung D, Park C, Park B. Capillary Tube Selection for HCFC22 Alternatives. International Journal of Refrigeration, 1999, 22: 604-614

42. Mortaheb H R, Kosuge H, Asano K. Hydrodynamics and Mass Transfer in Heterogeneous Distillation with Sieve Tray Column. Chemical Engineering Journal, 2002, 88: 59-69

43. Gabrielii C, Vamling L. Drop-in Replacement of R22 in Heat Pumps Used for District Heating—Influence of Equipment and Property Limitations. International Journal of Refrigeration, 2001, 24: 660-675

44. Imthias Ahamed T P, Rao N, Sastry P S. A Reinforcement Learning Approach to Automatic Generation Control. Electric Power Systems Research, 2002, 63: 9-26

45. Bhaskar K, Balasubramanyam G. Accurate Analysis of End-loaded Laminated Orthotropic Cylindrical Shells. Composite Structures, 2002, 58: 209-216

46. Van De Vanter M L. The Documentary Structure of Source Code. Information and Software Technology, 2002, 44: 767-782

47. Hawwa M A, Nayfeh A H. The General Problem of Thermoelastic Waves in Anisotropic Periodically Laminated Composites. Composites Engineering, 1995, 5(12): 1499-1517

48. Rito-Palomares M, Lyddiatt A. Process Integration Using Aqueous Two-phase Partition for the Recovery of Intracellular Proteins. Chemical Engineering Journal, 2002, 87: 313-319

49. Eiter T, Lukasiewicz T. Complexity Results for Structure-based Causality. Artificial Intelligence, 2002, 142: 53-89

50. Lee Y B, Ro S T. Frost Formation on a Vertical Plate in Simultaneously Developing Flow. Experimental Thermal and Fluid Science, 2002, 26: 939-945

51. Antoniol G, Villano U, Merlo E, et al. Analyzing Cloning Evolution in the Linux Kernel. Information and Software Technology, 2002, 44: 755-765

52. Rubinstein B Y, Bankoff S G, Davis S H. Instability of Subcooled Boiling Film on a Vertical Wall. International Journal of Heat and Mass Transfer, 2002, 45: 4937-4948

53. Yegnan A, Williamson D G, Graettinger A J. Uncertainty Analysis in Air Dispersion Modeling. Environmental Modeling & Software, 2002, 17: 639-649

54. Seifi H, Seifi A R. An Intelligent Tutoring System for a Power Plant Simulator. Electric Power Research, 2002, 62: 161-171

55. Gabrielii C, Vamling L. Changes in Optimal Distribution of Heat Exchanger Area Between the Evaporator and Suction Gas Heat Exchanger When Replacing R22 with R407C. Int J. Refrig., 1998, 21(6): 440-451

56. Bayham Y, Kayisoglu B, Gonulol E. Effect of Soil Compaction on Sunflower Growth.

Soil & Tillage Research, 2002, 68: 31-38

57. Rajapakse R K N D, Gross D. Transient Displacements of a Composite Medium with Defects Due to a Surface Pulse. Composites Engineering, 1995, 5(12): 1519-153658. Stanton N A, Baker C. Error by Disign: Methods for Predicting Device Usability. Design Studies, 2002, 23(4): 363-384

59. Celik D, Van Sciver S W. Tracer Particle Generation in Superfluid Helium Through Cryogenic Liquid Injection for Particle Image Velocimetry. Experimental Thermal and Fluid Science, 2002, 26: 971-975

60. Teichmann R, Oyama J. ARCP Soft-Switching Technique in Matrix Converters. IEEE Transactions on Industrial Electronics, 2002, 49(2): 353-361

61. Agranovski I E, Myojo T, Braddock R D, et al. Inclined Wettable Filter for Mist Purification. Chemical Engineering Journal, 2002, 89: 229-238

62. Wang Y, Vafai K. Transient Characterization of Flat Plate Heat Pipes During Startup and Shutdown Operations. International Journal of Heat and Mass Transfer, 2000, 43: 2641-2655

63. Asaeda T, Ca V T. Characteristics of Permeable Pavement During Hot Summer Weather and Impact on the Thermal Environment. Building and Environment, 2000, 35: 363-375

64. Zim C, Jastrab A, Sternberg A, et al. Description and Performance of a Near-Room Temperature Magnetic Refrigerator. Advances in Cryogenic Engineering. 1998, 43: 1759-1766

65. Barclay J A. Active and Passive Magnetic Regenerators in Gas/Magnetic Refrigerators. Journal of Alloys and Compounds, 1994, 207/208: 355-361

66. Smith J L, Iwasa Y Jr. Material and Cycle Considerations for Regenerative Magnetic Refrigeration. Advances in Cryogenic Engineering, 1990, 35: 1157-1164

67. Whitaker S. Forced Convection Heat Transfer Correlations for Flow in Pipes, Past Flat Plates, Single Cylinders, Single Spheres, and for Flow in Packed Beds and Tube Bundles. AIChE Journal, 1972, 18(2): 361-371

68. Ichinose T, Shimodozono K, Hanaki K. Impact of Anthropogenic Heat on Urban Climate in Tokyo. Atmospheric Environment, 1999, 33: 3897-3909

69. Stewart I D. Influence of Meteorological Conditions on the Intensity and Form of the Urban Heat Island Effect in Regina. The Canadian Geographer, 2000, 44(3): 271-285

70. Habeebullah M H, Akyurt M, Najjar Y S H, et al. Experimental Performance of a Waste Heat Recovery and Utilization System with a Looped Water-in-steel Heat Pipe. Applied Thermal Engineering, 1998, 18(7): 595-607

71. Collins T D, Fung P. A Visual Programming Approach for Teaching Cognitive

Modeling. Computer & Education, 2002, 39: 1-18

72. Ercetin ö, Krishnamurthy S, Dao S, et al. Provision of Guaranteed Services in Broadband LEO Satellites Networks. Computer Networks, 2002, 39: 61-77

73. Chun W, Kang Y H, Kwak H Y, et al. An Experimental Study of the Utilization of Heat Pipes for Solar Water Heaters. Applied Thermal Engineering, 1999, 19: 807-817

74. Gran H C, Hansen E W. Exchange Rates of Ethanol with Water in Water-Saturated Cement Pastes Probed by NMR. Advanced Cement Based Materials, 1998, 8: 108-117

75. Riffat S B, Omer S A, Ma X. A Novel Thermoelectric Refrigeration System Employing Heat Pipes and a Phase Change Material: an Experimental Investigation. Renewable Energy, 2001, 23: 313-323

76. Fossa M, Tanda G. Study of Free Convection Frost Formation on a Vertical Plate. Experimental Thermal and Fluid Science, 2002, 26: 661-668

77. Krishna R, Calero S, Smit B. Investigation of Entropy Effects during Sorption of Mixtures of Alkanes in MFI Zeolite. Chemical Engineering Journal, 2002, 88: 81-94

78. Chan Y T, Lee B H, Inkol R, et al. Direction Finding with a Four-Element Adcock-Butler Matrix Antenna Array. IEEE Transactions on Aerospace and Electronic Systems, 2001, 37: 1155-1162

79. Meurer C, Pietsch G, Haacke M. Electrical Properties of CFC-and HCFC-Substitutes. International Journal of Refrigeration, 2001, 24: 171-175

80. Zhu N, Vafai K. Analytical Modeling of the Startup Characteristics of Asymmetrical Flat-Plate and Disk-shaped Heat Pipes. International Journal of Heat Transfer, 1998, 41(17): 2619-2637

81. Tan X. Comparisons of Friction Models in Bulk Metal Forming. Tribology International, 2002, 35(6): 385-393

82. Cox D T, Ortega J A. Laboratory Observations of Green Water Overtopping a Fixed Deck. Ocean Engineering, 2002, 29: 1827-1840

83. Yamazaki T. A Mathematical Analysis of the Development of Oriented Receptive Fields in Linsker's Model. Neural Networks, 2002, 15(2): 201-207

84. Lee J, Kim S E. Lateral Buckling Analysis of Thin-Walled Laminated Channel-Section Beams. Composite Structures, 2002, 56(4): 391-399

85. Altmann J, Linev S, Wei β A. Acoustic-Seismic Detection and Classification of Military Vehicles—Developing Tools for Disarmament and Peace-Keeping. Applied Acoustics, 2002, 63(10): 1085-1107

86. Dejmal I, Tirosh J, Shirizly A, et al. On the Optimal Die Curvature in Deep Drawing Processes. International Journal of Mechanical Science, 2002, 44(6): 1245-1258

87. Ozmusul M S, Picu R C. Structures of Polymers in the Vicinity of Convex

Impenetrable Surfaces: the Thermal Case. Polymer, 2002, 43(17): 4657-4665

88. Golebiewski R, Makarewicz R. Engineering Formulas for Ground Effects on Broad-Band Noise. Applied Acoustics, 2002, 63(9): 993-1001

89. Bravo J M, Sinisterra J, Uris A, et al. Influence of Air Layers and Damping Layers Between Gypsum Boards on Sound Transmission. Applied Acoustics, 2002, 63(10): 1051-1059

90. Loeffler G, Hofbauer H. Does CO Burn in a Fluidized Bed? - a Detailed Chemical Kinetic Modeling Study. Combustion and Flame, 2002, 129(4): 439-452

91. Minh L Q, Tuong T P, van Mensvoort M E F, et al. Aluminum-Contaminant Transport by Surface Runoff and Bypass Flow from an acid Sulphate Soil. Agricultural Water Management, 2002, 56(3): 179-191

92. Taylor J G, Rogers M. A Control Model of the Movement of Attention. Neural Networks, 2002, 15(3): 309-326

93. Hidaka Y, Henmi Y, Ohonishi T, et al. Shock-Tube and Modeling Study of Diacetylene Pyrolysis and Oxidation. Combustion and Flame, 2002, 130(1-2): 62-82

94. Wels Susan. Stanford: Portrait of a University. Stanford: Stanford Alumni Association, 1999

95. Swift G W. Hybrid Thermoacoustic-Stirling Engines and Refrigerator. Proceedings of Symposium on Energy Engineering in the 21st Century (SEE 2000), 2000, 1: 2-17

96. Bull S R. Renewable Energy in the 21st Century. Proceedings of Symposium on Energy Engineering in the 21st Century (SEE 2000), 2000, 1: 18-30

97. Kaviany M, Oliveira A A M. Length Scales and Innovative Use of Nonequilibria in Combustion in Porous Media. Proceedings of Symposium on Energy Engineering in the 21st Century (SEE 2000), 2000, 1: 32-56

98. Gori F, Bossi L. Cooling of Two Cylinders in a Row by a Slot Jet of Air. Proceedings of Symposium on Energy Engineering in the 21st Century (SEE 2000), 2000, 1: 239-246

99. Chen X, Han P, Li H, et al. Heat Transfer and Fluid Flow for a Thermal Plasma Jet Impinging Normally on a Flat Plate. Proceedings of Symposium on Energy Engineering in the 21st Century (SEE 2000), 2000, 1: 270-278

100. Mutaf-Yardimci O, Saveliev A V, Fridman A A, et al. Thermal and Non-Thermal Regimes of Gliding Arc Discharges. Proceedings of Symposium on Energy Engineering in the 21st Century (SEE 2000), 2000, 1: 96-106

101. Chen T, Lou Y, Zheng J, et al. Boiling Heat Transfer and Frictional Pressure Drop in Internally Rebbed Tubes at High Pressures. Proceedings of Symposium on Energy Engineering in the 21st Century (SEE 2000), 2000, 1: 393-398

102. Eschenbacher J F, Joko M, Nakabe K, et al. Heat Transfer in the Wake Behind a Longitudinal Vortex Generator Immersed in Drag-Reducing Channel Flows. Proceedings of Symposium on Energy Engineering in the 21st Century (SEE 2000), 2000, 1: 262-269

103. Trinh E H, Chung S K, Sadhal S S. Experimental Study of the Flows Within a Levitated Spot-Heated Drop. Proceedings of Symposium on Energy Engineering in the 21st Century (SEE 2000), 2000, 1: 229-236

104. Zhu N. Heat Transfer Enhancement of Horizontal Cylinder by Ultrasound. Proceedings of Symposium on Energy Engineering in the 21st Century (SEE 2000), 2000, 1: 316-320

105. Han B, Goldstein R J. Effects of Tip Clearance and Rotation on Three Dimensional Flow Fields in Turbine Cascades. Proceedings of Symposium on Energy Engineering in the 21st Century (SEE 2000), 2000, 1: 206-211

106. Kuznetsov A V. Heat and Mass Transfer in Free Surface Flows with Solidification. Proceedings of Symposium on Energy Engineering in the 21st Century (SEE 2000), 2000, 2: 896-902

107. Feng Z, Serizawa A, Two-Phase Flow Patterns in an Ultra-Small-Scale Flowing Passage. Proceedings of Symposium on Energy Engineering in the 21st Century (SEE 2000), 2000, 2: 643-649

108. Fu H, Leong K C, Huang X, et al. Heat Transfer of a Porous Channel Heat Sink Subjected to Oscillating Flow. Proceedings of Symposium on Energy Engineering in the 21st Century (SEE 2000), 2000, 2: 497-504

109. Bi Q C, Zhao T S. A Visual Study of Slug Bubbles in Miniaturized Channels. Proceedings of Symposium on Energy Engineering in the 21st Century (SEE 2000), 2000, 2: 438-444

110. Guo X Q, Sun C Y, Rong S X, et al. Modeling of Viscosity and Thermal Conductivity of Hydrocarbons Based on Equation of State. Proceedings of Symposium on Energy Engineering in the 21st Century (SEE 2000), 2000, 2: 588-597

111. Chung B T F, Ma Z. Optimization of the Annular Fin with Base Wall Thermal Resistance. Proceedings of Symposium on Energy Engineering in the 21st Century (SEE 2000), 2000, 2: 581-587

112. Borzenko V I, Malyshenko S P. Rewetting Phenomena and Thermal Stability at Steam Generation on Surfaces With Porous Coatings. Proceedings of Symposium on Energy Engineering in the 21st Century (SEE 2000), 2000, 2: 512-520

113. He K X, Wang J C, Chow A, et al. Microscale Heat Transfer at Fast Time Studied by Novel Laser-Based Measurement Techniques. Proceedings of Symposium on Energy Engineering in the 21st Century (SEE 2000), 2000, 2: 680-686

114. Chan A M C, Elphick I G. Critical Two-Phase Flow in a Short Converging Nozzle. Proceedings of Symposium on Energy Engineering in the 21st Century (SEE 2000), 2000, 2: 408-415

115. Zhang H, Wong H. Self-Similar Growth of a Compound Layer in Thin-Film Binary Diffusion Couples. Proceedings of Symposium on Energy Engineering in the 21st Century (SEE 2000), 2000, 2: 621-627

116. Gerlach C, Eder A, Jordan M, et al. Acceleration of Flames and Transition From Deflagration to Detonation Due to the Influence of Highly Blocking Obstacles. Proceedings of Symposium on Energy Engineering in the 21st Century (SEE 2000), 2000, 3: 1273-1280

117. Hara T. Experimental Investigation of Cooled Air Injection in Thermoacoustic Refrigerator. Proceedings of Symposium on Energy Engineering in the 21st Century (SEE 2000), 2000, 3: 1178-1183

118. Zuo Z J, Dubble E H, Garner S D. Compact, Double Side Impinement, Air-to-Air Heat Exchanger. Proceedings of Symposium on Energy Engineering in the 21st Century (SEE 2000), 2000, 3: 1007-1014

119. Van Nguyen T. Direct Liquid Water Injection and Interdigitated Flow Field for Reactant Gas, Water and Thermal Management in Proton Exchange Membrane Fuel Cells. Proceedings of Symposium on Energy Engineering in the 21st Century (SEE 2000), 2000, 4: 1453-1459

120. Cui Y, Stubington J F. The Sensitivity of Pressurized Fluidized Bed Combustion of Char to In-Bed Processes and Their Parameters. Proceedings of Symposium on Energy Engineering in the 21st Century (SEE 2000), 2000, 4: 1662-1667

121. Guo Y, Chan C. Prediction of Gas-Particle Flows and Gas Combustion in a Cyclone Furnace. Proceedings of Symposium on Energy Engineering in the 21st Century (SEE 2000), 2000, 4: 1515-1523

122. Park K S, Choi M, Chung J D. Unsteady Heat and Mass Transfer for Multi-Component Particle Deposition in the Modified Chemical Vapor Deposition. Proceedings of Symposium on Energy Engineering in the 21st Century (SEE 2000), 2000, 4: 1532-1539

123. Mi J, Nathan G J. Precession Strouhal Numbers of a Self-Excited Processing Jet. Proceedings of Symposium on Energy Engineering in the 21st Century (SEE 2000), 2000, 4: 1609-1614

124. Wang C Y, Transport Phenomena in Proton Exchange Membrane Fuel Cells. Proceedings of Symposium on Energy Engineering in the 21st Century (SEE 2000), 2000, 4: 1460-1467

125. Lloyd A C. Meeting California's Air-Quality Goals: The Role of New Technologies

and Fuels. Proceedings of Symposium on Energy Engineering in the 21st Century (SEE 2000), 2000, 1: 138-147

126. 鄭易裡，黨鳳德，徐式穀等。英華大詞典。修訂二版。北京：商務印書館，1984

127. 張道真。實用英語語法。修訂二版。北京：商務印書館，1990

128. 徐立吾。當代英語實用語法。長沙：湖南人民出版社，1982

129. 章振邦。新編英語語法教程。上海：上海外語教育出版社，1984

130. 薄冰，趙德鑫。英語語法手冊。修訂三版。北京：商務印書館，1990

131. 杭寶桐，朱鍾毅。英漢雙解常用英語同義詞手冊。南寧：廣西人民出版社，1986

132. 天津大學化工精儀系外語教研組。科技英語閱讀手冊。北京：石油化學工業出版社，1979

133. 西安交通大學外語教研室。科技英語語法。西安：西安交通大學，1978

134. 清華大學外語系《英漢科學技術詞典》編寫組。英漢科學技術詞典。北京：國防工業出版社，1991

135. 張芳傑。牛津現代高級英漢雙解詞典（簡化漢字本）。北京：商務印書館，1988

136. 劉新民。再談英語論文寫作規範。外語與外語教育，2001(4): 30-32111111

國家圖書館出版品預行編目資料

科技英語論文寫作＝Practical guide to
scientific English writing／俞炳丰編著.
--初版.--臺北市：五南，2007 [民96]
面；　公分
參考書目：面
ISBN 978-957-11-4771-0（平裝）
1.科技英語－作文　　2.論文寫作法
805.175　　　　　　　　96008917

5A62
科技英語論文寫作
Practical Guide to Scientific English Writing

作　　者 － 俞炳丰

校　　訂 － 陸瑞強

發 行 人 － 楊榮川

總 編 輯 － 龐君豪

主　　編 － 穆文娟

文字編輯 － 陳書彥

責任編輯 － 蔡曉雯

封面設計 － 簡愷立

出 版 者 － 五南圖書出版股份有限公司

地　　址：106台北市大安區和平東路二段339號4樓

電　　話：(02)2705-5066　傳　　真：(02)2706-6100

網　　址：http://www.wunan.com.tw

電子郵件：wunan@wunan.com.tw

劃撥帳號：01068953

戶　　名：五南圖書出版股份有限公司

台中市駐區辦公室/台中市中區中山路6號

電　　話：(04)2223-0891　傳　　真：(04)2223-3549

高雄市駐區辦公室/高雄市新興區中山一路290號

電　　話：(07)2358-702　傳　　真：(07)2350-236

法律顧問　元貞聯合法律事務所　張澤平律師

出版日期　2007年6月初版一刷
　　　　　2009年7月初版三刷

定　　價　新臺幣520元